Plea.
s!

The Japanese Devil Fish Girl and Other Unnatural Attractions

The Japanese Devil Fish Girl and Other Unnatural Attractions

Robert Rankin FVSS*

* Fellow of the Victorian Steampunk Society

with illustrations by the author

GOLLANCZ
London

Copyright © Robert Rankin 2010
All rights reserved

The right of Robert Rankin to be identified as the author
of this work has been asserted by him in accordance with the
Copyright, Designs and Patents Act 1988.

First published in Great Britain in 2010 by Gollancz
An imprint of the Orion Publishing Group
Orion House, 5 Upper St Martin's Lane, London WC2H 9EA
An Hachette UK Company

A CIP catalogue record for this book is available from the British Library

ISBN 978 0 575 07873 4 (Cased)
ISBN 978 0 575 08853 5 (Export Trade Paperback)

1 3 5 7 9 10 8 6 4 2

Typeset at The Spartan Press Ltd,
Lymington, Hants

Printed and bound in the UK by
CPI Mackays, Chatham, Kent

The Orion Publishing Group's policy is to use papers that
are natural, renewable and recyclable products and
made from wood grown in sustainable forests. The logging
and manufacturing processes are expected to conform to
the environmental regulations of the country of origin.

www.thegoldensprout.com

www.orionbooks.co.uk

THIS BOOK IS DEDICATED TO

CONNOR

WITH LOTS OF LOVE FROM HIS GRANDAD.

Cut into the present and
the future leaks out.

William Burroughs

1895

1

he Grand Salon of the *Empress of Mars* was furnished to exquisite nicety.

The overstuffed couches, thoughtfully arranged before the tall Gothic viewing windows, were royally upholstered in the palest of Japanese silks. Tables for every occasion rose upon fluted cabriole legs to bear silver trays of sweet-meats, petits fours and fruits of exotic origin. On walls made beautiful by the fabrics of Sir William Morris, ornate crystal mirrors glittered in the light of electric candelabra. Octagonal carpets of the Jovian persuasion smothered the maple floor and orchids from the forests of Venus, rising from elegant French porcelain cache-pots, perfumed the rarefied air.

The Grand Salon was abuzz with conversation.

The very cream of London society, aristocrats of noble blood, rubbed suave and braided shoulders with potentates from other worlds. Champagne twinkled, amorous glances were exchanged. Military gentlemen, high-ranking officers of the Queen's Own Electric Fusiliers, their uniforms of blue displaying many cam-paign medals, shared jokes with portly princelings from the royal houses of Jupiter.

The men were debonair and dandified, the women

pale and enchanting, their tiny waists encircled by corse-
lets of filigreed brass, offset by flaring skirts and bustles
prettied with embellishments of peacock feathers, ostrich
plumes, waxen roses, jewels and further jewels. Upon
their heads, nestling midst the coiffured, pampered curls,
they wore the very latest thing: tiny silk top hats adorned
with inlaid evening goggles.

Beyond the Grand Salon, upon the promenade deck,
ladies and gentlemen strolled and took in the views. For
on the warm and tender evening of this maiden flight,
the views were well worth taking in.

Above, a clear night sky all draped with stars, and
planets that might be viewed through one of the many
astronomical telescopes arranged at regular intervals
along the handrail.

Beneath, the City of London.

The *Empress of Mars* drifted silently over the great
metropolis, a sleek silver air-form, one-third of a mile
in length. The first of its kind, an aerial pleasure ship.

Sadly, upon this night of nights the capital was
wreathed in fog. Another industrial pea-souper. The
dome of St Paul's peeked above the murk, as did the
tessellated tower of the Babbage Institute for the
Advancement of Science. And towards the south, a
golden glow as of some rich and royal treasure could be
discerned atop the hill at Sydenham. From the destination of this wondrous aircraft. The Crystal Palace.

For tonight a concert of celebration was to be held
for the exalted company aboard the *Empress of Mars*.
Titurel de Schentefleur would conduct Mazael's
Mechanical Orchestra in the performance of a cosmic
operetta, created by Messrs William Gilbert and Arthur
Sullivan:

Of Mars and Mankind
(A stirring and exemplary tale as characterised by this Age of Moral Rectitude)

This stirring and exemplary tale had been expressly commissioned by the Prime Minister, Mr Gladstone. This stirring and exemplary pillar of society had taken it unto himself to oversee and vet the libretto, in order to ensure that the story of how British Forces defeated the Martians and extended the British Empire to the Red Planet be told in a manner that was altogether favourable to all involved. A manner that laid great emphasis upon the selfless, loyal bravery of the victorious Queen's Own Electric Fusiliers and the callous cruelty and innate cowardice of the denizens of Mars.

That such a victory might in any way have a 'tainted' quality about it would appear outrageous to the all and sundry who had consumed the ongoing details of this singular interplanetary campaign via the pages of *The Times* newspaper. But nevertheless . . .

There were those who knew all of the truth. And others who wished to keep all of the truth from those who did not know it.

War of any kind is never less than ugly and an inter-species war, as of Mars against Earth and the subsequent genocidal retaliation, entered realms of ugliness previously only inhabited by certain debauched human exhibits in the Celebrated Professor Coffin's Cabinet of Human Curiosities.

In brief, the true tale is as follows.

It has been well recorded by the pen of Mr Herbert Wells and set down in his episodic chronicle, *The War of the Worlds*, all that came to pass when soldiers of Mars descended to British soil in their machines of war and wrought a terrible carnage.

This appalling circumstance, which resulted in the loss of many lives and the destruction of much property, was luckily, if such a word can indeed be suitably applied, confined to the southern counties of England alone. As will be known and understood by those who have read the work of Mr Wells, the Martians were defeated not by selfless, loyal bravery, but by falling prey to Earthly bacteria against which their unearthly bodies held no natural resistance. The invaders drooped and died. Their three-legged chariots of death rocked and tumbled.

Earth and the British Empire survived. Triumphed.

Celebrations followed and folk danced gaily in garlanded streets and cheered for Queen and for country.

In Westminster, however, behind closed doors, ministers took stock . . .

A secret conclave met in a secret room . . . The year was 1885.

At the table's head sat Mr Gladstone, flanked by two fellows of funereal aspect. These two fellows' names remain unrecorded and a matter of ongoing speculation. To the right of Gladstone and seated next to one of the anonymous fellows was to be found that eminent scientist and mathematician Charles Babbage, a jolly red-faced man, well swaddled in a great abundance of tweed. And directly opposite him, a gaunt but dapper personage of foreign extraction who answered to the name of Nikola Tesla. A surname the future would know as 'the derived SI unit of magnetic flux density equal to a flux of one weber in an area of one square metre'. Beside him was an empty chair. And opposite this chair, next to Mr Babbage, sat Silas Faircloud, newly appointed Astronomer Royal, tubercular and frail.

The secret conclave was called to order, and Mr Gladstone spoke.

'Gentlemen,' he began, 'we meet here under what we must all consider to be the gravest of circumstances: the concern that further enemy forces might even now be amassing upon Mars, readying themselves for attack. Mr Faircloud, what think you of this?'

'Ahem,' went Mr Faircloud, a-clearing of his throat. 'The possibility must be apportioned strong. Astronomers around the country, indeed throughout the civilised world, have their instruments trained upon that planet. As yet there are no signs of further martial activity, but—'

'Pardon me,' said Mr Babbage⋆, 'but I am unaware of the existence of optical systems capable of observing the face of Mars to the degree that space-going vessels might be clearly discerned.'

'I am working on such matters even now,' claimed Mr Tesla, 'although mine are not optics of glass, but of a more metaphysical disemblement that will penetrate the ether of space via the medium of radionic waves.'

'Quite so.' Mr Gladstone struck the table with a folded fist. 'But we must all agree that the possibility of another attack is strong.'

Silas Faircloud made so-so motions with the bobbing of his head. 'We can only speculate as to whether further forces of a Martian military nature even exist. It is

⋆ History records that Charles Babbage died in 1871 – but history, as Henry Ford so aptly observed, 'is bunk'.

possible that they flung their entire might against us. That we took all they had and triumphed, as it were.'

'What think you of this, Mr Babbage?' asked the Prime Minister. 'Would this adhere to your mathematical principles?'

'Oh, very much so, sir.' And Mr Babbage smiled. A big broad beamer bringing warmth to all. 'Although the modes of thought employed by Martians have few echoes amongst we folk of Earth – and I have here the autopsy reports on the examinations of Martian bodies carried out at the London Hospital by the noted surgeon, and Her Majesty's physician, Sir Frederick Treves, which suggest that the Martian brain has more in common with the shark or the porpoise than with that of the human being – regardless of these differences, logic of any kind surely dictates that if you choose to wage war upon another planet, you would do well to overwhelm your enemy as speedily and judiciously as possible. To wit, fling all you have in a great big all-out attack.'

Mr Gladstone nodded thoughtfully. 'Which might be to say,' said he, 'that should the fight be carried to Mars, an all-over British victory might be accomplished.'

'Carried to Mars?' asked Silas Faircloud. 'How so might this be?'

'Mr Babbage once more,' said the PM, indicating same.

'Through a process of what Mr Tesla here has named "back-engineering". To put it simply, we repair and restore the Martian ships of space. Convert their controls for human piloting. Fly to Mars and wreak—'

'Revenge,' said Mr Gladstone. 'An ugly word, I know, but war is an ugly business. It would be my proposal that regiments of the Queen's Own Electric

Fusiliers be put on standby. Your comments please, Mr Faircloud.'

'Well,' puffed the Astronomer Royal, 'if it is to be done then it had best be done speedily. At this time, Mars is at its closest for some years to come. The opportunity presents itself, but fearful consequences might result.'

'Specifically?' asked Mr Gladstone.

'One might only speculate. Perhaps a virulence exists upon Mars to which its inhabitants are immune, but which might well lay waste to soldiers from Earth.'

'Unlikely,' said Nikola Tesla. 'My own researches suggest that the Martian atmosphere is thinner than our own, perhaps equivalent to that upon a mountain peak. As such, solar radiation cleanses the planet of bacteria. Mars, I believe, is a totally sterile environment. I would stake my reputation upon this.'

'And such a reputation it is,' said Mr Gladstone. 'I understand that you have recently made great strides forward in the field of, what is it — teletalkation?'

'Telecommunications,' said Mr Tesla, nodding modestly. 'The ability to communicate verbally, across great distances, without recourse to wires, cables or suchlike mediums of transmission.'

'Extraordinary,' wheezed the Astronomer Royal. 'Would that I will live to see such wonders. But I still have fear for our soldier boys. These Martian vessels must be stocked with compressed air and sufficient rations. Much planning will be necessary. And who knows what awaits on Mars? Mighty armaments trained upon the sky? Who can say?'

'Who can say, indeed.' Mr Gladstone took out his cigar case and relieved it of a smoke. This he cut with a clipper on his watch fob and placed between his lips. 'Speed and force,' said he, though slightly mumbled. 'Speed and force must be of the essence, and to this end I propose that we engage the services of a young gentleman who has lately distinguished himself in the African troubles. I am putting him in command of the strike force. Mr Babbage, you are nearest – would you open up the door and bid him enter?'

Charles Babbage rose, pushed back his chair, took himself to the door and opened it. A slight young man with the face of a baby grinned into the room.

'Gentlemen,' said the Prime Minister, 'allow me to introduce you to Mr Winston Churchill.'

2

istory does *not* record that Winston Churchill organised the assault against Mars. Nor indeed did the libretto of *Of Mars and Mankind*. There was some controversy.

Mr Gladstone bade the young man enter.

Mr Churchill entered with a smile.

Mr Gladstone indicated a vacant chair and Mr Churchill placed himself upon it. Mr Gladstone said, 'The floor is yours.'

Mr Churchill rose and bowed politely. 'I am gratified,' said he, 'to be chosen for this task. One that will garner no glory for myself, but one that will be of enormous significance to the future of the British Empire.'

Mr Faircloud coughed a little. 'Sir,' said he, 'we have not been introduced but—'

'You are the Astronomer Royal,' said Mr Churchill. 'And here I see the noted Mr Babbage and the equally noted Mr Tesla. And the two funereal gentlemen are—'

Mr Gladstone put a finger to his lips. 'One does not disclose the names of the Gentlemen in Black.'

'Quite so,' said the smiling Mr Churchill.

'But how—' asked Silas Faircloud.

'I have my contacts,' said Mr Churchill. 'An intelligence network. It is necessary to know who is whom. And whom may be trusted with what.'

'All may be trusted here.' The Prime Minister inclined his head towards Mr Churchill, and then asked, 'And why, might I enquire, do you feel that you will garner no praise for your part in this noble enterprise?'

The young man with the infant face produced a sheaf of papers. 'Because the method by which we will achieve success must never be made public. For reasons which will immediately become apparent once I have explained them.'

'Then please do so, sir,' said Mr Gladstone.

'*Sir?*' asked Winston Churchill.

'There are many ways of rewarding a servant of the Crown.'

And Mr Churchill smiled once more. '*Your* servant, sir,' said he. And he read from a typewritten page. ' "From the eight extant Martian vehicles of interplanetary transport surviving, three can be put into serviceable condition, fuelled with an equivalent to Martian propulsive fuel, stocked with compressed air and foodstuffs sufficient to—" '

'That is *my* report,' said Mr Babbage. 'How—'

'How is not important.' Mr Churchill's smile increased in size but not in warmth. 'Three craft can be flown to Mars. Each craft is capable of transporting five hundred soldiers of the Queen, with full packs and Royal Enfield rifles. Fifteen hundred troops against the might of an entire planet.'

'British troops,' said Mr Gladstone, proudly. 'The finest in the world.'

'In *this* world,' said Mr Churchill. 'But untrained to fight in the unknown conditions of another.'

'Highly adaptable,' said Mr Gladstone. 'At present we have several thousand men serving in Afghanistan. Soon that errant nation will be brought to book and no more trouble will this world know from it.'

Mr Churchill declined to comment. 'Mars,' said he, 'presents us with a challenge. My solution is simple and will prove wholly effective. It will, however, garner me no praise, as I have said.'

'Then please let us hear this plan,' said Mr Gladstone, taking the opportunity to light the cigar that had been all a-quiver 'tween his moving lips.

'We will send *no* troops,' said Mr Churchill. Pausing to let his words take effect.

'No troops?' said Mr Babbage. 'But then how—'

'Fifteen hundred civilians,' said Mr Churchill. 'No full packs or Royal Enfields. Just the clothes they stand up in. Or perhaps lie.'

'Please explain yourself,' said Mr Babbage.

'The Ministry of Defence has lately been experimenting with certain new forms of weaponry. Sophisticated modern weaponry that will make the bullet a thing of the past.'

Mr Babbage groaned. 'You speak of poison gas,' said he. 'I have heard rumours of this awful stuff.'

'Something to do with custard, isn't it?' asked Silas Faircloud.

'Mustard,' said Mr Churchill. 'Mustard gas. Hideously effective. But the Ministry is moving beyond this. In fact, regarding the Martian campaign and the Martians' obvious susceptibility to Earthly microbes, you might term my proposal "Germ Warfare".'

Certain breaths were sharply taken in.

Mr Faircloud coughed a bit and said, 'Not very, how shall I put this, British.'

'Nor indeed the method of distribution.' Mr Churchill darted eyes about the table. 'The fifteen hundred souls aboard the three Martian craft will be incurables. Terminal cases. Consumptives. Those suffering from whooping cough, scarlet fever, diphtheria, cholera, typhus, genital crabs—'

'People don't die from genital crabs,' said Mr Babbage.

'They do if they give them to *me*,' said Mr Churchill.

There was a brief moment of silence then, before Mr Gladstone said, 'Dignity *please*, gentlemen. I allowed the "custard" remark to pass unchallenged, but if we are to descend to the humour of the music halls, I will be forced to call these proceedings to a halt.'

'My apologies,' said Mr Churchill. 'Syphilitics, those in the advanced stages of any sexually or otherwise transmitted and transmittable terminal diseases. Three space-borne plague ships bound on a voyage of no return.'

'My word,' said Silas Faircloud. 'I trust that I will not be recruited to this hapless jaunt.'

'By no means, sir.' The smile remained on Winston Churchill's face. 'At a stroke we will empty fifteen hundred beds in chronic wards. Where would be the loss, when everything, it would seem, would be the gain?'

'As long as nobody knows.' Mr Faircloud gave a little shiver. 'It is a terrible thing. But in its way a noble thing. Viewing it dispassionately I ask myself, where would be the harm? But as a humanitarian, to sanction such a thing would be—'

'Not for you to trouble yourself with.' Mr Churchill bowed towards the Astronomer Royal. 'I will take full responsibility. Which is to say that I will make all the necessary arrangements. We will deliver these wretches to Mars. Hopefully the Martians will not open fire upon their own ships. Once they have landed and the ports are opened, nature will take its course. I would suggest that one or two months later, during which time more Martian craft can be "back-engineered", we will send out a contingent of Fusiliers. Hopefully they will meet with neither resistance nor indeed a single live Martian. Gentlemen, such is my proposal.'

Mr Churchill reseated himself.

To no applause whatsoever.

'Would you care for a cigar?' asked Mr Gladstone.

'Indeed,' replied the youthful Mr Churchill. 'I have always wondered just what they might taste like.'

But so it came to pass. And so to great success. Few questions were asked regarding the fifteen hundred terminally ill patients who vanished from their beds of pain. And questions asked regarding the human bodies found upon Mars, when the Queen's Own Electric Fusiliers yomped down the gangways and onto the surface of the now lifeless planet, were capably answered in Parliament by a young buck named Churchill, who was building a reputation for himself.

'I am aware,' he stated, 'that something I understand to be called a "Conspiracy Theory" exists regarding the human corpses found – and disposed of in a Christian manner – upon Mars. This theory states that for years prior to the Martian invasion of Earth, beings from Mars had visited this planet and abducted humans for experimental purposes that are far too horrific to dwell upon. The theory that I have lately heard, which may or may not bear credence, is that the French authorities had for years colluded with these unspeakable aliens, supplying their needs in exchange for certain advanced machinery. I have heard it stated that this intelligence came to the ears of Her Majesty Queen Victoria, who ordered that all such abominable transactions cease immediately. It was this cessation that led to the Martian attack upon England. Which led in its inevitable turn to a retaliatory attack culminating in the extermination of the vile Martians and the extension of the British Empire to Mars. God save the Queen.'

And that was that.

Or nearly was.

Because it transpired that there was a degree of truth to the words spoken by Mr Churchill. Beings from other planets had indeed been visiting Earth for several decades. These visitors had not, however, been from Mars.

They had been from Venus and from Jupiter. Two more of the four inhabited planets of this solar system. These beings came in peace and in secrecy. But when the men from Planet Earth wiped out the unsavoury Martians, the men from Venus and Jupiter presented themselves to Her Majesty the Queen. Earth joined a congress of planets and a new age of interplanetary travel and discourse began.

That year was eighteen eighty-five, and ten years later, in this year of our Lord known as eighteen ninety-five, the *Empress of Mars*, its panoramic maiden joyride completed, settled down onto the landing strip of the Royal London Spaceport, at Sydenham, just to the south of the Crystal Palace. Gangways were lowered and Queen Victoria, Queen of England, Empress of India and Mars, cast her regal shadow onto a red carpet that extended from the airship, across the landing strip, past the Terminal One building that mirrored so perfectly the architecture of the Houses of Parliament, and all the way up the hill to the palace of crystal, where tonight would be held the concert of celebration for the tenth anniversary of Britannia's triumph over the Martians.

Her Majesty would be greatly amused this night by the comic capers of Gilbert and Sullivan and their musical evocation of British vim and valour. The truth, although out there, would never be known to her.

3

he pickled Martian's tentacles were fraying at the ends. A foul and healthless fetor filled the air. The showman's wagon that housed this 'Most Meritorious Unnatural Attraction' trundled uncertainly upon its broad iron wheels. The constant clamour and shudderings of steam that arose from the traction engine hauling this wagon contributed no joy whatsoever to the chap in its cramped interior.

George Fox was a lanky lad whose legs needed plenty of room. As a wagon wheel plunged into yet another pothole, George found himself flung forwards, his face all squashed against the cold glass of the pickled Martian's tank. He swore, briefly but greatly to the point, and made an attempt to straighten himself. This attempt was met with failure and George sank back on his bottom.

What there was to be seen of George, illuminated yet vaguely in profile by a guttering candle within a bull's-eye lantern, looked reasonable enough. A noble profile with a striking chin. A blue eye all a-twinkle and a rather spiffing sideburn. A good head of wavy brown hair. A shirt with a collar in need of a scrub. And the costume of a showman's assistant. Loud, that suit, very loud.

George Fox eschewed the word 'zany', although this was the title his employer Professor Cagliostro Coffin had thrust upon him.

'One who engenders warmth and sympathy in the growing crowd by means of gambols, pratfalls and tricks above ground. A noble craft, my boy. A noble craft.'

A noble craft! George Fox held his fingers to his nose. He was nothing more than a clown to a shiftless trickster. And now *this*. George viewed the pickled alien that bobbed within its glassy prison. A gruesome creature, all tentacles and bulbous bits and bobs, its pale and scaly skin a jigsaw puzzle of autopsy stitchings.

George's duties had recently been extended to the care and maintenance of this hideous specimen. And George hated the pickled Martian. Not just as one of a species would hate a natural enemy, but with specific, personal malice. Somehow that dead beasty had it in for George, and George in return had it in for the beasty. He was rapidly reaching the conclusion that this line of work did not suit him and that he should seek another position, one more trimmed to the skills he possessed.

Whatever those skills might be.

The wagon gave another lurch and George was drenched in formalin that spilled from the Martian's tank. He did grittings of the teeth and gave himself to loathing.

At length, the wagon grumbled to a halt and hands threw the rear doors wide.

'Sleeping?' called the voice of the professor. 'The life of luxury it is that you live, to be sure.'

George made grumblings of his own and rose most carefully. The contents of the wagon were many and various and all, according to Professor Coffin, 'of great value and irreplaceability'.

An 'Holistical Mirror', in which could be viewed the reflection of all of the world and all of its people thereto.

A stone from the Tower of Babel.

A grimoire penned in a universal language that could be read by anyone of any race, had they the knowledge of reading or not.

A clockwork pig of destiny, which solved mathematical conundrums and gauged the age of ladies by the shape of their unseen knees.

The stuffed remains of not only Brutus the Canine Escapologist, but also a mermaid lately taken by fisherman off the Island of Feegee.

All had been spoken of by Professor Coffin.

None, however, had been viewed by George Fox.

The boxes that housed these treasures rose to all sides of George in precarious towerings.

George stepped warily out into the night.

'Where are we?' he asked the professor. 'Are we where we should be?'

'Aha,' said Professor Coffin, rising on the toes of his pointy boots. 'It is for such questions that I retain your services, young Mr Fox. We have reached our destination. The Common Fields to the East of the Sydenham Spaceport. Here, tonight, we display our pickled companion. Although—' And here the professor took to the sniffing of young George Fox. 'It would appear that you have been applying the contents of his tank to your good self as an evening cologne. I fear you'll fail to attract the ladies. Best you have a wash.'

'Lead me to the nearest bathhouse,' said George, with hope in his voice.

'A horse trough presents itself yonder,' crooned Professor Coffin, singing the words as one would a music-hall ballad and performing as he did so a curious high-stepping dance.

George Fox viewed his employer with a jaundiced eye. The professor was far from young. Sixty, perhaps? It was hard for George to tell, for he was in his teens and all men over thirty appeared quite aged.

Sprightly, though, the professor was, and slim as a dolly mop's promise of faithfulness. And he had charisma. A presence. And almost poetic it was.

His face was that of Mr Punch, with a smile as wide as can be. His suit was louder than that of George, the broadcloth was Burberry. He twirled a cane with a skeleton's head and he laughed as often as not and he called men 'Rubes' and trusted none except for the carnival lot. His accent was a queer one and his origins unknown. If ever asked he'd swear that all the universe were home.

And grudgingly George was forced to admit that he liked the professor very much. Although he would never have been able to bring himself to say this out loud. For it would probably have caused great embarrassment to the both of them if he had.

George Fox sighed, glanced in the direction of the horse trough and then set free a great and mighty gasp.

'What, pray, is *that*?' he enquired when he was able.

'That, my boy, is the *Empress of Mars*.'

Cabled to its mooring masts, the great pleasure ship filled a quarter of the horizon, its twinkling underbelly lit by naphtha spotlights and modern electrical bulbs. Although constructed by British craftsmen in the hangars of Northolt, under the strict supervision of its designer Sir Ernest Lovell, the *Empress of Mars* was a thing of unworldly beauty. That it was the single largest feat of engineering since the construction of the Great Pyramid had been a fact much trumpeted in Grub Street.

George took a step back and blew out a breath. 'It is truly the most beautiful and indeed fearsome thing that I have ever seen in my short life. And—'

'Please do not say it,' the professor said.

'Say what?' asked young George.

'Say, "And one day, when I have made my fortune, I shall travel upon it." Or some such tragic phrase.'

'Ah,' said George. 'I say that kind of thing often, do I?'

Professor Coffin nodded with his napper. A napper onto which he had now placed a top hat, whose fabric matched his suit. 'Do you recall Liverpool, where I took you to the Philharmonic Dining Rooms? "One day I shall own an establishment such as this," you said. Or in Paris, regarding that ghastly iron eyesore designed by the Frenchie, Alexandre Eiffel.'

George had to concede that he had indeed coveted the Eiffel Tower. And if it came down to the matter of a personal lack, highlighted by the words hitherto spoken by Professor Coffin, it could be said that George lacked the natural contempt for the French that was seemingly held by all 'good' British folk. That Martian he hated, but the French were all right.

'Sorry,' said George, all downcast once more.

'Not a bit of it, my boy.' Professor Coffin patted George, then wiped his fingers on an oversized red gingham hankie. 'You have ambition. The seeds of greatness were sown within you at birth. You will achieve wonderful things. Believe me, I know such stuff.'

'You really do think so?' asked George, with hope once more in his voice.

'Of course, of course. But one thing at a time. I will secure our pitch and then you must pitch our tent. And when all is neat and nice, then you will pitch to the crowd.'

'Me?' said George. 'Me on the bally, giving the pitch to the crowd? Not you? But this is—'

'An honour?' asked Professor Coffin. 'Think nothing of it, my boy.'

'I was going to say a "royal liberty",' said George, 'as you will no doubt fail to increase my wages accordingly.'

Professor Coffin doffed his topper, then skipped off in search of a pitch.

George sat down on the wagon's rear steps and gazed off into the night. Beyond the spaceport and the *Empress of Mars* rose Sydenham Hill and at the crest, the Crystal Palace, ablaze with light and wondrous to behold.

George set free another sigh. This was indeed an age of miracles. An age, it seemed, when almost anything was possible. Each week brought some new marvel. Each daily news-sheet spoke of the latest adventure. There had never been a time such as this. And George was here and this was *his* time and he knew that he must do something.

Make somehow a name for himself.

Succeed.

George took to further great sighings and hunched his head down low.

'Good sir.'

And George remained hunched.

'Good sir, if you please.'

And George raised his head. Then raised his body too and stood politely. 'Madam,' said George. 'How might I be of assistance?'

A young woman looked up at George. She was a beautiful young woman. This was evident even though her face was modestly shaded by a riding veil, which depended from the tiny top hat nestling midst a tumbling of bright-red curls.

By the clothes that she wore, she was clearly a gal of the gentry. The flounced shoulders of her nip-wasted jacket, cut in the continental style of the inimitable Pierre Antoine Berquin de Rambouillet, glistened with pearls. Her brass corset showed traces of turquoise. Naphtha light reflected in her ivory-framed evening goggles.

'Your servant, ma'am,' declared George Fox, bowing almost to the ground.

The young woman tittered and raised her modesty fan. As the plumes unfurled, George was made conscious of a delicate perfume that breathed from this gorgeous item.

'I fear that I have become lost,' said this lady, a damsel in distress. 'I somehow became separated from my party. It is my own fault, I confess. I became entranced by a showman's exhibit – an "Holistical Mirror" in which could be viewed the reflection of all of the world and all of its people thereto.'

'Indeed?' said George. 'Indeed?'

'And now I have become a-feared. There are so many rough types here and myself unchaperoned and oh so vulnerable.'

George sought to detect the hint of a certain eroticism in these words. Surely just his wishful thinking.

'Allow me to offer my protection,' said he, with all the gallantry of Don Quixote, or indeed the Chevalier Tannhäuser. 'And if you know the destination of your party, then please do not think me forward in offering to accompany you to this very destination.'

'You are charm personified.' And the young lady curtseyed a little. 'I have lately arrived upon the *Empress of Mars* to attend the concert at the Crystal Palace. But I am somewhat short of sight and know not even how this concert hall might look. If you would be so kind as to escort me there, I would be more than willing to reward you for your trouble.'

'To have assisted such a lady as yourself would be sufficient reward in itself,' said George, who could feel himself rising to certain heights of gallantry.

'As you wish,' the young lady replied. 'But I do have a spare ticket and it would be such a shame if it went all to waste.'

'A spare ticket?' said George. 'To the concert?' said George. 'To the royal celebratory concert?' said George.

'Indeed,' said the lady. 'Indeed.'

'Then, madam, I would be grateful beyond words to accept this most generous offer.'

'I am not interrupting you? From your work, perhaps?'

'My work, perhaps?' George glanced all around and about. There was much coming and going of many people, but no sign whatsoever of Professor Coffin. 'I hold to no work,' said George, of a sudden. 'I am a gentleman of independent means.' And he extended his arm to the lady and smiled.

The lady returned a shaded smile to George. 'Only one small thing,' said she.

'And that is?'

'Perhaps you might care to take a small dip in yonder horse trough. You reek rather poorly at present.'

4

ords were penned by George in a hasty missive to his employer, to the effect that he had been called away upon an important matter, would return soon and was regretful of any inconvenience that his absence might cause.

Solicitous and to the point, George considered as he folded the note and wedged it into the door crack of the showman's wagon. A brisk sojourn at the horse trough, a don of his bowler and George was on his way.

There was, in truth, no great difficulty in finding the way to the Crystal Palace. It stood out upon the hill in the manner that a performing porker pig will stand out at a dowager's *petit déjeuner*. Strikingly.

As George made his solemn and dignified approach, revelling in every moment that he had the beautiful woman on his arm, it occurred to him just how much he would love to own such a structure, and perhaps convert it into an indoor country park, where carriage rides might be taken and rare fowl cultivated. George's face took on a wistful expression that did not go unnoticed.

'You appear troubled,' said the beautiful woman on his arm. 'What is it that troubles you?'

George glanced down at the lovely creature and realised for the first time that he did not know her name.

'I know that we have not been formally introduced,' he said, 'as one might be in high society, but allow me to introduce myself to you. I am George Geoffrey Arthur Fox and I am proud to escort you.'

The lovely creature giggled girlishly. 'You are a gentleman, Mr Fox,' she said. 'My name is Ada Lovelace.'

'Your servant, ma'am.' And George did doffings of his bowler.

It was a pleasant moment, strolling towards the mighty palace of glass, lit to a dazzling brilliance from within. On every side the folk of fashion, gorgeous in their finery, folk of this world and beyond. The crème de la crème of this belle époque.

George gave guarded looks to all and sundry: to the provosts and paladins and papal nuncios, the plutocrats and panjandrums and princely potentates. He viewed the hospodars and shahanshahs, commissioners and commissars, the oligarchs and grand viziers, the emperors and subadars, the ecclesiasts of Venus, with their vestments and perfumers, the merry trolls of Jupiter, in pantalettes and bloomers . . .

'This would be the life,' said George unto himself.

Ada beckoned George and whispered, 'Do you like Venusians?'

'I do not really know,' George replied. 'I have never met one.'

'I've met several.' Ada's voice was soft, but George was listening intently. 'And I don't like them at all. You cannot tell what they are thinking.'

George did shruggings and said that he rarely knew what anyone was thinking.

'And they have three sexes,' Ada said.

George, though tall, stopped short in his tracks. 'What did you say?' he asked.

'They have three sexes,' said Ada once more. 'Male, female and "of the spirit". And their spaceships do not have motors in them. They are powered by faith. They call them "Holier-than-Air craft".'

'That sounds most unlikely,' said George, expressing doubts.

'But it is true,' said Ada. 'Aether ships they also call them. And I have heard that their intention is to convert all the people of Earth to their religion. They have their own bible called *The Book of Sayito* and speak of a "Goddess of the Stars" who will manifest herself to all in a time not far from this, when the "Great Revelation" will occur.'

'Ah,' said George. 'Please do not consider me impious, but I hold to be prudent those men who do not offer to explain the Book of Revelation.'

'Well, I find Venusians fearful,' whispered Ada. 'Sleek and beautiful perhaps, but so too is a fencing foil.'

A tall Venusian passed them by, then paused and turned them a glance. George could see the beauty, but he could not sense a threat. The being of Venus, man, or woman, or be what else it was, stood tall and slender to behold, with hair as white as alabaster and teased to dizzying plumes. The face was gaunt, the cheekbones angled, the eyes pure gold and radiant. The high-shouldered vestments were pinched at the waist and reached all the way to the ground. The perfumer, without which no Venusian was ever to be seen, swung censer-like from the being's pale left hand. Small whispers of luminous green smoke issued from the perfumer. Human yet inhuman was the creature. George wondered how such beings as this had managed to move incognito amongst the peoples of Earth for quite so long. Masters, mistresses or otherwises of disguise, George supposed, although their innate 'otherness' would surely be hard to conceal.

But no further words were said upon the matter of Venusians, as George and Ada had now reached the entrance of the Crystal Palace. George looked up at the dizzying walls of glass, the great distant swirl of the high façade. The golden glow of light within, provided tonight, George overheard a fellow remark, by Mr Nikola Tesla, who had positioned ten thousand neon tubes around and about the vast glazed building, brought to fluorescence by an induction loop of cable that did not actually touch the tubes themselves.

'One day all domestic lighting will be as this,' George heard the fellow say.

And then they were within. Within that vastness, with its tall statuary, hewn from silica mined from Earth's moon. Her Majesty's moon, where the first flag planted was the Union Jack. The humming of the neon tubes, the static crackle of a thousand educated voices. The glamour and the beauty.

George was entranced.

This was the company he belonged with.

This was the place for him.

They stood upon a red carpet now, bounded by velvet ropes on brassy stands. The queue for admittance to the concert hall. George was most excited.

'I need to go somewhere,' Ada whispered to him.

'Where else would be a better place for us than here?' George asked.

'A ladies' somewhere,' hissed Ada. 'It has been a long walk and I have a frail constitution.'

'Oh,' said George. 'Most sorry,' said George. 'Perhaps,' said George, 'that fellow?'

And George pointed towards a tall and swarthy fellow, in turban, coronation dress, buskins and puttees. He wore a very fierce beard, with tightly curled moustaches.

'You ask him,' said Ada. 'I would faint from embarrassment.'

'Ah,' said George, 'indeed.'

And so George pressed forwards through the queue, much to the disgust of margraves, viceroys and the occasional rajah. He spoke urgent words into the tall and swarthy fellow's ear and this fellow beckoned to Ada.

She hurried through the grumbling throng, ducked under the velvet rope that barred the way ahead and slipped away to a certain ladies' somewhere.

George returned to his place in the queue.

'She needed a wee-wee,' he explained to a crusty cardinal, who stood a-tut-tut-tutting.

And slowly the queue moved forwards as tickets were checked and directions given by the tall and swarthy fellow, now joined by several others of his ilk.

As George reached the head of the queue he began to fret. 'She had better return soon,' he fretted to himself. 'She has both tickets and by the way these folk are a-sniffing at my person, it is certain that I shall not gain entrance without one.'

It was only after the unpleasantness occurred that it

fully dawned upon George that he had not actually seen the actual tickets. He had not been given the opportunity to vouch for their authenticity.

Or indeed their very existence.

He made loud his protests, of course. Explaining that the lady had the tickets. That the lady would shortly return. That all would be well when she did so.

But the lady did not return.

The lady was not for returning.

And who was there, amongst gentlemen, who was prepared to believe that a gentleman would possibly trust a mere woman to mind the tickets? George bristled somewhat at that. But then, it was explained to George, George was clearly *not* a gentleman. George was a common fairground hobbledehoy, seeking to slip into an affair many levels above his lowly station in life, to dare to mingle with his betters.

George not only bristled at this.

George swore somewhat too.

Which led to much of the aforementioned unpleasantness. With George being frogmarched from the Crystal Palace between two swarthy turbaned types. Both of whom, George noted in passing, owned too many medals. No doubt from the soon-to-be-concluded campaign in Afghanistan.

In the shadow of some beech trees George received a thorough trouncing and was left there unconscious to dwell upon his folly.

5

eorge awoke in darkness. In darkness, but to movement. A rumbling rattling movement it was, and as George awoke to it he also became aware of a most maleficent smell.

'Oh no.' George did groanings and worried at his head.

Delved into his waistcoat, recovered his match case, removed and struck fire to a Lucifer.

The pickled Martian fixed him with a pickled baleful eye. George did groanings once again, then took to a fitful sleep.

He awoke this time to the wagon's rear doors being flung open and a great deal of bright white sunshine flooding in all over the place.

'Up, my sorry fellow,' called the voice of Professor Coffin. 'Another fine day awaits your late arrival.'

George did the regulation blinkings of the eyes and, upon finding his voice, asked, 'What happened?'

'I worried for your safety, as well I might,' replied the professor, all in silhouette before the beastly morning light. 'And not without good cause, as I found you in the grounds of the Crystal Palace, all bleeding, broken and banjoed.'

'Banjoed?'

'Done for. Patched your bruises, so I did, then brought you back to your home.'

Even in his loosely semi-conscious state, George could sense a certain duplicity in these words. It was not, as it might be put, the whole story.

'But another day has dawned.' Professor Coffin leaned into the wagon and tousled George's hair. 'You are fit and well once more, or certainly will be once you have some vittles housed 'neath your belt, and together we must make up for our loss of earnings last night.'

'And where are we now?' asked George, squinting into the light and discerning a humble cottage or two.

'A tiny rural hamlet by the name of Brentford.' Professor Coffin straightened up and twirled his cane a little. 'Upon the northern bank of the Thames, opposite Her Majesty's Royal Gardens of Kew.'

George did strugglings from the wagon and took in pleasant surroundings.

'Yonder inn.' Professor Coffin pointed with his cane. 'The Flying Swan. We shall take our breakfast there.'

The Flying Swan served a goodly breakfast. Specialising as it did in the popular dishes of the day, George enjoyed amongst other such popular dishes a helping of chibberlings, two portions of Melbury chubs, three wifters (finely sliced) and a quick-fired crad that would have done credit to Her Majesty's breakfasting table at Windsor. And all washed down with porter. Splendid stuff.

George drew a jacket cuff across his mouth and

nodded his approval. 'Would you like to tell me what really happened last night?' he asked.

Professor Coffin swallowed a slice of Corby snaffler. 'Would *you*?' was his reply.

'I made a mistake,' said George. 'And I abandoned you, my employer. I apologise for this. I paid a price for my thoughtless behaviour.'

'We will speak no more of the matter.' Professor Coffin gulped porter. 'Tit for tat, black for white, the balance of equipoise is maintained.'

'Professor.' George Fox looked up from his breakfast. 'Have you ever met a Venusian?'

'Many, my boy. Most many. And not a single one of them would I trust.'

'But for why? They have such rare beauty and seem so benign in their manners.'

'They have three sexes, you know?' Professor Coffin forked up a rumpling and popped it into his mouth.

'Male, female and "of the spirit",' said George, knowledgeably.

'No,' said the professor. 'All in a single being. They are what are called "tri-maphrodites". They can self-reproduce. They do not require sexual partners.'

'They have sex with themselves?' George spat out breakfast.

'Well, don't think I haven't seen you doing it.'

George now choked on his breakfast.

'Jesting, of course,' said Professor Coffin. 'Don't cough your minced pappings into my porter, please.'

George took sup from his own porter pot.

'I don't trust the blighters.' Professor Coffin made the face of disgust. 'They are all too sweet and kindly. And I have heard it said that they have no machines whatsoever. They cause things to happen through the power of their minds. Move their ships of space through the heavens by the power of faith alone.'

'I did hear that,' said George, reapplying himself to his breakfast.

'Venusians are a bunch of black magicians,' said Professor Coffin, spitting onto the sawdust on the floor.

'Steady on now,' said George. 'Black magicians, you say? That is rather strong, surely?'

'Then think on this,' said the professor. 'You would call yourself a Christian boy, would you not?'

'That is the way that I was brought up.'

'That is not what I asked.'

'Then I *am* a Christian, yes. I believe in God.'

'And do you believe in magic?'

'Witchcraft, do you mean?'

Professor Coffin's head went bob-bob-bob. 'Magic is presently quite the fashion amongst the London toffs. Seances are regularly held in the parlours of the gentry.'

George nodded to this intelligence. The papers were filled with stories about a certain Daniel Dunglas Home, who held such seances. And in whose spiritual presence tables moved of their own accord, instruments played themselves and Mr Home himself had been known to levitate. Mr Home was quite the darling of the upper classes, lionised by ladies of the court. A certain expression crossed George's face.

'Do *not* even think about it,' said his employer. 'Your future does not lie in spiritualism.'

George tucked into his tucker.

'My point is this,' the professor continued. 'Magic *is* practised here on Earth, but in my opinion to little or no effect. I concede that conditions upon another planet might be conducive to practical magic. Magic that is controllable and employable. But is this *Godly* magic, or is it the work of the Devil?'

'I have always wondered,' said George, giving his mouth another cuff-wipe, 'who was the very first magician? Magicians always claim to have these ancient books of magic. Grimoires penned by Paracelsus, or your namesake Cagliostro. But who wrote the very first one? And where did the information come from? That is what I would like to know.'

'Then I will tell you.' Professor Coffin finished his porter and called for more from the bar. 'From Moses is the answer to that. When Moses ascended Mount Sinai and received the tablets of stone upon which God had hewn the Ten Commandments, God took Moses into his confidence. God gave Moses more than just the Ten Commandments. He gave him the very first grimoire. Or rather he dictated it to Moses, who wrote it all down.'

'But why?' asked George.

'For the improvement and advancement of Mankind. Moses was to employ the magic at his discretion.'

'And did he?'

'You know that he did *not*. When he came down from the mountain the first time and found the Israelites worshipping a golden calf, he flung down not only the tablets of stone, but also the grimoire.'

'So how does that make Moses the very first magician if he threw down the very first grimoire and never used it?'

'I said that it was dictated to him. This gave him the status of being the very first magician. The only man

35

ever to receive magic directly from God. He flung down the grimoire but it was not destroyed in flames. It was recovered, and passed from hand to hand and generation to generation. Few could interpret it correctly. The magic got all dissipated. The world would no doubt be a different place if the Israelites had not made that golden calf. Mind you . . .' Professor Coffin made a significant pause.

'Go on,' said George. 'You have me hooked.'

'Some do say that this event gave birth to the very first conspiracy theory. That the making of the golden calf took place through the influence of a certain evil Israelite who planned the whole thing, knowing that Moses, who was noted for the shortness of his temper, would be so upset when he came down from the mountain bearing God's words and saw that calf being worshipped that he would fling down whatever he had been given and get in a proper huff.'

'Ah,' said George. 'I understand. And then this evil man would hastily avail himself of whatever it was that Moses threw down in a huff.'

'Quite so. And what was intended as "good" white magic by God, as a present to Man, ended up as "bad" black magic, in the hands of bad black magicians.'

'It is a good story,' said George, who had now finished his breakfast. 'But let me put this to you. What if God not only put an Adam and Eve upon this planet, but also upon Venus, Mars and Jupiter? And what if the Moses of Venus was not caused to cast down his grimoire? Then the magic employed by Venusians would be good magic, would it not?'

Professor Coffin made grumbling sounds underneath his breath.

'Well, I have nothing personal against Venusians,' said George. 'They have yet to do me wrong. Young women of Earth, however, are quite another matter.'

'I knew it!' Professor Coffin rose to his feet and danced a little jig. 'I just knew it. You were befuddled and befooled by a pretty young thing last night. I just knew it.'

George made a mumbled assent.

'Do not feel bad about it, my boy. It happens to us all. Try to learn from your mistakes. You never know, you might prove to be the first man in the history of the planet who actually *can* learn from his mistakes. And now,' Professor Coffin bowed before George, 'the show must go on. We are bound for the fair at Hounslow and I for one would be gratified if we turned a shiny penny or two before this day is out.'

George Fox smiled and rose to his feet and dusted crumbs from his waistcoat.

Professor Coffin drove the traction engine. George, on this occasion, stood beside him. The traction engine was marvellous, all barley-twists of polished brass, great whirling flywheels, sniffs of smoke and oil. This wondrous vehicle had but recently come into the hands of Professor Coffin. He had been fortunate enough to win it during a game of cards with a carnival proprietor named Mandible Haxan, who advertised himself as 'the Sorcerer Genius' and presented an attraction known as 'the Hieronymous Machine' or 'Intuitive Prognosticator' – a construction of brass, ivory, leather and tinted gutta-percha that took questions from members of the crowd and replied to them by means of a mechanical voice. The Hieronymous Machine cast horoscopes and offered those who chose to pay an extra florin 'accurate foretellings of the future'.

Clearly Mr Mandible Haxan had not had recourse to employ the Hieronymous Machine to predict his own immediate future, before engaging Professor Cagliostro Coffin in that fateful game of cards.

George Fox knew well the professor's skill at cards. George Fox had once owned a gold pocket watch. This gold pocket watch now resided in the waistcoat watch pocket of Professor Cagliostro Coffin.

George *had* learned from *that* particular mistake. He would never play another game of cards with his employer.

The road between Brentford and Hounslow passes by the Park of Syon, that great estate that was the property of Lord Brentford himself. The high walls topped by the distinctive urns of Robert Adam shielded George's gaze from the cultivated gardens and pleasure domes within. It was rumoured that Lord Brentford had twenty concubines and a monkey butler that wore a fez and an embroidered waistcoat. It was also rumoured that His Lordship, when not pushing though reform bills in the House of Lords to benefit the poor at the expense of the wealthy, engaged in the practice of those *Artes Diabolique* of which Professor Coffin had accused the Venusians.

George knew that he was beginning to make that face once again and so he tore his eyes away from the high walls of the opulent estate and fixed them on the road ahead. Beyond the farms and wayside coaching inns lay

Hounslow. Hounslow with the Hounslow Fair, that wonderful famous fair.

George Fox flicked coal-smuts from his jacket and gave himself up to optimistic thoughts.

6

'n this year of our Lord eighteen hundred and ninety-five,' called Professor Coffin above the cacophony of the steam traction engine, 'there are nearly one hundred travelling circuses plying their trade across England. Countless more lesser travelling shows and single sideshow attractions. Hounslow Fair is a yearly event that can be traced back five hundred years. You will see much to amaze and amuse you, but do keep your hands in your pockets.'

George Fox made a thoughtful face.

'Keep a firm hand on your purse.'

'I see.'

As they approached Hounslow it was clear that there would be considerable competition in the field of the 'Educational Attraction'. George espied the rear ends of several wagons that he recognised. 'Toby the Sentient Swine', 'The Dark of the Moon Monster Medicine Show', 'Pinchbeck's Automated Minstrels', 'The Travelling Formbys', 'Soft Napoleon and the Screaming Nova'. George raised his eyebrows to that one. 'Dick, Dack and Dock, the Siamese Triplets' and the ever-popular 'Mechanical Turk', which had once soundly thrashed George at chess.

More than just 'considerable competition', perhaps, was this varied ensemble. And the day, to George's growing misgivings, looked to be turning into a hot one. Which would not suit a small tent housing an evil-smelling pickled Martian.

Such thoughts as these clearly also entered the head of Professor Coffin, who said to George, 'You, my boy, will hasten upon our arrival to the nearest pharmacy and purchase five cannisters of formaldehyde and ten of distilled water. Also violet nosegays, to the number one hundred, and two of those new facial masks worn by surgeons at the London Hospital.'

'And all of that they have on hand in Hounslow?'

'Surely you know the musical hall song,' said Professor Coffin, who, without waiting for a reply, launched into it.

> *If you need a lady's bonnet*
> *With fine dinky goggles on it,*
> *Or a stately coat for strolling up and down,*
> *If they ain't got one in Brentford,*
> *Or in Neasden, Penge or Deptford,*
> *They're bound to have the lot in Hounslow Town.*
> *Oh—*

But George cut Professor Coffin short. 'I will seek out the items you require,' he said, 'as long as I am furnished with the financial means so to do.'

'Good boy, we'll see what might be taken on account.'

George Fox shook his head. Slowly and firmly. 'Look at the state of me,' he said. 'Ragged and besmutted and stinking of a Martian's foul and fetor. Trust me upon this, Professor, no apothecary, chemist or fellow of the pharmaceutical persuasion will offer *me* any credit.'

Professor Coffin did smackings of the lips. 'You really must be prevailed upon to spend some of the generous largesse I heap about your person to purchase new duds. The Rubes take not to an evil-smelling zany.'

'Assistant,' said George Fox. 'Assistant.'

'Quite so. A trusted and valued assistant.'

George smiled proudly at this.

'Who I will now require to stoke up the firebox, as pressure is dropping in the boiler.'

An hour later saw the professor's engine, wagon and all, positioned on Hounslow Heath. Dick Turpin had once robbed the rich upon this very land. Certain parallels might be drawn upon this very day.

Professor Coffin pressed a pound note into the out-stretched palm of George Fox. 'I will erect the tent myself, whilst you hasten off to the pharmacy,' he said.

George, although an honest lad, looked long and hard at that pound.

'If you choose to abscond with the money,' Professor Coffin told him, 'I will of course be forced to have you pursued, tracked down and murthered.'

'Murthered?' queried George.

'Murdered,' said the professor. 'A word sometimes employed by Mr Charles Dickens, who would have it that working folk go about doffing their caps to the gentry and saying such things as "fank you werry much, your 'oliness".'

'I have never held a pound note before,' said George Fox.

Professor Coffin nodded thoughtfully. 'So you were simply thrilling to the experience – I understand.'

'No,' said George. 'Not precisely that. I was simply wondering whether an experienced pharmacist, with such knowledge of chemicals as he must necessarily attain to, would recognise, as I most instantly did, that this one pound note has been rendered in crayon and ink. And is indeed a fraud.'

With another of those grumbling sounds, Professor Coffin snatched back the bogus one pound note and furnished George with a real one.

'I will be as expeditious in my endeavours as it is possible to be,' said George.

'And take the handcart,' said the professor.

'And bring it back!' he added.

George Fox reasoned that the transportation of so noxious a substance as formaldehyde was something that should be entered into with considerable care. You just could not rush a thing like that. You had to take your time. Any employer, such as his own, who knew about the volatile nature of such a chemical, would naturally know that such things *did* take time. He would not expect George to return for at least an hour or two.

Surely not.

And so George strode off pushing the cart, but soon slowed to a stroll.

There was just so much to see. So many marvels.

Certainly George's time in the employ of a showman had taught him that what you saw was not necessarily what it was claimed to be. The verbiage splashed across the showmen's wagons in letters big and bold promised a great deal more than it actually delivered. That gorgeous pouting beauty, with the long golden hair showering over her naked breasts as she coquettishly fondled her fish's tail, was not entirely representative of the exhibit that lurked within the showman's enclosure. That wrinkled, varnished, wretched thing, an ungodly chimera of monkey and halibut that was hailed as a captured mermaid.

But the magic of the showground would never be lost upon George. After all, he *had* run away from a perfectly respectable family in order to join the circus. And after discovering that the circus did not require his unskilled services, he had taken various lowly jobs in various doubtful showmen's booths, prior to meeting the professor.

The professor certainly engaged in numerous doubtful practices. But it did have to be said that at least his Martian was real. Whether the means by which he had acquired it were wholly creditable, who was George to say? But it *was* a real exhibit.

Though George Fox hated it!

George steered the handcart in between the showmen's tents and through the growing crowd. Not the sophisticated crowd of worthies who had attended the concert the previous evening at the Crystal Palace, this. This was more your common crowd of roughs and ne'er-do-wells. The cackles of laughter from toothless hags and the drunken oaths of their partners failed to raise the spirits of George.

These were not his kind of folk. Perhaps he should just return to his family. Become an apprentice at this father's firm, which produced the Tantalus. George gave an inward shiver. He did not want to do that. He wanted adventure and advancement. He wanted to experience the zeitgeist.

The voice of a 'barker' reached George's ears, bawling out to the crowd. George caught sight of a colourful fellow mounted upon a high podium. Above him and spelled out in the new electric light bulbs flashed the words:

MACMOYSTER FARL
THE APOCALYPTICAL EXAMINER

The barker wore a red velvet suit of the formal persuasion, topped with a red velvet topper. The hues of his nose mirrored those of his clothes and his fine waxed mustachios coiled like twin watch-springs and jiggled to each exhortation. The substance of the barker's words caught George's interest. They held a certain relevance to his breakfast conversation with Professor Coffin.

'Gather round,' bawled the barker, raising his cane, 'and hearken unto me. Would you know your own futures? Would you care to speak directly to the dead? You, sir—' and he caught a passing fellow's eye '—you, sir, I feel, have recently suffered loss.'

'That is true for the truth of it,' said the fellow, halting so as to speak. 'My dear daughter Mary went down with the consumption a week ago. Just as her mother, my dear wife Mary, did a decade past. Though she was one of those carried off to Heaven in the early Rapture, by all accounts. Or at least that was what was telled us by the doctors when I came to view her empty bed.'

'And would you wish to speak with your dear ones again?'

'Would that I could, sir. Would that I could. But these seance-callers and spiritualists are naught but a pack of rogues, to my thinking.'

'And mine too,' agreed the barker, calling the fellow forwards into the gathering crowd. 'But within this tent sits a man who can speak with the spirits. A scientist of Christian worth and high moral rectitude. He learned his craft in a secret Government ministry – what think you of that?'

'I think I would care to know more,' said the fellow.

'Macmoyster Farl,' quoth the barker, making expansive circlings with his cane, 'who learned his craft at the secret Ministry of Serendipity where he worked with a team of psychic prestidigitators who were engaged in contacting the dead with a view to extending the British Empire into the realm of the hereafter.'

'Oooh,' went the crowd, for *this* was a revelation.

'Yes,' cried the barker. 'A revelation, is it not? And whilst on the subject of Revelations, Macmoyster Farl witnessed a seance where the intention was to invoke the Beast of Revelation also.'

'My oh my,' went some of the crowd. Others expressed themselves more crudely.

'I must add,' the barker added, 'that *that* seance was a *French* seance.'

Which caused the crowd to cheer somewhat and blow out raspberries too.

'For a shiny penny, nothing more, my friends,' the barker continued, 'you may speak with Macmoyster Farl, who will intercede with spirits upon your behalf. If not entirely genuine and if not every question satisfied with an appropriate answer, your money will be returned to you. What have you to lose, when you have so much to gain?'

'Count me in,' cried the fellow who had lost both his Marys. 'I will trust to the words of this eminent fellow. Here, take my penny that I might take a place to the fore of the auditorium before the crowd of hundreds marches in.'

And with that he tossed his penny to the barker and vanished into the tent.

George Fox did rootings in his pockets. It was probably all nonsense, he knew. Macmoyster Farl was most likely an impostor, claiming gifts he did not possess. But something was drawing George Fox in, into the tent. Something saying, 'Come.'

'Come, young master,' called the barker to George. 'My senses tell me that you are a young man seeking something. A young man with an itch he cannot scratch. Although not from lice, as I spy you as a clean 'un.'

George did further rootings in his pockets. He brought to light a piece of string, a hunk of sealing wax, a half-eaten toffee that he really should have finished.

And a bright and shiny, fine large copper penny.

George turned this coin upon his palm and, 'Count me in,' he said.

7

s George entered the show tent auditorium of Mr Macmoyster Farl, 'The Apocalyptical Examiner', he became immediately aware of a number of things. That it was a large tent, easily capable of housing an audience of at least one hundred people. That it was a clean and freshly smelling tent and a cool one too. George blew breath from his mouth and saw it steam as on a winter's day. Now how was *that* done? George asked himself. And another thing, too – George viewed the quality of the seating. Not your usual benches or bleachers here, but individual chairs and of excellent quality.

George ran his hand along the back of one. Mahogany.

To the front rose a stage all lit by new electric. A brass pulpit affair wrought with exquisite craftsmanship into the likeness of an angel, wings spread wide and holding an open book above her lovely head.

'Quality,' said George in a most approving tone. And he almost made that face again, but did not. Professor Coffin had told him, without uncertainty, that a career in spiritualism was *not* for George. And although George did not exactly hang upon the professor's every word, or take each to be the truth of the Gospel, he knew in his heart of hearts that he did *not* wish to become a spiritualist's barker, no matter how prosperous that spiritualist appeared to be. Spiritualism was, after all, to do with communicating with the dead, and communicating with the dead did amount to necromancy, no matter how politely you chose to put it.

George took a seat three rows from the front; many more patrons were bustling in behind him. George folded his arms and glanced all about and wondered, quite rightly, *exactly* why he had entered.

Had he felt a compulsion, a fateful compulsion? George simply shrugged and knew not. He would give it a quarter of an hour or so and if it was all a lot of toot and tosh, he would go off about his employer's business, a penny lighter, but a wiser man.

Within a few minutes all who were to be seated, were, the tent flap to the outer world dropped down and there was silence. It was an intense silence, a surprising silence considering the racket without. And it clearly had a profound effect upon those present. Toothless cacklings and drunken oaths dropped to whispers and died. George did further glancings around. There were fewer than thirty Rubes, including George himself. No great takings at a penny a piece. A meagre half-a-crown's worth. And such fine furnishings as these?

Then George's thoughts, whatever they were and were about to become, were interrupted by mighty beatings on a gong. A voice – coming, George supposed, through a concealed voice-trumpet – stung the silent air.

'My lords, my ladies and my gentlemen. Discerning and noble patrons, welcome to this Academy of Spiritual Science. He has travelled the inhabited worlds in search of esoteric knowledge. Consorted with the lamas of Tibet, the tribal hexmen of the Kalahari Desert, the monks of Parnassus, the ecclesiastics of Venus, the coenobites of Jupiter. Pythonesses, priests and pujaris have taken him into their confidence and passed on their arcane wisdom. He has daily congress with the Secret Chiefs of the Great White Brotherhood. He is the Ascended Master. He is Macmoyster Farl.'

The audience, driven to deeper silence by this litany of metaphysical qualifications, were at a loss whether to now applaud, or respectfully steeple their fingers in prayer. So most just simply sat.

Another intonation of the hidden gong, a fluorescent flash and here he was. Before the crowd, onstage by the brazen angel.

George was most impressed by this dramatic entrance. The stage looked solid enough, no apparent trapdoors or springboards. A very neat trick indeed, thought George, and a mighty presence too.

Macmoyster Farl was a most remarkable man. He was of a terrible tallness, a towering terrible tallness, and of a thinness too that hurt the eye to gaze upon. Of the fantastical costume that clothed him, George had never seen the like before. Surely these were the robes of a medieval wizard, adorned with Cabalistic characters, runes and cryptic symbols, wrought silver on a crimson silken background. And oh, of his turbaned headwear. The confusion and profusion of gemstones that speckled this outré bonnet. Chrysoprase and tourmaline and moonstone and jasper, ruby and sapphire and heliotrope. It was a rajah's ransom and all on a single hat.

And as to the face of this formidable figure, such a face it was. Bewhiskered with wild white mustachios that flared to either side of a visage so pinched and stretched of skin as to be scarcely more than a skull. But the nose was long and the eyes were bright and bluer than a turquoise to behold.

Silence, only silence.

Then he spoke.

'Fellow travellers,' he said, in a voice so deep of timbre as to be a further marvel, as it issued from so slim and fragile a frame. 'I am amongst you to pass on the wisdom I have learned. To answer your questions no matter what they be. To speak on your behalf to loved ones on the other side and convey their replies, which are whispered in my ear, unto you. So, hold not to reticence or shyness, ask anything of me. Ask anything.'

There was a further silence. As if a collective breath had been drawn in and held. At last a fellow spoke.

'My Marys,' said he, for he was the fellow who had lost his wife and daughter to consumption. 'I would speak to them. I would know that they are at peace.'

Macmoyster Farl raised a long and twig-like finger and put its tip to his left temple. He closed his eyes and rocked gently upon his toes.

And then he did something that caused a collective gasp to rise from the audience.

He rose.

Rose gently upwards, into the air, to hover there in defiance of the well-known law of gravity, a full ten inches above the stage. And all, it seemed, without wires.

George looked on approvingly. This was worth sixpence on its own. He had at least got value for this penny.

'Your daughter lies at rest in the paupers' plot at

Spitalfields,' said he. Which caused the questioner's head to bob up and down. 'But your wife—' Macmoyster paused, fluttering slightly in the air, as if caught by a gentle breeze. 'She lies not within the bosom of soil which is our blessed home.'

'What means this?' asked the fellow.

'Mars,' the voice of Macmoyster boomed. 'She was cremated on Mars.'

'But that cannot be.' The fellow rose from his chair and wrung his hands. 'You are mistaken, you speak not of *my* Mary.'

'Mary Harcourt,' intoned the voice of Farl. 'Born third of March, eighteen sixty-two. Died fifteenth of April, eighteen eighty-five.'

'Upon Mars?' The fellow shook his head again and again.

'She is exalted in spirit.' Macmoyster's voice grew even deeper still. 'Behold and I will bring her to you.'

Then things, already odd enough, took an odder turn yet.

The lights within the tent auditorium dimmed, Macmoyster Farl produced a lit candle from somewhere about his person and this presented the only light that there was.

Now there came a soft and gentle whispering, so it seemed to be, of vespers sung. Or of a choir in a distant chapel, or might it be the angels? Or perhaps the cherubim?

'My Mary,' cried the fellow, as there on the stage a woman appeared, transparent, a ghost-like wraith. She wore white robes and a coronet of violets upon the languid tresses of her head.

George's eyes were all but popping from *his* head. He

knew of the illusion known as Pepper's Ghost – it was a well-loved, music-hall presentation. But it required a vast sheet of angled glass and a false lower stage with cunning light effects.

This was none of *that*.

The white-robed phantom raised a pale hand and spoke as from a great distance. 'Shed no more tears for me, Johnny,' she said. 'I am part of the one which is all, now. I am at peace, be likewise.'

With which she was gone. Of a sudden. Just gone.

The electrical lighting returned to full force. The candle extinguished itself. Macmoyster Farl descended to the stage and folded his hands on his chest.

Now as George knew well, a crowd can be a volatile thing to handle. One moment in your palm with seeming solidity, the next slipping through your fingers like quicksilver.

The crowd's response to the incredible spectacle that had just occurred could go either way, in George's opinion. Thunderous applause, or screaming fearful flight.

It was the latter. Indeed.

The man who had lost his Marys led the way. He ran screaming from the tent auditorium, hotly pursued by the crowd. There were no calls for the return of their pennies but they had seen enough. Felt enough. Experienced enough. The crowd craved the dull safe reality of the outer world. The crowd made a mighty rush for it, overturning quality chairs, tripping over one another.

Presently George found himself all alone in the tent auditorium. All alone but for Mr Macmoyster Farl, who stood all alone on the stage. George shook his head and offered a shrug. Though George's mouth hung open.

'Fiddle de, fiddle dum,' said Macmoyster Farl, his voice now somewhat higher and nearer to the normal. 'To use the current argot of the showmen's world, it would appear that I "peaked too early and made a werry 'am-fist of a two-bob cert".'

George had no comment to make.

'My first performance, you see,' explained Macmoyster Farl, removing his gem-spattered turban to expose a baldy head. 'I will have to pace the presentations more carefully, I feel.'

'It is a remarkably accomplished act,' said George. 'The levitation was first rate and the ghostly illusion superb.'

'*Act?*' said Macmoyster Farl. '*Illusion?*' said Macmoyster Farl.

'Very impressive,' said George. 'And I speak as one who is in your profession.'

'A medium? Yourself?'

'A showman,' said George. 'Though no illusionist, me. I present an educational exhibit.'

'*Showman?*' went Macmoyster Farl, and his pale face grew steadily red. 'No showman, I. All you saw and experienced was one hundred per cent genuine. Will you not believe the evidence of your own eyes?'

'It was most convincing,' said George, 'but—'

'But me no buts, young man. I have devoted my life to the metaphysical and I seek now to share the knowledge and wisdom I have attained. You saw that fellow's Mary, did you not?'

George now cocked his head upon one side. 'Now wait,' said he. 'I think to detect sincerity in your words. Are you truly telling me that all I just saw was not the polished art of a master prestidigitator, but rather of a genuine mystic capable of communicating with the spirit world?'

Macmoyster Farl bowed his baldy head and cradled his turban beneath his right arm. He put his long left finger to his temple and once again rose from the stage.

'You,' and the deep dark voice was back, 'you, George Geoffrey Arthur Fox, zany to Mr Charles Milverton Snodgrass, who presents himself as Professor Cagliostro Coffin, would you know your future?'

'Well,' said George. 'I don't know,' said George. 'Charlie Milverton Snodgrass?' said George also.

'The book,' boomed Macmoyster Farl. '*The Book of Sayito* will be opened unto you. You will find Her, young George Fox. Upon your shoulders will rest the future of the planets.'

Macmoyster Farl took in a deep breath.

George asked, 'What do you mean?'

But before that question could be answered there came a great hustling and bustling into the auditorium tent.

'That's him,' a voice called out. And George Fox saw the policemen. They came in a fearsome company, big and bluely clad. And with them came two odd funereal-looking fellows, who appeared to be in charge of what was clearly an arrest. Two Gentlemen in Black were these, and George liked not the look of them.

Macmoyster Farl was wrestled from the stage. Hand-cuffs were enclosed about his delicate wrists, and amidst much clamour he was dragged away.

George looked on, agog.

Macmoyster Farl's voice called back to George. 'The future will depend on you,' it called.

And George was left alone.

But for a moment.

One of the funereal Gentlemen in Black returned to the tent, leaned low and whispered into George's ear.

'Forget about all this,' he whispered. 'You saw nothing, you heard nothing. Do you understand?'

George Fox opened up his mouth.

A pistol clicked at his neck.

'Nothing,' said George. 'I saw nothing and I heard nothing.'

'Good boy, then.'

And George was once more alone.

Somewhat later and considerably shaken, George Fox left the tent auditorium. There was no sign of Macmoyster Farl, the fearsome policemen or the Gentlemen in Black. George Fox sighed and shivered.

Then discovered, to greater distress, that Professor Coffin's handcart had been stolen.

8

rofessor Coffin was not best pleased at George's return.

He was not best pleased by the lateness of George's return. Nor by the fact that George did not return in the company of the professor's handcart.

He did, however, take stock of George's condition.

George had an all-in look to him. A down-and-out and all-in look. Certainly George was exhausted physically. He had dragged upon a wooden pallet, begged from the pharmacist, five cannisters of formaldehyde and ten of distilled water. Violet nosegays, to the number one hundred, and a pair of those new facial masks that were presently quite the thing amongst the surgeons of the London Hospital.

Professor Coffin asked to be given his change.

George forked it over with a shaking hand.

Professor Coffin viewed his glum assistant.

'What ails you, boy?' he asked. 'You have a sorry look to you and it's not for the loss of my handcart.'

George sat himself down upon the rear steps of the showman's wagon and buried his face in his hands.

Professor Coffin heard the sniffling sounds and laid a hand upon young George's shoulder.

'Tell me all and tell it to me now,' said he. 'And if anyone has harmed you it will be the worse for them.'

It was approaching late afternoon now and although Professor Coffin had erected the exhibition tent, winched the Martian in its covered tank down from the wagon and single-handedly manoeuvred it into said tent, then hauled up the banner that announced the 'Most Meritorious Unnatural Attraction', set out the bally rostrum, climbed upon it and proclaimed the meritorious nature of his unnatural attraction, he had taken not a penny of a profit.

True, he'd drawn money from Rubes, but once inside the tent and almost brought to blindness by the reek of the pickled beasty, all had made with knotted fists and demanded back their coin.

Sorely vexed, Professor Coffin was, but not too vexed to see another's pain. He sat himself down beside the sorrowful lad and asked once more to be told what was what.

George then told his tale, most dismally.

'Macmoyster Farl,' said the professor, when the tale was done. 'There is a name that brings back memories.'

'You know him?' asked young George. 'Then is he genuine? He knew my name and yours too, Mr Snodgrass.'

'Ah, and plah.' Professor Coffin spat. ''Tis true enough for me, I so regret. But I have never met the man, only heard the stories.'

'He claims that he has travelled to the planets and he spoke to me of very curious things.'

'A hero of the Crown,' said the professor. 'A captain of the Middlesex Regiment of the Queen's Own Electric Fusiliers. He served in the Martian campaign and to all accounts saw terrible things upon that Godforsaken planet. He won the OCE – the Order of the Celestial Empire – for deeds of bravery, but on a second tour of duty became somehow marooned. He wandered alone upon that lifeless world for five years before an archaeological expedition sent out by the Royal Society found him.

'Of course, Mars is now part of the Grand Tour if you have the wherewithal to pay for your flight, but five years back, before the dawn of passenger travel in space, the visits to Mars were few and far between.'

'A hero of the Crown,' said George. 'You would not think today that he had ever been a soldier.'

'When archaeologists fetched him up from Mars he was stark roaring mad. He was committed to St Mary of Bethlem's asylum, otherwise known as Bedlam.'

'And there perhaps he has been returned,' said a sighing George. 'The manner of his arrest was most curious. Two pale bodies in funeral black took charge of the affair. And one of them—' And George once more buried his face in his hands.

'A Gentleman in Black,' said Professor Coffin, gravely. 'No good ever came from crossing the path of one of those terrible fellows.'

'Who are they?' asked George, from between his fingers.

'It is better not to know.'

'He threatened me.'

'I am sure that he did.'

'He frightened me.'

'I am sorry.'

George Fox lifted up his head and gazed at the professor.

'I am so sorry,' he said. 'Once again I have let you down. I am no good to you, best I seek employment elsewhere.'

'No, not a bit of it, my boy. I agree that of late you have cost me more than somewhat. But such is the showman's lot. One day a feast, the next an empty platter. But we will triumph somehow. Tell me more of what Macmoyster said.'

'He said that the book would be opened to me. That I would find Her. And that upon my shoulders would rest the future of the planets.'

'I see your cause for glumness. But what of this book of which he spoke?'

'*The Book of Sayito*', said George.

Professor Coffin smiled. 'Otherwise known as the Venusian Bible.'

'Indeed,' said George, recalling his conversation with Ada Lovelace, she of unhappy memory. 'But what *that* would have to do with me would be any person's guess but my own.'

Professor Coffin rose to his feet and gave a twirl of his cane. 'I will give my thoughts to these matters and should revelations whisper at my ear, I will whisper at yours. But for now,' and he gave a bow to George, 'the temperature drops and my thinking is that if we drain friend Martian's tank and speedily refill it, deck our tent with nosegays and set you upon the bally, we might turn a profit by evening time and fill our bellies withal. What say you to this, my loyal z— *assistant*?'

'I say yes to it,' said George. And shook the professor's hand.

★

In less than an hour, the horrid work done, George took his place on the bally. Barker for the evening, he sought to make the professor proud.

And so George Fox called out to passing Rubes. Tonight the Most Meritorious Unnatural Attraction took on new life, breathed into it by George.

'Come one, come all,' he called to all and sundry. 'View the fiend in all of its terrible form. Behind this wall of canvas lurks the most evil being in all of the universe. Phnaarg by name, the King of all the Martians. Brought to book by General Sir Macmoyster Farl OCE, hero of the British Empire, who engaged the wicked monster in swordplay one upon one.' And George enthusiastically mimed such swordplay, cut and slash and parry with Professor Coffin's cane. 'Come see for yourself and marvel and thrill. No unaccompanied ladies or children under five.'

When the distant chimes of ten were heard from Hounslow clock tower and the crowds had melted away and were gone, Professor Coffin smiled.

'Splendid,' he cried, a–counting of coin. 'Positively splendid.'

'Did I make you proud, sir?' asked George Fox.

'Beyond all words, my boy, beyond all words.' Professor Coffin danced a copper penny on his palm. 'The take is more than a pound, my boy, and what do you think of that?'

'I think,' said George, 'as I counted them in, that it is considerably more than that. In fact, it is precisely—'

'Two pounds, one and tuppence,' said Professor Coffin.

'Yes, precisely that.'

'And one–third of it is yours.'

'A third?' said George. 'But you only pay me one-quarter.'

'But you did magnificently. We will make a showman of you yet.'

It took much time to fold the tent, winch the Martian back into the showman's wagon, lock all and sundry within *and* disable the traction engine (for Professor Coffin had spied minions of Mandible Haxan lurking in the crowd), but finally the professor and his valued assistant set off for sustenance and ale.

The taverns of Hounslow never closed during the Hounslow Fair. They served beer and victuals twenty-four hours of the day. Professor Coffin led young George past many a rowdy alehouse before tuning into a narrow side street and walking up to an unlit door.

'A more select establishment,' he explained to George, whose stomach rumbled loudly. 'But just one thing before we enter. This is where the exclusive brotherhood raise their cups.'

'The exclusive brotherhood?' George Fox queried.

'Come, boy,' said the professor. 'The unique ones. The very special people. Many are close friends of mine and have worked with me in the past. You will find most as charming as can be. If you show politeness to them, it will be returned to you.'

'I am confused,' said George. 'But perhaps it is from lack of food.'

'And you'll dine well tonight and I will buy you ale.' Professor Coffin knocked upon the door.

There was a moment's pause and then the sounds of drawing bolts and then a face peered out into the darkness.

'Quenten, my good friend and fellow.' Professor Coffin stepped from the dark and gave the fellow hugs.

The fellow said, 'My good friend Cagliostro.'

And as this hugging went about its friendly business, George stared on. Somewhat goggle-eyed and roundly lipped in the mouth department.

For Quenten was not as other men. There was a difference to the face of Quenten that cut him out from the crowd. A quality of uniqueness. Something very special.

Quenten winked over Professor Coffin's shoulder.

Winked at George.

Winked at George with a single eye.

In the very centre of his forehead.

9

'uenten Vamberry the Third,' said Professor Coffin, making the introductions. 'And this is my assistant, George Fox.'

Quenten Vamberry parted from the professor's embrace and wrung George Fox's hand between his own. 'Damnably fine to meet you, George,' he said.

'And me you, sir, yes.'

George found himself led into a comfortable room that smelled of hops and tobacco smoke. Lamps fuelled by whale oil with dark heavy shades hung in wall sconces and dropped pools of light upon scrubbed oaken tables. The hubbub of merry conversation did not cease as George entered this room, no one looked up at him, no one paid him any mind.

'Porter?' asked Quenten of George and the professor. 'Porter and supper, I'm thinking.'

'Yes indeed, indeed.' Professor Coffin grinned a mighty grin. He settled himself down into a chair at an empty table and beckoned George to do the very same.

George sat himself down, took off his bowler, diddled its brim with his fingers. His eyes did cautious wanderings about the clientele.

They were indeed most very special people.

A dwarf, his face tattooed after the fashion of the Maori, played at chess with a princely personage from the Indian subcontinent. This gentleman wore a neat white turban affixed with a single ruby, a high-collared shirt, a white bow tie, a double-breasted evening jacket of dark stuff with broad lapels of silk. This jacket, however, bulged curiously, and when the time came for this personage to make his move, a tiny hand sneaked out from the front of the jacket and moved the chess piece for him.

'Laloo, the Indian double boy,' said Professor Coffin, following the direction of George's wandering eyes. 'A parasitic twin sprouts from his chest. He calls it Anna, but it is a he. And plays a finer game than does Laloo.'

George Fox shook his head in wonder. 'What marvellous folk,' said he.

'And many of them, as I told you, my good friends.' Professor Coffin, through polite indication and no pointing whatsoever, drew George's attention to a number of the establishment's most notable patrons.

'Fedor Jeftichew,' said Professor Coffin. 'Exhibited as Jo Jo, the Russian Dog-Faced Boy. Although a thick coat of hazel-coloured hair adorns him from top to toe and his face resembles that of a Skye terrier, no more charming and personable a young man could you wish to meet.'

Fedor caught the gaze of George and waved at him with a hairy hand. George smiled back and nodded and gave a little wave.

'Carl Untham,' the professor continued. 'The Armless Prodigy. Born without upper limbs, he can do with his feet what any man can do with his hands. And he plays a virtuoso violin. Perhaps he will favour us with a tune later. But do not push the matter – he can become truculent when in his cups and has been known to kick the occasional nuisance out of the window.'

'I will bear that in mind,' George said.

Professor Coffin went on. He named a bearded lady and a frog-boy known as Hopp, a pair of beautiful Siamese twin ladies, a Wild Man of Borneo, a pinhead fop named Zip and an albino called Unzie, whose plaited hair hung down to his knees.

And then the suppers arrived. Two brimming bowls of nadger, with pickled frips on the side and a generous platter of dolly-bread that none would turn their nose up to. Even on a Tuesday, when the world preferred blunt rolls. George and the professor got stuck in to their suppers and George felt rather glad to be alive.

He had one of those moments that folk sometimes have and are grateful for. Moments of realisation and happiness, for good food and better friendship.

'You smile as you chew,' observed the professor. 'A good sign, that, by my reckoning.'

George smiled somewhat more and swallowed as he did so. 'I do enjoy working with you, Professor. Life on the road can never be said to be dull. Although . . .' And here George's face clouded somewhat. 'I must confess to hatred of that Martian.'

Laughter choked Professor Coffin, who spat frips over George.

'Pardon me,' he said, a-wiping at his chin, 'but you and that pickled horror are not a loving partnership.'

George continued with his feeding.

'And in truth,' continued the professor, dabbing once more about his Mr Punch chin, 'I do not know how much longer we can keep that thing on display. It is coming apart all over and soon may be nothing but soup.'

'My heart will not break when we flush it away,' said George.

'No, but your belly will rumble. We turned a fine penny tonight, young George. You are a natural on the bally. If we lose our Martian we must have something even better to replace him with.'

'Perhaps someone here is presently unemployed,' was George's suggestion.

Professor Coffin shushed that one to silence.

'These are top-class acts,' said he, 'who deserve and attain to top-class wages.'

'But if they draw in the Rubes, then they surely deserve their pay.'

'It can be complicated.' Professor Coffin pressed on with his supper, presently finished same, dabbed himself hugely with his oversized red gingham handkerchief and leaned back in his seat, a-stroking of his belly.

George mopped up the last of his gravy with a slice of dolly-bread and made satisfied smackings with his lips. 'I really did enjoy that meal,' he said.

'Fiddle de, fiddle dum.' Professor Coffin supped upon porter. 'It sets me to thinking, though.'

'About what?' asked George Fox.

'As to what might replace our reeking Red Planet reprobate.'

A chuckle came from a table nearby and Laloo turned smiles upon them.

'We overhear you, Cagliostro,' said the well-clad fellow.

'It is ever the showman's lot to suffer hardship and privation,' said Professor Coffin. 'Whilst great folk such as you accrue kingly pensions, we showmen must fork out countless expenses, bear the heavy weight of responsibility and deposit but a few meagre pennies into our patched pockets.'

Laloo let out another chuckle. 'And see that,' he said to George. 'He says all that without ever breaking a smile.'

'And believe me, it is not easy,' said Professor Coffin, breaking one now, and a large one too. 'Years of practice, it takes, and I am getting no younger.'

'In truth,' said Laloo, 'the days of the live show, with a prodigy of nature on display, may well be numbered. Mechanical marvels fill the public's imagination and gaffs are everywhere.'

'Gaffs?' asked George, who was a stranger to the term.

'Fakes,' said Laloo. 'As the professor observed, although obliquely, a live performer needs food, accommodation and payment. A bouncer, by contrast, needs none of these things.'

'Bouncer?' queried George.

'Or "pickled punk". A two-headed baby, or unborn Siamese twins, created from wax and hair and mounted in a display bottle. On a recent tour of America, I visited a company in New York by the name of Merz and Hansen – "Manufacturers of Petrified Mummies, Two-Headed Giants, Sea Serpents, Double Babies, etc." They boast that they can create anything your imagination runs to and they only require twenty-one days to create it – the time it takes for the papier mâché to thoroughly dry.'

'Incredible,' said George.

'And a death knell to the travelling show,' said the professor. 'Perhaps we have become an anachronism.

Our time is past. Soon it will be electrical whirligigs and · bumping motor carriages.'

'You sing a dismal song,' said Laloo, 'but one that lacks for candour on your part. Yes, perhaps we cannot do battle with the new, but why would we try? To do so would be foolhardy. We must adapt, as all must, as Man moves forwards into the future. And who knows this better than you, who has presented so many varied attractions, each in its way tailored to the current fashions?'

''Tis true,' said Professor Coffin, raising his porter pot to Laloo and calling out for further ales. 'But it is every showman's dream to find *the* attraction. That most wonderful attraction that ever there was. Something that all of the world would pay to see. And also the other worlds too.'

'There are wonderful beings about,' said Laloo.

'There is Joseph,' said the dwarf with the tattooed face. 'Some say he's the greatest of our age.'

'Joseph?' asked George.

'Joseph Carey Merrick*,' said Professor Coffin, 'advertised as "the Elephant Man". An extraordinary fellow by all accounts. But he has long retired from the travelling life and lives now at the London Hospital, on a special pension.'

'Your Martian came from there, did it not?' asked George.

'Through the kind donation of Sir Frederick Treves, Mr Merrick's sponsor and friend. I have obliged him

---

* History does record that Joseph Carey Merrick died in 1890. History must therefore have got it wrong once again.

with a few specimens over the years. He was quite eager to lend me the Martian.'

'Glad to be rid of the smell,' said George.

'I now believe this to be the case, yes. And he told me a strange thing, too, as it happens.'

'Go on,' said George, as he, Laloo and the tattooed dwarf drew in close to hear the professor's words.

'In eighteen eighty-eight there were seven murders in Whitechapel.'

'Jack the Ripper,' said George.

'Precisely. And several displaying wounds thought to have been inflicted by surgical instruments. And every murder within a stone's throw of the London Hospital.'

'A surgeon?' said George.

Professor Coffin shook his head. 'Not according to Mr Treves. Mr Treves says Joseph Merrick did them. He says that Mr Merrick confessed to him whilst drunken with champagne.'

'A sensational tale,' said Laloo.

'And one that will never find its way before the public,' said Professor Coffin, in a whisper. 'Mr Merrick is the darling of the gentry and in failing health. He will die loved and that will be how history will record him.'

'But—' went George.

'I did not say it was "just",' said Professor Coffin, 'only that that is how it will be.'

There was a certain silence then, each man alone with his thoughts.

'Of course,' said the tattooed dwarf, 'we all know what the greatest attraction in the world *would be*, if anyone could attain it.'

'Ah,' said Laloo.

And Professor Coffin nodded.

'What is it, then?' asked George. 'What might this be?'

'A legend,' said Professor Coffin. 'A tall tale told in pot-rooms.'

'I know of a man who claims that he saw Her,' said Laloo. 'Or claims that he knows of a man who did, or suchlike.'

'What is it?' George asked once again.

'I heard,' said the dwarf, 'that Barnum* is even now in negotiations. That he hopes to present Her in London before the Queen's Jubilee.'

'What is it?' asked George. Once more. Again.

'I have heard that you cannot gaze upon Her without the use of special goggles,' said Jo Jo, the Russian Dog-Faced Boy. 'That Her glance can turn you to stone just like the Medusa's.'

'If someone does not tell me at once,' said George, 'I will be forced to start a fight.'

'Then out of the window you will go,' said the armless Mr Untham.

'Someone tell me, please.'

'She is known by many names,' said Laloo, 'and there are many tales regarding Her origins. Some say that She is an unnatural prodigy, a genuine chimera of woman and of fish.'

'A mermaid?' said George. 'A genuine mermaid?'

'Not a mermaid,' said the dwarf. 'Although there is the involvement of fish. She is the last survivor of Atlantis. She breathes through gills but walks upon two legs.'

'Atlantis,' went Mr Untham. 'Plah. She was born

* And history also records that Barnum died in 1891. Ludicrous!

from an alchemist's vat. Created by the last of all the Magi. Grown in a girl-shaped vase and brought to life by words drawn from the Grimoire of Moses.'

George glanced to Professor Coffin.

Professor Coffin shrugged. 'There are many, many theories,' he said, 'but all agree that She *does* exist somewhere. And that She is the most wonderful creature in all of the universe. They call Her the Japanese Devil Fish Girl.'

'They call Her Sayito,' said the dwarf.

10

ventually they returned to Hounslow Heath, somewhat mellow from drink. As the air within the showman's wagon was once more ill-favoured by Martian taint, the professor pulled out blankets and suggested to George that as the night was warm, they should bivouac on the roof.

A deal of alcohol-induced comedy climbing up there concluded with the two of them side by side and flat upon their backs, gazing up at the stars.

'You knew,' said George. 'And do not deny that you did.'

'I assume you refer to the Japanese Devil Fish Girl,' Professor Coffin said.

'You knew that She is known as Sayito. And because Macmoyster Farl said that I would one day open *The Book of Sayito* and meet *Her*, you took me to that very alehouse and steered the conversation around to that very subject.'

'You give me credit for subtlety and subversiveness that I would be proud to possess.'

'So it is all just a coincidence?' George gave a drunken hiccup.

'On this occasion, yes. Although some might discern

the finger of Fate pointing, pointing, pointing.' Professor Coffin pointed a finger at George. 'Pointing at you, young George.'

'I am no one special,' said George. 'Although I know I would like to be.'

'Then perhaps this is your moment. This very day the turning point in your life.'

'Really?' said George. 'Do you really think so?'

'I believe that everyone has such a moment. But few are they who recognise it as such and follow where Fate leads them.'

'Well,' said George. 'I do not know what to say.'

A shooting star passed across the sky and George Fox wished upon it.

The dawn brought with it spots of rain, and the rooftop lost its charm.

'Where to now?' asked George, as he took to blearily raking out the firebox of the traction engine. 'Onward with the wagons to another fair, or what?'

Professor Coffin brought forth a hip flask, poured a tot of 'Mother's Ruin' into its cap and offered this to George.

'An early-morning enlivener,' he said. 'But surely you recall our late-night conversation?'

'That my moment has come and I must follow where Fate will lead?'

'The very same. What are your thoughts upon this matter this morning?'

George gazed off all around and about. The show folk were stirring from their tents and caravans. Loading up their gaily painted wagons. Priming their steam engines, stoking coal. Romany women washed their clothes in oversized zinc baths. Ragged children played amongst the show boards and rolled canvas.

George took a deep and steadying breath. 'I love this life,' he said.

Professor Coffin eyed him thoughtfully. 'You are a natural to it,' he said. 'But it will not suit for ever. There is more to you, young George. More that is still to be discovered.'

'And the Japanese Devil Fish Girl?' George asked.

'Whom some call Sayito?'

George made a face that had no expression. 'What do you make of it all?'

'It is what *you* make of it all that matters, George. You are the one who has been offered prophecy. If *you* were to ask *me* to join you in a search for the most wonderful being in all of the universe, the greatest sideshow attraction that ever ever existed, what do *you* think *my* answer might be?'

'I can smell Martian from here,' said George. 'I think your answer would be "yes".'

'So, do we seek Her? What do you think?'

'I think we *do*,' said George.

Professor Coffin did a little dance. He spat into the palm of his right hand and smacked it into George's. 'When you find this wonder,' he said merrily, 'and I do mean when and not if. *When* you find this wonder, you must promise me that we will go fifty-fifty on all of the takings.'

'Fifty-fifty?' said George.

'If that suits you, my boy.'

'It does indeed.'

'Then that is the deal shaken on.'

This deal shaken on, the two of them stood with their hands in their pockets gazing around and about.

'So,' said George.

'So indeed,' said the professor.

'Right,' said George.

'As right as a nine-penny portion,' said the professor.

'Cheese,' said George.

And, 'Cheese?' said the professor.

'I have run out of things to say,' said George.

'Fiddle de, fiddle dum. We must formulate a plan of campaign.'

'I would not reject breakfast out of hand,' said George.

'A plan of campaign,' said Professor Coffin. 'If we are to discover this wonder, it would be well for us to have some inkling of where to search. Do you not agree?'

'Japan,' said George. Without hesitation.

'It would seem the logical place to start.' Professor Coffin took to pacing up and down, measuring his strides with his cane.

'We shall cross the Channel,' said George, 'work our way through Europe, then traverse Russia, then China, then down the Korean Peninsula to Japan.'

'Your knowledge of geography is profound,' said the professor.

'It was one of my favourite subjects at school.'

'And arithmetic?' Professor Coffin asked.

'I have some skills in that discipline, yes.'

'Then perhaps you would care to calculate how many days it would take a traction engine with a top speed of five miles per hour to span the continent of Europe, cross Russia, China and Korea and fetch up in Tokyo?'

George attempted certain mental calculations. He folded his brow with the effort.

'Let me spare you a banjoing of the brain, George,' said the professor. 'A very, very, very long time would be the answer to that. And whether the engine would even hold up past Calais, I would not care to wager upon.'

'Then we are lost,' said George. 'It cannot be done.'

'There are other modes of transport,' the professor said. 'We live in the Modern Age, remember. There are steam trains now that can travel at sixty miles an hour. And other vessels faster still than that.'

'Ah,' said George. 'You speak of course of spaceships. They may take the wealthy upon the Grand Tour, but there are no spaceports in Japan.'

'True,' said Professor Coffin. 'There are no spaceports anywhere upon this Earth but London. But there are other craft that fly in the sky and one that is bound for Japan.'

George lifted his bowler hat and gave a scratch to his head.

'You marvelled at it only two days back, young George.' Professor Coffin fished into his waistcoat pocket and pulled out a printed flysheet. 'I saw this a-blowing along the road. I do not know why I picked it up, but I did. This, young George, is how we will reach Japan.'

George took the crumpled paper, unfolded same and put his gaze upon it.

AROUND THE WORLD IN SEVENTY-NINE DAYS

he read.

GREAT FLIGHT OF WONDER
SEVENTEEN CAPITAL CITIES TO BE VISITED
UPON THIS STUPENDOUS
AERIAL PERAMBULATION OF THE PLANET
PARIS – ROME – MOSCOW – TOKYO ETC.

THE EMPRESS OF MARS
THE WORLD'S MOST MODERN AIRSHIP
TAKES FLIGHTS FROM
THE ROYAL LONDON SPACEPORT AT SYDENHAM
27TH JULY 1895

Tickets from 200 gns

George looked up at Professor Coffin. 'The *Empress of Mars?*' he said.

'And she takes flight three days from now.'

'But two hundred guineas a ticket,' George said. 'How could we come by such wealth?'

'Ah,' said the professor. 'It might be done. In such a noble and adventurous cause, we might sell the wagon and its contents.'

'The Martian?' said George, with relish in his voice.

'And the traction engine. Mandible Haxan would willingly purchase it back.'

'But four hundred guineas?'

'It will require enterprise on both our parts. This is a huge commitment for me, young George. I will be parting with everything. We will have to live entirely on our wits alone. Does that thrill you, or fill you full of fear?'

'A little of both, as it happens,' said George.

'So, shall we do it, my boy?'

'The *Empress of Mars*,' said George, wistfully. 'To fly on the *Empress of Mars*.'

'To seek the Japanese Devil Fish Girl,' said Professor Coffin.

11

rom its very genesis, Earth's first spaceport gave cause for concern and controversy. The British Empire's back-engineering of crashed Martian spaceships and subsequent annihilation of the Martian race brought forth worldwide rejoicings. And the arrival of emissaries from Venus and Jupiter, to welcome Earth into the fellowship of planets (a fellowship from which Mars had been notably excluded due to its people's warlike nature and expansionist policies), with the emissaries presenting themselves before the court of Queen Victoria, gave rise to further exultations of joy.

But there the fun and jollification and the elation at opening trade and communing between planets ceased. For anyone other than the wealthy of the British Empire. The British Empire owned the Martian spaceships. The British Empire had exclusive use of these spaceships to commune between the planets. The British Empire signed treaties and trade agreements with the Venusians and Jovians.

The British Empire would build the Earth's first *and only* spaceport. In London.

The Americans were not best pleased. They wanted a spaceport built in Washington. P. T. Barnum, considered by most, if not all, to be the world's greatest show-man, had even promised to finance the building of the Washington Spaceport (as long as he might be allowed to run the food concessions there and establish a permanent circus in the arrivals building).

Requests had been put in from France, the Prussian Empire and Czarist Russia. The British Empire held firm. The one and only spaceport would be in London.

Then came the matter of design, for the build-ings, hangars, landing platforms and so forth. Naturally, only British architects and engineers would be given consideration. And – and here once more conspiracy theories came into their own – it was said that only high-ranking Freemasons need apply. A fist fight broke out in the House of Commons between Isambard King-dom Brunel, designer of the Great Western Railway and just about anything else that could be constructed from iron and steel, and Alfred Waterhouse, architect of the Natural History Museum and pretty much anything else that might be raised from terracotta brick.

Brunel won the fight, but Waterhouse took the contract with a design based upon Charles Barry's neo-Gothic masterpiece, the Houses of Parliament. The architectural designs were passed personally by Her Majesty Queen Victoria, who considered them emi-nently suitable. For, to quote her words: 'As the Houses of Parliament pass bills to convey fairness, justice, truth and virtue throughout this world, so such a design will convey these concepts to travellers from other worlds.'

Whether these travellers from other worlds would embrace British democracy or indeed seek to influence Earthly politics and political thinkings was another cause for concern. Particularly when it came to matters theological.

The invaders from Mars, proving, as they did, that intelligent life existed upon other worlds, caused considerable stir amongst this world's religious bodies. Earth had, up until then, cornered the market in God, so to speak. That other planets were inhabited and that the denizens of these worlds held to other religious faiths that did not precisely mirror our own was sorely vexing to the Earthly church hierarchies.

The Pope decreed that as no mention of life outside the Earth had been made in the Bible (which was, after all, *the* Word of God), off-worlders must be considered pagan and ripe for conversion to Christianity. The Archbishop of Westminster held to similar views, but was reticent about passing on to Her Majesty a message from the Pope that Rome would send missionaries to Venus and Mars to deal with the peoples there in the manner in which, several centuries before, they had dealt so successfully and kindly with the folk of South America.

It was all going to get rather complicated.

The matter of interplanetary trade gave rise to more gasps of disbelief from those outside of the British Empire. When they learned that England alone, having signed the exclusive treaties and trade agreements, would be taking care of *all* interplanetary business. 'To ensure fairness, justice, truth and virtue,' Queen Victoria explained.

Mr Gladstone put it in a manner that was understandable to all. 'As representatives of Planet Earth, the British Government has entered into a meaningful alliance with the Governments of Venus and Jupiter, an alliance both mercantile and military, which offers a combination of strength and security.' Adding, 'If Johnny Foreigner cares not for this, then so much the worse for Johnny Foreigner.'

So that was all sorted! To the Empire's satisfaction at least.

Which cleared the stage for more important matters.

Such as the actual name that the spaceport was to be given.

Mr Charles Babbage, who had been appointed head of the British Empire's Space Programme, put forward a number of suggestions that he considered suitable. These included:

The Charles Babbage Grand Astronautical Interplanetarium

The Charles Babbage Celestio-Pantechnicon Kinetic Harbour

The Charles Babbage Tri-World Transportarium

And perhaps the most obvious:

The Charles Babbage Astro-drome

All, however, were rejected, possibly because all were prefixed by the words 'The Charles Babbage . . .'

The name finally fixed upon was:

The Royal London Spaceport

And so it would remain.

And so, upon the twenty-seventh of July in the year eighteen hundred and ninety-five, a wondrous silver airship dandled elegantly above runways one to six. The day was of the sunniest and although another pea-souper held London firmly by the throat, here, in this delightful rural setting 'neath the great hill surmounted by the

Crystal Palace, the sky was blue, the birdies sang and all was right with the Empire.

Around and about the spaceport, strictly segregated according to their planetary origins, stood craft from other worlds.

Bulky merchant packets from Jupiter, all burnished copper (or the Jovian equivalent thereof), with swollen sides and riveted flanks and small, glazed piloting 'pimples'. These sprouted at irregular intervals above, below and to all sides of the bulbous craft, like the symptoms of a mechanical disease.

The pleasure-craft of Jupiter were quite another matter. Sleek and steely arrowheads with outboard power units.

But what drew the Earthman's eye upon this or any other morning were the spaceships from Venus. These interplanetary vessels were of surpassing beauty. The folk of Venus did not, of course, refer to their own planet as Venus. That was the name the folk of this world had given to it. The folk of Venus referred to their world as Magonia. And to their spacecraft as 'cloud-ships'. The cloud-ships of Magonia. And they *were* of surpassing beauty.

They were aptly named 'ships' because they resembled exotic galleons. Constructed not from metal but from some semi-translucent organic material, which offered up a rainbow sheen whilst seeming also to constantly shift through a spectrum of colours, these ships appeared to display no aerodynamic features whatsoever. They were the product of whimsy, fairy-tale castles, towers topped by conical roofs rising from galleon decks, with billowing, all-but-transparent sails set one upon another. To catch the solar winds, some said, but others doubted this.

It was claimed that these magical ships travelled through magical means, powered by faith alone and referred to by the Magonians as Holier-than-Air craft. Magonians *thought* their way across the vastnesses of space, it was said. And as they offered little in the manner of trade goods, discouraged any form of Earth tourism upon their planet and seemed to seek only to proselytise, they were viewed with a mixture of wonder and suspicion.

It was approaching midday and the last of the luggage and straggling rich folk were boarding the *Empress of Mars*. The cargo gangways fairly groaned beneath the weight of oak-bound steamer trunks and sharkskin portmanteaus. Ladies' dressing cases designed by Peter Carl Fabergé and Louis Vuitton. Delicately packed with exquisite perfumes, powders, lipsticks, smelling bottles by Crawfords of Piccadilly, lace handkerchiefs, countless kid gloves, elaborately hand-stitched 'unmentionables', brass corsetry and the entire pantheon of female under and over attire, shoes and hats and parasols and goggles for every occasion.

Gentlemen's 'diddy boxes' containing ivory-handled shaving paraphernalia, enamelled moustache-wax cases, inlaid snuff caskets, travelling Tantalus sets, firearms to enforce one's point in foreign parts, smoking accoutrements and all the tweeds and linen suits and formal wear and hattery that a gentlemen of means required when travelling abroad.

Add to this crates of the finest champagnes, medical essentials, travellers' libraries, picnicking hampers, ukuleles and mechanical musicolas, Sir Digby Pendleton's horse, Belerathon, without which he refused to travel anywhere, and Lord Brentford's monkey butler Darwin.

The mighty sky-ship sparkled in the sunlight, casting a great cigar-shaped shadow over the spaceport's cobbles.

The last of the luggage was finally aboard and the cargo gangways were mechanically winched into the upright position. The promenade decks were made gay with jostling gentry, waving their farewells to less-fortunate relatives, who could only stand and wave and aspire to emotions that did not include jealousy. The gentry aboard disported themselves in their finest 'out-going' attire. Gentlemen in 'morning formals' in soft pastel shades with matching top hats and gloves. Ladies in a riot of silks and tumbling lace with fans of pale satin embellished with bons mots and tasteful erotic drawings, wrought by the pen of Aubrey Vincent Beardsley.

Oscar Wilde was aboard, of course. And so too were Bram Stoker, Dame Nellie Melba, who had been engaged to provide entertainment in the Grand Salon, Mr Babbage, Nikola Tesla, Little Tich, who was travelling to New York, the first port of call, to take up a six-month residency at Carnegie Hall, and a host of other London glitterati. Charles Darwin* (unaware that his simian namesake gibbered in the cargo hold) shared a joke with the mystic and adventurer Hugo Rune. Princess Elsie, one of Queen Victoria's lesser known daughters, spoke in whispered tones to an enigmatic figure swaddled in the blackest of blacks with a velvet face mask and hat of outlandish size. This gentleman was rumoured to be none other than the society favourite

* Who clearly did *not* die in 1892, as history so inaccurately records.

Joseph Carey Merrick, famously known as the Elephant Man.

And so the summer sun shone down. The gentlemen smoked their expensive cigars in blatant disregard of any health and safety implications and toasted each other with glasses of deep-cut crystal. The ladies fluttered their fans and gently turned their parasols. The waiters and sky-men, serving folk, menials, menservants and maids, in uniforms starched and immaculately laundered, came and went about their business. Lines were dropped and bosun's whistle blown. The *Empress of Mars* prepared once more to rise into the sky.

But then calls were to be heard. Calls to hold hard and please to hold on for one moment. A honking of a hansom's horn as one of these horse-drawn conveyances was being driven at reckless speed across the cobbled space towards the airship, scattering members of the grounded waving crowd before it.

The cab drew up as the passenger gangway was rising. Two men, dressed in the most fashionable attire, hastened from the vehicle burdened by their luggage and pell-mell leapt to the rising ramp and boarded the *Empress of Mars*.

This late arrival elicited much mirth and applause from the assembled multitude, as 'fashionable lateness' had only recently begun to find favour.

'Your names please, gentlemen,' said the airship's major-domo, bowing to the stylish latecomers and snapping his fingers at bellboys to take the gentlemen's luggage.

The elder of the two twirled an ebony dandy cane topped with a silver skull. 'Professor Coffin,' he said. 'And my youthful ward and student, Lord George Fox.'

12

‘*ord* George Fox?’ asked plain George Fox, turning a shining brass ‘Aristocratic Cabin’ key upon his kid-gloved palm. ‘And how did I come by this title?’

Professor Coffin shushed the lad to silence with a fluttering of fingers. ‘A little conceit of my own invention,’ he whispered, ‘which you will come to appreciate when communicating with these swells.’

George Fox grinned and stroked at his striking chin. ‘It is a pity that we do not have friends and family here to wave us off,’ said he. ‘If my mother could see me now . . .’ But George’s voice trailed away, as it saddened him to think of his parents. Perhaps he would send them postcards from exotic ports of call. Wish them well, bid them love, ask forgiveness for running away.

George Fox sighed and waved at strangers, and then he cried, ‘Oh – look.’

Professor Coffin followed the direction of George’s now-pointings to view wheeled conveyances being driven at dangerous speed, to the considerable alarm of the ground-level wavers, and bound for the great airship.

‘Other late arrivals,’ called George to the majordomo. ‘Do not leave without them.’

‘All are ticked off on the manifest, Your Lordship,’

this fellow replied. 'But see, they are tradespeople, I believe.'

George looked on and said, 'Oh yes, they are.'

For oh yes, they were tradespeople indeed.

George spied a high-sided wagon upon which the words

JONATHAN CRAWFORD
Suiting to the Gentry

were emblazoned.

'We had our suits made there,' George observed.

Also a steam cart being steered with reckless abandon:

ELIAS MAINWARING
Quality Canes and Umbrellas

'We got our new dandy canes from there,' George observed.

A yellow brougham, drawn by two pairs of matched black geldings:

LOUIS VUITTON

'And our luggage came from—' And George's voice once more trailed away. He gave hard looks towards Professor Coffin, who shrugged.

The landing lines dropped, the ground anchor was weighed and the *Empress of Mars* rose gracefully into the sky.

George gave Professor Coffin further hard looks. 'I think I hear my name being called out by those tradespeople below,' he said. 'My name, prefixed with the title "Lord".'

Professor Coffin shrugged once more, though somewhat painfully it seemed. 'What could I do?' he whispered to George. 'We needed new clothes, new canes, new luggage. You could hardly have come aboard in your old suit, stinking of Martian, now could you?'

George shook his head, somewhat sadly.

'They are snobs to a man, those tradesmen,' Professor Coffin continued. 'They would not have extended credit to common folk like us, but to a "lord", oh yes indeed.'

'So you represented me as a lord. And they found out to the contrary.'

'Fiddle de, fiddle dum,' said Professor Coffin. 'When you return to England with gold in great store you can pay them off if you so choose.'

'Indeed I will,' said George.

'And please do not think unkindly of me,' said the professor. 'I sold all that I owned in order to purchase the tickets. You do not begrudge me a suit of clothes, surely?'

And surely George did not. He smiled a bit at this, did George, and stared out at the landscape spreading beneath them.

The Crystal Palace diamond studding the hilltop. The sprawl of outer London edging its way into the countryside. The village of Penge in all its beauty.

'It is all too beautiful,' said George, enthralled.

'It is something to be marvelled at,' agreed the professor. 'But all that dust raised by the hooves of the hansom cab's horse—'

'You failed to pay the driver,' said George.

'Have given me a throat most dry,' Professor Coffin said. 'And so I suggest we adjourn to the bar.'

'There is a bar on board?' George asked.

'Two, I understand, and a billiard hall. And a gaming lounge where one might engage in card games, or chess or suchlike, with one's fellow passengers.'

'Card games?' said George, recalling his lost gold watch.

'And I have something for you,' said Professor Coffin, producing same from his waistcoat pocket. 'His Lordship requires a timepiece, do you not think?'

George received the returned timepiece with gratitude. 'Well, thank you very much indeed,' he said.

'Think nothing of it, my boy. We are partners now, fifty-fifty all the way. Now what say you to a gin and Indian tonic water?'

'I say yes to that.'

The bar for gentlemen only was on an upper deck. It lurked, and 'lurked' was surely the word, within the bowels of the ship. It boasted no natural light, nor outside windows, and was already filling nicely with cigar smoke.

Big-bellied beings in acres of tweed, with pork-chop whiskers and multiple chins, tugged upon Cuban cigars and cradled brandy balloons in pink-sausage fingers. On their heads they wore sola topis; perched on these, colourful goggles.

'Tourists from Jupiter all set for a tiger hunt,' explained Professor Coffin.

A strange angular personage, wearing a frock coat of the Regency period, a high violet-tinted peruke and a veritable galaxy of gemstones upon his waistcoat area, was entertaining these Jovian tourists by conjuring all manner of unlikely objects from his delicate pocket handkerchief.

Professor Coffin ordered drinks and, unknown to George, charged these to Lord Fox's account. Then he joined George, who had seated himself at a Britannia-style public house table, wrought ingeniously from aluminium and balsa wood. George was giving this a good looking-over.

'Everything is light of weight,' he said. 'This is all such a wonder to me.'

'I am happy that you find it to your liking,' the professor said.

And George truly did. Being here was beyond anything he could possibly have imagined. Although he rather fancied getting back to the promenade deck as soon as he and the professor had done with their drinks. It was, although lavish in its way, somewhat stuffy in this gentlemen's bar and there was so much to be seen all over the rest of the marvellous pleasure ship.

'Which includes your accommodation,' said the professor, as if attuned to George's thoughts. 'You have a cabin with a view. You will not be disappointed.'

'I am so grateful for it all,' said George. 'I only hope that I do not disappoint *you*. You have ventured all on this expedition of ours. I hope that we find what we seek. The Jap—'

But the professor placed his hand lightly over George's mouth. 'Best not to speak the name aloud,' said he. 'It is our sacred secret, yours and mine, fifty-fifty – do you not agree?'

'Indeed,' said George, as a waiter arrived with the drinks.

'Just sign for those, if you would,' said the professor.

'Lord' George did so.

At length the angular gentleman in the Georgian finery concluded his entertainment, bowed to his portly alien audience and, having asked whether he might do so, and having been told that he might, seated himself at George and the professor's table.

'I spy,' said he, a-smiling at Professor Coffin, 'a fellow traveller.' And he reached out his hand and received a certain handshake.

'Professor Cagliostro Coffin,' said the showman. 'Celtic Lodge Five Hundred and Sixteen.'

'The Count de Saint-Germain,' said the other. 'Prague Four Hundred and Twenty-seven.'

Knowing nods came into play. George looked on, bewildered.

'My young charge, Lord George Fox,' said the professor.

George put out his hand in the hope of a certain shake, but received in return one of standard issue.

'Whence bound?' asked the professor of the count.

'All points, all cities. So much progress has been made, so many new sights to be seen. So much to be learned.'

'I am taking my charge on the Grand Tour,' said Professor Coffin. 'It will be an education for both of us, I am thinking.'

'Are you presenting an entertainment?' enquired the count.

'Oh no,' said the professor. 'I am temporarily retired from the showman's life.'

'But it never leaves your blood.' The count diddled

with his hankie and produced a live chicken. This he set upon his knee and tickled at its feathered neck.

'You have great skills,' said the professor, 'yet I do not recognise your name from any poster.'

'Prestidigitation is nothing more than a hobby for me at present,' said the count. 'I retired from the itinerant life many years ago. I am a chemist now. I formulate perfumes.'

'There would be many pennies to be made in that calling, should a man pursue it with sufficient knowledge at his fingertips.'

'Which is to say,' the count said, 'that it is a profession guarded by much secrecy. As, though, is any other.'

George felt that perhaps he should withdraw now to the promenade deck in the company of his gin. This conversation, he felt, was not likely to become particularly interesting. A yawn escaped George's lips and George apologised for it.

'Methinks,' said the count, 'that your charge finds my profession dull.'

'I am just tired,' said George. Who was not.

'Yet I could tell you things and show you things that would make your hair stand on end.'

'Really?' said George. Who doubted this.

The count smiled hugely upon George, who noted that he wore a great deal of face powder. And upon closer inspection, there was something of the museum mummy about him.

'Have you ever heard of the Scent of Unknowing?' the count asked of George.

George shook his head.

'It is a legendary perfume,' said Professor Coffin, who appeared to know something about most things. 'A perfume that, once sniffed, puts the sniffer into a state of trance, making them suggestible to almost anything.'

'To *absolutely* anything,' said the count. 'One sniff and you fall under its spell. The dream of every man is to have such a cologne, or any woman such a perfume.'

'And such a thing exists?' asked George.

'I seek it,' said the count. 'The Holy Grail of perfumes, one might say.'

George almost said that he and the professor were on a likewise quest, but recalling the professor's earlier words, he did not.

'I think you would become very rich indeed if you could make such a perfume,' said George. 'But I find it hard to believe that such a magical thing could really exist.'

'Really?' The Count de Saint-Germain raised a powdered eyebrow. 'So have you never heard of the Evil Breath?'

George shook his head and said, 'I have had such a thing upon a morning after too much drinking, I believe.'

'Not such as this,' said the count. 'Would you care for me to explain? And when I have done so, demonstrate?'

George now felt somewhat uncomfortable. 'Perhaps I might,' he said. 'I do not really know.'

'This boy must come to no harm,' said Professor Coffin to the count. 'I have heard of the Evil Breath, but I have never seen it demonstrated. I was informed that the effects can prove fatal.'

'Your charge will come to no harm,' said the count. 'Although he might experience some mild discomfort.'

And then he went on to tell a tale that put the wind up George.

13

‘ou must know,' said the Count de Saint-Germain, folding his arms in their quilted sleeves across his sparkling chest, 'that I have travelled greatly during my lifetime and fetched up upon many a foreign shore. I have wandered in the wastelands, jaunted through the jungles, mooched about the marshes, high-stepped o'er the hinterlands and tripped the light fantastic in the Garden of Earthly Delights.'

George Fox glanced towards the door and thought about the sunshine.

'And you must know,' the count continued, 'that the world traveller must be capable of defending himself against footpads, pirates, brigands and sundry rapscallions.'

'Which is why I acquired for us a brace of pistols,' said Professor Coffin to George.

'Which would be why I observed a gunsmith's wagon tearing towards us as the airship ascended,' said George. 'Although I did not comment on this at the time.'

'Might I continue?' asked the count. Receiving nods in the affirmative from his companions, he continued, 'Then it is this way. I have studied many forms of the martial arts. I have mastered samurai swordsmanship,

Baritso stick fighting and Irish Knobkerrie-Knocking-All-About. I learned Kung Fu, which means literally "empty hand", at a Shaolin temple in China. The monks there have developed a system of self-defence which involves no weaponry, for they are forbidden to carry such. Their techniques allow them to disarm even the most skilled swordsman. It is remarkable what they are capable of. Word reached me of secret techniques that did not involve strenuous punches or kicks, rather light but significant touches to the body that effected a complete collapse upon the part of the attacker. The system is known as Dimac, or the Death-Touch. One trained in Dimac can skilfully touch a person, thereby causing them to react fatally to this touch several days later.'

'That would not be much good if you were actually having a fight with them,' said George.

'I am leading to my point,' said the count. 'I learned also that there are certain practitioners of Dimac who claim to be able to disable an opponent without actually touching him at all, so adept have they become.'

'That would surely be impossible,' said George. 'You cannot affect someone like that without actually touching them.'

'So you might think. But it is indeed the case. The professor here will probably recall how popular mesmerism became some years ago.'

Professor Coffin nodded. 'It was doubted at the time,' said he, 'but now it has been refined into hypnotism. And, as the count says, one certainly can influence someone without actually touching them through the use of hypnotism.'

George nodded thoughtfully. He had watched a hypnotist's act at one of the popular music halls. He was not altogether certain, however, as to whether he truly believed in it or not.

'I see doubt once more upon your face, Your young Lordship,' said the count. 'But we shall see what we shall see. The Japanese masters created a martial system known as *Kiai-jutsu* or the Shout. As a soprano can shatter a champagne glass through the projection of a high-register note, so can one of these deadly fellows injure an assailant with a properly attuned cry.'

George's face looked no less doubtful.

'Then if you doubt *that*, Your Lordship, I have no reason to believe that you will not doubt me when I inform you that it is possible for an adept who has learned a secret technique to disable an opponent simply by breathing upon him.'

George sought to get up and take his leave. The professor suggested he stay.

'The Evil Breath,' said the Count de Saint-Germain. 'It took me seven years to develop, but I am now the master – indeed the *only* master – of this particular technique. I sought to create a breath so terrible that any man it struck would sink instantly into unconsciousness. I experimented with herbs and spices that I had collected upon my world travels, refining the combinations into my daily meals. I found that I could disable first a canary, then later rodents, and later still a fully grown mastiff. My problem, however, was that I could never tell exactly when I might be attacked on the road and could hardly gulp down herbs and spices at the approach of every suspicious-looking fellow.

'I continued with my experimentation, using certain breathing techniques I had learned in the Orient and adding the herbs and spices daily to my meals. At long last I have perfected the technique. I can summon the Evil Breath from deep within myself and project it over a distance of six or more feet, to the distress and disablement of any who would mean me harm.'

George Fox shook his head slowly. The thoughts now moving through his mind were to the effect of, *Is there any chance at all that one single word of any of that is true?* George concluded that, *No, there probably is not.*

The count grinned at the professor, who made a pained expression. Then the count drew back in his seat, inhaled a mighty breath, held it for but a moment, then breathed upon George.

George became instantly aware of the arrival at his nasal openings of the rankest, foulest, vilest, most foetid and disgusting stink that it had ever been his gravest misfortune to experience. It far outranked the pong of the pickled Martian and inhabited a cursèd kingdom of rotting corpses, sewerage scrapings and dog excrement.

George gasped, gagged, clawed at the air and fainted dead away. Professor Coffin caught him as he sank towards the table. 'That was a bitter lemon,' he told the count. 'From a detached point of view an amusing one. But if you have injured my charge it will be the worse for you, Evil Breath or no, believe me on this.'

'You clearly hold this young fellow in the highest regard,' said the count, removing from his waistcoat pocket a slim phial of liquid and carefully unscrewing its cap. 'I projected but the mildest of breaths. This will aid his recovery.'

'A smelling bottle?' said Professor Coffin.

'Not as such,' said the count.

He waggled the uncapped bottle beneath the nose of

George, who all of a sudden jerked once more into consciousness.

'You have experienced nothing but pleasure,' the count told him. 'You have no recollection of an Evil Breath, nor indeed any conversation concerning it. You fancy a nice stroll upon the promenade deck. Goodbye to you now, my boy, it was a pleasure to meet you.'

George Fox rose, placed his topper once more onto his head, bowed slightly towards the count, said, 'It was a pleasure to meet you, sir,' then left the gentlemen's bar.

Professor Coffin gazed at the phial of liquid as the Count de Saint-Germain rescrewed its cap.

'The Scent of Unknowing,' he said to the count.

'The same,' the other replied.

The *Empress of Mars* was travelling steadily west. The gentle murmur of the electric turbines, Mr Tesla's invaluable contribution to the craft, did nothing to mar the enjoyment of the exalted folk who strolled the promenade deck.

George Fox strolled amongst them, topper tipped at that angle known as rakish, dandy cane a-twirl between gloved fingers. George took in great breaths of healthy air. How perfect was this indeed. He experienced a certain queasiness of stomach, but attributed this to altitude sickness as this was his first time aboard a sky-going craft. George straightened his shoulders and grinned a little grin. No one was staring at him, or sniffing at him as they had done upon his ill-fated visit to the Crystal Palace. He looked the part and felt the part and folk thought him one of their own.

George took himself to the guardrail and leaned upon

it, gazing down upon England. Below was Bath, its streets and buildings laid out in a pattern only understood by high-ranking Freemasons. George did sighings at the beauty.

This *was* the life for him. It was, it really was. George recalled a line of Oscar Wilde's, to the effect that 'every man eventually finds his true position in life, whether it is above or below the one he was born into'.

And George gave the moment to thought.

All this had happened so suddenly. His encounter with Macmoyster Farl, 'the Apocalyptical Examiner', who had made his prediction to George. A prediction that George remembered word for word. '*The Book of Sayito* will be opened unto you. You will find Her, young George Fox. Upon your shoulders will rest the future of the planets.'

A shudder passed up George's spine. A tiny chill ran through him. Macmoyster Farl had been hauled from his levitation by police minions under the command of the Gentlemen in Black. George wondered what had become of him. Nothing good, he concluded. But then he smiled a little. There was nothing that he, personally, could do for Macmoyster Farl. Other than to travel on this quest with the professor. It might lead to great things, or indeed terrible things, but that was for the future. A future that included several exciting destinations.

The *Empress of Mars* would be docking in New York as its first port of call. Then San Francisco. Then Hawaii. Then Tokyo. And there they might find the Japanese Devil Fish Girl. Who could say? But this *was* the journey of a lifetime. Aboard the most amazing craft ever built upon Earth, in the company of London's most glamorous folk, George was surely one 'blessed of God'. George's smile spread wider.

So George did twirlings of his cane and further perambulations. He acquired a plan of the sky-ship and wandered here and there, taking in the great dining hall, the casino, the concert auditorium, the mixed bathing pool, the absinthe boudoir, the Grand Salon and finally his own cabin. An 'Aristocratic Cabin'. George found each and every thing very much to his liking.

He closed the cabin door, flung his topper onto a faux marble washstand and flung himself fully clothed onto his bed.

The bed dipped to one side and George was cast to the floor.

Regaining his feet, if not entirely his dignity, George now viewed his bed with suspicion. Then noted that it swung hammock-like from four aluminium chains, each affixed to a separate bedpost and each meeting at a central ceiling stanchion.

'No doubt for comfort in rough weather,' said George, carefully mounting his bed.

Suitably settled, George Fox put his hands behind his head and, smiling contentedly, took to an afternoon nap.

14

eorge Fox dreamed of a terrible stench and awoke with a terrible start. It was evening now and pale moonlight showed beyond his cabin porthole. George arose and straightened himself, smoothing down the crumpled parts and dusting at his shoulders. He took himself over to the washstand, turned a brass stopcock and took pleasure from the cool water that splashed between his outstretched fingers. He flicked some onto the face of him and dried with the towel provided. George felt a growing sense of excitement. His first night upon the wondrous sky-ship, what exotic pleasures awaited him? Professor Coffin had whispered that there was a Nympharium on board, but George had his doubts about that. There would be dinner of course, in the great dining hall. But George had worries for this. There was bound to be considerable cutlery involved and George had no idea as to the appropriate etiquette, knife and fork and strangely dimpled spoon-wise. The *Empress of Mars* was bound to offer room service. Perhaps it would be safer to dine in his cabin, rather than risk some social gaffe that would reveal his humble status to this world amongst the clouds.

George examined his reflection in the full-length

cheval glass. He certainly did *look* the part, even if he was unsure, in so many ways, of exactly how to act it.

But he would learn.

George returned his topper to his head and with his dandy cane once more in kid-gloved hands he left the cabin.

The promenade deck was deserted. Grand folk were dressing for dinner. George took joy in the sudden solitude of the vast expanse of decking. He dawdled along the rows of steamer chairs, past the tennis court and the shuttlecock area, sauntered to the edge of the deck and ran his gloved fingers along the guardrail. Chancing to look over, he viewed the lifeboats slung beneath, each canvas-covered and tethered by hawsers. George Fox cocked his head upon one side.

'Lifeboats?' he said to no one but himself. 'If this mighty craft was to plummet suddenly from the heavens, I am not quite certain how the lifeboats would help.'

Then George caught a glimpse of something untoward. A flicker of movement above one of the lifeboats. The canvas covering was being rolled back by someone within. George looked on as a colourful head emerged into vision, followed by naked shapely shoulders. Then George saw a washing bowl being lifted and tipped over the side. George's heart gave a tiny little jump. A stowaway on board!

George crouched down lest he be seen and peeped over the edge of the deck. The stowaway was clearly a rather attractive young woman with bright-red hair in swirling ringlets, sporting a jaunty little topper with a pair of evening goggles.

And nothing whatsoever more.

The stowaway was naked as could be.

George's mouth hung open and his eyes grew round and starey.

The stowaway was naughty Ada Lovelace.

George ducked back and rose to his feet and smiled very broadly. Ada Lovelace, who had used him so wickedly to gain entrance to the Crystal Palace. She *had* told George that she had arrived in London upon the *Empress of Mars*, but in the light of her wickedness he had come to doubt this. It would never have crossed his mind that she travelled upon the airship as a stowaway.

George took himself over to the nearest steamer chair and settled himself into it. This was indeed a 'situation', and one, George considered, that might in some way be turned to *his* advantage. He was not a vindictive lad, far from it. The concept of vengeance was alien to him. But perhaps some tiny punishment might be meted out, to teach the errant young woman to pursue less evil ways.

'The promenade deck is deserted,' said George to himself. 'I could perhaps do a wee-wee down upon her.'

But then, appalled that such a terrible thought had entered his head, he modified it to the emptying of an ice bucket. But then considering that this would be rather cruel, George took to wondering what else he might do.

Then he shrugged and sighed. Nothing whatever nasty, it simply was not in him. George returned to the guardrail, leaned upon it and gazed down. Ada was half-decent now, in glorious drawers and a singlet.

George licked his lips and then called down, 'Miss Lovelace, we meet again.'

George saw the lovely woman freeze, then frightened eyes glanced up to meet his smiling gaze.

'You,' she said in scarce but a whisper. 'You are here. But how?'

And then, suddenly aware of how little she was wearing, Ada Lovelace ducked away beneath the canvas covering and George took in the heavens with a grin.

The airship drifted just above the clouds of early evening. Above, the sky spread out in all its black and star-strewn beauty. George, who knew a little of astronomy, could discern the simple constellations, plus Venus there and also Mars, all pink and gently shimmering.

At length he heard movement below and was given to some surprise when a neatly dressed Ada Lovelace swarmed up the lifeboat's mooring hawser and climbed onto the deck.

'You have risen somewhat in the world, George Fox,' she said, with scarce a hint of breathlessness.

'*Lord* George Fox,' said George. 'You met me when I was travelling incognito. I believe I mentioned to you that I was of independent means.'

Ada Lovelace made one of those faces that is capable of saying so much without actually having to vocalise anything.

'And I find you in such regrettable circumstances,' said George. 'I will summon the major-domo at once and demand he upgrade your accommodation.'

'Pray sir, no,' said Ada. 'I believe you understand my circumstances well enough. I apologise for using you so poorly, it was unforgivable of me. But I am in dire need and you have the advantage of me. If it is your wish to use me as you will, so be it, if in return you do *not* report me to the major-domo.'

'Use you as I will?' George's eyes widened once

more. That of course would be one way of 'settling the score', as it were. And Ada was a very lovely woman.

'No,' said George. 'I am a gentleman and to take such advantage of a helpless woman would be anathema to me.'

'Oh,' said Ada. And there was perhaps a certain hint of disappointment in the manner of her saying it. 'Well, I thank you, kind sir,' and she curtseyed.

'We will put it into the hands of the major-domo,' said George. 'He will know what to do for the best.'

'Oh no, Lord George, please no.'

'I am joking,' said George. 'Are you hungry?'

'I am rarely anything *but* hungry. I come out and scavenge at this time of day, when the posh are dressing for dinner, and later when they have all gone to their bunks.'

'Come dine with me,' said George.

'In the great dining hall? I could not. I have no ticket and therefore no seat at a table.'

'It is a beautiful evening,' said George. 'Perhaps we might dine right here. Al fresco, as it were. I am sure that one of the bellboys might be prevailed upon to bring us something.'

Ada Lovelace gazed up into George's eyes.

The eyes of Ada Lovelace were large and green. Lit by the moonlight, George viewed twin reflections of himself therein. It seemed to George a moment of surpassing intimacy. 'Seat yourself there at that wicker table,' said George, 'and I will arrange everything.'

He turned to take his leave and then turned back. 'You will still be here when I return?' said he.

'I will,' said Ada. 'I promise.'

★

They dined upon roasted quail and sweet potatoes, asparagus tips and broccoli spears. They drank champagne from fluted glasses, munched upon truffles and sweet petits fours.

And all alone upon that deck they toasted each other and the stars and George was very happy.

'Tell me,' he said, when he thought that the time might be right, 'why have you been reduced to living such a life? You are clearly a young lady of some refinement. Has Fate used you cruelly?'

Ada Lovelace stared into her glass. 'I might ask such questions of you,' she replied. 'You were not badly brought up. Your accent, however, is not one of a public school and when we first met you reeked of embalming fluid and wore the costume of a showman's zany.'

'Assistant,' said George. 'Assistant.'

'And you do *not* possess a title. *Lord* Fox indeed.'

'It has a certain ring to it,' said George, viewing his lovely dining companion through his champagne glass. 'And one day, who knows, I might become a lord.'

'And I a lady,' said Ada. 'Or perhaps the Queen of Sheba is as likely.'

'You are evading offering an answer to my question,' said George. 'I have treated you with kindness and furnished you with food and drink – am I asking too much to learn of your misfortunes? Perhaps I might even be able to help you in some way.'

Ada Lovelace said that she was sorry. She was used now to being alone and fending for herself. She was of a respectable background but it had been discerned early that she possessed the most extraordinary skills in the field of mathematics. She was in fact a child prodigy.

But, and here a big but sadly presented itself. No university would take on this arithmetically inclined child genius because she was a girl. She yearned to take employment in some scientific field of endeavour, possibly something to do with the development of Mr Babbage's Difference Engine or the further understanding and back-engineering of captured Martian technology. But she would never be granted such opportunities in England and so she was running away, or indeed being carried away, to America, aboard the *Empress of Mars*, to seek a position suited to her prodigious talents in a land that offered greater prospects to a woman than did her own home country.

'Well,' said George, when Ada's tale was done. 'I wish you all the bestest for it. Everyone should have the opportunity to follow their dream, and I have heard it said that America offers many opportunities. I hope that you will find what you seek in America.'

'Thank you, Lord George,' said Ada, gazing up at George and fluttering her eyelids. 'You are a very nice young gentleman and it would please me greatly to call you my friend.'

George smiled somewhat wanly. Young ladies always said that to him. They always wanted just to be his friend, though *best friend* some of them said. And though George was eager to take a lover and experience the joys that sexual intercourse were promised to offer, it seemed that this was unlikely to occur before he met with a young woman who wanted *more* than simply friendship.

Although, if she wanted marriage, she might make George *wait*.

Sudden sounds drew George's attention. Time had passed more quickly than he had supposed. Dinner was over and folk were now issuing onto the promenade deck for after-dinner strollings, cocktails and cheroots.

'I have so enjoyed this evening together,' said George.

But, turning, he found only a half-empty glass upon the wicker table.

Ada Lovelace had slipped away.

And George was all alone.

15

p on high amongst the clouds the airship took but fifteen hours to span the great Atlantic. Which was a remarkably good start to a journey that was scheduled to last for seventy-nine days. George, who had been having a bit of a lie-in, awoke to the professor's knockings at his cabin door and was amazed to discover that the *Empress of Mars* was already approaching New York.

But rather saddened too was George, because he had hoped to spend more time with Ada. More time, he had hoped, that might lead to something greater than just friendship. But here, so swiftly, was New York and here she would jump ship.

'And whatever happened to you last night?' Professor Coffin bustled all about in George's cabin. Interfering with things, toying about with George's brand-new, ivory-handled, badger-haired shaving brush. Needlessly dusting at George's top hat. 'I missed you at dinner. Shared a table with a Russian research chemist named Orflekoff, and his grandson, Ivan.'

George did not rise to that one.

'Also an American false-limb manufacturer by the name of Fischel and his little son, Artie.'

Nor that one.

'And an upper-class Shakespearian actor called Ornott-Tobee and his brother, Toby.'

'Indeed?' said George. 'And did you by any chance meet with the highly hyphenated Mr Good-mind-to-give-you-a-punch-on-the-chin-if-you-do-not-stop-making-all-these-terrible-name-jokes, and his son, Ivor?'

'No,' said Professor Coffin. 'Nor do I wish to. So—' And he danced his sprightly dance. 'Up and about with you, my bonny lad. New York awaits us and we have people to see.'

'We do?' asked George. 'What people?'

'One in particular, George, my boy, and that one is Phineas T. Barnum.'

They took a late breakfast in the great dining hall, a vast room that easily accommodated the thousand or more passengers.

Over a feast of croissants, ginger marmalade, coddled eggs, boiled ham, an assortment of cheeses and coffee from a proper copper coffee pot, Professor Coffin passed bad news to George.

'There was an accident last night,' he told the lad, who was ladling a coddled egg into his mouth. 'The whole ship is abuzz with it and it is better that you hear it from me than from some bellboy or bootblack.'

George did wonderings at what was to come.

Professor Coffin told him. 'You will recall the Count de Saint-Germain, whom we encountered in the gentlemen-only bar?'

George nodded and chewed as he did so.

'A charming fellow,' said the professor.

'It was a pleasure to meet him,' said George. 'Although curiously I cannot recall what it was that we spoke about.'

'No matter,' said Professor Coffin. 'Know only this tragic news. The count imbibed rather too freely in the absinthe boudoir last night, took a stroll upon the promenade deck to clear his head and pitched over the guardrail.'

George did chokings upon coddled egg.

'Such a pity,' said the professor. 'Such a learned man.'

'And he fell down, *all the way* down, into the sea?' asked George, quite horrified by the thought.

'From an altitude of eight thousand feet. No man has ever fallen so far before. I was speaking earlier with a Mr Guinness, who is thinking to compile some kind of record book. He is considering putting the count in as the very first entry, so I suppose he will get some kind of posthumous fame.'

'Awful,' said George. 'Quite awful.'

'Oh, I don't know,' said the professor. 'It might prove to be a most interesting book.'

'That is even less funny than the silly name business earlier,' said George. Then he asked, 'How *do* you coddle an egg?'

After breakfast the two took themselves off to the promenade deck to view New York as the airship came in to land. George marvelled at the sky-scraping towers, the Statue of Liberty, the great cruise liners that lay at berth in Manhattan Harbour. All was wonderful to George, who held very tight to the guardrail for fear that he might join the count.

★

There was far less fuss with the disembarking and the actual setting foot upon American soil than George had supposed there would be. The professor presented officials with 'Papers of Recognition' and George observed the certain handshake being brought once more into play.

The *Empress of Mars* had taken moorings above Central Park, and having passed successfully through Customs and Immigration Control, George and the professor strolled from the park and hailed a New York cab.

The cab itself was much as a London hansom in design, although with wider wheels and painted yellow. The cabbie wore a racoon-skin top hat and fringed buckskin Ulster coat. Upon learning the nationality of his fares, he informed them that if there was anything – '*anything*, do you hear me, *anything*' – that they required whilst in New York, then he, Mr Frontier, or if not he then his son, Wilde, would be happy to meet those very requirements. The excessive degree of lewd eyelid pulling and exaggerated winking told George all he needed to know regarding what was meant by *that*.

'Wilde Frontier,' said Professor Coffin, nudging George in the ribs.

Barnum's American Museum stood upon Broadway in the theatre district of New York. It had so far been burned to the ground twice, the first time by Confederate soldiers during the American Civil War, but each time it rose again, a shameless, preening, gaily coloured phoenix from the ashes.

Having alighted from their conveyance and after a period of intense negotiation regarding payment, as neither George nor the professor owned any American currency, the two men stood looking up at the gaudy façade.

American Gothic, characterised by more frivolous and architectural adornment than the eye could comfortably encompass. A profusion of pinkly bummed cherubim fussed about swags of terracotta, amidst carven beasts of mythical origin, flowers and fruits and fripperies. The vast arched central window was of stained glass, the work of Dante Gabriel Rossetti, who had taken the commission from Barnum whilst holidaying in the New York borough of Queens. It depicted the great showman as Noah, the ark behind him upon Mount Ararat and two of every kind issuing from it. Two of every kind of a kind that could be viewed at Barnum's American Museum.

'The man is a god,' said Professor Coffin, bowing before the mad building. George just shook his head.

The driver of the cab had accepted a 'diamond' ring from the professor in payment for the fare. One that had apparently been in the professor's family for several generations. Although one that George felt sure he recognised from a job lot the professor had purchased for one shilling several months before. At the entrance booth of Barnum's museum there was no problem regarding the exchange of non-American currency.

The personable young lady who sat in the booth, wearing a costume that showed much bosom, worked upon a brass contrivance with many cogs and levers that with the touch of a numerical keyboard could be made to display the exchange rates of any currency that there was.

Both George and the professor were very impressed by this extraordinary mechanism. Although perhaps a mite dismayed to learn just how unfavourably the value of an English pound compared to that of an American dollar.

Professor Coffin parted with two English pounds and he and George entered the so-called 'Dime Museum'.

There were five whole floors loaded down with wonders. There were marvels of many ages, wondrous beasts, live savages and a two-headed giant. There was the famed Feegee Mermaid, a troupe of performing monkeys, and even a selection of automatic beds.

'Automatic beds?' George asked, as he viewed a poetic poster advertising same.

'There are marvels here of the scientific persuasion as well as those appertaining to natural philosophy.'

'This place is heaven for you, is it not?' asked George.

'It is in the blood, my boy.' Professor Coffin tapped his cane upon the body area that contained his heart. 'It is either there, or it is not. Mr Barnum has raised the showman's craft to an exalted level. Look there, George.'

The professor drew George's attention to an enormous showcase that housed an exquisitely detailed diorama of the Battle of Waterloo.

At the touch of a button – and Professor Coffin touched this button – cogs engaged and the workings of complicated animation began: soldiers marched, muskets fired, men and horses fell.

George looked on and shook his head anew.

'I do not recall, when studying history at school,' said he, 'that dirigibles were involved in the Battle of Waterloo.'

·'Poetic licence,' explained Professor Coffin. 'The iron-sided gunboats are perhaps a mite too modern also.'

They wandered through the marvellous museum. Viewed the dancing of Zulu warriors. The shrinking of a human head by Jivaro tribesmen. An exhibition of toad juggling. A pig race. A 'Sapient Horse of Distinction' that offered tips on the New York Stock Exchange. Giraffe-necked ladies and plate-lipped lasses. A giant called Tomaso and General Tom Thumb.

Barnum's famous midget had circled the globe several times on his sell-out tours. He had been presented before Queen Victoria and almost every European house of royalty. He had gained great wealth and, more than that, great love.

General Tom Thumb sang several humorous songs, danced a solo gavotte and left the stage to riotous applause.

'Now *he*,' said George, 'is arguably the greatest showman's attraction ever to pull in the Rubes.'

''Tis true,' said the professor. 'Undoubtedly the most financially successful attraction in history. But we will do better than that.'

'I am beginning to wonder about that,' said George. 'I am so filled with awe by all that I have seen and experienced of late that at times I wonder whether I am simply dreaming. But do think on this, Professor. There may be no truth at all to what we seek. She may just be legend. There may be no truth to Sayito.'

Professor Coffin flapped a hand at George. 'Shush, my boy,' said he. 'We must have words with the proprietor of this esteemed establishment regarding that which we seek. But we must do it in such a fashion that the

117

fabulous showman gleans no hint that we actually seek what we seek. Do you understand?'

'I might if I put my mind hard to it,' said George. 'Do you think he is actually here?'

'Yonder,' said Professor Coffin, pointing with his cane.

To stage left stood a portly fellow, chatting with Tom Thumb.

He wore a grey suit cut in the American fashion, with portmanteau sleeves and a cuttlefish-skin, triple-breasted waistcoat. Upon his back was strapped an intricate contrivance of polished pine and burnished brass, which belched the occasional puff of smoke from a stovepipe chimney attached to his tall dark hat. The intricate contrivance was linked to the portly fellow's high brass boots by a complicated system of leather belt-drives and hissing pistons.

George looked on, a-gawp.

And as he looked on at the portly gentleman and the extraordinary mechanical paraphernalia that adorned him, matters took a sudden and most unexpected twist.

'Oh,' and, 'Ow!' cried P. T. Barnum, leaping suddenly high.

General Tom Thumb scuttled away as the clearly rattled Mr Barnum now performed what appeared to be an extravagantly high-stepping dance all about the stage, accompanied by further vocal outcries which rose to an uncomfortable crescendo.

'He is on fire,' observed George. 'And his bodily machinery is out of control.'

'Fiddle de, fiddle dum,' said Professor Coffin. 'Do something quickly, George.'

But George did not hear him say this, as George was

already hastening to assist the smoking showman cavorting about on the stage. George leapt up onto the stage and tore down one of the curtains. This he threw over P. T. Barnum and wrestled that man to the floor.

There were great hissings and splutterings of steam and Barnum's legs thrashed wildly. But George held him down and beat at the smoking firebox that fuelled the apparatus.

Presently, and much to the relief of all concerned, there was silence and stillness and George unwrapped the showman and helped him to his feet.

'Are you all right?' George asked him. 'Or should I summon a medic?'

P. T. Barnum divested himself of his belligerent backpack, unclipped the linkages to his brass footwear and booted all and sundry across the stage.

'Thank you, young man,' he said to George. 'That demonic contrivance would surely have done for me had you not intervened with such inspiration. I fear the world is not yet ready for Barnum's Patent Pneumatic Pedestrian Perambulators. Mechanical walking aids. I think I might just reconsider Mr Henry Ford's invitation to invest in his horseless carriage arrangement. Indeed, by golly, yessiree.'

'I am glad I was able to offer assistance,' said George. 'You are sure that you are undamaged?'

'Right and round as a silver dollar.' Barnum dusted himself down. 'And forever in your debt for sparing me from torment. My name is Phineas Taylor Barnum and I would be honoured to learn of yours.'

'I am George Fox,' said young George Fox. And shook the showman's hand.

16

T. Barnum's office was a wonder to behold. George, to whom wonders had been falling upon of late with such frequent rapidity that he felt he could surely accommodate a few more, just gawped about the crowded room with lower jaw a-dangle.

George had introduced Mr Barnum to the professor. That certain handshake had come once more into play and the great showman had welcomed the lesser showman as a fellow traveller and invited both he and George to enjoy a drink in private quarters.

Mr Barnum's desk was simply huge. Carved from elephants' tusks, inlaid with tiger teeth and topped with rolled leather from koala pelts, it dwarfed a full-size billiard table and was littered with more curiosa than could reasonably be described. George discerned domes of glass containing foetal skeletons mounted in tableaus representing historic events. The Siege of Troy. The coronation of Queen Elizabeth the First. The Storming of the Alamo. An American planting the Stars and Stripes flag upon the surface of the moon. George rolled his eyes at that one. The wall-mounted heads of stuffed bison and bears gazed down upon George with their glassy stares. A suit of samurai armour, all tortoiseshell and porcupine quills, stood in one corner. A waxwork figure of Jesus Christ, blessing fingers raised above a map of America, stood in another. And many too were the mechanical instruments of copper, brass and steel.

'Seat yourselves where you can,' advised Mr Barnum, seeking out a bottle of Jack Daniel's whisky and three crystal tumblers. Professor Coffin cleared circus posters from a green leather swivel chair and settled upon it. George wheeled over a massive elephant-foot stool and lowered his bottom upon that. Mr Barnum decanted liquor and pushed the glasses as far as he could across the spacious desk. With much strained reachings and assistance from George, Professor Coffin availed himself of the drinks and took to toasting Mr Barnum.

'Not a bit of it,' said that man. 'To George, for saving my Baltimore bacon.'

'To George,' said the professor, raising his glass.

Drinks were drunk and lips were smacked approvingly.

'And so,' said P. T. Barnum, 'what are you two gentlemen doing upon this side of the Great Pond?'

'We are circumnavigating the globe,' said the professor, 'aboard the *Empress of Mars*. The eighth wonder of the world, I believe she has been called.'

'Hm,' went P. T. Barnum. 'I have recently been having some discussions with the President of this fair land regarding the construction of a larger and more luxurious version of this airship.'

George Fox raised his eyebrows and sipped some more at his drink.

'As we were in New York,' continued Professor Coffin, 'we just had to visit your museum. It is famous throughout the world. It was not to be missed.'

'One does what one can to provide entertainment, education, enlightenment and edification. I trust that you have not been disappointed.'

'Well . . .' said the professor, and he paused.

'Well?' asked Mr Barnum. 'What should I make of this "well"?'

'I believe that we were misinformed,' said Professor Coffin. 'We were told that you had a most wonderful attraction here. *The* most wonderful attraction that ever there was. What was it called again, George? The Chinese Fish Woman or something, was it?'

George Fox noted the guarded wink. 'Something like that,' he said. 'Japanese, I think, yes, that was it – the Japanese Devil Fish Girl.'

P. T. Barnum leaned back in his chair, beyond his desk. His round head nodded gently and he made a thoughtful face. 'The Japanese Devil Fish Girl,' he said slowly. 'Well now, there is a thing.'

'We would very much like to see her,' said George. 'Is she presently engaged as one of your resident artistes?'

Mr Barnum's face now gained a quizzical expression. 'One of my resident artistes?' he said. 'Well, there's another thing.'

'Opinions in England vary,' said Professor Coffin, 'as to what she actually is. Some say a mermaid, others some kind of exotic being the like of which has never been viewed in the West. If you do have her here we would very much like to see her.'

'Would you now?' said P. T. Barnum. 'Would you now indeed?'

'Yes, sir, very much so,' said George.

Professor Coffin nodded.

'Well, gentlemen,' said Phineas Taylor Barnum,

emptying the remaining contents of his glass into his mouth and swallowing them back, 'I have been more than sixty years in this profession and I have met with every variety of shyster, double-dealer, sleight-of-hand merchant, huckster and bamboozler, but few of them could indeed hold a candle to you two gentlemen. The subtle charm of the English, is it? Well now, there's a thing.'

'I fail to understand your words,' said George.

'I fear that I do all too well,' Professor Coffin replied.

'And I,' said P. T. Barnum, rising from behind his desk now and taking up a sword that it was said had once belonged to Major Robert E. Lee, 'must applaud your audacity and indeed your ingenuity. How was it done, eh? You somehow sabotaged the workings of my Pneumatic Pedestrian Perambulator, that you might be on hand to save me and then inveigle yourselves into my confidence? What?'

'Nothing of the sort, sir,' said George, all bewildered. 'I do not know what you are talking about.'

'Oh really?' cried Barnum. 'Oh really? I think rather that you would seek to steal from me the Greatest Showman's Treasure of this or any other age.'

'Then you *do* have her,' said Professor Coffin.

'What I have or do not have is nothing of your business. Leave my premises at once or I will summon my monkey butler Charles to fling you into the street.'

Another monkey butler, thought George, with a certain envy.

'Out!' shouted Mr Barnum. 'Villains! Footpads! Outlaws! Rustlers!' And he waved his sword.

'This is all a big mistake,' said George.

'Let it lie, my friend,' said the professor. 'The game is

up for us, we must make a dignified retreat. My apologies to you, Mr Barnum. We were foolhardy to think that we could ever pull any wool over your observant eyes. That you would be aware of such obfustication should have been obvious to us. We shall take our leave now and trouble you no more. Come, George.'

'But—' went George.

'Come, George!'

George Fox rose from his elephant-foot stool and bowed his head before the master showman.

'We did not mean to trick you in any way, sir,' he said. 'We only wanted to know whether you had the Japanese Devil Fish Girl in your employ or not. Surely that is not so outrageous.'

'Out!' cried Mr Barnum. 'Out!'

'Quite so,' said the professor, backing towards the door. 'Sorry to have bothered you. Goodbye and a fond farewell.'

'This is ridiculous,' said George, but he too backed towards the door before the waving sword.

At the office door things became a little more confusing for George. He and the professor became somehow jammed into the opening. George could not for the life of him understand how, given the size of the opening, the two of them had become so jammed. It was almost as if the professor was doing the jamming on purpose.

P. T. Barnum stormed towards them, swinging his sword on high. George became suddenly aware of the words, 'Drop to your knees, George,' being hoarsely whispered into his ear by the professor. And George in an almost instinctive manner dropped straight to his knees.

Then there was confusion and tumbling as P. T. Barnum tripped over George and fell forwards into the corridor, dropping his sword, which Professor Coffin kicked beyond his reach. Then there was a considerable struggle as Professor Coffin leapt onto the prone show-man and bestraddled his chest, pinioning his arms and restraining him in a most undignified manner.

George stared on in disbelief as Professor Coffin now produced a slim glass phial from his waistcoat, carefully unscrewed the cap and then held it to the nose of Mr Barnum.

'We are going to return to your office now,' said Professor Coffin to the now non-struggling showman, 'and there you will tell us everything that you know about the Japanese Devil Fish Girl. Do you understand me, Mr Barnum?'

Mr P. T. Barnum nodded. 'Everything I know,' said he.

17

hey returned to Phineas Barnum's office, and George was most perplexed. Mr Barnum moved like an automaton. All stiff-legged and staring ahead, he crossed to his ample desk, then dropped into his chair like a sack of potatoes.

'Whatever have you done to him?' George asked of the professor.

Professor Coffin counselled silence. 'Just leave this to me. Please close the office door, George. And I spy a key on this side, so kindly lock it also.'

George did as he was bid, with much shaking of his head, and some worries too, for what was going on here seemed altogether odd.

'Sit down, George,' Professor Coffin told him. 'I don't want you to miss any of this. It might prove most important.'

George reseated himself upon the elephant-foot stool and looked on as Professor Coffin settled down once more into the green leather swivel chair and spoke across the desk to Mr Barnum.

'It would please me, sir,' said he, 'if you would now tell George and I everything that you know about the Japanese Devil Fish Girl. Omit nothing. Tell us *everything.*'

The great showman's eyes looked glazed and sightless.

Softly then he cleared his throat. 'I will tell you everything,' he said. 'I have kept this terrible secret for too long – I will be glad to tell you the tale.'

Professor Coffin nodded. 'Tell your tale to us,' he said.

The eyes of P. T. Barnum seemed to focus, as upon some far and distant point. 'So long ago,' he said, 'so very long ago . . . I have, as you know, lived a long and extraordinary life in my chosen profession. I believe that I have eclipsed all those who have gone before me in the world of showmanship. I have presented to the public many unique attractions and all of the very special people that I have exhibited have profited from their professional relationships with me. I—'

But Professor Coffin raised his hand. 'I am well aware of your venerable career – I own a copy of your autobiography. Please speak only upon the subject that I requested you to speak of. The Japanese Devil Fish Girl.'

'There are always rumours,' said P. T. Barnum, 'in the showman's world, of some great attraction, far greater than all the rest. Always beyond the next hill, in the next country, far across the next ocean. In the area upon the old maps that reads "HERE BE DRAGONS". I first heard of the being of which you speak whilst I was in Oregon. There is a mysterious area there, a few miles from Grants Pass, that is known as the Oregon Vortex. A weird magnetic geographical anomaly, where gravity plays tricks with you and nothing is quite what it seems. I was considering the idea of purchasing the area and opening it to the American public as the Strangest Place on Earth. It was there that I met a man by the name of Farl.'

'Macmoyster Farl?' asked George, amazed.

'His father, Sebastian Farl. At this time two sisters were wooing American audiences with their spiritualist performances, clicking the joints of their toes to mimic replies from the deceased to those sad folk who sought their solace with them. Sebastian Farl mocked the two sisters – he recognised them at once as charlatans and he presented himself to me as one of the few true psychics upon the planet who could actually communicate with the dead. I could see that there was novelty to this act and that if presented as the only true Apocalyptical Examiner, he might become the very epitome of sensationalism. It was necessary, however, for me to test his claims in some way. Not necessarily to prove them genuine, you understand, but to see how convincing they appeared.'

'And were you convinced?' asked Professor Coffin. 'And where, pray, is this leading?'

'It is leading to me answering your enquiries.' P. T. Barnum's voice became shrill. 'You demand answers from me and I feel compelled to supply them. You asked me to omit nothing, therefore allow me to tell my tale.'

George glanced towards Professor Coffin. There was something deeply wrong about all of this. It made George feel sick at heart and he felt that he wanted no more.

'This is very important,' Professor Coffin whispered to George, sensing all too well the young man's concern. 'This may not be altogether pleasant, but it is necessary.

This is your fate, young George. This is of the utmost importance.'

George held his counsel and P. T. Barnum continued.

'Sebastian Farl held a seance in the cabin on the edge of the Oregon Vortex and there I spoke with the spirits.'

'The spirits of the dead?' asked George, the hairs rising up on his arms.

'So I was given to understand at the time and jolly convincing it was too. Sebastian Farl coined the term "channelling" to describe what he did. He "channelled the spirits", but not of the dead, as I found out to my cost. All over the country, and indeed all over the world at the time, there were others such as Farl, each believing that they spoke with the dead. None of them actually charlatans, but none of them actually "channelling" the spirits of the dead.'

'I fail to understand,' said George. 'They were communicating with something, but *not* the spirits of the dead?'

'Correct,' said P. T. Barnum. 'They were communicating with beings from another world. They were communicating with the ecclesiastics of Venus.'

'Oh,' said George. 'Is that true?'

'True enough,' said Mr Barnum. 'But I did not know this until five years ago and by that time it was too late for me and too late for all of us, I fear.'

George glanced at the professor, who shrugged.

'Shall we drink some more of that remarkable liquor of yours?' asked the professor. 'I have a feeling way deep down in my very bones that we might be needing it.'

'Indeed you will,' said the great showman, and he topped full the glasses all round. Sinking back into his chair he continued with his tale. The pain showed in his face as he spoke and the reasons were shortly apparent.

'I myself was convinced that Farl was a genuine medium who spoke directly with the dead,' Mr Barnum continued. 'I asked him to communicate with my mother, ask her specific questions, the answers to which only she could provide. The answers he relayed to me were correct in every detail.'

'Then he *did* speak with the dead,' said George, most confused.

'No,' said Mr Barnum. 'The answers were correct, but my dear mother was not dead at the time. She was brightly alive upon her homestead.'

'It was a mind-reading act,' said Professor Coffin. 'I have observed such performances. They appear inexplicable, but the medium in fact gleans the required information from the client consulting them through unconscious gestures and body movements.'

'You fail to understand,' said P. T. Barnum. 'As did I at the time. All is interconnected. All − the living, the dead, the folk of this planet and any other − all are part of a single entity. A world soul, a universal soul. The very soul of God.

'I will tell you,' Mr Barnum went on, 'tell you what happened and what is to happen. I was obviously sceptical regarding Mr Farl's performance. The replies were correct, yet my mother still lived. I engaged in further experimentation with him. He began to receive messages from an entity that named itself Hieronymous who issued Farl with a set of instructions to construct a mechanical contrivance that was to be a wishing machine. This machine was designed to perform a single function. Seek something precious that had been lost.

Something of supreme importance. Something by the name of Sayito.

'Sebastian Farl had now convinced himself, and myself also, I confess, that he was speaking directly to angels. This wishing machine was to be a kind of nineteenth-century version of the Ark of the Covenant. It would be the link between Mankind and Sayito—'

'But what *is* Sayito?' George asked. 'What *is* the Japanese Devil Fish Girl?'

'She is a Goddess,' said P. T. Barnum. 'A living, breathing Goddess. And the ecclesiastics of Venus who were communicating with Mr Farl and whom Mr Farl believed to be angels had discerned that this living Goddess was to be found somewhere upon the Earth. They were dictating plans for the machine that could locate Her to Mr Farl so that he could locate Her for them.'

'This does not make sense to me,' said George. 'We now know that the folk of Venus and Jupiter have been visiting this planet for years and years. They could surely have discovered this Goddess for themselves without having to elicit any help from human beings.'

'If it had indeed been the case that the folk of Venus and Jupiter moved inconspicuously and anonymously amongst us, then indeed this would probably be the case. But they did not and do not to this day. An organisation of enlightened men exists, linked to every Government on Earth, monitoring the movements of those who travel to us from planets other than this. They owe their allegiance first to the Vatican and their order was originally formed at the time of the Inquisition. They are known only as the Gentlemen in Black.'

George's head was spinning now and so he raised his hands. 'Now please slow down, sir, if you will,' said he.

'You are telling us, or so it seems to me, that a living Goddess by the name of Sayito truly exists and that the ecclesiastics of Venus seek to somehow acquire Her, kidnap Her from this planet – is that what you are suggesting?'

'That is indeed the case,' said Mr Barnum. 'The Gentlemen in Black have for centuries thwarted their attempts to get up to whatever chicanery they sought to get up to upon this world. Which is why they took to employing new tactics. Most plain-thinking people consider mediums to be harmless cranks. Should some half-mad medium construct some dotty wishing machine, who would ever consider that some dark motive existed behind its construction? And you must understand, George Fox, it was not until after the beings of Venus made public contact with the folk on this planet that I realised that the messages were not those of angels, but of beings from another world. I learned of their sacred book, *The Book of Sayito*, a grimoire that is written in their language but which can be understood by anyone. But by then the point was moot. I oversaw and paid for the construction of the machine for purely selfish motives – that I might acquire and exhibit the greatest attraction on Earth, a living Goddess. Imagine that, if you will. A living Goddess.'

George Fox nodded thoughtfully and then asked whether the Hieronymous Machine had actually ever been constructed.

'Indeed so,' said Mr Barnum. 'At preposterous expense to myself. And tested, just the once. *Eleven years ago.*'

George Fox looked into Mr Barnum's eyes. 'Is there a significance to that?' he enquired.

'I fear so,' said Mr Barnum. 'The machine was constructed in London. Two of the finest minds alive were engaged in its construction – a Mr Charles Babbage and a Mr Nikola Tesla. I do not fully comprehend the inner workings of this infernal machine, only that when it was set into motion it created a burst of stupendous energy that radiated about this world and beyond it. Such I suppose was its intended purpose, that by some aetheric waves its message would be received upon Venus. That it would discover the location of what was sought and relay this to the ecclesiastics upon that distant orb.'

'I have read of such things,' said George. 'The work of Mr Tesla, messages transmitted through the air from one location to another. Telegraphy it is called.'

'And so between the worlds,' said P. T. Barnum. 'But, as history does *not* record, this message reached another world. A world of warlike beings. Who then sought to acquire the greatest treasure of the universe for themselves.'

'The Martians,' said George. 'The Martians received the message.'

P. T. Barnum bowed his head. 'Thus and so,' he replied.

'Then you—' said George.

'Then I,' said P. T. Barnum, 'through my own folly and through my desire to possess the greatest treasure in the universe – a living Goddess, no less – I financed the construction of the Hieronymous Machine and *I* am responsible for what your English author H. G. Wells described as *The War of the Worlds*.'

18

eorge was left quite speechless at this. Professor Coffin was not.

'The Goddess,' said he. 'Sayito. Did this Hieronymous Machine divine Her location?'

'I grow weary,' said Mr Barnum. 'I can speak no more of these matters.'

'Upon the contrary.' Professor Coffin rose from his seat, skirted the mighty desk and once more held the slim phial of liquid beneath the showman's nose. 'Where is Sayito?' he asked P. T. Barnum. 'Where is the Japanese Devil Fish Girl?'

'I do not know,' cried Mr Barnum, swaying precariously. 'The machine destroyed itself – as I believe it was intended so to do. Whatever message it relayed I remain unaware of. The Martians attacked and closed upon London, the machine's former location, and eventually succumbed to Earthly bacteria.'

Professor Coffin shook Mr Barnum about.

'Do not do that to him,' said George. 'He has told us everything he knows. And chilling stuff it all is too.'

Professor Coffin raised his hands. 'And that is *all* you know?' he asked the showman. 'I ask you a straight question. Do you know where She is to be found?'

'I know something more,' said Mr Barnum, 'but I do not wish to say it.'

'I *insist* that you say it,' said the professor. 'Say it to me and *now.*'

'Only this.' P. T. Barnum was struggling not to speak, but found himself compelled to do so. 'When the machine destroyed itself, Sebastian Farl spoke two words and then he dropped down dead.'

'What did he say?' the professor asked.

'He said *"Umbilicus Mundi".*'

'What does that mean?' asked the professor.

'Literally, "the navel of the world".'

'The Centre of the Earth, do you think?'

'The navel of the world, that is all I know.'

'Absolutely all?' demanded the professor.

'All,' said P. T. Barnum. 'But still I am persecuted by folk such as you. The search must cease. Sayito must be left in peace. I believe Her to be the last of the Gods. The last of the ancient pantheon. She is not for mortal men to gaze upon, nor a sideshow attraction to be gawped at by the Rubes. If it is your endeavour to seek Her, turn back while you still can. No good can come from your search, only evil.'

'All right,' said the professor. 'I will trouble you no more. Sleep now and awaken a half of an hour from now. Upon waking you will have no recollection of this conversation, or that you even met us. You will be happy and at peace. Now sleep, if you will.'

Phineas Taylor Barnum, the world's greatest show-man, settled his head upon his desk and took to tuneful snorings.

'Come, George,' said Professor Coffin. 'We have

learned all there is to be learned here – our search must continue elsewhere.'

George looked up at the professor. 'What are you saying?' he asked.

'That we know that Sayito exists. Our visit here has not been wasted.'

'No,' said George. And, 'No, no, no. Do you not understand? That man did a terrible thing. He sought to find Sayito and his greed led to the deaths of thousands. As he said himself – "No good can come from your search, only evil."'

'He exhibits a gloomy disposition at times,' said Professor Coffin, 'but such can often be the way with great folk. I myself am occasionally troubled by misgivings.'

'You are not listening to me,' said George. 'We must abandon the search. I am done with it. All is over. All this is awful stuff.'

Professor Coffin shook his head. 'George, George, George,' he said. 'Do you not understand? Macmoyster Farl, the son of Sebastian Farl, made the prophecy. *You* will find Sayito. It is your destiny, George.'

'No,' said George, rising once more from the elephant-foot stool. 'I will have no more part of it. I am sorry, Professor. You have invested all you had in this quest, but it is a fool's errand. We are dealing with mystical forces here, godly forces. They are not for us to tamper with.'

'Fiddle de, fiddle dum,' said Professor Coffin. 'I comprehend. So that is how it is.'

'It *is* how it is,' said George. 'I am sorry, but that is that.'

'All right, George, I appreciate all that you say. You

are a good and honest fellow and to force you to do something against your will would be wrong. I understand that.'

'It *would* be wrong,' said George. 'And I would not do it.'

'I understand that.' Professor Coffin looked George up and down. 'Are you all right?' he asked of the lad. 'You seem a mite shaky and pale in the face.'

'This has all been rather upsetting,' said George. 'But I will be all right.'

'I am not so sure,' said Professor Coffin. 'And your health and well-being are my uppermost concern. I wish no ill to come to you. Here, take a small pick-me-up.'

'A small *what*?' asked George.

But that was all that he asked, because of a sudden, a slim phial of liquid was being held beneath his nose and George said nothing more for a little while.

He became aware of the coffee. The coffee smelled very good.

'They certainly know how to brew up a cup of coffee,' said Professor Coffin. 'This blend is flavoured with vanilla.'

George took a sniff and sipped from his cup. 'It is very nice,' said he. And then, suddenly aware that he was not quite certain where he was and how he had come to be where he was, he sought this information from the professor.

Who said to him, 'Come, come, George.'

They sat upon cane chairs before a delicatessen called Delmonico's, coffee on a table and cheroots to hand.

'You said that you fancied a cup of American coffee,'

said Professor Coffin. 'You *do* remember saying that, George, don't you?'

'Oh yes,' said George and he glanced all around. It was afternoon now, with the post-noon sunlight slanting down between the scrapers of sky and casting angled shadows. 'Were we not supposed to be visiting Barnum's American Museum?' George asked. 'I recall you mentioned it earlier.'

'I think not,' said the professor, lighting up a cheroot. 'I do not feel there is anything useful to be learned there. We will press on with our search elsewhere, I think.'

'All right,' said George, tasting coffee. 'Whatever you think is best.'

Professor Coffin nodded and smiled. 'Whatever I think is best.'

They returned at length to the *Empress of Mars*, the time being a little past four.

'Take yourself off for an afternoon nap,' Professor Coffin told George. 'We will meet at eight in the great dining hall for supper and then we will attend a talk in the lecture theatre.'

'There is a lecture theatre on this airship?' said George.

'Next to the concert hall. Between it and the gymnasium.'

'And what is this talk about?'

' "Advanced Calculus and Euclid's Proposition".'

'I generally like to take a little stroll upon the promenade deck after I have eaten,' said George.

'This talk is being given by Mr Charles Babbage,' said Professor Coffin. 'And Mr Babbage has much to tell us.'

And with this he winked at George in a knowing fashion, which made George a little confused.

He felt no less confused when he returned to his cabin and settled down to take an afternoon nap. As he dropped off to sleep, he wondered just why it was that he seemed to get so tired in the afternoons nowadays. And he wondered whether there might be something going slightly wrong inside of his head. Queer thoughts nagged away at George. Thoughts regarding *precisely* what he had done that day. There appeared to be something missing. George could recall leaving the airship and climbing into a canary-coloured cab. But then the next thing he remembered was drinking vanilla-flavoured coffee outside Delmonico's Delicatessen. And surely several hours had passed between the two. George did heartfelt sighings. He would question the professor on the matter when he awoke.

The professor would set his mind at rest.

The professor knew what was for the best.

Rocking gently in his hammock bunk, George dropped off to sleep . . .

To be awoken most violently from a curious dream about a portly man in a very weird room. Awoken by a deafening bang and a shock wave that overturned George's washstand and pitched him from his bunk.

George arose from the floor to the sounds of screaming and loud alarm bells.

Something really terrible had happened.

19

eorge slid open his cabin door to find the corridor beyond crammed up with scream-ing people. Some in states of indecent undress, all in panic and fright.

'What has happened?' shouted George, attempting to make himself heard above the unwhole-some din. 'What has happened? Someone tell me, please.'

No one seemed particularly interested in answering George's enquiry. All, it seemed, had gone completely insane.

George spied a bootboy getting all squashed up in the thick of it and hauled him by the scruff of his neck in through the cabin doorway.

'Unhand me, please,' cried the youth. 'The ship goes down, we are doomed.'

'You will be crushed to death out there,' said George, drawing shut the cabin door. 'Now tell me what has happened.'

'We are under attack,' wailed the wretched child. 'Anarchists have bombed the ship. We must flee for our lives.'

'That might prove somewhat problematic,' said George, and then he viewed the open porthole.

'We can't go that way, sir,' said the bootboy, all a-shiver. 'The anarchists are in the trees, sniping at us with rifles.'

'Indeed?' said George. 'And I thought to detect a hint of smoke in the corridor. Are we ablaze, by any chance?'

'We are, sir, yes. A bomb went off in the Kinema. A terrible fire there is.'

'Kinema?' queried George.

'It's on the upper deck, between the indoor golf course and the ice rink.'

'Indeed,' said George. Quite slowly. 'Well, it is stay and fry or risk the porthole. What think you to this?'

'I will follow *you* through the porthole,' said the lad. Thoughtfully.

'The porthole is quite high,' said George. With equal thought. 'Best if I help you up and through it, I am thinking.'

And the bootboy *was* smaller than George. And George *was*, after all, saving him from death by smoke and flame.

'And out you *go*,' went George as he pushed the bootboy through the open porthole.

He did not tumble to his doom, nor indeed get sniped by a sniper. He dropped safely onto the service deck three feet beneath the porthole, as George had known he would. It was a bit of a squeeze for George, but fear of impending doom will put a spring into your step and spur you on to greater efforts than might otherwise be the norm.

George tumbled down to the deck beside the lad. 'It looks safe enough,' said he. 'Which way is the Kinema?'

The bootboy pointed.

'Then we should flee in the other direction. Come, stay close to me.'

Now George knew, as many aboard the great airship *did* know, that its mighty bladder was filled with helium. And that helium was an inert and non-flammable gas. So there was not likely to be an almighty, all-encompassing explosion that would wipe the airship's passengers, the airship itself, Central Park and a chunk of New York from the map. But fire was fire and a fearful mob was fearsome.

Folk were already throwing themselves over the side. They were dropping into the trees and some into the lake. And the lake was probably where those who were thoroughly over-crowding the lifeboats were hoping to head for.

In the ballroom the band played on. As was ever the way.

'I am thinking,' said George to the bootboy, as the two of them caught glimpses of chaos and mayhem, 'that, although this might appear counter-intuitive—'

'Counter-*what*?' asked the lad.

'Against common sense,' George explained. 'But I think we would do well to climb higher, rather than risk jumping down.'

'Climb higher?' asked the lad, and he strained to lean back his head and peer up at the vast acreages of silver canvas filling most of the sky. 'Climb up there? Are you mad?'

'They will probably get the fire put out soon,' said George. 'And if you jump down there, you will probably break something, or someone will fall on you, or one of the anarchist snipers will shoot you. What think you of this?'

'I think I will follow *you* once more,' said the lad, who lacked not for astuteness.

So they climbed up. Up service gangways, up hawsers and lines, hand over hand and so forth. It was as if they were scaling a wondrous mountain, fairy-tale silver and shining. The wonder of it was not lost upon George, although he did harbour certain fears regarding what might happen if the gas bag got well and truly punctured. It would be a very, very long way to fall indeed, and although George naturally worried for his own welfare, he actually worried even more for that of the bootboy, who had now become, to George's mind, *his* responsibility.

'If the gas bag gets punctured—' began the lad.

'It will not,' said George, 'trust me.'

The views were rather splendid from the heights of the *Empress of Mars*. The chaos below was thankfully obscured by the airship's bulging sides, so the views were mostly panoramic and pleasurable. The parkland and the high-rising buildings beyond. A pall of smoke billowing from the *Empress of Mars* did blot out much of what lay to the east, however.

'Are you all right?' George asked the lad. 'Make sure you hold on tightly to something.'

The lad looked into George's face and managed a bit of a smile. 'You're not like those other toffs, sir,' said he. 'You saved me from a squashing for sure. I've you to thank for the life of me, I'm thinking.'

'I did what anybody would have done,' said George. But he knew in his heart of hearts that this was not the case.

'I wonder why anarchists would want to blow up this airship?' he wondered aloud.

'Because probably they ain't anarchists,' replied the bootboy. 'They probably is them Creationists that hate them Venusian people.'

'What of this?' asked George.

'It's been in all the papers here, sir,' said the lad. 'I reads the papers, me. Read them in England, then picked up some here to read. I am hoping to be a writer, sir. When I grow up.'

'A laudable ambition,' said George. 'Writing is a noble profession.'

'Not the kind of writing I have in mind, sir. I want to specialise in adult literature. Erotic works, or smut as it is more commonly known. But like I says, no mention in the London papers that this here airship was going to be under threat the moment it arrived in New York. The papers here say that a Fundamentalist Christian group, a "cult" the papers call them, seeks to destroy the *Empress of Mars* and all aboard her. They claim she is a sky-flying Sodom and Gomorrah and that Venusians and Jupiterians are the spawn of Satan, come to Earth to bring on the End Times before these times are truly due.'

George managed a slack-jawed, 'Indeed?' but that was as far as it went.

'They ain't got souls, you see,' said the bootboy.

'Who?' George managed. 'The Fundamentalist Christians?'

'No, the blokes from Venus and Jupiter. They ain't like us. We've got souls because the Garden of Eden was here on *this* planet. We are God's true people. Them lot up there are the Devil's brood. They should all go back to their own evil worlds.'

'And the Christian Fundamentalists believe this, do they?' George asked.

'Doesn't everyone?' asked the bootboy. 'Makes common sense to me.'

George shook his head somewhat sadly. 'I think we should all try to live in peace with one another,' said he.

'Oh, me too, sir. Once we've sent those alien swine back to where they come from.'

George momentarily considered pitching the bootboy over the side. Did the world really need a racist pornographer? Did it already have sufficient? Or if it had none, did it actually need any at all?

'You're looking at me in a right queer fashion,' said the bootboy. 'In case there is any misunderstanding, please allow me to disillusion you. Just because a young man chooses to pursue a career in filthy literature, it does not necessarily follow that such a young man is a sexual pervert eager to engage in acts of sodomy.'

'Stop right there,' said George. 'I was certainly not thinking what you might think that I am thinking.'

'I am thinking that, to judge by that sentence, a career in any kind of literature is probably not for you,' said the lad.

And for his outspokenness he received a buffet to the head that sent him reeling.

'Sorry,' said George. 'But you *really* asked for *that*.'

'Quite so, sir,' said the bootboy. 'Violence is the eloquence of the unlettered, I always say. And always safer meted out to one smaller than yourself.'

'That is quite enough,' said George. 'Sit quietly there until things calm down and the fire is extinguished, then we will descend and go about our separate business. Do you understand?'

'I do, sir, yes.' And the bootboy took to silence.

But not quite as a duck will do to water.

He fidgeted about, eager to hold forth upon anything and everything. George sighed inwardly and stared all around and about. Somewhere in the distance he caught a glimpse of colour upon the airship's silver upper parts. A little glimpse of red amidst that silver. George shielded his eyes to the setting sun and stared very hard indeed. And then he told the bootboy to stay where he was and George marched off across the vast surface at a trot.

She was seated most comfortably. She had a picnic hamper open beside her. Freshly cut sandwiches laid out on two plates. A fine selection of cakes. As George approached, she smiled upon him and raised a champagne glass.

'I rather hoped,' said Ada Lovelace, passing up a glass of bubbly to George, 'that if anyone had the presence of mind to climb *up*, rather than jump *down*, that someone might be you.'

George smiled hugely, accepted the glass and sipped champagne from it. 'How lovely to meet you once more,' he said. 'Would you mind if I joined you for tea?'

But George did not get to take tea, because another explosion and yet another shock wave knocked him from his feet.

20

lat on his back on the top of an airship, George gazed up at the sky. The sun was sinking low now and the stars were coming out. George could just see Venus rising with them, winking its mystical eye . . .

When an awful rushing roaring sound banged his ears about.

'What now?' moaned George, and, 'When will this madness end?'

'Quite shortly, I believe,' said Ada Lovelace, helping George into a seated position and refilling his rather spilled glass.

'That noise?' George did bashings at the side of his head, whilst holding his glass steadily in the other hand to avoid any further champagne spillage. 'What was that horrible noise?'

Then George followed this question up with another, to the effect of, 'What is happening *now*?'

'The *Empress of Mars* is taking off,' said Ada Lovelace, carefully pouring champagne. 'And in answer to your first question – "What was that horrible noise?" – that would be the ship's onboard defence and retaliatory systems finally engaging. One of Mr Tesla's innovations.

Reverse-engineered Martian technology. A heat ray, it's commonly called.'

'What?' went George, and now most seriously all agape, he sought to make some kind of sense of all that was going on around him.

Had George been granted a three-hundred-and-sixty-degree all-around overview of what was happening beneath, he would have seen that the great airship was now ringed by a wall of fire. The trees of Central Park were ablaze. Anarchist snipers, or perhaps they were Christian Fundamentalists, were leaping on-fire from branches. Surviving jumpers were patting at their flaming selves. And the great airship was rising. Up and up and up some more. It was most alarming.

Mooring lines strained and snapped, the *Empress of Mars* swung about, cleaving the sky in a mighty arc. And fire poured down from its weaponry, raking over Central Park, striking the high office towers surrounding it.

Ada Lovelace clung to George and George was glad for this clinging. Up and away went the *Empress of Mars*, trailing fire behind her.

George and Ada remained atop the airship. They watched as New York fell astern, as the flames became but a dim and distant glow that presently was gone into the evening.

'I do believe,' said George, 'that a great deal of New York City is now gone up in flames.'

Ada Lovelace shrugged and said, 'They started it.'

Which caused George to think of the bootboy and wonder whether he had survived.

'If you are thinking of me, I'm fine, guv'nor,' said that very lad. Who was safely to be seen sitting by Ada's picnic hamper and tucking into the fruit cake.

'This is madness,' said George, much rattled. 'All of this is madness.'

'I do not think that the crew that manned the heat ray actually meant to do that amount of damage,' said Ada. 'Although they might have got carried away in all the excitement.'

'How do you know about this heat ray, anyway?' George asked.

'I know every inch of this craft,' said Ada. 'I've been living aboard it since it was first launched. They have many secrets hidden on this ship, but none are hidden from me.'

'You are a most extraordinary young woman,' George observed. 'Do you think that it is safe to go down now?'

'I should think so. But I expect that tonight's Kinematic presentation will have to be cancelled.'

The promenade deck had lost much of its charm. Wounded folk were laid out on the steamer chairs. Others who had moved beyond the wounded state, into that state known as death, were covered head to toe with towels and blankets. There was general all-around moaning and grief and all traces of the previous gaiety had departed. Those who could walk were for the most part doing their best to minister to those who could not, but the deck had the look of a war zone to it, very grim indeed.

George caught with difficulty the eye of a wine waiter, who was doing his best to avoid eye contact and make himself appear as tiny as could be.

'Do you know what is happening?' George asked this fellow. 'Are we heading back to London, do you know?'

'I don't think so, sir,' the other replied. 'San Francisco next stop and making good time with the wind behind us.'

'We are going *on* with the journey?' George said.

'According to the captain.' The wine waiter put on a professional face. 'People have paid a lot of money for this trip, sir. We can't go letting them down now, can we?'

'What?' went George. 'Not let them down? How many dead, I ask you?'

'Dead?' said the wine waiter. 'Dead? Dead is such an ugly word, isn't it? I myself prefer the term "non-dining passengers".'

'How many *dead*?' George demanded to be told.

'I believe there will be one hundred and eighty-nine vacant seats in the dining hall tonight, sir. I might possibly be able to give you and your lovely companion here an upgrade. Lord Brentford's table has become available. But for his monkey butler and I am sure you would not mind sharing with him.'

George looked the wine waiter up and down. That *was* insolence, wasn't it? Just like the bootboy. The menials aboard this sky-ship really held the passengers in considerable contempt.

'Yes,' said George. 'My name is *Lord* George Fox and Lord Brentford's table will be fine. Lead us to it at once, my man. And bring us a bottle of bubbly.'

The folk in the dining hall were not looking altogether well. Those who weren't actually charred were rather red of face, sunburned in appearance, peripheral victims of the airship's onboard defence and retaliatory systems.

Most appeared to be in a state of shock. Few were actually eating.

The wine waiter did polite pullings-out and pushings-back of chairs. George and Ada smiled upon him.

'Bring the champagne,' said George.

The wine waiter sauntered away without haste.

George shrugged his shoulders to Ada.

Ada, however, did not see this shrug. She was leafing through the vellum pages of the menu and salivating somewhat as she did so. She did, however, look up, just the once, at George.

'Can I order *any*thing?' she asked him.

'Anything you like,' said George. 'Anything you like.'

And then he thought about the settling up of the bill. Which caused him to think about Professor Coffin. Which in turn caused George to think about what a terrible person he, George, must be, not to have thought about the professor earlier. What if he was dead?

'Oh no,' said George. 'How terrible of me. What a foul fellow am I?'

'Are you?' asked Ada, without looking up.

'My travelling companion, the professor – he might be dead and I am sitting here with you and—'

'He isn't dead,' said Ada.

'You know him?' George asked. 'You know who I am talking about?'

'The shifty fellow who took you to Barnum's American Museum this morning.'

'What?' went George, of a sudden.

'I slipped off the airship just after you, George. I saw you enter the cab. I heard him tell the cabbie where to drive to.'

'The American Museum?' George did wrackings of

his brain, but no memories of the American Museum came to him.

'It is all very odd,' said George. 'But how do you know the professor is not dead?'

'Because he is coming this way now,' said Ada. 'Do you think I should leave?'

'Certainly not,' George told her. 'I do not really approve of lying, but I will not contradict anything you care to tell him. Should you wish to elevate your social status to "Her Ladyship", or whatever.'

And George smiled at Ada, who smiled back at George, and then both of them smiled at the professor.

'Fiddle de, fiddle dum,' said that fellow, dancing up and bowing low. 'You are in good health, young George, the saints be thanked for it. I have been scouring the ship for you, in fear that you might have taken a spill. But you are well and in the company of a beautiful young woman *and* at Lord Brentford's table. Good evening, Darwin.'

Lord Brentford's monkey butler gibbered in reply.

'I am well,' said George, 'and very pleased to see that you are too and this is—'

'Ada Fox,' said Ada. 'I am George's sister.'

'*Sister?*' said Professor Coffin, falling back in surprise. '*Sister*, George? You never spoke to me of any sister. This is a great surprise to me.'

'No more than it is to me,' said George. 'Which is to say, of course, that I did not know that my sister was on board. We are not a close family. My sister has come to America to seek work as a—'

'Dancer,' said Ada 'Fox'.

'Mathematician?' said George.

'Champagne, sir?' said the wine waiter. 'And will your sinister grandparent be joining you for dinner?'

'What did you say?' asked Professor Coffin of the wine waiter.

'I asked whether the *superior* grandparent – to wit yourself, sir – would be joining His young Lordship here for dinner.'

'I certainly will,' said Professor Coffin, and, throwing back the tails of his coat, flung himself down onto a chair.

Champagne was danced around. Grand food was ordered and consumed, conversation married itself and at least on Lord George's table everyone was having a good time.

'Can we keep the monkey butler?' George asked Professor Coffin. 'He is an orphan now, it seems.'

Professor Coffin made a jolly face. 'Certainly,' said he. 'Did you and your sister have pets when you were children?'

'Yes,' said Ada.

'No,' said George.

But both spoke together.

'Which is to say,' said George, 'that yes, Ada did, but no, I did not.'

'And what pets did you have?' asked the professor.

'Dog,' said George.

And, 'Cat,' said Ada.

Once more both together.

'It was a cat,' said George. 'Although it looked a lot like a dog. I used to walk it on a lead, people used to think it was a dog.'

'All becomes *very* clear,' said the professor. Making a knowing smile.

'George tells me that you are taking him on the Grand Tour,' said Ada, smiling beautifully upon Professor Coffin. 'He has told me so much about you. He holds you in very high esteem.'

'Of course I do,' said George.

'And I likewise do you,' said the professor, offering a guarded look to Ada as he did so. 'But I think I should leave you two young people to your conversation. You must have so many things to catch up upon. I spy Mr Charles Babbage at yonder table, not looking too much the worse for wear. I have certain questions that I wish to ask him. If you will pardon me.' Professor Coffin rose from his chair, dabbed a napkin to his lips, saluted Ada, bowed stiffly, turned and departed.

'He really is such a very nice fellow,' said George, smiling after him.

Ada Lovelace slowly shook her head. She turned her beautiful green eyes upon George Fox and looked at him long and hard.

'I do not know,' she said to George, 'whether you might trust that unquantifiable something that is known as "female intuition".'

George Fox shrugged and sipped a little champagne.

'Well, upon this occasion I would advise you to do so,' said Ada Lovelace. 'For your companion, George, is undoubtedly by far the most evil man that it has ever been my misfortune to encounter.'

21

‘h no,' cried George, most terribly shocked. 'You are wrong about the professor.'

Darwin the monkey butler refreshed George's glass and George thanked him for doing so.

'Trust me,' said Ada Lovelace. 'I know these things. I am a woman.'

'Trust *you*?' said George, and his face expressed some doubts.

'George,' said Ada, 'I know I used you and I have apologised for that. You are an extremely nice young man and I consider us now to be friends.'

'Friends,' agreed George, with only tiny little grindings of his teeth.

'Then trust me when I say to you that the professor is evil. As well as having inbuilt intuition, women also have this other thing, this rather unfortunate thing.'

George almost said, 'The menstrual cycle?' But he did not, because he knew that had he done so, he would then have had to take recourse to 'the gentleman's way out' and throw himself over the side.

'An almost hypnotic fascination *for* and attraction *to* wicked men,' said Ada. 'Women find evil men, how shall I put this, well, *sexually* attractive.'

Darwin the monkey butler hid his face.

'I am sorry,' said Ada, 'and I wish it were not so. But it *is* so and therefore I have to conclude that, as I find Professor Coffin to be almost a veritable Love God, yet consider the looks of him to be thoroughly repellent, he is an evil monster.'

'No,' said George, a-shaking of his head. 'He looks after me. He cares about me. He treats me almost royally.'

'Does he?' said Ada. 'Does he indeed?'

'Yes he does.' George quaffed champagne. 'And he financed our trip out of his own pocket. I have paid for nothing.'

'Really?' said Ada. 'Do you know the second time I heard your name?'

'No,' said George. 'But that is a strange question. The first time, I recall, was when I told it to you. On the night of the concert at the Crystal Palace.'

'Quite so.' Ada Lovelace sipped champagne, the liquid reflecting in her eyes. 'The second time was when it was being shouted loudly by various tradesmen in various trade wagons that were rushing towards the *Empress of Mars* as it rose from the Royal London Spaceport.'

'Ah,' said George. 'I do remember that.'

'I had a very good view from my nest in the lifeboat. Those tradesmen looked upset.'

'Ah,' said George, once more. 'Indeed they did.'

'But it was definitely *your* name they were calling out and not that of the professor.'

'He explained that to me,' said George, gulping down further champagne. 'He needed to use an aristocratic name to get credit with the tailors and makers of toiletry items and spat manufacturers and royally appointed cane merchants and—'

'It never occurred to him to call *himself* Lord Coffin?'

'Ah,' said George, for a third time. 'But he did sell everything that he owned to pay for our tickets.'

'To take you on the Grand Tour? That was very generous of him. Almost altruistic, one might say.'

'One might,' agreed George.

'Assuming it to be the truth,' said Ada. 'And that there was no ulterior motive. That the professor did not want something in return. Something that you could provide him with.'

George groaned. 'You are twisting it all about,' said he. 'He is a good man. He looks after me.'

The wine waiter appeared once more at the table. 'I do hope everything has been to your liking,' he said, in a tone that George felt lacked for a certain sincerity. 'Only it has been a rather rough day for some of us and I would like to creep away to the sorry wooden bunk that has been provided for me and get two hours of sleep before I am called back onto duty.'

'Quite so,' said George.

'So there is the matter of the bill,' said the wine waiter.

'Perhaps Professor Coffin will be covering it,' suggested Ada Lovelace.

'No, madam, I fear not,' said the wine waiter. 'I just encountered that gentleman purchasing absinthe for Mr Charles Babbage. He said that *you* would be signing for the meal, Lord George.'

George ordered further champagne. And a pint of porter for Darwin.

'So,' said he to Ada. 'An evil man, you think?'

'I fear that I do, George. Sorry, but it is true.'

'Things certainly have been a bit odd lately.' George passed a drinking straw to Darwin, who was having problems with his porter. 'The staff are turning somewhat surly – I almost fear for a mutiny, and then all this hideous violence and I have been experiencing periods of missing time. My memory is fragmented.'

Ada Lovelace raised a beautiful eyebrow. 'Why are you *really* on this voyage?' she asked. 'What does the professor *really* want from you?'

George Fox sighed and glanced around. He did not know what he should say.

'You can tell me the truth,' said Ada. 'What harm could it possibly do?'

'I do not think that *you* tell *me* all of the truth,' George said.

'I am perhaps given to the occasional slight exaggeration,' said Ada, fluttering her eyelids at George. 'Perhaps prone to storytelling, but it is a hereditary thing. Quite out of my control.'

'As with your attraction to wicked men?'

'Not unlike,' Ada agreed. 'It is a family thing. It would surprise you, indeed, were you to learn the name of my father.'

'Strangely, I feel it would *not*,' said George.

'Lord Byron,' said Ada Lovelace.

Darwin the monkey butler hastened to dab at George with an oversized red gingham serviette. For George had spluttered champers down his front.

'Lord Byron?' said George. 'I do think *not*.'

Ada Lovelace dipped into her sequined evening purse and produced a folded newspaper cutting. This she handed to George, who unfolded same and read from it aloud.

POET'S DAUGHTER VANISHES

he read:

> The daughter of renowned poet and substance abuser George Gordon Byron was reported missing yesterday. Investigations led by Scotland Yard's leading detective Inspector Lestrade have so far proved fruitless. It is thought that the family of Miss Ada may seek to employ the services of the renowned consulting detective Mr Sherlock Holmes.'

'And there is a photograph,' said George. 'And that photograph is of you.'

Ada Lovelace smiled upon George and took back the newspaper cutting.

'Mr Sherlock Holmes will find you,' said George. 'He is the best detective in the whole wide world.'

'He is afeared of heights,' said Ada Lovelace. 'After that business at the Reichenbach Falls with Professor Moriarty — another evil professor, you will notice — he cannot stand heights. Thus I fled upon the very means of transportation that soars to the highest of heights.'

'To find work as a mathematician in America?' George asked.

'To find adventure,' said Ada, a green fire sparkling in her eyes. 'I am a girl adventurer. An adventuress. These are exciting times, George Fox, and we are lucky to be young and living in them.'

'There has not been too much luck about today,' George observed. 'Sorry to deaden the conversation, but nearly two hundred people have died to my knowledge and who knows how many more in New York.'

'Not too many,' said Ada. 'Although I did overhear some people at that table over there saying that Barnum's American Museum burned to the ground.'

'Oh dear,' said George. 'I would have liked to have visited that. But listen, this is all an awful affair. These people who have died were not just hoi polloi, they were titled folk.'

'And that makes their lives more valuable?' Ada asked.

'No,' said George. 'I do not mean that. All life is equally valuable.'

'Even alien life?' asked Ada, turning her head towards a party of Venusians who had lately entered the great dining hall and were now elegantly seating themselves.

George looked on as they did so.

Tall and gorgeous they were, with their high plumed albino locks, their startling cheekbones and golden eyes. George recalled how Ada Lovelace had told him that she found Venusians fearful and George could understand how their very 'otherness' made Earth folk uncomfortable. To the extent that today Fundamentalist Christians had sought to murder those aboard the *Empress of Mars*.

The Venusian sitters looked aloof, detached from the everyday. If the events earlier had affected them in any way there was no evidence of that here. They placed their perfumers before them on the table and engaged in prayers in their native tongue.

'Cold,' whispered Ada. 'Cold as fish, they have no emotions at all.'

'I worry for all of this,' said George. 'What if the Fundamentalist Christians had succeeded in murdering these Venusians today? It might have sparked off, how shall I put this, an *interplanetary* incident, as well as an international one. They travel under the protection of Queen Victoria, as do all aboard.'

'And all men are equal, no matter what their race?' said Ada.

'Of course,' said George. 'How could it be otherwise?'

'And no matter the planet of their birth? I do not recall the Martians coming in peace for all Mankind.'

'They were mad, those Martians,' said George. 'But they are all dead now, thank goodness.'

'George,' said Ada, 'you are a lovely man. You care about everybody. But this world, and no doubt others also, are not peopled by lovely men like you. People are bigots, religious or racial or both. I do not like Venusians, I admit it. I do not wish to kill them, but in truth I wish they were not here. They make me uneasy. I know they are up to something.'

'Well, I do not know,' said George. 'I think that what happened today was appalling. I think that this airship should return to London where the dead can be given proper burial. And—'

'What of you, George Fox? What of you?'

'I do not know,' said George. 'You have put certain doubts in my head. I do not know what to think any more.'

'Perhaps a little more champagne might help.'

George Fox stroked at his striking chin. 'Perhaps it might,' he agreed.

★

The evening passed away most pleasantly. George tried quite successfully to turn a blind eye to the scorched diners and the aloof Venusians, whom he noticed did not dine, but only took glasses of water. Ada Lovelace was a skilled and witty conversationalist and as George looked into her entrancing green eyes he could only think of how lucky he was to be sitting right here, right now, at this table with such a beautiful woman.

George did his best to put all thoughts from him for anything but Ada. And found this not altogether impossible.

George finally signed a bill of prodigious price without any thought of adding a tip, dismissed Darwin the monkey butler for the night and escorted Ada Lovelace for a stroll on the promenade deck.

It had been cleared now of the wounded and the dead and was once more a picture in the moonlight.

'We will not walk too closely to the guardrail,' said George. 'A drunken fellow pitched over it last night.'

'He did so after a struggle with someone,' said Ada, 'and bounced right off my lifeboat when he fell.'

'Well,' said George, 'we had best be careful. It is a beautiful night.'

The moon shone in the star-struck sky, the clouds below and all of heaven above. George and Ada strolled the deck, arm in arm and at peace.

And when Ada turned up her face to be kissed, George kissed it tenderly.

22

ude awakenings now held little surprise for George, so when a mighty rapping upon his cabin door jarred him into consciousness he did not complain *too* loudly. In fact, he hardly complained at all; he did not have it in him. George swung his legs gently over the edge of his dangling bunk, cradled his head in his hands and moaned softly. George had a terrible hangover.

A sudden thought gripped him and he glanced back to the bunk, but the thought was a vain one and Ada Lovelace was not to be found sleeping there, her lovely red head upon the pillow, those emerald eyes closed in peaceful sleep.

George felt his way to the cabin door and eased it open a crack, and the bootboy's grinning face displayed itself.

'Lord bless my soul, guv'nor,' said the mouth of this face. 'You've a sorry look to yourself and no mistake.'

'What do you want?' asked George in a growly tone.

'I've been sent to knock up all the passengers.' The bootboy spoke in a chirpy voice. 'Sorry if you were a sleeping.'

'I am not a violent man,' George managed to say, 'but you surely try my patience.'

'The captain would like a word in your ear,' said the bootboy. 'Not just yours, as it happens, but those of all on board. There is to be a big meeting in the concert hall in half of an hour. The captain apologises for any inconvenience, but would appreciate your presence.'

George closed the cabin door on the lad and sought a glass of water.

The concert hall of the *Empress of Mars* was an exact reproduction of the interior of the Hackney Empire Theatre. Which would cause much interest to future architectural historians, in that the Hackney Empire Theatre was not built until the year nineteen hundred and one*.

Three balconies rose above the stalls, gorgeous and fussy with all the rococo trimmings. Muses and cherubim, angels and demons, masks of comedy, tragedy and more. Clusters of fruits and columns and finials, domed faux temples either side of the stage.

George had once seen Little Tich perform his now legendary Big Boot Dance at the Hackney Empire. And once one has seen an act like that, one is pretty much spoiled for anything else.

In the gorgeous gilded foyer, George was met by the wine waiter who had served him the previous evening. The wine waiter held a board with an ornate brass clip on the top. A list of names was attached to this board.

'Oh,' said the wine waiter, without enthusiasm. 'It is you.'

'And it is *you*,' observed George. 'In yet another role, so versatile you are.'

---

* And once more proof that history is simply *not* to be trusted.

'And other roles to come,' said the wine waiter, in that tone that is known, and universally unloved, as 'grumpy'. 'Half the crew jumped ship in New York, which is why I am so overworked.'

'That explains much regarding, how shall I put this, your attitude,' said George. 'Where should I sit, any-where?'

'Oh no,' said the wine waiter. 'Seats are allocated according to status. You are . . .' And he ran his finger down the list. 'In the back row,' he said.

'Back row of the stalls?' asked George.

'Back row of the gods.'

Whatever humour there had originally been in naming the very topmost balcony of a theatre 'the gods' was lost upon all who could only afford seats in 'the gods' and who had to walk up all of those steps to be so far from the stage.

George walked up with a slouch in his steps. He was hungry and wanted some breakfast. He had a right old hangovered grump on by the time he found his seat, but was not disappointed to find Ada Lovelace in the seat next to his and Darwin the monkey butler next to her.

'Good morning,' said George, smiling bravely.

'Good morning to you,' said Ada.

Darwin the monkey had nothing to say. He just picked at his nose.

There was a great deal of mumbling and grumbling in the concert hall. George viewed surly faces, many red and raw. He also viewed the royal box, where sat Venusians. Distracted and removed from it all, elegant and effete.

There was no orchestra in the pit and when a bosun

piped the captain onto the stage, the captain received no applause.

The captain wore an elaborately decorated dress uniform, all swirling flourishes of golden thread upon a background of royal blue. He sported extravagantly flounced jodhpurs, highly polished knee boots and a high-crowned sola topi with silvered goggle accessories.

'My lords, ladies and gentlemen, ecclesiastics of Venus and burghers of Jupiter,' said this man, clearing his throat politely and offering to all a professional smile. 'My name is Captain Bigglesworth, overall commander of the *Empress of Mars*.' He paused there in the hope of applause. Upon not receiving any, he continued, 'It is with the deepest regret that I must inform you that due to the unfortunate incident in New York, the work of a mad anarchist faction, I understand that the toll of non-dining passengers stands at two hundred and two.'

George whistled softly between his teeth. A general gasp of displeasure rose up throughout the concert hall.

'Most regrettable indeed,' the captain continued. 'A full list of the non-diners will be posted in the vestibule of the great dining hall; a collection will be taken up later. It has been proposed that a burial at sea, with full honours for those of military rank and a Christian service for all, courtesy of the ship's chaplain, will be held at three this afternoon when we reach the Pacific Ocean. It has been decided that we will *not* be stopping at San Francisco as was originally planned. It is considered unsafe to do so in the light of recent events, and let us be entirely frank here – the folk of the West Coast of America are to say the least volatile and eccentric. Was it not our own Charles Rennie Mackintosh who said, "if you turn America on its side, everything that isn't screwed down rolls to California"?'

The captain paused now, possibly in the hope of a laugh. But upon not receiving one he went on with what he had to say.

'We will be pressing on,' said he, 'to our next port of call on the itinerary: the paradisiacal island of Hawaii. You will find the natives there *extremely* friendly, eager to please and given to gay caprice. We have encountered an unfortunate incident, but we will not let that stand in our way. We are British and we possess this.' And he pointed to his stiff upper lip. 'Let us put the past behind us and press on with this voyage of a lifetime. What say you to this?'

The applause was polite, and it rippled through the audience, but ripple indeed it did, *and* applause it *was*.

George just shook his head and shrugged his shoulders.

'So that is *it*, is it?' he said to Ada. 'The show must go on.'

'It is the British way of doing things,' said Ada.

'So,' continued the captain, 'we will reach Hawaii tomorrow evening, hopefully in time to see the sun set upon it. I am told it is a thing of great beauty to behold. The natives of Hawaii have many quaint customs, one of which is their evening ritual of the setting sun. They believe that the volcano upon their island gave birth to the sun, a belief that goes back to the very dawn of their civilisation. The Greeks, who visited Hawaii one thousand years ago, named it the *Umbilicus Mundi* – the Navel of the World.'

★

George was one of the last to leave the concert hall. It is as far *down* from the gods as it is *up* and there were a lot of people mooching down before him.

When he gained the foyer he was surprised to find Professor Coffin bouncing up and down and looking very pleased indeed to see him.

'What splendid news it is, my boy,' he said to George, a-wringing of his hands. 'It is fate indeed, is it not? Your fate.'

'I know not quite of what you speak,' said George.

'The *Umbilicus Mundi*,' crowed Professor Coffin, and he fairly crowed. 'The Navel of the World, my boy.'

'It means nothing to me,' said George.

'Ah no, of course it would not. But it is the destination that we seek, my boy. Hawaii is where lies the object of our quest.'

'Object of your quest?' asked Ada Lovelace.

'Ah!' went the professor. 'Fiddle de, fiddle dum. I did not see you there, Miss Fox, all hid behind your brother.'

'He is such a *big* boy,' said Ada, 'and I a mere slip of a girl.'

'Quite so. Well, come, George, we have much to speak of.'

'You may speak in front of me,' said Ada. 'George has no secrets from his sister, do you, George?'

'Really?' said Professor Coffin, looking hard at Ada. 'Well, I have no wish to bother you with manly business. I am sure there are feminine matters that require your close attention.'

'So nothing that I should bother my pretty little head with?'

'Quite so,' said the professor once more. And, 'Come, George,' he also said.

'I have some misgivings, Professor,' said George. 'There are certain things bothering me.'

Professor Coffin's fingers toyed at his waistcoat pocket. Within this waistcoat pocket lay a slim glass phial of colourless liquid.

'If you will excuse us, dear lady,' Professor Coffin said to Ada. 'A few words in private with your brother and then I will return him to you as good as new.'

'What a queer choice of words,' said Ada Lovelace.

'Well, be that as it may, come, George.'

George Fox scratched at his striking chin and made a doubtful face.

'Whatever is the matter, my boy?' asked the professor.

'It is about our quest,' said George. 'I am having second thoughts.'

'Then come, George, *please*, and we'll sort this matter out.'

'George is not feeling very well,' said Ada, squeezing George's hand. 'He is still very upset about what happened yesterday.'

'*Very* upset,' agreed George.

Professor Coffin jigged about from one foot to the other.

'Perhaps George and I might see you for lunch, Professor,' said Ada.

Professor Coffin's knuckles whitened on the skull-top of his cane. 'Yes indeed,' he said. 'Well, no matter, these things can wait.' He looked long and hard at Ada Lovelace. 'We do not arrive at Hawaii until tomorrow evening and who knows what might happen in the meantime?'

And, bowing deeply, he turned on his heel and marched away at the double.

Ada Lovelace let out a breath. Her hand in George's shook.

'I fear,' said Ada Lovelace, in a still, small voice, 'that I have made a mortal enemy.'

23

rofessor Coffin was absent from lunch and also absent from tea. George and Ada paid their respects to the departed at the afternoon funeral service and George looked on in awe as tightly shrouded bodies were dispatched over the guardrail of the promenade deck to fall down and down to the rolling ocean below.

The Pacific Ocean spread towards foreverness. An endless expanse of blue, it seemed, broken only by the airship's mighty shadow. George marvelled greatly at the speed of the airship. Capable, as it was, of spanning America in a single day. George might well have found himself lost once more in awestruck reverie, had not Ada Lovelace nudged him in the ribs and suggested that they do something adventurous to exercise their minds.

'Darwin and I were thinking to visit the casino,' she said.

Darwin grinned a simian grin and raised a simian thumb.

'The casino?' said George. 'But I do not have any money.'

'I do,' said Ada. 'And also Darwin. He has put himself in charge of his deceased master's goods and chattels.'

'An enterprising ape,' said George, and thought to

himself that if all else failed, he and the professor might well exhibit such an ape to an appreciative public.

The casino of the *Empress of Mars* fairly beggared description. It was decorated all about in the style called erotic-exotique. It certainly outdid the bathing rooms of Cardinal La Motte, or the suave and gracious boudoir of La Marquise du Deffand. It was rich with royal stuffs and furnished with frescoes that would have done justice to the Rabelaisian Abbey of Thélème.

George kept his gaze low and tried to move with seeming ease and confidence between pillars that arose like hymns in praise of carnal revelry.

Ada Lovelace glanced up at George. 'Your cheeks are red,' said she.

George did whispered shushings in reply. 'The pictures are frankly obscene,' said he. 'I cannot believe that images such as these should be on board this ship.'

'You have clearly not visited the Nympharium,' said Ada.

'I do not even know what that means,' whispered George.

And Ada spoke words into his ear.

'No!' said George, growing redder than ever. 'That is outrageous. No.'

'The rich will not be denied their indulgences,' said Ada. 'But the art displayed here is rather beautiful, to my thinking. It is the work of Mr Aubrey Beardsley, who also designed a lot of the ladies' fans that you might have seen fluttering about.'

'What shall we play, then?' asked George of a sudden. 'I do not really know how to gamble.'

'Let us just drift about a little and see what takes our

fancy,' said Ada. 'Ah, look though, Darwin has already found his way to the Snap table.'

'The Snap table?' George Fox asked.

'Now do not tell me that you don't know how to play Snap,' said Ada. 'Everybody knows how to play Snap.'

'Snap?' said George. 'In a casino? Snap?'

'There is Snap,' said Ada, and then she pointed. 'And over there I see Ludo and there Happy Families, Noughts and Crosses, Snakes and Ladders, Hunt the Thimble and Tiddlywinks. And there is Boggle. Although I confess that I have never quite understood Boggle.'

'But these are children's games,' protested George. 'I had assumed that there would be roulette and poker and pontoon.'

'I have never heard of those,' said Ada. 'Let's watch Darwin playing.'

Darwin the monkey butler gave a good account of himself at the Snap table. He won five rounds in succession, but was then out-snapped by the dealer, whom George recognised almost at once to be none other than the wine waiter he now so regularly encountered.

'What is your name?' enquired George. 'We meet up so often, I feel I should address you by name.'

The wine waiter/dealer wore a decorated golden turban and matching robes. The casino staff look was distinctive. He wiggled a gloved hand at George and counselled silence.

'I cannot speak now, sir, I—'

'Snap!' went Darwin.

And, 'Snap!' went the dealer also.

'The monkey won that one,' said George.

'You distracted me,' complained the dealer. 'Please do not speak when I'm playing, it—'

'Snap!' went Darwin once more.

'And he definitely won that one,' said George.

'Sir, I must ask you not to speak at the table,' said the dealer, 'because I—'

'Snap!' went Darwin once more again.

'That was never Snap,' cried the dealer. 'That was a two and a three. You cannot call Snap on a two and a three.'

'It was two twos,' said George. 'You laid that three after the monkey called Snap.'

'I did nothing of the kind, I—'

'Snap!' went Darwin.

'Stop it!' cried the dealer, flinging his cards to the table. 'I cannot concentrate on the game when someone is constantly distracting me. It is outrageous.'

'I am sorry,' said George. 'I did not mean to upset you.'

'It is all too much.' The dealer now kicked at the Snap table, hurting his toes and resulting in much comedic hopping about.

'Calm yourself down,' said George.

'Snap!' went Darwin one more time and loudly.

'I resign,' shouted the dealer. 'Here, take all the money, I don't care. I have had enough.' And with that said he thrust piles of gambling chips in Darwin's direction, tore off his turban and flung it to the inlaid floor and flounced from the casino in the very worst of moods.

George stared after him, then turned back to the Snap table, rubbed his palms together and sought to avail himself of the dealer's largesse.

'Ah, sorry now, sir, but we cannot have *that*.' Another young man in casino livery stepped swiftly behind the table and drew the gambling chips beyond George's reach. 'That boy will receive the thrashing he deserves. My apologies for his behaviour, sir, but what can one expect when one employs Austrians?'

'Austrians?' queried George. 'He did not have an Austrian accent.'

'And what, pray, does an Austrian accent sound like, sir?'

'Fair enough,' said George. 'And I never did learn his name.'

'His name is Hitler,' said the new dealer. 'Adolf Hitler, the little tyke, he'll come to no good, mark my words.'

George smiled at Ada who smiled back at him. 'I am sure there is some lesson to be learned from all of this,' George told her, 'but for the very life of me I have absolutely no idea just what it might be.'

'Do you fancy a game of Marbles?' asked Ada.

'I certainly do,' said George.

And so they spent a pleasant hour or two. There were some moments, however, that were slightly less pleasant. Such as when Darwin the monkey butler was caught cheating at Hopscotch and was escorted from the casino. Or when he returned shortly afterwards with something very much less than pleasant in his hairy hand and proceeded to hurl it into the face of the casino's horrified Hopscotcher.

George and Ada turned away their faces. George suggested they should take their leave.

★

Once more upon the promenade deck, in steamer chairs with cocktails and cakes, George toasted Ada and remarked that he had had a most entertaining afternoon and thank you very much for it.

Ada flashed her emerald eyes and took to counting money.

'You did rather well at the casino,' said George. 'Your skills at Happy Families would seem to be unrivalled. Winning that last big pot was a triumph. I thought the dealer was going to win and he would have done too if he had been able to come up with all of the Baker's family. Luck was also on your side, it would seem.'

'So it would seem,' agreed Ada. But as she continued with her money counting, George was somewhat saddened to see several cards fall from her lace-cuffed sleeve. Master Bun the Baker's son being one of them.

Darwin the monkey butler came bouncing along the deck.

'I hope you have washed your hands,' George said to him.

The monkey butler grinned at George and helped himself to a cake.

'I must go and powder my nose,' said Ada Lovelace. 'Do not let Darwin eat any more cakes – I want the chocolate eclair.'

She rose from her chair and smiled down at George, then stopped and kissed his cheek.

'I like being with you, George,' she said. 'I like you very much.'

George looked on as she walked away and a small tear formed in his eye. For George Fox knew more than anything else that he was in love with Ada.

Ahead crackled something of a storm. High, dark

clouds upon the horizon. And there was of a sudden a certain chill to the air and George hunched his shoulders and rubbed his hands together and wondered much regarding the future.

The *Empress of Mars* boasted to the most luxurious Ladies' Accommodation. Etched-glass mirrors and faux marble fixtures and fittings of brass and of copper. Specific needs such as the unlacing and relacing of corsetry were attended to by a female servant, the 'feminine needs facilitator', known colloquially as the 'toilette fairy'. The toilette fairy was not in residence upon this particular afternoon, but Ada Lovelace, skilled in lacework of her own corset, had no need for her.

Ada repaired to the cubicle and did what ladies do.

She tugged at the ivory handle of the Rupert Fairglass Patent Sanitizing Ceramic-bowl-de-fustigator, set herself to decency and emerged from the cubicle.

To find herself most unexpectedly confronted by Professor Cagliostro Coffin.

'You see, Darwin,' George told the monkey butler, 'it could be a most wonderful world, wonderful *worlds* in fact, if people just took time to care for each other rather than be so nasty.'

Darwin nodded his hairy head. His thoughts were, however, elsewhere.

'Take yourself as an example,' said George. 'I expect you would rather be back in the jungle, swinging about in the trees with your relatives.'

Darwin, who had been born in Brentford and preferred the wearing of fine livery and kid gloves to the prospect of naked ramblings in treetops, had no comment to make.

'You are discriminated against because you are not human,' said George. 'Folk look down on you. Not *me*, of course, but other folk do, trust me on this. Everybody seems to be suspicious of everybody else and if there are folk who are different, then they get treated badly.' George had something of a bee in his top-hat bonnet and as Darwin made no objection to his diatribe, George continued with it.

'I am supposedly on a sacred quest,' he said. 'A prophecy was made to me. My fate, it seems, is sealed. And maybe that is true. But the more I see of this world, the less I like it. I do not think I have enjoyed this journey.'

'Not enjoyed the journey?'

At the sound of these words George looked up, to view the smiling professor. 'We are near our goal,' said he to George. 'Trust me, all will be well.'

'Trust?' said George, in reply to this. 'I am having trouble with trust.'

'You do too much thinking, my boy. Too much cerebral concentration gives rise to an anxious disposition. Follow my lead and be joyous in your outlook.' Professor Coffin did a little dance. 'We are a happy crowd of travellers and must put all differences aside if we are to succeed in our goal. Do you not agree with me, dear Ada?'

George looked beyond the professor. He had not seen Ada return.

'I agree with everything that you say, Professor Coffin,' said Ada Lovelace, with a faraway look in her eyes. 'You must trust this gentleman, George, he wishes you only well.'

George Fox stared at Ada Lovelace. 'But?' was the word that he spoke.

'I was wrong,' said Ada. 'I am a foolish girl. The professor can be trusted absolutely. We must do whatever he says. Whatever he thinks is for the best.'

Professor Coffin smiled upon Ada. 'Whatever I think is best.'

24

he evening proved to be less fun than had been the afternoon.

The sparkle had departed Ada Lovelace. The lovely girl sat at the late Lord Brentford's table, speaking only when she was spoken to and only then in monosyllables. George was most distraught about her drastic change in demeanour and asked repeatedly regarding the state of her health.

'I am fine,' she said, each time that he asked.

But George was far from convinced.

The storm that had crackled on the horizon was all about them now and the captain had been unable to take the ship up above the clouds. Rain smashed down on the *Empress of Mars*, and lightning tore about it.

Captain Bigglesworth's voice rang sharply through the great dining hall, twanging through huge tuba-like, brass-bell public address systems, which were linked by speaking tubes to the bridge.

'My lords, ladies and gentlemen, ecclesiastics of Venus, burghers of Jupiter, we are presently travelling through a period of light drizzle. You might experience some mild discomfort. Please remain indoors and away from the promenade deck. Enjoy your meals. Tonight's entertainment is provided by Guru Gurami the Indian

Swami, who will perform the celebrated Indian Rope Trick and other acts of subcontinental metaphysical transubstantiation. Employing the transperambulation of psuedo-cosmic—'

But few were listening to him. Thunder rattled the windowpanes and shook at the cutlery, the great ship quivered fretfully, the turbines wheezed and trembled.

Young Master Hitler, sporting a rather dramatic black eye, served them at table. George settled on a simple swordfish casserole, Ada said she was not hungry and Professor Coffin rubbed his palms together and ordered most of the menu.

Darwin made selections from the wine list, but only Professor Coffin seemed to appreciate the choices.

'Cheer it up there, young George,' he said to his dismal companion. 'We shall soon reach Hawaii and while I do not expect that we will be enjoying any sunsets over the volcano, we will be near to reaching our goal. Can you not feel it, George? *I* feel it.'

'I am sorry, Professor,' said George, 'but things have been getting me down lately. And now this storm and Ada looking so poorly—'

'The storm will pass.' Professor Coffin clapped his hands together. 'And Ada will arouse herself from her stupor. Won't you, my dear? Cheer yourself up for your brother. Do it for me *now*.'

A smile spread over Ada's face. But this smile lacked for conviction.

'Perhaps you should take yourself off to your bunk,' said George to Ada. 'Sleep out the storm, as it were.'

'A capital idea,' said Professor Coffin. 'I will escort the young lady. Upon which deck is her cabin?'

'On second thoughts,' said George, 'perhaps it would

be better if she remained here, where I can keep an eye on her.'

'Perhaps,' said the professor. 'Ah, see, here comes the "turn".'

The 'turn' wore golden robes not unlikened to those worn by the airship's casino staff. He sported a larger turban though, with many encrustments of pearl. And he wore upon his feet a pair of those curl-up-toed slippers that find great favour with genies.

Some tables had been cleared away from the central area of the dining hall and a small round stage assembled. Guru Gurami the Indian Swami climbed onto this stage. He bowed to all and sundry, was acknowledged by no one, clasped his hands together and vanished.

Just like that.

In a big puff of smoke.

'Not the most entertaining of acts,' said Professor Coffin, 'but it has brevity on its side, so let us be grateful for that.'

'Sir?' came a voice at Professor Coffin's ear. Professor Coffin ducked away in shock.

'Sorry to startle you,' said Guru Gurami the Indian Swami, for it, indeed, was he, 'but I require the services of an assistant upon stage – would you do me the honour to oblige?'

Professor Coffin gathered his wits, and he was rarely rattled. 'Not I,' said he. 'A bit of a game leg, caught by a Jezail bullet in the Afghan campaign. But that will be over by Christmas.'

'I have my doubts as to that,' said the swami, 'but if not yourself, then perhaps your lovely granddaughter?'

'My *what*?' Professor Coffin bridled.

'You then, sir,' said the swami unto George.

'Not really,' said George. 'I have a casserole due and—'

There was a deafening crack of thunder and the ship took a lurch. Glasses tinkled to the floor, occasional ladies fainted.

'I think you will find the experience uplifting,' said the swami, now helping George from his chair. 'Let us enliven the company and take people's minds from the raging storm beyond.'

And indeed the storm was truly raging now. Up upon the bridge the captain clung to the wheel. Sky-men cranked at stopcocks, consulted big brass-bound pressure gauges, swung mighty levers, worried at flickering dials. Lightning tore the sky apart, and the great ship quivered and shook.

George was now upon the stage and most embarrassed was he.

'Have you ever met me before, young man?' asked the swami.

'No, I have not, sir,' said George. 'I do not know you at all.'

'Well done, son,' said the swami. 'It is good to know that some of your mother's and my good manners have rubbed off upon you.'

The swami grinned out at the audience. The audience ignored him.

'What a miserable, stuck-up bunch,' whispered the swami to George. 'I'd rather do a Friday night at the Glasgow Empire.'

'Can we just get this over with?' George asked. 'I do not want my casserole getting cold.'

'All right then,' said the swami, and once more he addressed the dining passengers. 'Good folk,' called he, 'offer me please your attention. I present for you this evening a metaphysical manifestation second to none. An elliptical navigation through the aethers of oblivion. A polymorphic endochromatical calcification, utilising serendipitous—'

'You are really just making this up as you go along,' whispered George to the swami. 'None of that makes any sense.'

'You expect sense, do you, George?' asked the swami. 'Amidst this Hellish maelstrom?'

And the Hellish maelstrom was growing by the minute.

'Hold on there,' said George to the swami. 'I never told you my name.'

'You are George Geoffrey Arthur Fox,' said Guru Gurami the Indian Swami. 'Here on a sacred quest.'

'Oh no you do not,' said George. 'I see through your game. The professor put you up to this, did he not? He told you my name. You do not fool me.'

'That man is the very Devil himself,' the swami's voice hissed at George's ear. But it was *not* the voice of the swami. It was the voice of Macmoyster Farl. 'Take care, young George,' said the voice of Farl. 'Take care in whom you would trust.'

'And I command you, *rise!*' The voice was that of the swami once more and shouted with terrible force.

George felt suddenly very odd, as if detached from himself. He was there, but he was not, so to speak.

George cried, 'What are you doing to me?' And then he just went, 'Waaaaaaaaaah!'

For George no longer stood upon the stage. George

now floated in the air. The few diners who were actually watching this happen halted their takings of dinner. Forkfuls of loveliness hovered in mid-air, glasses paused before lips.

'Oh,' wailed George Fox. 'Let me down. I do not like it up here at all.'

But George was rising even higher now. Up towards the gilded frescoed ceiling. Up towards the crystal chandeliers. And the diners who viewed this now did nudgings at their companions. Nudgings were all the rage.

George spied from his uneasy eyrie a party of jovial Jovians, seated at table and giggling with mirth. It flashed briefly into George's consciousness, as he hung there in open defiance of gravity's best-known law, how quite unlike the folk of Venus these were. Big and jolly, given to raucous laughter, the burghers of Jupiter bustled and bumbled about the Earth seemingly meaning no harm. Did Earth people hate them as much as they hated Venusians? George wondered. Although obviously not all Earth people, but—

'Help!' cried George. 'Help!'

The party of Jovians cheered.

Professor Coffin clapped his hands. Ada stared on, speechless. Darwin the monkey gibbered and jigged. Young Master Hitler did spittings in somebody's casserole.

'Down please, now,' called George to the swami. 'I have had enough now, thanks.' And as George struggled upon high, to the admiration of some, but still the complete lack of interest of others, a bolt of lightning struck the ship and it slewed wildly to port.

Tables and chairs, diners and waiters took to a sudden rush. Crockery tumbled, diners upended, falling glass shattered, chaos ensued. Another great flash and the ship slewed to starboard. Chairs, tables, diners and all rushed back. Up on high and seemingly cocooned against gravity's urgent callings, George looked on in horror. Folk were being bowled about like dolls in a giant's toy box. A chandelier fell from the ceiling, statues toppled and smashed.

'Get me down,' cried George. 'Get me down!'

But Guru Gurami the Indian Swami had rolled away under a table. George caught sight of Ada Lovelace sliding by upon a waiter's tray and Professor Coffin clinging for his own dear life to the side of the makeshift stage.

Flashings of lightning, roarings of thunder, then a terrible grinding sound. More terrible, this, than the elemental thrashings in the sky, the sound was of machinery tortured into high-pitched whinings, growing to a devastating scream.

And then the voice of the captain came once more over the public address system. 'Ladies and gentlemen, er, lords and ladies and gentlemen and, er – we are experiencing some problems with the electric turbines. We will—'

And his voice died away.

To the port side once more rushed all and sundry, hideously twisting, screaming and struggling.

Back came the voice of the captain once again.

'We regret that we will be forced to make an unscheduled landing. Unfortunately we are still some ten nautical miles from the paradisiacal island of Hawaii—'

And once more his voice died away.

An awful explosion roared from the rear of the airship.

The starboard turbine tore itself loose and plummeted down to the sea.

'. . . passengers will please make their way to the lifeboats,' came the voice of the captain, then to be silenced for ever.

The lights went out in the great dining hall.

The *Empress of Mars* was going down.

25

he ill-starred airship's maiden voyage was coming to an end. A bitter and sorry end was this. The great doomed pleasure-craft wallowed and sank, down through the hideous maelstrom, gas bag ruptured, turbine mountings broken and ablaze.

Thrashing and clawing at one another like lost souls in one of Dante's less-than-cheerful lower circles of Hell, the screaming multitude in the great dining hall sought the salvation of the lifeboats. The credo of 'women and children first' found few followers here.

George looked down in horror as the living and the dead were hurled together in some ghastly *danse macabre*.

Where was Ada? Was she dead? And where was the professor?

George struggled vainly and sought release from the magical force that held him, but it was as if he were enclosed within an invisible shell, protecting him from harm, whilst rendering him helpless to offer what assistance he could in this monstrous calamity.

The *Empress of Mars* suddenly all but upended. Passengers and crew, Earthfolk and others from elsewhere, tables, chairs and all the fine paraphernalia of first-class dining, now joined by the stage, the grand piano, statues, pillars and whatnots, took one final terrible trip, over the dining hall floor, out through the windows and onto the storm-lashed promenade deck.

And after them all travelled George, in surprising comfort considering the apocalyptic circumstances. He wafted gently, light as a bubble from a child's soap-sud meerschaum. Out and away into the sky.

Untouched by the storm, undampened by the rain, but reaching a point close to madness, George drummed his fists upon the interior of his invisible prison and called the name of Ada Lovelace again and again and again. And as he floated away from the airship, he viewed its terrible end. Lit by spreading fires now and the lightning's awful blaze, the *Empress of Mars*, billowing and broken-backed, plunged into the storm-whipped ocean. Folk were fighting for the lifeboats now and overloaded vessels were tearing free of their moorings. The destruction was titanic, decks imploding, cabins tearing open. George looked on as the concert hall turned inside out, spewing seating and balconies into the foaming waves.

And George Fox turned his face away, for he could bear no more.

Shortly before the coming of dawn the storm lost its fury and ceased with its howlings and wrath. The gales dropped away, the lightning departed, the thunder no more to be feared. The ocean calmed to a palette of blues as sunlight fell upon it.

George awoke from troubled sleep to find himself alone.

Alone upon a beautiful beach and freed from his eerie cocoon. His fingers touched on silver sand, warm sunlight kissed at his striking chin. George rose upon his elbows, for he was flat on his back. Took in the idyllic surroundings, smiled to himself and then recalled all that had happened.

George's face did cloudings-over, George's stomach knotted. He climbed to his feet and he shouted Ada's name, but George was all alone. Before him, a sea of infinite blue; behind, a rising jungle.

George shielded his eyes from the early sun and scanned the distant horizon. Debris, bodies, lifeboats? George saw only blue.

Was he the sole survivor saved from the watery grave? Saved somehow by magic, or by God? George's thoughts went racing – how had it come to this? Was what had happened his fault? Was he somehow horribly jinxed? A modern-day Jonah bringing doom to all he met?

George Fox sank down onto his knees and cradled his hands in prayer.

'Please, God,' prayed George, 'let Ada live. Send my soul to Hell in trade, but please let Ada live.'

A monkey shrieked somewhere in the jungle, causing George to lose his concentration. Had Darwin the monkey butler been washed ashore alive? A monkey butler would prove a most useful creature to a ship-wrecked fellow on an uninhabited island.

But then George's thoughts became further confused. What if this was *not* an uninhabited island? Putting two and two together, George came up with a seemingly appropriate four by concluding that if not uninhabited, the island must therefore *be* inhabited. By cannibals!

'Oh please spare me, baby Jesus,' prayed George Fox, so suddenly devout. Then George's stomach rumbled somewhat, adding further confusion by reminding George that he had missed his dinner the previous evening and was now extremely hungry.

George Fox sank once more to the sand and buried his face in his hands.

The sun rose higher in the sky, the tide gently nibbled the beach.

At length George rose to his feet once more and dusted sand from himself. He needed food. He needed to know how large the island was and what natural resources it had to offer. And most of all he needed to know if Ada Lovelace had come ashore alive, unharmed and well.

And then George's thoughts moved on to what it would be like if only Ada had been washed ashore, leaving only her and George upon the island. The thought of *this* made George's spirits rise. He could picture the two of them building a tree house to live in, and of course employing the services of a monkey butler. Perhaps even raising a family. Before being rescued and brought back to London, where the royalties from the best-selling book of their adventures would comfortably keep them in a Mayfair mansion for the rest of their lives.

George smiled broadly and stroked at his striking chin. Then he took a great big breath and marched along the beach.

'My stride,' said George, to no one but himself, 'would be approximately one yard. So if I count my footsteps I will be able to gauge the circumference of this island when I eventually return to the point of my departure.' It was logical thinking and George was pleased with it, and so, counting loudly to himself, he strode along the beach.

George whistled as he counted, a popular music-hall ditty of the day: 'Don't Jump off the Roof, Dad, You'll Make a Hole in the Yard'. George had but recently seen demonstrated at the music hall Mr Thomas Edison's patent wax-cylinder phonograph – a wonder of modern-day acoustic science, whereby music could actually be recorded upon revolving waxen cylinders and then re-played by the application of a needle linked to a brass horn affair. And George *had* wondered at the time, were he ever to be marooned alone upon a desert island, which eight waxed cylinders he would like to take with him. And which book also, assuming he already had a Bible and the works of Shakespeare.

George plodded on, for plod he now did, his stride being all but gone. He had counted his way through three thousand footsteps, and he was all but done. But then George suddenly gave up the count and found a new spring to his step. Ahead along the beach lay wreckage. George ran forwards in hope.

This hope, however, was unfulfilled and George stopped dead in his tracks. It was certainly wreckage that lay on the beach, and considerable wreckage was this. But it was not the wreckage of the *Empress of Mars* – this was old and crusted.

A galleon? thought George. Perhaps. *A pirate ship washed up with chests of treasure?*

There was not much that had not been recently cov-ered by the mercurial mind of George Fox. Cannibals and tree houses. He and Ada as Adam and Eve and the desert island waxings. But *this* was unexpected.

This was something different.

George approached this something gingerly. Not because he feared for his safety, but more through simple amazement.

That *was* what he thought that it was, was it not?

Broken, ancient, barnacle-crusted and wrecked on a tropical beach, it had clearly been there a very long time, but it *was* what he thought that it was.

'It is a spaceship,' said George in amazement. 'It is an old-fashioned spaceship.'

And there was no doubt at all in George's mind that *that* was exactly what it was. An old crashed spaceship. Centuries old by its looks. It was a big one too, although much of it was sunken into the beach and much more hidden from view beneath the incoming tide. Easily the size of a Martian war hulk or a Jovian trading vessel.

A Martian war hulk? George's thoughts grew busy again. Martians ate humans, this was well known. And where can you flee to on an island?

'No,' said George. 'They must all be long dead. Or rescued, probably rescued.' Would there be anything to salvage from the spaceship? George's stomach rumbled urgently. Probably no food, George concluded, and he really needed some food.

Thoughts of food had not left George since he started his hike along the shoreline. But he had not been keen to enter the jungle. Jungles George knew to be fearsome. He had already covered their fearsome potential. Explorers of the Empire were forever leading pioneering expeditions into jungles such as this one. Many never to be seen again. Small brown men with bones through their noses and blowpipes at their lips lurked in jungles such as this one. They shot at you with poisoned darts. Cooked and ate your tasty parts. Shrank your head and hung it on the wall. Why, small brown men with bones through their noses might well have eaten the crew of the fallen spaceship. So they would certainly make short work of George, and he knew it.

'I am done,' said George. 'Doomed and done.'

And with that said he sat back down upon the sand, buried his face once more in his hands and had a good big cry.

And he would probably have continued to sit there upon that tropical beach, blubbering away and bewailing his lot, had not something brought this to an end.

It was a very sudden something and George did not see it coming. It struck him on the top of his head and felled him like a tree.

When George Fox woke up once again to find things not to his liking, it honestly did not surprise him at all. He was growing more than used to it by now. The only logical solution that he could call to mind would be *not* to sleep at all. Sleeping led to waking and waking led to trouble.

George awoke to trouble and did so with resignation.

He did manage a mentally exhausted, 'What *now*?' but when he saw quite how matters stood, he viewed them fatalistically and did not make a fuss.

George was in a native village, in a clearing in the middle of the jungle. There was a ring of mud huts and George was at its centre. Little brown men with bones through their noses danced about all around George.

The style of their dancing was unknown to George, but he applauded its vigour. Or would have indeed applauded it had he been able to get his hands free. But George could not get his hands free because they were bound tightly to his sides. A feast was clearly being prepared as George could smell the soup. Vegetable soup, deliciously exotic.

George did sniffings at this soup. For he was very near to this soup. *In* this soup in fact was George.

In a cooking pot.

26

ow many in such circumstances would have cried for mercy. Begged their tormentors for release. But George put on the bravest face and not a word said he. For after all, he had done a deal with God.

He *had* prayed that the good Lord would take his life in exchange for sparing Ada's.

True, he had shortly after revoked this plea with a plaintive, 'Oh please spare me, baby Jesus.' But the Almighty was not to be toyed around with and if He, in His ultimate wisdom, had decreed that the deal was done, then so the deal was done.

George shifted uncomfortably. It was growing hot.

'I hope these natives put me out of my misery before the real cooking sets in,' said George, perhaps addressing God. 'Although I have read that the more terrible the martyrdom, the more rewards are stored up in Heaven for the martyr. Not that I consider myself to be a martyr, of course. I confess that I have not been the very best of Christians and for that I apologise— Ow – ouch!'

A native, with a bone through his nose, and no doubt a blowpipe back in his hut, tossed a few more faggots of wood onto the fire that crackled away beneath the cooking pot.

Other natives held what looked to be marshmallows upon sticks towards the flames.

'Nice for starters,' George observed. Then carried on his one-sided chit-chat with God.

'I have *tried* to be a good person – ouch!' he continued. 'I do not think that I have ever – ow – knowingly done – ooh that hurts – harm to anyone and I was supposed to be on some kind of sacred quest. I think perhaps I should have spoken to you personally about that, but I – oh – ohh – ow – aaaaaagh . . .'

And that was that for George's conversation.

'Help!' screamed George at the top of his voice. 'Somebody help me, ple—'

And a native with a bone through his nose, and a catapult in his hut, for he was too young for a blowpipe, stuck an apple, or indeed the tropical equivalent thereof, right into George's mouth, staunching further screams from the coming dinner.

George thrashed about as best he could, which was not much at all. It was all hurting far too greatly now to permit any lucid thought of further colloquy with the Almighty.

It is strange indeed what fills your head when you think that your end is near. The possibilities are almost infinite. Repentance for past transgressions. Regret for not having done the things that one should have done. Thoughts of loved ones and of hated ones. Thoughts of the unfairness of life in general. Thoughts of God in particular.

Though rarely enough, it might be supposed, a muse upon 'irony'.

'How damned ironic,' went words in George's head,

for they no longer left his mouth. 'I am hungrier now than I ever have been and I end my days as food.'

And there might, of course, have been a moral there, but if so it was lost upon poor George.

The natives continued their dinner dance, the sun shone down from on high, the jungle in its beauty rose around.

George did inward screamings that his misery would cease.

But George knew that his life was almost done.

So he missed it when the first of the natives screamed and fell to the ground. He also missed the second, third and fourth. He became aware quite shortly thereafter, though, that something odd was afoot when, howling madly, all the natives ran.

And he would have a vague recollection of hairy figures bounding into the village hurling coconuts. And one, who wore a salt-stained fez, hauling him from the pot.

George Fox opened wide his eyes and then beheld an angel.

'Well,' said George. 'At least I have gone to Heaven.'

Or indeed he might well have said something very much like this had he been able to speak, but as there was an apple jammed into his mouth, he did not.

But then the apple was wrenched from his mouth and George beheld a demon. He had not reached Heaven at all, but gone to the other place.

The demon sniffed at the apple, then took to munching upon it. The angel, once more in George's vision, asked, 'George, are you all right?'

George did blinkings of the eyes, as anyone would do in such circumstances, then said, 'Ada . . .'

Then he said no more.

When George awoke this time he found Ada's face anxiously looking down upon his own. He became aware that he was lying on a bed of straw, within a rude mud hut. A blowpipe hung on an earthen wall, beside a shrunken head.

'Ada,' said George. 'Ada, you are alive.'

'And you also,' said Ada. 'Although it was touch and go.'

'But how?' asked George, and Ada told him how.

'It was all too mad,' said Ada Lovelace. 'All too terribly mad. The horrors of the great dining hall with people being bowled about as if they were nothing at all. And you up in the air in your magic bubble – how ever was that done?'

But George just shook his head.

'Then there was all the mad fighting over the lifeboats. People were overcrowding them and they didn't know how to get them loose from the wreck. Now, as you know, I was well acquainted with one particular lifeboat and I made my way to it as best I could. I had it all to myself, then Darwin arrived, carrying the professor, who had been knocked unconscious. And obviously I could not leave him behind, because he is such a good man and knows what is for the best.'

George let this one pass without comment and Ada continued with her tale.

'I released the lifeboat and rowed very hard,' said Ada.

'*You* rowed?' said George.

'The professor felt that it was for the best.'

And George Fox ground his teeth.

'The lifeboat was not too crowded. There was just me, Darwin, the professor and young Master Hitler, the wine waiter.'

'Ah,' said George. 'Well, I am *so* happy that *he* came to no harm.'

Ada gave George a certain look, then carried on with her tale.

'It was simply awful, George,' she said. 'I saw you sail away into the sky and there was nothing I could do. I could only hope that you would be safe. Not a lot of people survived the crash, I don't think. Half a dozen lifeboats full at most. I saw a lifeboat with the Venusians in and another with those fat Jovians. Laughing away like mad they were, enjoying every minute. But then the Empress sank and the storm went on for hours. When dawn came we saw the island and came ashore. Only three other lifeboats survived, I think, or perhaps the others made land on another island. We all made camp on the beach, then the professor told me that it would be for the best if I went into the jungle to forage for food. Darwin came with me and we met with a tribe of monkeys. They led us here and here we found you in the pot. Which is all of my story really – what did you think of it?'

'I think I am impressed,' said George, now sitting up and feeling at his parts. 'I think most of it is true.'

'*All* of it is true,' said Ada, making a wounded face.

'Which is why I am impressed,' said George. 'In the recent past you would have probably made up some far-fetched fiction.'

'Well, I don't do that any more,' said Ada. 'Not with you.'

'And I am glad,' said George in reply. 'And very grateful to you for saving my life.' And Ada gave George a bit of a hug and that really hurt poor George.

He was not too badly burned, though, as it happened, and this was probably due to the protective attributes of his quality suit, although it had shrunk somewhat in the cooking pot's water and now had a music-hall look.

Ada served George food and drink and George was grateful for it.

'Does anyone have any idea where we are?' asked George, as he munched upon a marshmallow. 'I do not suppose one of the sky-pilots survived with a map or a compass?'

'There has been some very funny talk,' said Ada, 'especially amongst the Jupiterian tourists. They have maps of Earth woven into the linings of their jackets apparently, and I overhead them saying that this island is not on their maps.'

'Then we are truly marooned,' said George, drinking from half a coconut. 'If it is not on the map then it is not near a shipping lane.'

'I think that goes without saying,' said Ada. 'Cannibal natives do not find favour in tourist resorts. And this is very much a paradise island. Mr Thomas Cook would probably be more than happy to add it to his brochure.'

'Well,' said George, 'looking on the bright side – and as I have been saved from a horrible death and you are with me once again, I feel I *can* look on the bright side – we will not starve upon this island. The natives have been able to sustain themselves and once we have dealt with them, so shall we.'

' "Dealt with them" – as in exterminate them?' Ada queried.

'You know me to be a charitable fellow,' said George, 'in no way racially bigoted and meaning harm to no man. But those evil fellows tried to cook me. I do not think I will mourn for their loss.'

'So we should just wipe them out and take over their island?' asked Ada.

'Well.' George paused. 'When you put it like *that*—'

'Oh, do not get me wrong,' said Ada. 'I have no problems with that at all. We might even think of salting some of them down and storing them away to be consumed at a later date.'

George was somewhat speechless at this and felt he was done with his dinner.

But there was no getting away from the fact that the prospect of life upon a paradise island with Ada Lovelace held to enormous charm. Adam and Eve in the Garden of Eden, near as near could be. He would just have to grin and bear it while the natives were put down. It was for the common good, there was no help but to do it.

All will be well, thought George to himself. And he thanked the Lord for salvation. Everything had been so brutal lately. But everything had led to him being here. Upon this beautiful island with Ada. It was clearly God's will. What God had in mind for him. And any previous doubts he might have had throughout his short life thus far as to the existence of God had now all blown away.

George had become a believer.

George, indeed, had found God.

And so George had a bit of a pray and thanked his God for all. For having spared Ada from drowning and him from the cooking pot. Clearly, George concluded, it had been God's plan all along to send George here, that he and Ada might live in the new Garden of Eden as the new Adam and Eve.

'I thank you very much,' said George to God, 'for everything you have done for us and for providing us with this new Eden. One,' George added, 'superior to the first, as it lacks for the terrible serpent.'

'Do I hear you praying, George?' asked the voice of Professor Coffin.

27

ow positively wonderful to see you.' Professor Coffin danced his little dance. 'I feared that I had lost you for ever, but once more we are reunited. What a happy happenstance.'

'Indeed,' said George. And, 'Yes,' also and, 'Indeed,' once more.

'No injuries, I trust? No permanent disfigurings?'

'I am somewhat scalded but I will survive.'

'Most splendid,' cried the professor. 'And so you must gather some sleep to your person, for tomorrow the big march begins.'

'Big march?' George asked. 'And what big march is this?'

'To the temple, young fellow. To *Her* temple.'

'I am missing something,' said George. 'And a most substantial something, so it seems.'

'Fiddle de dum diddle, thus and so.' Professor Coffin bowed. 'Of course, dear boy,' he said to George, 'you were not perhaps made privy to the topological and indeed archaeological anomalies when you were transported to this dismal village.'

'They bonked me on the head,' said George.

'Quite so. You see, at the very heart of this island rises

a great volcano and upon its rim rises something more –
a temple, my boy – the temple of Sayito.'

'That is an impossible assumption to make,' said
George. 'It might be any old temple.'

'Yes, you would think so, would you not? However,
the native we captured somewhat earlier spoke the name
without too much in the way of prompting.'

George let that one slip by. The professor clearly had
quite extraordinary powers of persuasion.

'So,' said Professor Coffin, 'we will set out with the
cracking of the dawn. The burghers of Jupiter will
accompany us. They apparently came to Earth to hunt
tigers, and I suggested that tigers *might* be found in the
jungles of this island.'

George sighed softly and shook his head.

'No sadness now, my sweet fellow. Those Jupiterians
will provide a sturdy guard for us, against natives and
who knows whatever else.'

'There is worse than natives on this island?'

'The captured native seemed at first most fearful of
something lurking on the slopes. But he will lead the
way for us as a guide. I explained to him as best I could
that I knew what was for the best.'

Professor Coffin wished George a good night's sleep.
He patted George kindly upon the shoulder and assured
him that all would be well. 'Tomorrow should prove to
be a most exciting day,' he said.

And George felt no reason to doubt this.

Professor Coffin departed and this time, to the
accompaniment of a background din provided by many
jungle beasties, George said his prayers as a good boy
should and then dropped off to sleep.

★

It had all the makings of a proper expedition, so much in the way of equipment there was to be seen. Sleeping bags and picnic hampers, hammocks and mosquito nets. Bottled water and provisions, beer and crates of cigarettes. Tents and special umbrellas, big game rifle ray guns too. A folding canvas gents excuse-me. Sola topis, red and blue.

George was handed a sola topi, turquoise blue with fine big brass jungle goggles.

'Where did all this wonderful stuff come from?' asked George of the professor. 'I cannot believe it all just washed ashore.'

'The burghers of Jupiter, as you will have observed, are somewhat jolly fellows,' Professor Coffin explained. 'One reason for this is that they are always prepared. For *anything*, really. They work on the principle that "well prepared is best prepared". They were first into a lifeboat. A lifeboat that they had previously packed with all this paraphernalia "just in case".'

'They clearly possess superior foresight,' said George, putting on his sola topi. 'How do I look?'

'Absurd,' said the professor. 'But it will keep the mosquitoes out of your hair and the sun off the back of your neck. Mind you, with that hat and your shrunken suit you'd cut a comic dash on the stage of the Hackney Empire.'

'Professor,' said George, steering the showman away to a quieter place where he might speak confidentially. 'Do you really think that we will find Sayito in this temple?'

'I have every confidence, my boy.'

'And you believe She is a Goddess, correct?'

Professor Coffin shrugged. 'I believe only this,' he

said to George, 'that whatever She is, She is unique. And if we return with Her to the civilised world, She will make our fortunes.'

'I do see a flaw in such reasoning,' said George. 'Whoever, or whatever, She is, She may not wish to accompany us.'

'We will cross that bridge when we come to it. I feel confident that I have the means to persuade Her. George, we are not here by any accident. All of this has been preordained. All of this is fate. *Your* fate.'

'But *why*?' asked George. 'Why *me*?'

'I have no doubt that all will eventually become clear, to everyone's satisfaction.'

George was not altogether convinced.

'So are you ready to leave?' asked the professor.

'As ready as I will ever be, I suppose,' said George.

'And you have done your business and washed your hands?'

'*What?*' went George, appalled.

'You really do not ever want to get caught short in the jungle,' Professor Coffin explained. 'Too many red ants' nests or horrible fishes that swim up your old John Thomas if you are having a wee-wee in the river—'

'Stop, Professor, *please!*' went George. 'And I *have* been, thank you.'

Professor Coffin gave him a look.

'And washed my hands *too*. Now stop.'

The captive native, secured about the waist by a length of sturdy rope for fear that some untoward circumstance might cause him to desert his position, led the way. Behind him two Jupiterians, heavily built and armed in the likewise persuasion. Then Ada and Darwin, then

George and the professor, and then four further burghers of Jupiter, the final two armed with their big game rifle ray guns and walking backwards.

'As long as we are not attacked from the sides we have every chance of survival,' said George.

Professor Coffin said nothing.

It was going to be an uphill struggle in every sense of the words. The fellows from Jupiter, enthusiastic and full of beans as they were, were not built for uphill travel. Jupiter was a great big planet with heavier gravity than the Earth, and as a consequence the folk of Jupiter were very solidly built. So although they experienced a certain lightness of step when they set foot upon Planet Earth, this had a tendency to be negated by the heroic quantities of Earthly food they proceeded to consume.

George did not know quite what to make of them.

They were certainly more human than were the ecclesiastics of Venus. They appeared to really love life. They laughed, they sang, they gambolled and they laughed some more. And were it not for certain subtle differences – their lack of an index finger, the length of their ear lobes, the close set of their eyes – they were really all but human in appearance.

And they did not seem to bother with religion. They came, they traded, they spent the money they earned from their trading and then they all went home.

They were a racist's delight.

George eyed them as they puffed and plodded and climbed ever higher and higher.

On every hour they took a break and sat down for a rest. George sat close to Ada, who had divested herself of her normal travelling clothes and now wore only her vest, corset and bloomers, and looked *just* the way that a girl adventurer should. Together they gazed out over the jungle. It truly was paradise, the lush green trees, the silver sands, the gorgeous ocean beyond.

'Tell me,' said George to Ada, 'do you still have your female intuition?'

'I hope so,' said Ada. 'Why do you ask?'

'Because even though I obviously do not possess it to a single degree, I have a *very* bad feeling about how all of this is going to end.'

'The professor knows what is—'

'Stop that,' said George once more.

'Everything sweet as a sweet little nut?' asked the professor, ambling over. 'I thought I heard you saying "stop", young George.'

'Everything is fine.' George lifted his sola topi and wiped away sweat from his forehead. 'How much longer do you think it will take us to reach the summit?'

'If we continue unmolested, an hour perhaps. We have, however, been followed for at least the last hour by small brown men with bones through their noses.'

George gave a terrible shudder. 'I expect they want our guide returned to them.'

'And us in their cooking pot. But it is not really for the natives that I have concerns regarding our safety.'

'No?' said George. 'Then for what?'

'Look up,' said the professor. 'Up into the sky.'

George glanced up to the dazzling sky.

'Apply your goggles, George,' said the professor.

George lowered his goggles from his headwear and scanned the heavens above. At length he lifted his goggles once more and said, very quietly, 'What are those?'

'I am of two opinions,' said Professor Coffin, 'and I am torn between the two.'

Ada Lovelace did glancings upwards, donned *her* goggles and stared. 'Oh dear no,' said Ada Lovelace. 'I do not believe *that*.'

'Whether or not they fit into your belief system,' said Professor Coffin, 'is probably neither here, nor there. They circle above us large as life, but somewhat twice as terrible.'

'Vultures?' said George. 'Or great bats? But certainly horrible creatures.'

'Ah,' said Professor Coffin, 'your goggles lack for a magnifying lens. They are neither of the above, young George. They are either harpies or they are ptero-dactyls.'

George took in the enormity of this.

Ada all but fainted.

'Just think,' said Professor Coffin, 'if we could get one of *those* back to London alive. I have heard tales of an island where there lives a gigantic ape. Long King Dong I think they call him, but that is probably just a tall tale. Those, however,' and he pointed to the sky, 'those look real enough to me. If they attack us – and I feel that they will – we must do everything in our power to net one.'

George Fox rolled his eyes. 'You never let an oppor-tunity slip by, do you, Professor?' he said.

'I am a professional, George. I tucked half a dozen shrunken heads into that knapsack you are carrying – the Rubes will pay a goodly penny to see *those* in London.'

'Aaaagh,' went George, a-tearing off his knapsack. 'Those are people's heads.'

'Onwards and upwards, George.' The professor

laughed. 'Indeed onwards and upwards everybody, we will soon be there.'

Another half an hour of plodding upwards found the party upon a grassy promontory, several hundred yards below the summit.

'Oh yes indeed, indeed,' said the professor. 'What think you of that, George? What think you?'

Above them loomed the temple. A vast construction clinging to the rim of the volcano. George had once seen an etching of the Potala Palace in Tibet and there was much of that extraordinary edifice evident here. But there was so much more to be amazed by. Golden rooftops pitched at eccentric angles; turrets, seemingly of pearl, rising to dwindle in dizzying perspective. This building was Gothic, it was Chinese, it was Indian and Japanese and Javanese and Balinese, Taiwanese as well. And parts even bore a striking resemblance to the Prince Regent's pavilion in Brighton. There were statues of many Gods, Judaic, heathen, pagan. Symbols inlaid into stone. The hexagram of Solomon, Böhme's wheel of anguish, the lapis sigil of the alchemists. Fludd's Trinitarian heaven enclosed within the sacred triangle. The squared circle of Pythagoras. The Rosicrucian 'Tree of Pansophia'. The tenfold universal spheres of Hermes Trismegistus. These and more, in stone beneath the sunlight.

'I am afeared,' said George to the professor. 'We are in a sacred place and we have not come here to worship. We must turn back, Professor. We must go no further.'

'Oh my word no,' said Professor Coffin. 'We might well be the first civilised men to have visited this place in a thousand years. We cannot turn back now, not when we are so close. My entire life has led to this moment, George, and yours also. It is our fate, do you understand me? It is *your* fate.'

George looked hard at the professor, whose eyes, shaded by the brim of his solar toupee, seemed to glow from within, lit by some dark fire.

'It is wrong,' said George. 'All wrong. We are not fit to enter.'

Professor Coffin's hand moved to his waistcoat pocket.

'Step aside with me a moment, George,' said he.

28

eorge stepped aside with the professor. He was not too keen to do so though and when the showman put his arm about George's shoulders, the young man shrugged him off. Politely.

'Come, come, George,' said Professor Coffin. 'You look all in and tired.'

'I am not too bad,' said George. 'I do not particularly want to leave Ada alone, though, with those wild things all circling in the sky.'

'We will be but a moment. There is something I would like you to see. Something I would like you to smell, in fact.'

'To *smell*? I do not understand.'

Professor Coffin dipped in his waistcoat pocket. Drew out a slim glass phial with a screw-on cap. 'This will not take but a moment,' he said to George. 'And then all will be well—'

But George said, 'No,' very loudly and pushed past the professor. 'I cannot leave Ada,' he told the showman. 'You will have to show me later.'

Professor Coffin watched the lad returning to his love.

'Be assured,' said he, beneath his breath, 'I *will* show you later.'

★

Ada Lovelace, looking very pretty, was sipping water from a brass canteen. Her emerald eyes turned up towards George as he approached her and she asked, 'Is everything satisfactory between yourself and the professor?'

'Yes,' said George, rather sharply, and he settled down beside her. 'He wants to enter the temple. *I* do *not*.'

'Then why not just wait here for him? After all, he does know what is—'

George cut her off in mid-flow. 'Ada,' he said, 'I do not know what that man did to you, but I know he did something. Your about-turn regarding your opinion of him is overwhelmingly suspicious. Young ladies such as yourself are *not* for turning.'

George looked Ada deep in the eyes. '*Did* he do something?' he asked.

Ada Lovelace made a puzzled face; a pretty face it still remained, but puzzled. 'Something happened,' she said slowly. 'Something in the Ladies' Accommodation aboard the *Empress of Mars*. But it is blurry and indistinct. Some of my memories are missing.'

Two and two were making four with George. 'The same thing happened to me,' said he. 'Both times in the company of the professor.'

'Yes,' said Ada, her green eyes growing wide. 'The professor. He was—' But she never finished.

Instead she screamed at the top of her voice and pushed George to the side.

The expedition was suddenly under attack.

Down they plunged from the sky, those horrid beasties. And as they swooped and dived towards the party upon the exposed promontory, it was clearly apparent that they were neither harpies nor pterodactyls.

'They are flying monkeys,' cried George, scooping up his knapsack filled with shrunken heads and whirling it about at the attackers.

Darwin the monkey butler, exhibiting a wisdom which spoke highly of the evolutionary link between ape and man, ducked away to silent cover and hid himself at the jungle's edge.

Professor Coffin took to hurling stones.

Jovial Jovians cocked their mighty weapons.

The flying monkeys were really quite horrid, with nasty red faces and bad bat wings. They wore little waistcoats and big baggy trousers and muttered and hissed the most terrible things.

'I think they are actually swearing at us,' shouted George to Ada. 'Take cover in the trees. I will do my best to keep them at bay.'

Ada fled to where Darwin lay hiding, while George continued with his swinging of the knapsack.

Which, although not actually serving as much of a deterrent, did at least create something of a diversion.

The Jovians, however, made a greater show of force.

They swung up their ray guns towards their attackers and beams of energy crissed and crossed the sky.

'Those certainly put the old Royal Enfields in the shade,' said Professor Coffin, appreciatively. 'Oh mercy me!'

A flying monkey swinging close was atomised before him.

'There wouldn't be too much left of a tiger,' said the professor, now hastening in pursuit of Ada Lovelace.

'Come, George,' he called. 'Let's leave this to the fellows with the space guns.'

And it did have to be said, the fellows with the space guns were making a considerable impact upon their aerial attackers. Flying monkeys exploded at the touch of fearsome rays. Alien technology, it appeared, was more than a match for mythic monsters made flesh.

It fleetingly entered George's mind that there might well be a moral in there, or a lesson to be learned, or something, but just as fleetingly such thoughts were gone as George ran howling for cover.

The laughing burghers of Jupiter had arranged themselves into a kind of battle formation: a circle with their big broad backs towards the middle. And they were laying down devastating fire upon their swooping enemies.

'I think we might just win this one,' said George, flinging himself into cover and dropping down beside Ada and the professor.

'Perhaps they might be persuaded to just *wing* one,' said Professor Coffin. 'I am indeed *shocked* and also *awed* by the magnitude of their firepower.'

'We are winning the battle, though,' said George. 'And that, I suppose, is all that matters. Although—'
And here George paused.

'Although?' asked the professor.

'Just what is *that*?' said George, and he pointed.

A swirling black cloud was billowing in the distance. Tumbling over and over in the sky. George had once spent a pleasant evening upon Brighton beach watching the vast flocks of starlings at play above the West Pier. And there was a certain similarity here. That swooping and twisting. That—

'No!' cried George. 'Flying monkeys, thousands of them!'

The Jovian hunters saw them too. And realising themselves to be outnumbered beyond all reasonable, or indeed unreasonable, hope of victory or survival, they broke ranks and fled to the jungle's edge.

The creatures came down like a swarm of locusts, blackening the sky. George was given to a fleeting wonderment as to where they could all have possibly come from, for surely this island could not sustain their dining for a single day. But again this was only a fleeting wonderment. George had more important things on his mind.

'Run back down deeper into the jungle,' cried George. 'Everyone hurry, do.'

'Ah,' said the professor. 'Maybe not.'

'Not?' said George, preparing to flee. 'I do think so – come, Ada.'

'George, no, don't. The natives – look.' Professor Coffin pointed.

And sure as sure and bad as luck could be, many little brown faces, with bones though the noses, were to be seen. Many, many brown faces.

'Natives!' cried George. 'Thousands of them.'

'It rather looks,' said Professor Coffin, 'as if *our* villagers have sought the assistance of most of the nearby villages. Which leaves us somewhere between the Devil and the deep blue sea, I do believe.'

'I do not like to say "I told you so"—' said George.

'Then kindly do not, it will not advance our situation by one iota.'

And they were suddenly in all but darkness, flying monkeys blackening the heavens. Down came these

Hellish simians, intent upon no good whatsoever. The Jovians, no longer quite so jovial, mashed their way into the jungle, squinted towards the upcoming natives and trained their guns upon them.

The flying monkeys tore at the treetops, ripping away at the foliage. Natives raised their blowpipes.

A mighty battle ensued.

Caught in the very midst of it, without any weapons and not a lot of hope, George clung to Ada, who clung right back to George, and Darwin clung to the professor.

'We are doomed,' cried the professor. 'It should not come to this. Do something, George, save us all.'

'Me?' cried George, as blowpipe darts went whizzing by his head and ray-gun rays set the jungle on fire. 'Why me?'

And a flying monkey stole his sola topi.

If the horrible goings-on in the great dining hall of the *Empress of Mars* when the airship went down had resembled a scene from Dante's *Inferno*, then the present mayhem held more to the fevered imaginings of Hieronymus Bosch, after a hard night down at his local upon whatever was the fifteenth-century equivalent of absinthe.

The screaming and the swearing and the ripping and the tearing of the monkeys.

The horrible destruction of each awful terror gun.

The war-chants of the natives and the blowings of their blowpipes.

The fear and flames, the blood and death and all upon an island.

In a sea of blue beneath a summer sun.

'To the temple,' cried Professor Coffin, 'to claim sanctuary. It is our only hope.'

'I do not know what to do,' shouted George.

'Trust the professor,' said Ada.

George Fox threw up his fists in despair.

As the worst that could occur did.

They were suddenly all about him, scratching and savaging. His hand was torn from Ada's and as George looked on, horror-struck and in mortal fear, several of the flying, screaming horde plucked up Ada and bore her into the sky.

'No!' cried George. 'Shoot those monsters, someone.'

But the Jovian huntsmen were otherwise engaged.

George watched, as best he could amongst the flapping wings and scrabbling claws that were all about him now, and saw Ada carried up and up and then in through one of the windows in the dwindling towers of pearl that soared above.

'This way,' shouted the professor. 'Here, George, come with me.' And Professor Coffin dragged George after him, to what looked like some kind of oversized rabbit burrow, and pushed George ahead of him into it.

It was dark and smelled poorly of dung. And when something moved, George nearly died right there and then from absolute terror. But a friendly hairy hand laid hold of George and Darwin cooed gibberings of comfort into his ear. Above, the sounds of battle were terrific. And seemed to go on hour after hour. George huddled low and rocked to and fro. Professor Coffin hid his face and said certain prayers of his own.

Perhaps hours had passed, for George had lost all sense of time. But when all became finally silent, Professor

Coffin peeped from the hideaway and, once assured that all was safe as it could be, whispered for George to follow him.

George did so.

George saw carnage. Trees reduced to blackened stumps. Bodies strewn, two burghers of Jupiter dead. And the smell of death, that ghastly miasma, hung like a shroud over all.

'My God,' said George. But that was all he could say.

Professor Coffin rummaged all about himself, unearthed his cigar case, took out a cigar, bit off the end and spat it out. He applied the fire from a Lucifer and drew in calming breaths.

Darwin directed certain urgent sounds towards the showman and Professor Coffin shared his cigar with the ape.

'All is lost,' said George, when he could find more words to speak. 'Everything is lost.'

Professor Coffin opened his mouth, then slowly closed it again.

'But,' and George looked up, to the temple rising above, 'she might still be alive.'

'She?' said the professor. 'The Goddess? That She?'

'I mean Ada,' said George. 'The creatures carried her away into a window high in that tower.' And George pointed. 'She might still be alive. I have to find her.'

'Find her?' And Professor Coffin smiled. It was not a pleasant smile and he turned his face away so George should not see it. 'Find Ada,' said Professor Coffin. 'Somewhere in the temple. Oh yes. That would be for the best.'

29

owers of pearl glittered in afternoon sun-
light and rooftops of gold glittered too.
Through the shimmering haze climbed
George, the professor and Darwin the
monkey, each alone with their thoughts –
dire thoughts, of what might lie ahead.

They had taken the precaution of arming themselves
and although George felt it instinctively wrong to enter
a temple of any religious persuasion carrying a weapon,
his only thoughts at this time were for Ada Lovelace.

He and the professor carried long unearthly rifle ray
guns, taken from the bodies of the fallen Jupitarians.
Darwin the monkey held a blowpipe. Several bandoleers
of poisoned darts and as many canteens of water swung
from his now most shabby waistcoat.

George himself looked very much the worse for wear.
His ludicrously shrunken suit was thoroughly besmutted, his hair was matted, his face begrimed, and
lines of sweat ran down from his forehead to drip from
his striking chin. George was not in the finest of moods
and Professor Coffin felt it for the best not to engage
him in idle conversation.

Above, the marvellous temple pierced the sky. A
rugged pilgrims' trail snaked up against the naked rock.

The heat was fearfully oppressive. The dismal party soldiered on.

Finally George spoke. 'We rescue Ada,' he said. 'If she is still alive we rescue her. Nothing more. I want no part of any Japanese Devil Fish Girl. This entire journey was cursed from the very beginning.'

Professor Coffin nodded thoughtfully. He had many homilies readily to hand regarding the warrior spirit of the Britons. And how the forging of a mighty empire had been brought about through the enduring of hardships by men of noble valour. Who had soldiered on, as indeed the two of them and the monkey were now doing, to achieve the glory they so truly deserved. These homilies, however, he kept to himself. 'Whatever you say, my boy,' he said.

George Fox glanced at his companion. For on this occasion he certainly knew a lie when he heard one.

They scrambled higher and higher, in terror of falling at times as chunks of the narrow path gave beneath their feet and plunged down and down to the jungle below. And always in terror of a renewed attack from the flying monkeys. For surely they had never been more vulnerable than now.

'We are almost there,' said Professor Coffin. 'Darwin, go ahead and see that all is safe.'

Darwin the monkey butler rolled his eyes, then slowly shook his head.

'Obstinate wretch,' said Professor Coffin, raising a knotted fist.

Darwin put a blowpipe to his lips and pointed same at the professor.

'No hard feelings, old chap.' Professor Coffin affected a grin. 'Naturally I will go first.'

'*I* will go first,' said George. 'And if anything gets in my way I will kill it.'

There was such determination in the voice of George Fox that Professor Coffin limited his own words to asking George whether he had the safety catch off, on his big rifle ray gun.

George made affirmative gruntings and made his way ahead.

A plateau hewn from living rock and paved with Rose Aurora marble spread before the entrance to the wonderful temple. A film of volcanic dust covered the marble pavement, undisturbed by footfall, so it seemed, for many ages past.

The mighty temple doors were of tropical timber carved with the most fantastic of creatures. Beasts resembling tri-pedal crocodiles writhed amongst fish-headed lions and snakes with the faces of men.

George plodded forwards, Professor Coffin followed.

'Have you ever seen such horrors?' the professor asked of George. 'Unnatural and nasty, the spawn of the Bottomless Pit.'

'Un*worldly* is the word,' said George. 'These things are not of this Earth.'

The eyes of the carven creatures were inlaid with precious stones. Professor Coffin drew most near to feast his eyes upon them.

'There is a fortune to be had here alone,' said he. Thoughtfully.

'When Ada is safe you can do what you like. I care not at all.' George gazed up, beyond the mighty temple doors to vertical walls of stone. Painted were these walls, after the fashion of ancient Thebes. But not with the profiled likenesses of Rameses II. Rather with those of a beautiful woman. Although time had weathered her features to a blur.

George Fox put his shoulder to one of the temple doors and applied pressure. It gave a touch but then refused to open further.

George stepped back and once more looked aloft. 'We cannot possibly batter these doors open,' he said.

'Stand aside there, then, George,' said Professor Coffin, cocking his big rifle ray gun, 'and I will blast our way in.'

George glared at the professor. 'I am a desperate man,' said he, 'but such wanton vandalism may not be necessary. Look – see there what appears to be a large letterbox.'

'That is a votive embrasure,' Professor Coffin explained. 'You see them in European churches of the Middle Ages. Lepers and those smitten with the pox were not allowed entry to the church. They passed their pennies through such openings and the priests blessed them in return. From a safe distance, as it were.'

'Be that as it may,' said George, unmoved by the professor's knowledge, 'it might be possible to squeeze through the opening, drop down and open the doors from the inside.'

'You would not fit and neither would I,' said the professor.

'Darwin . . .' called George.

Darwin lacked for a certain enthusiasm. Even when Professor Coffin expounded homilies of warrior Britons and empire-building heroes upon his hairy person.

'As many bananas as you can eat,' said George. 'A complete new outfit, including fez and spats.'

Darwin looked thoughtfully at George. And scratched about himself at a flea or two.

'I promise,' said George and crossed his heart as he did so.

Darwin reached up and shook George's hand. Then laid down his blowpipe, divested himself of bandoleers and water canteens, gave a perfunctory gibber, scampered up the temple door and in through the votive embrasure.

George Fox held his breath and prayed a bit. He hoped very much that he had not sent Darwin to his doom. But how else might entry be gained? George put his ear to one of the doors and listened. Sounds of a struggle? The drawing of a bolt?

And George fell forwards as the great door swung open before him.

It groaned dramatically upon its ancient hinges, but swung with a certain ease. George dragged himself once more into the vertical plane and congratulated Darwin for his efforts. Darwin swaggered past George and retrieved his blowpipe, darts and *one* water canteen.

'Bring them *all*, please,' said George.

Darwin brought them all.

The temple was all but in darkness within, save for what sunlight welled in through the half-open door.

George swung this door fully open and then the other one too. Sunlight illuminated a floor of turquoise stone, deliciously inlaid with intricate patterns, symbols, sigils and writings. If words indeed were these, they were no words known to George, or indeed to the professor, who had travelled widely and entered many temples.

'Japanese, do you think?' asked George.

Professor Coffin shook his head. 'I have seen such symbols somewhere, though,' he said. 'But not in a temple, I feel.'

'Well, I care not,' said George, cocking his rifle ray gun. 'I want only Ada.'

The three of them moved forwards, slowly, warily, with care. For it *is* well known to anyone who reads adventure stories that places such as these are always wrought with deadly traps. A misplaced footstep onto a secret button leading to spears striking out from hidden recesses, or great stone pendulums swinging down from above. Floors that open to plunge the unwary explorer down onto sharpened stakes below, there to dwell amongst the skeletons of the formerly unwary.

As a child, George had read such adventure stories. So had the professor, though Darwin had not.

They were to all appearances within a great cathedral, like Notre Dame, or Salisbury, or St Paul's. Gothic fan vaulting, mullioned truss-work and a dome adorned with stars and a vision of a God upon high. But was it a God, or a Goddess? So high above and in such poor light, it was impossible to tell.

There were no pews or benches, nor any furnishings at all.

Just a vast expanse of inlaid floor and walls that rose and rose.

'I wonder just what *that* is?' whispered Professor Coffin, his whispered words echoing eerily about the vastness of the temple as he drew George's gaze towards something that bulked ahead.

It was certainly huge and stood at the furthest end of the enormous cathedralesque hall. But whatever it was it was covered, as if by some builder's dustsheet, and offered little clue to its identity.

'A pagan idol?' George suggested. 'Some heathen horror, I have no doubt.'

And stepping with the utmost care, the three of them moved forwards. Two of them at least testing every footfall. One with a blowpipe to his lips and showing the whites of his eyes.

'Shall we see what lurks under the dustsheet?' asked the professor.

'It is of no concern to me,' said George. 'I seek only staircases to reach the pinnacle where Ada was carried. And frankly I see no other doors, do you?'

Professor Coffin shook his head. 'Perhaps under the dustsheet?' he suggested.

George squinted in his direction and many others. The only doorway into this mighty chamber appeared to be the one through which they had entered. But there surely had to be another. 'Go on then,' George said to the professor. 'Pull down the sheet.'

'Go on then, Darwin,' said the professor. 'Do what the nice man asks. I bet he will give you more bananas.'

Darwin made a thoughtful face and cocked his head on one side. Then once more he laid down his weaponry and water flasks and sauntered slowly forwards.

The sheeting that covered the monumental something was not some builder's coarse-cloth. It was silk of the finest quality, delicately embroidered. The effect was of a beautiful tapestry, once bright colours dimmed to pastels by the passing of time. The depictions were in panels almost after the fashion of a penny comic book. An epic saga created by the hands of skilled artisans, surely the work of several lifetimes, so gorgeous to be—

Darwin took the silk in his hairy hands and ripped it away. It tore, the sound like a cry of anguish, and fluttered down, countless yards of silk, onto the monkey.

Darwin struggled and freed himself and backed away to look up.

George and the professor looked on, transfixed by what rose up before them.

It was the statue of a Goddess. But unlike any other Goddess was She. No huntress like Diana, nor ancient Roman love queen Venus, nor Aphrodite to the Greeks, nor Bel to the Babylonians. This was not Freya, Viking Goddess of beauty, nor Ix Chel, the Lady Rainbow of the early Mayan Empire. Nor was She Anu, Celtic Goddess of fertility, nor indeed the virgin mother of Christ.

None of these was this Goddess, though somehow She encompassed all.

George tried to take in the wonder before him. A statue wrought from gold and silver, bronze and copper and lapis lazuli. The wings of an angel and a mermaid's fishlike tail, arms spread in an open posture of beatitude, face raised towards the heavens. Atop bronzed ringlets, a helmet belikened to that of the samurai, a silvered disc with a crescent moon and the image of a devil fish.

Professor Coffin shook his head and whistled through his teeth.

George stared on, most wholly rapt in wonder.

About the angled, slender, gilded neck hung many pendants and gemstoned necklets, adorned with the symbols of deities. Hindu, Jain, Judaic, Christian, Taoist, Shinto, one upon another.

And George took in all that he thought that he could. And then saw something more.

'It is Her,' whispered Professor Coffin. 'The fish scales, the symbol on the helmet. It is the Japanese Devil Fish Girl, there can be no doubt.'

George shook his head and rocked upon his heels. 'But do you not see it?' said he.

'I see it,' said Professor Coffin. 'I see it. And yes, I *claim it* on behalf of the British Empire. I had hoped for some living specimen of course, but this surpasses all of Western art. This will truly be the greatest attraction of this or any age.'

'No,' said George. 'You do not see it.'

'I do, my boy, believe me that I do.'

'The face,' said George Fox, slowly.

'Golden,' said Professor Coffin. 'With emeralds the size of a man's fists for eyes and fringed by copper ringlets.'

'The face,' said George. 'The face of the Goddess. The face of Ada Lovelace.'

30

rofessor Coffin viewed the gorgeous statue. He looked from it to George and back again. The resemblance to Ada was uncanny. He put a hand on George's shoulder, felt the young man's pain.

'There are certain similarities,' he said softly. 'Ada is a beautiful young woman.'

'And *I* must find her,' said George. 'Find her and make some sense of all of this.'

Darwin the monkey butler took to a sudden bouncing and to certain squawking squealing sounds.

'Silence, you loquacious simian.' Professor Coffin mimed rifle-shootings at Darwin.

'He is trying to tell us something,' George observed. 'What is it, Darwin? Show us what it is.'

The ape danced forwards to the base of the statue. To the base where the fish-scaled feet of the Goddess rested. Upon this base was carved the resemblance of a mighty book, its title engraved upon it. The carven symbols were of an unknown language, but George instinctively knew what they meant.

'*The Book of Sayito,*' said he.

Darwin bounced a little more and rapped a hairy knuckle on the big carved book.

A dull hollow echo was to be heard. Coming from within.

'Let me see,' said George, stepping forwards. 'Ah yes, Professor, see this.'

Professor Coffin hastened to join George and watched as the young man ran his fingers about the edges of the carved book cover. 'It is a door,' said George. 'The cover of the book must open, like a door.'

'Step aside, George,' said Professor Coffin, once more cocking his gun.

'You are not firing that thing anywhere near this statue,' George told the professor. 'Darwin seems rather good with doors. Can you open it, Darwin?'

The monkey butler thumbed at his waistcoat lapels and bowed, then turned to the statue's base. Did *something* and then stood back. The book-cover door swung open.

George stepped forwards to peruse the ape's doings. 'Ah,' said he. 'You turned the key. I really should have noticed that. Well done.'

Professor Coffin came forwards and peered into the opening. Struck fire to a Lucifer, held it within. 'Stairs,' said he, 'going down, but you wanted to go up.'

'Let us follow where they lead and see what happens.' George took the professor by the elbow. 'You have the fire,' he said, 'so you should lead the way.'

'Darwin—' said Professor Coffin.

But Darwin now skulked to the rear.

'Then I shall lead,' said Professor Coffin. 'And remember our deal – we split whatever we find fifty-fifty.'

'I want nothing but Ada,' said George. 'And I want one hundred per cent of her.'

The steps led down, as steps will do, when they are not leading up. Down and down and down some more, with a terrible tedious downness.

'It would be for the best,' said Professor Coffin, holding fire before him as he stepped forever down, 'if we do not inform the other survivors of the airship of what we have discovered here. It would be better to keep it private, I think. They will all be anxious to leave the island and will probably harbour no longings to return.'

'We do not even know where we are,' said George. 'This island is not on the map.'

'No present-day map, no, my boy. But it is upon *a* map. A map that I once saw in the British Library.'

'And what were *you* doing in *there*?' George asked.

'Seeking authentication for a book I had acquired. A handwritten manuscript. A play, it was. *Romeo and Juliet* by Shakespeare.'

'You had acquired an original Shakespeare manuscript?'

'So I believed. But it was not so. The Head of Literary Antiquities identified the handwriting – it was not Mr Shakespeare's.'

'Tough luck,' said George, in a tone which implied that he meant it.

'It was the handwriting of a certain Francis Bacon,' said the professor. 'The Head of Literary Antiquities became most animated. He paid me almost twice the price I had intended to ask.'

'Now stop there just one moment,' said George. 'Whilst still continuing to walk down this staircase, of course. But are you now telling me that you possessed a manuscript that proves that Francis Bacon wrote Shakespeare?'

'I am not *precisely* telling you *that*,' replied Professor Coffin. 'When I say that it was the handwriting of a certain Francis Bacon, that is not to say that it *was actually* the handwriting of a certain Francis Bacon. More perhaps that it was so very close in resemblance to the handwriting of that fellow as to be easily accepted as the same.'

'It was a forgery!' said George.

'I prefer the term "imaginative reimaging". People will believe what they want to believe, George.'

'There is a moral to that, then, is there?' said George.

'I use it as an example to illustrate a point. You saw the face of Ada Lovelace upon the statue, I did not.'

'It was her face,' said George.

'Maybe so,' said the professor. 'And when we return with it to London, the Rubes can make up their own minds as to the resemblance. We could exhibit Ada along with the statue, dressed as the Goddess perhaps.'

'Absolutely *not*,' said George.

'Well, it is open to discussion.'

'It is *not*,' said George. 'Believe me on this. And anyway we have yet to leave the island, which I recall mentioning only a moment ago is *not* on any map.'

'It *is* on the map I saw at the British Library.' Professor Coffin fanned at his face. 'The air is rank,' said he.

'Tell me about the map,' said George, with a sigh. 'Tell me what you know.'

'Myth has it,' said the professor, 'that at the dawning of time three great civilisations were born. One from the children of Adam and Eve. Centred about the Euphrates, this civilisation spread across the planet. We are all the many times great-grandchildren of Adam and Eve. But there were two other civilisations. Perhaps not wholly blessed by God, perhaps not God's creation. Or not the creation of *our* God, but of another. These two existed upon other continents, cut off from each other by many sea miles. One in the Atlantic, Atlantis. The other in the Pacific, here, Lemuria.'

'We are on Lemuria?' said George.

'*In*, it seems at the present. But yes, that is what I believe. The remains of ancient Lemuria, a tiny part of a now sunken continent.'

'It is as good a tale as any,' said George. 'And it is my dearest hope that these steps will lead us somehow to Ada. If they lead merely to a dead end, where excavations were terminated, it is going to be a very dismal climb back up again. We have surely been walking for hours.'

'Perhaps Darwin will offer us a piggyback.'

Darwin pinched Professor Coffin's bottom.

'Or perhaps *not*,' said the professor. 'But look – I see a light ahead. What do you make of *that*, George?'

And with that the steps simply ended. They had reached wherever it was they led to.

George, the professor and Darwin looked on. The professor extinguished his Lucifer and as three pairs of eyes adjusted to the soft light that offered a gently crepuscular illumination, two mouths opened wide and drew in breaths.

'A subterranean city,' said George.

'Lemuria,' said the professor.

'And more.' And George made gesturings before him. Gesturings that the professor followed.

These were no sunken ruins. No fallen temples and

rubble-strewn carriageways. No city gone to dust to haunt the speculations of present-day archaeologists. This was an ancient city, yes, but one most fiercely alive.

This city flowered within a cavern so vast as to seem a veritable hollow Earth. Sleek towers rose towards a rocky ceiling lost to vision. And between these towers moved airships of advanced design.

Design that was not of this Earth.

'Oh dear me,' said Professor Coffin. 'Fiddle de, fiddle dum, fiddle dum-de-dum-de-dum.'

'Why are you fiddle-dee-ing so much?' asked George.

'Because all becomes most frighteningly clear, my dear fellow.'

'Then please take this opportunity to enlighten me,' said George, 'because I am surely all in the dark.'

'The symbols,' said Professor Coffin, 'on the floor of the temple above – I told you that I felt I knew them from somewhere. That I had seen them before, but not in a temple.'

'Go on,' said George. 'Please tell me.'

'Recall, if you will, our dear old friend the pickled Martian,' said Professor Coffin. 'When I collected him from the London Hospital, there were various alien artefacts to be seen, which were being studied by the surgeon Sir Frederick Treves. Amongst these were what was believed to be the "user's manual" for one of the Martian warships. The symbols were identical, George. This underworld is peopled by surviving Martians.'

George took in the enormity of this and then he said, 'Hold on there. This is an ancient civilisation. The inlaid symbols on the floor of the temple above, the statue of the Goddess – all of this is ancient. Are you saying that the Martians were the original inhabitants of Lemuria?'

'I can only speculate upon what my eyes are telling me,' the professor replied. 'Photographs of the cities of Mars were published in the press. Look at those towers, George, and those aircraft also. Martian in design. There is no doubt.'

'I am well and truly confused,' said George. 'Are you suggesting that the original Martians were born on this planet? That they lived in Lemuria and when it sank beneath the waves, well, they sank with it and here they are?'

'Something, if not similar, then precisely the same.'

'I do believe,' said George, 'that as exhausting as it might be, we might retrace our steps and continue our search for Ada upon a higher level.'

'I am right behind you there, young man. Or possibly even in front of you.'

Darwin now made squealing and squawking sounds.

'Yes, I am sure you agree,' said George, and sought to give him a pat. But Darwin was not to be patted. Darwin was backing away.

'No need to be stand-offish,' said George. 'You know that I am your friend.'

But then George saw that Professor Coffin was also backing away.

And gazing into the strange dim light, George saw just why this was.

Something was approaching them. Something heavily armed.

It pointed its prodigious weapon at George and gargled something in an alien tongue.

Its alien tongue moved within a head resembling the shell of a crab, beneath which trailed and curled many tentacles. The creature gargled something more. Barked and gargled this also as an order.

George Fox dropped his weapon and slowly raised his hands as the Martian with the ray gun slid towards him.

31

‘ough on him, George,' cried Professor Coffin. 'Give him some of your germs.'

George was about to reply that, in his opinion, these particular Martians had most likely long ago developed an immunity to Earthly bacteria. Further conversation between himself and the professor was, however, staunched by more urgent garglings from the Martian, accompanied by most violent wavings of its gun.

'Yes,' said George. 'I understand – you would like us to come with you.'

The Martian now gargled *very* loudly and gestured towards the staircase.

'And I think that means *you too*,' called George to Darwin.

Darwin peeped out, hung his head and sidled over to George.

The Martian growled and gestured once more with his weapon. Two men and a monkey moved along before him.

'So tell me, young George,' Professor Coffin whispered. 'What manner of plan are you hatching?'

'Me?' said George. 'Plan?' said George. 'Hatching?' said George also.

'Of course, my boy. You are surely one blessed of the Almighty. You have followed where Fate led you. Fulfilled your destiny.'

'I think that you are correct when you apply the word "followed",' said George. 'I *have* been *led*. None of this is under my control.'

'You will save us all,' the professor assured him. 'Did not that prophecy say that the fate of the planets would depend upon you?'

'And I take little comfort from *that*.' And George hung his head, with his striking chin on his chest.

The Martian slid and slithered along behind them, occasionally and unnecessarily poking them with his monstrous weapon.

'They really *do* pong, don't they?' whispered the professor. 'Alive or dead, they hum like a sewer in summer.'

'Actually,' George whispered back, 'I wonder if this lot down here know that Mars is now a dead world.'

'Best not to bring it up in conversation with them, I am thinking.' Professor Coffin made a thoughtful face. 'Now, if we could bring back one of these fellows *alive* to London – *that* might pull in the Rubes.'

George Fox raised his head and shook it. 'Unbelievable,' he said.

'I have faith in you, George. We will triumph, I am certain. We have not come so far to just— Oh dear . . .'

And George saw what the professor saw and George said, 'Oh dear,' too.

They had entered the city proper. Sleek towers loomed and soared to every side. There was something of a central plaza here, gained by shallow steps, as Martians, it appeared, moved in the manner of slugs.

To the centre of this plaza rose a stepped pyramid of the Inca persuasion. But one not wrought in brick, but built from human skulls.

'Now *that* I find *most* discouraging,' said George.

Professor Coffin nodded thoughtfully. 'The Martians' eating habits have never been particularly endearing,' he said. 'It is to be hoped that Darwin will do what is expected of him and rescue you once more from the cooking pot in the very nick of time.'

But Darwin did not at present appear to have much of the liberating angel about him. He had a downcast and sorry slouch to his gait. Darwin looked a most put-upon monkey.

'We will be fine,' said Professor Coffin. '*Somehow*, we will be fine.'

'Pardon me if I do not share your bundles of optimism,' said George. 'I am *not* fine now and I have little confidence that I will *ever* be fine again.'

There were many Martians now upon the central plaza.

Gargling away they were and pointing with their tentacles and nips.

There were large and small ones too. And some quite in-between.

But all of equal nastiness.

And smelliness and ghastliness.

For they would eat a fellow up, as one might fish and chips.

George maintained a brooding silence as he moved along before the muzzle of the Martian's monstrous weapon. Professor Coffin found that his feet had altogether lost their dance and Darwin grumbled in Neanderthal tones and scowled at all and sundry.

Onwards they plodded, happily past the skull-piled pyramid. Down broad streets they were urged at ray-gun-point, where curious vehicles, horseless and outré, moved with a silent whiz. Conveying Martians to whatever business it was that they were about.

'One of those would cut a dash in the Mall,' said the professor. 'If we can somehow strike a deal with these fellows that does not involve us lining their stomachs, matters might be adjusted to our advantage.'

'Ah,' said George, as their Martian tormentor drew him, the professor and Darwin to a sudden halt. 'It would appear that we have reached our destination.'

'A hotel, perhaps,' said the professor. 'The prodding about with the ray gun might just be their way of leading us to a suite reserved for honoured guests.'

George had no comment to make.

A building tall and black rose up before them. The Martian urged them all in at the hurry-up.

Within was even dimmer than without, and the reek of Martian bodies overwhelming. George and the professor held their noses and squinted all about.

They stood within a vestibule, blackly walled and floored and ceilinged. Up ahead, a wall of glass and a wonderful machine.

It somewhat resembled a pumping engine, with many cogs and wheels and big ball governors. There was a big brass trumpet horn of a thing that strongly resembled the public address system of the *Empress of Mars*, with many knobs and dials and pressure gauges and all of this merrily in motion.

'Quite a pretty thing,' said the professor. 'Assuming of course that it is *not* an instrument of torture.'

'I like the champhered grommet mountings,' said George.

'And I the flanged seals on drazy hoops,' said the professor, in an admiring tone.

Both agreed that the burnished housings of the knurdling gears had much to recommend them, aesthetically speaking, yet mourned for the lack of a rectifying valve that would have topped the whole off to perfection.

They would no doubt have continued their discourse on the merits of the gybo-straddling of the instrument panel, discussing the numerous features that indicated that this intricate contraption might well be powered by the now-legendary transperambulation of pseudo-comic anti-matter, had it not been for the Martian, who clobbered George on the head.

'No need for *that!*' cried George. 'I was only admiring the piston fillets on the cross-threaded sprocket drive.'

'I do believe,' whispered Professor Coffin, 'that the secret might well be in knowing when to stop.'

The Martian now tinkered at the remarkable machine with a tentacle or two and a couple of nips, which set further wondrous bits in motion, accompanied by the occasional puff of steam.

The Martian now gargled loudly into the brass trumpet horn affair and then paused as if awaiting some reply.

This came moments later, with less gargled words.

Professor Coffin listened hard. 'Japanese,' he said.

George looked on at the wonderful machine. 'It translates language,' he said.

'I once exhibited a lesser version,' said the professor, 'a talking head that could enunciate most clearly, through the manipulation of air-pressure valves and the tuned reeds of woodwind instruments. The Cerebral Prognosticator it was called and—'

Professor Coffin received a buffet to the head that sent him staggering. 'No need for *that*!' howled he.

Creaks and groans now issued from the marvellous machine. Clickings of subtle readjustments, hints of fine-tunings and the rearrangement of things.

'Good afternoon to you, sir,' came a mechanised voice from the brass trumpet horn affair. 'And how might I be of service?'

'There,' said Professor Coffin to George. 'What did I tell you? We are to be welcomed as weary travellers and offered the best that there is.'

Professor Coffin now addressed himself to the machine. 'My name is King Coffin,' he announced. '*Good King Coffin* to my many subjects. I am here upon a trading mission, to share with you the abundant largesse of my lands, in return for a small trinket or two.'

A pause, then a whirring of wheels and a clicking of parts.

'Papers,' came the voice from the brazen trumpet.

'Papers?' asked Professor Coffin. 'What is this talk of papers?'

'Papers of indenture and permission to travel. An entry visa to Lemuria, accompanied of course by letters of recommendation sealed with the authorisation of at least three diplomatic envoys who can vouch for your honesty and good character and have known you for at least—'

'Hold hard, please,' said Professor Coffin. 'I am of a royal household – I have no need for such trivial documents.'

'I have not yet even begun to enumerate the *trivial*

documents,' replied the mechanical speaker. 'You also require foodstuff importation permits, not to mention for the introduction into Lemuria of an unclassified hairy-boy.'

'An unclassified hairy-boy?' Professor Coffin asked.

'I told you not to mention that.'

A tiny silence followed. Darwin broke it with a raspberry.

'And where are your medals?' asked the voice.

'Back in my palace?' Professor Coffin suggested.

'A pilgrim without votive medals?' The voice, although monotone and lacking all inflections, seemed somehow to take a graver turn.

'Votive medals? Ah, I see,' said the professor. 'Naturally, as pilgrims, having travelled halfway across the planet to offer our devotions to the Goddess, we indeed had many votive medals. But our journey has been fraught with peril at every turn. We have been attacked and set upon time and again. All of our belongings were stolen.'

Had George been wearing a hat he would now have taken it off to Professor Coffin. The showman certainly knew how to 'think on his feet', as it were.

The Martian leaned past the professor and gargled once more into the machine.

'Weapons?' queried the voice. 'We are informed that not only did you fail to pass through immigration control at the crater, but you were attempting to smuggle weaponry into Lemuria.'

'Ah,' said the professor. 'There does seem to be some misunderstanding.' Professor Coffin cast George a desperate glance.

'Do not look at me,' said George. 'You were doing so nicely on your own. Carry on.'

Clickings, whirrings, cog-intermeshings, marvellous puffings of steam. Then more words issued in cold blank monotone.

'The details of your neglect in providing correct and appropriate documentation, illegal entry to Lemuria, arms smuggling, unlicensed importation of an un-classified hairy-boy – these and numerous other misdemeanours and breaches of protocol, some genuine, others whimsical and unjust but prompted by the enor-mity and scale of the offences, are now being punched onto card and entered into the Patent Adjudicator.'

George Fox rolled his eyes about. 'We do not require the services of a Cerebral Prognosticator to predict what is coming next,' said he.

'Execution,' said the machine.

'No surprise there then,' said George.

'Public execution, followed by ritual dismemberment and the dispersal of meat stuffs to the population.'

'Hold hard there,' cried Professor Coffin. 'That is utterly outrageous.'

There was a pause, then the voice spoke once again.

'Indeed,' it said. 'I do apologise. So many mis-demeanours have overloaded the data operation system. The sentence should be prolonged torture, *then* ritual dismemberment, *then* execution and the dispersal of meat stuffs.'

'I protest,' Professor Coffin protested. 'I demand a reappraisal, an opportunity to appeal against each separ-ate charge before a jury of my peers. The representation of an accredited legal advisor. A—'

The gun butt caught him a terrible blow and felled him to the floor.

'Carry your fellow criminal to the cell provided,' the voice from the machine told George, 'and counsel him upon reawakening to make no further protests or his tongue parts will be severed from his head.'

George Fox made a gloomy face and gathered up the professor. Things now looked impossibly hopeless. Which made George impossibly sad.

32

he accommodation, to say the least, was wretched. No full board with free drinks from the bar. Dark and dank and grim and glum and gloomy. Smelling rank and, if even listed in *The Gentleman Traveller's Guide to Prison Cells of the World*, scarcely even rating half a star.

George sat fuming in the rank and murkiness. Occasionally puffings and blowings escaped his lips. All indicative of extreme irritation and fury.

Professor Coffin toyed with his gold pocket watch. He had acquired this whilst aboard the *Empress of Mars* to replace that of George's which he had returned to the lad. This beautiful timepiece not only chimed the hour, but went for five whole days without winding.

There was absolutely no telling how long it would go for if you *did* wind it.

Inside the face cover were engraved the words

To Nikola Tesla

From all the Backroom Boffins

26th July 1895

Professor Coffin held the watch to his ear. 'We have been in this cell for nearly twelve hours,' he said to George.

'And I have hated every minute,' George replied. *'And,'* he added, 'I had no idea that a single ape can go to the toilet quite so many times.'

'He is a somewhat prodigious piddler,' Professor Coffin agreed. 'Which does not improve the ambience one little bit. But—'

'Do not even begin,' said George. 'If you tell me one more time that all will be well, I will fall upon you and wring the life from your neck with my bare hands alone.'

'Come, come, George,' said the professor. 'All *will* be well. But you are out of sorts. I have something here that will raise your spirits.' And he dipped into his waistcoat pocket to draw out a slim glass phial.

'Oh no,' croaked the professor. 'It is gone.'

'Gone?' asked George. 'What is gone?'

'Something rather special. Something that I felt might aid our escape from here. In all of our comings and goings it must have fallen from my pocket.'

'Tell me of this something,' said George Fox.

'It does not matter now,' said the professor.

'No,' said George, 'for we are soon to die most horribly. So where would be the harm in you telling me?'

'It was something I acquired whilst on board the airship. Something called the Scent of Unknowing.'

George did noddings of his head and stroked his striking chin.

'A perfume that I thought to be of myth. One sniff and the sniffer becomes totally compliant. Whatever the sniffer is told to do, or told to think, so shall it be for the sniffer.'

Professor Coffin might have added more, but of a sudden was quite unable to speak. George's hands were fastened around his throat and George was glaring fiercely and shaking the showman about.

'You thoroughgoing swine!' shouted George. 'At last all falls into place. My periods of missing time. Ada's most dramatic change of opinion concerning you.'

Professor Coffin floundered about. Though sprightly he, for the age of himself, no match was he for George.

Darwin the monkey set up a shrieking. Became a self-appointed referee.

'All right,' said George. 'All right.' He elbowed aside the chattering ape and let the showman fall.

'I am sorry, George,' croaked the professor, when he could once more find a voice to speak with. 'You might think me wrong. But I did it for the best of motives—'

'Your own financial advancement,' said George Fox.

'And yours too. Fifty-fifty.'

'Or at least until you had what you wanted. At which time you would most likely have had me take a little sniff of the scent and confess that I no longer had any interest at all in taking my fifty per cent.'

Professor Coffin tried very hard indeed to make the words 'I swear that I had no such thing in mind' sound convincing.

George was *not* convinced.

'We are finished, you and I,' he said. 'Our partnership is no more. If somehow I survive and somehow I find Ada, I will return with her, *somehow*, to England and take a respectable job.'

'Ha,' said the professor, with some difficulty because

it hurt his throat. 'Do not give me any of that, my boy. You have loved every minute of this. The thrills and high adventure.'

'Loved every minute?' George was all but speechless. 'I have lost all count of how many people died on the *Empress of Mars*. Then the natives. Then the flying monkeys and now *this*.'

'But you still live,' said the professor. 'And have you ever felt so truly alive before? You will find your love, George. I just know that you will and if you do return to England and take a respectable job, you will constantly recall our adventures and hanker after such excitement again.'

George Fox folded his arms in a huff and took to a sulking silence.

They did not get an evening meal, nor indeed a breakfast.

Which George felt the dying man deserved. And after all, if they were going to the cooking pot, then fattening them up was surely logical.

A Martian's slidy foot did slurpings in the corridor outside. Intricate brass coggery was set into motion, and bolts slid back upon the grim cell door.

'About time,' said Professor Coffin. 'No doubt some letter of apology from some high muckamuck at the Ministry of Immigration. Or possibly our breakfast.'

George Fox ground his teeth and knotted his fists.

The muzzle of a Martian terror weapon entered the cell. Gargly shouts of an urgent nature entered with it.

'Time, it seems, to go,' said George. 'And Darwin,' he said to the monkey butler, 'you have my most sincere apologies. You saved my life and I in turn threw it away. Taking yours with it, I regret.'

Darwin the monkey shook George by the hand.

The three then left the cell.

There was something of a carnival atmosphere upon the streets of Lemuria. Bunting swagged from building to building.

Somewhere music played.

Unrecognisable was this to an Earthly ear, appearing more a discordant jangle, accompanied by rattlings. But it had the desired effect upon the considerable crowd that lined the streets. Martians jigged their nips and tentacles and street-side vendors with colourful carts sold bottles of Martian beer.

Professor Coffin waved gaily. Some of the crowd waved back.

Professor Coffin did not, however, consider it politic to tell George that he still retained a degree of confidence that all would end happily.

George Fox stalked and Darwin scampered. Behind them the well-armed Martian slid along.

It came as absolutely no surprise at all to either George or the professor to find that their final destination was the pyramid of skulls in the central plaza.

George did desperate glancings all about. There had to be some way he could make his escape. Well, some way *they* could make *their* escape. As George wanted no harm to come to Darwin. Perhaps some low-flying aircraft might be leapt onto. Perhaps the surviving Jupiterians would arrive in the very nick of time to rescue them. Perhaps Darwin might have something up his hairy sleeve.

Perhaps.

Or, perhaps, simply, George would die here. Die in this subterranean city. Die and be eaten, or other-ways about. But have his head bone join the hill of skulls. Be just another unnamed victim, dead in a faraway place.

George wished for Ada.

George wished he was back in England.

George Fox thought of his parents.

George missed his mum.

Up the shallow steps went George at the urge of an alien gun. Step after step and up and up, skulls to either side.

Upon the very summit, flat-topped, plateaued, stood a Martian of considerable stature. Before him a table and this spread with instruments designed for nothing but torture.

Except, perhaps, for meat butchery.

And serving up.

George glanced back. The professor joined him, Darwin too.

The Martian with the gun made further garglings.

'Interlopers, insurgents, iconoclasts—'

The words boomed from the wonderful translating machine, which had been wheeled to the foot of the pyramid.

Amplified garglings followed, which George considered were probably a Martian translation of the words of English. Then—

'We speak to you in your own tongue, that you may understand the error of your ways. And that your flippancy and casual attitude to official paperwork has led you to receive just punishment.'

A gargled Martian version of all this followed.

'It is tragic that at a time such as this, when the prophecies are being fulfilled, that you did not come amongst us as penitent pilgrims armed with all the necessary correctly filled application forms and officially endorsed visas.'

Professor Coffin sighed and shrugged.

George said, 'Prophecies fulfilled?'

'Now is our time of great rejoicing,' the voice continued. 'And as such it is fitting that you should serve as part of our feast of celebration. Bow now and hide your faces from the Marvel that you are not fit to gaze upon.'

'What of *this*?' asked George.

But ask nothing more would he. Other than perhaps that God should forgive him all his trespasses. And recall the deal that George had formerly suggested, regarding the sparing of Ada's life in exchange for his own.

The very large Martian with the table-load of tortures cast his tentacles about George and dragged him from his feet. Other tentacles ensnared Darwin and the professor. Curled about their mouths, stifling their cries for mercy, holding them with a hideous strength.

'Death to the infidels!' cried the mechanical voice. And then took once more to ghastly gargles.

A blur of tentacles scooped up horrible cutting tools, fiendish things a-dazzle with corkscrew blades.

The Martian crowd made free with joyful cheerings.

The instruments of torment swept down upon the joyless three.

33

 mighty cry rose up above all. A hideous gargling shriek.

It stilled the Martian crowd to silence. The torture weapons halted in mid-swing.

A further gargled torrent of words and tentacles retracted.

George was suddenly free and gasped for air. His ears seemed to pop from the all-consuming silence. Gingerly George climbed to his feet. The professor, he observed, was doing likewise. Darwin was up upon his haunches.

The Martian executioner was replacing his terrible implements.

Professor Coffin offered George a shrug.

More amplified garglings issued forth. The huge executioner flung himself down to the paved plateau and set free plaintive moanings.

From his vantage point upon high, George could see that the countless Martians below were now sinking to the knee-like parts of themselves and bowing their horrible heads.

Further commands, for such these obviously were, poured from the translating machine. Uncomfortably, on its knees, the crowd did backings away.

And George looked down at the being who spoke the

commands into the wonderful translating machine and George beheld a great wonder.

George beheld the Marvel to which the previous speaker had alluded. The Marvel that they were 'not fit to gaze upon'.

The Marvel that had been made manifest at this time 'when the prophecies are being fulfilled'.

The Marvel was clothed in robes of gold and silver, bronze and copper and lapis lazuli. She wore the wings of an angel and a helmet likened to that of a samurai. Upon this was a crescent moon and a most distinctive image.

The being's face was golden, Her eyes of the purest green, and burnished copper ringlets framed Her lovely upturned face.

'It is Her,' cried Professor Coffin, and he bowed extravagantly. 'It is the Japanese Devil Fish Girl Herself.'

George found that he was bowing too and swaying slightly also. Dizzy from hunger and half-gone with madness for fear of it all, George could manage but three brief words, before he fainted away.

'It is Ada,' said George Fox, as blackness closed about him.

He awoke upon a bed of many comforts, with pillowings of swansdown and cushionings of silk. The air was rich with exotic perfumes, trays of rare confectionary were near at hand, and to George it all appeared most heavenly.

'I have died,' cried George as he woke to this vision of loveliness. 'And I have *not* gone to the bad place, thank you, God.'

'You have certainly found religion,' said a voice.

And George looked to the speaker and tears came into his eyes and George said, 'Ada, Ada – it *is* you.'

'It certainly *is*.' Ada, who had evidently been leaning over George, mopping at his brow with lavender water, straightened, twirled and went slowly through one of those provocative dances that never lose their popularity at the music hall.

George looked on appreciatively and would probably have clapped when she was done and called for an encore, but for the nausea that he felt and the growling of his stomach.

'Oh yes,' said Ada, ceasing her voluptuous motions. 'You must be very hungry. I will attend to that.' She turned and swept away, a veritable fairy queen in all her marvellous raiments and trappings, a veritable Goddess indeed.

George heard words barking and gargling from the translating machine. Ada Lovelace returned to him and settled down on the fantastic bed.

'Breakfast soon,' she said to George. 'And over it I will tell you all. For it is a wonderful story.'

The breakfast was delicious, of course. For how could it have been otherwise? For surely it was ambrosia. That food consumed by the Gods.

Ada Lovelace tasted this and that from the golden salvers set before her on a low carved table of the Turkish persuasion.

George sat opposite her. They both sat on tapestried cushions.

'Is Darwin all right?' George asked.

Ada Lovelace nodded, then made a pained expression.

'This helmet is somewhat tight,' she said, 'but I thought it imprudent to mention that it really isn't my size.'

George continued with his eating.

'You're not going to ask how the professor is?' asked Ada.

George shook his head and munched on. 'I could not care less,' said he.

'An evil man,' said Ada Lovelace.

George looked up. 'Thank God you have come to your senses,' he said. 'I know what he did to us.'

'Poisoned us somehow,' said Ada.

'Poisoned us with *this*.' George drew from *his* waist-coat pocket the slim glass phial with the screw-on cap. 'The Scent of Unknowing. I had Darwin liberate it from the professor's pocket. And the professor confessed to me as to what it did when he thought it was lost for ever.'

'I do not remember at all,' said Ada, and she shivered slightly. 'And I fear for what that terrible man might have chosen to do to me when he and I were alone.'

George Fox made a ferocious face.

'It is all right,' said Ada. 'He has no more power over us. We are safe from him.'

George poured out something and sipped at it. 'Are you sure that I am not dreaming this?' he asked.

'I *did* wonder if *I* was,' said Ada, 'but no. Would you like to hear the story?'

'Very much,' said George Fox, and he settled back to listen.

'This island is a sacred island,' began Ada Lovelace. 'Sacred to every religion, on this planet and off it. The statue of the Goddess in the temple above is as old as time itself. It is the most sacred object in all of the universe. *The Book of Sayito* the Goddess is here and I have read from this book.

'Allow me to explain all. The flying monkey creatures carried me away – not to do me harm, but to rescue me from amidst the battle. The natives are not allowed to climb so near to the temple. They protect the lower slopes, that is their job. The monkeys protect the temple.

'The Martians here see all, you see. All about this island anyway. They have camera devices hidden all over the island that relay images here. They saw me. And they recognised me to be Sayito, the Japanese Devil Fish Girl.'

'But you are not really Her,' said George. 'Or *are* you?'

'Of course I am *not*,' said Ada Lovelace. 'Although I do, it seems, somewhat resemble Her. My eyes, my hair. And remember, no woman has set foot upon this island for one thousand years or more. Their prophecies said that Sayito would come. An easy mistake to make.'

George went, 'Hm,' quite loudly. Sometimes things can be just *too* convenient to be altogether likely.

'The flying monkeys carried me to a tower and I was brought down here in a lift. And George, I have to tell you, I was terrified, I cried for you, I truly did. A city full of Martians right here beneath the surface of our world? How fearful a thing is this? But I was led to the translating machine and told that I was the Goddess and that all was mine, for my return had fulfilled part of the prophecies.'

'Incredible,' said George Fox, and not, he felt, without reason. 'And what of these prophecies?'

'I was taken to the inner temple. There is a great temple above that I did not visit.'

'I did,' said George. 'It is very large, with a fine big statue that really does look like you.'

'Then I would like to see *that*. But, as I say, I was led to the inner temple. Ritually bathed, which I did not like much, because those smelly Martians were rather too intimate with their washings. Then I was clothed in the raiments of the Goddess, which I really *did* like. But then who wouldn't? Then made up in golden cosmetics, and shown the sacred book, *The Book of Sayito*.'

'I am most confused about this,' said George. 'This and so many other things besides. When we first met, I recall you telling me that *The Book of Sayito* was the Venusian Bible. What are the Martians doing with it?'

'Exactly what I wondered, George. But it is all in the book. The book, you see, is a grimoire, written in a universal language that can be understood by anyone of any race. It is a magic book, George. Of the very first magic. I was shown it and I opened it, but when I read from it, I read the first chapter of Genesis. And I thought, this cannot be right, this is the Judaic Bible. So I flicked back a few pages and the next time I read it, it was all different. A different creation myth. This time the one of the Martians.'

'I would dearly like to see this book,' said George.

'And you will. But allow me to continue. In this myth there is *no* beginning, *no* creation, simply cycles that repeat themselves and go on and on and on. In the version I read, two great kings in two great cities wage war upon one another. But the daughter of one king and the son of the other have fallen in love. And so to share their love they run away together. They take with them the great books of knowledge and they escape their planet in a spaceship.'

'And they come *here*?' asked George. 'Why, I saw an ancient crashed spaceship upon the beach. Is this story true then?'

'I believe so. The spaceship crashes, they climb to the peak of the volcano and there they find the temple of Sayito, which has always been there, George. It was never actually built, it has *always* been here.'

George had his doubts as to the logic of this, but he was enthusiastic about allowing Ada to continue.

'They find the temple, they open a book at the base of a statue—'

'That is how we came here,' said George. 'Sorry, please continue.'

'They descend to these caverns and here they remain. They become Adam and Eve on this world. They have the books of knowledge with them, science, maths, engineering. Their children, their children's children, their children's children's children, build this mighty city.'

'Where did *The Book of Sayito* come from?' George asked.

'They took it from the hands of the statue of the Goddess.'

'Please continue,' said George.

'There is not much more to tell. There are prophecies in the book that one day the Goddess will return in a living body to free them from imprisonment.'

'What imprisonment?' asked George.

'Oh, they cannot leave these caverns,' said Ada. 'The upper air is poison to them. They would die as their brethren from Mars who attacked the Earth all died.'

'Then how are they going to be freed from their imprisonment? Are they intending to return to Mars?'

'They cannot. The spacecraft the prince and princess arrived in is broken beyond repair and there are certain minerals necessary to power the drive systems that only exist upon Mars.'

'You learned an awful lot from that book,' said George.

'I felt it best that I did. I did not wish to be asked certain questions that only the genuine Goddess would be able to answer and come up short, as it were.'

'Incredible,' said George. 'But tell me more about this fulfilling of the prophecies business.'

'Ah yes,' said Ada. 'That is the rather important part. Over the centuries the Martians here have been building more and more. They had the books to teach them how. They raised this remarkable city. They constructed the guns, the horseless carriages and the flying machines. They built and they planned and they waited until the prophecy was fulfilled and Sayito appeared to them in living form. Then, as I said, it would be time to leave their imprisonment. Travel above in their specially sealed war craft and lay waste to all that dwell upon the surface of the planet. This would happen because the infidels of the upper world would commit the Great Blasphemy, and for this they would have to be punished. By death.'

'And what is the Great Blasphemy?' George asked.

'That I do not know for certain. But it will result in the complete annihilation of Mankind, if the book is anything to go by.'

George Fox choked on a tasty viand. Ada patted his back.

'Sorry,' said George, 'but this is very bad.'

'Very bad,' agreed Ada. 'But I have not as yet mentioned the worst bit. The Martians will rise from the volcano's crater in their aerial warships and head across the planet spreading death. It will all end in an Apocalyptic Battle. Which, as far as I have been able to make out, no matter how many times I flick backwards and forwards through the pages of *The Book of Sayito*, is how the Bible of every single belief ends. The Apocalyptic Battle between Good and Evil. The forces of Good will defeat the forces of Evil.'

'That at least is comforting,' said George.

'Not as such,' said Ada Lovelace. 'The Martians naturally consider themselves to be the forces of Good. They will, after all, be led to the world above by the living Goddess Sayito.

'The forces of Evil who will have committed the Great Blasphemy and will be defeated hail from what the book describes as "the seat of all Evil". Or London, as it is otherwise described.'

'Oh dear, oh dear,' said George. 'That is very much the worst.'

'Not quite,' said Ada. 'There is one extra bit. The leader of the forces of Evil. He is named throughout the book. And his name is George.'

34

‘This has to be stopped,’ said George to Ada. ‘And somehow *we* have to stop it.’

The lovely Ada Lovelace touched at the golden make-up on her cheek. ‘I was thinking,’ said she, ‘that I might be able to stop it by telling them that *I, Sayito,* have come in peace for all races and that there must be no war and no killing, and that they must all stay right here and live happily ever after.’

‘I do like the sound of that,’ said George. ‘But what about what it says in the book?’

‘I think that as a living Goddess I hold the right to contradict an old book, don’t you?’

George Fox cocked his head on one side and made a certain face.

‘And,’ continued Ada, ‘I was actually thinking of destroying the book and having done with it.’

‘Ah,’ said George. ‘That might not be the brightest of plans. That might well constitute this Great Blasphemy that will spur them into the Apocalypse.’

‘You think so?’ Ada asked.

‘Unless it was my arrival with the professor that is deemed to be the Great Blasphemy.’

‘I have squared *that,*’ said Ada. ‘When I discovered

that I had been invited to an execution and that it was *your* execution, I spoke to them through the translating machine and told them that you and the professor were my servants. They do not have you down for blasphemers.'

George looked into Ada's eyes. 'I cannot tell you, Ada,' said he, 'how happy I am to see you alive and well. And being a Goddess certainly suits you. You really look the part. I missed you so much and was so afraid that something terrible had happened to you.' George Fox gave a little sigh. Ada squeezed his hand.

'The question is,' she said, 'how do we escape from here? They will not go on believing for ever that I am a Goddess. What if the *real* Goddess shows up?'

'I do not think that likely,' said George.

'George,' said Ada, 'do you not recall what happened to you when the *Empress of Mars* was going down? How you floated away in a magic bubble? That is not your everyday occurrence, now is it? That is the sort of mystical thing that only happens in a time that is the very End of Days.'

'You really think so?' said George. 'It is true that I was led here by a prophecy and thought myself to be on a holy quest.'

'And you could well find yourself leading the losing side in the final Holy War.'

'That is *not* going to happen.'

'Not if *we* can stop it.'

George looked hard at Ada Lovelace. 'Would I be right in believing,' he asked, 'that you have come up with a plan?'

★

Professor Coffin, George and Ada and Darwin the monkey butler sat in a little council of war atop the skull pyramid.

'I do *not* like it *at all* up here,' said George to all and sundry up there.

'Be that as it may,' said Ada, 'we can speak here without being overheard. They follow me around with that translating machine. I do hope they are not yet beginning to suspect.'

'All will be well, I am sure,' said Professor Coffin. 'Which is to say,' he continued, taking in the fullness of George's fearsome glare, 'that all is *presently* well and if the delightful Ada here, whom we all have to thank for our lives, has the kind of plan that I just know she has, we will be out of here and off on our way as soon as soon can be.'

George Fox looked towards Ada. Darwin the monkey did likewise.

'I am proposing *this*,' said Ada. 'I am not proud of my proposal, but I make it in the hope of saving Mankind.'

'There is much to be proud of there,' said the professor.

'Be quiet and let her speak,' said George.

'Quite so.'

'Thank you, George. My proposal is this. The Martians here have a fleet of flying warships. Not spaceships, but craft that can skim through the air and wreak havoc in any part of the globe. I propose that we commandeer one of them.'

'Steal it, you mean?' said George.

'No,' said Ada. 'I will tell them that I wish to travel aloft. Spy out the camps of our wicked enemies.

Plan stratagems, et cetera. We will have a Martian pilot fly us out of here.'

'And?' said George. 'Go on.'

'We will tell the Martians here to await my return. To do nothing until I return. I will tell them that there will be a sign. But before that sign is to be seen, they must all stay put.'

'That sign could be the Great Blasphemy,' said George. 'As no one seems to know what that is, then they will not know if it happens.'

'I like that,' said Ada. 'Once aloft and away from here we will acquaint ourselves with the controls of the craft, overpower the pilot and pitch him into the sea.'

'A little job for you then, Darwin,' said Professor Coffin.

Darwin the monkey bared his teeth in reply.

'Naturally we will all muck in,' said the professor. 'George and myself. It will be most exciting. Although we could of course just stun the pilot and return with him to London.'

George Fox shook his head most firmly.

'No, quite so,' said Professor Coffin.

'Into the sea with the pilot,' said Ada. 'Then we pick up all the survivors from the *Empress of Mars*—'

'I had quite forgotten about *them*,' said George. 'I hope that young Master Hitler has come to no harm.'

Ada winked a wink at George, who blushed some-what in return.

'We pick up the survivors,' she continued. 'We all return to London. There we hand over the Martian airship to the authorities and give them the latitude and longitude of this island. I am thinking perhaps that an attack with the element of surprise on its side, high explosives dropped from the airship into the crater, and all the Martians might be killed with one single stroke.

'Which is why I am not particularly proud of this plan. But I think it is for the best, if Mankind is to survive.'

'I too think it for the best,' said Professor Coffin. 'Young woman, I consider that a most inspired plan. It will be my honour to assist in its fulfilment.'

'Thank you,' said Ada. 'But please let me make this quite clear. George told me all about the Scent of Unknowing and so I must warn you of this. One single piece of "funny business" on your part and George, myself and Darwin too, I so believe, will pitch you into the ocean, through which you can swim home to England.'

George gazed proudly upon Ada Lovelace. Her bravery was supreme. Should he tell her just how much he loved her?

Perhaps on the voyage home, thought George.

'So,' said Ada. '*That* is my plan. Are we all agreed?'

She put out her hand palm down. George placed his upon it. Professor Coffin placed his upon George's and Darwin placed his on the professor's. It was a very special moment.

A special moment of trust.

Behind his back Professor Coffin crossed a pair of fingers. Anything at all could happen on so long a voyage.

It all might well have seemed too good to be true.

That it was pushing the boundaries of credibility to a point where they dispersed into fanciful realms. And if this plan had been formulated by George, George felt it would surely have turned into the very shape of a pear.

Ada called together a great meeting of the Lemurian elders, clerics of the Church of Sayito, scholars who studied the book. She spoke eloquently through the translating machine, explaining that she must travel ahead and they must wait behind, doing absolutely nothing until the Great Blasphemy occurred. A Lemurian elder raised a number of tentacles and asked Ada, as She was indeed Sayito and so knew everything about *Her* book, what *precisely* was the Great Blasphemy? Ada, who had certainly been expecting, if not *that* particular question, then one most similar to it, answered that so Great was the Great Blasphemy that even She was not able to speak of it. But so *very* Great it was that there would be absolutely no confusing it with any minor blasphemy that could not be described and obviously seen as the very Greatest of all Great Blasphemies.

This appeared to satisfy the elder. Who went on to ask whether Sayito would be taking Her servants with Her? Or whether She would find new servants elsewhere, and care to leave the old ones here to be eaten.

'I will be taking them with me,' said Ada. 'They have sentimental value.'

There followed a period of feasting. Happily mostly of a vegetarian nature. A period of waiting about whilst a flying ship was fuelled and suitably provisioned. A period which Ada, George and the professor passed most nervously. And then a great procession. Much bunting and beer stands. Discordant music and a pleasant stroll to a bulky airship tethered atop the horrid pyramid of skulls.

Pleasantries were exchanged through the translating machine.

Ada offered many blessings and stressed again and again that absolutely *nothing* must occur until the time of the Great Blasphemy. She gratefully accepted a large casket of oversized jewels as a going-away present, held her nose and kissed a Martian baby.

Then she, George, the professor and Darwin scaled the pyramid of skulls, stepped up the gangway onto the flying ship, waved final farewells.

And prayed very hard as the airship rose aloft.

A roof within the volcano's crater slid open. The airship drifted into the bluest of skies. The roof closed leaving no trace of its very existence.

Through the onboard translating machine Ada ordered the pilot to circle the island and demonstrate the craft's capabilities.

A pleasant hour was spent in this. And then Ada invited the pilot onto the open observation deck where they might take a little stroll together. She indeed took a little stroll, he a slime-trailed slurp.

Ada drew the pilot's attention to something in the distance. At which moment George, the professor and Darwin promptly pitched him over the guardrail and down to the sea beneath.

'Most ably done,' said Ada Lovelace. 'But should not one of you be steering the ship?'

The survivors of the *Empress of Mars* were most delighted to see them. Even little Master Hitler's face lit up.

'All aboard at the hurry-up,' called Ada. Recalling that Martian cameras monitored the island and hoping that none were presently active.

All aboard it was and bound for home.

Ada and George were gratified to hear that a surviving sky-man from the *Empress of Mars* had worked out the map location of the island with the aid of the Jupiterian hunters who had survived the assault of the flying monkeys and fled back to the beach.

There were sufficient provisions on board to accommodate all on the voyage home and all agreed that God had spared them and that they were blessèd indeed.

As evening fell, George left Darwin to steer the ship and walked with Ada on the open observation deck.

'Will all be well?' he asked of her. 'Do you believe we are safe?'

'All *will* be well,' said Ada. 'The worst is over for us.'

'I *am* thinking,' said George, 'that perhaps those Martians might just be left alone. Do not get me wrong – I do not like them and they would have eaten me – but if they never attack us and spend the next thousand years awaiting the Great Blasphemy, where would be the harm in that?'

Ada linked her arm with George's, smiled at him and said, 'I was myself thinking something along those lines. You are a good man, George. A very dear man indeed.'

Moonlight bathed the observation deck. A gentle breeze whispered, a high-flying parrot cooed softly.

George took Ada in his arms and kissed her.

'Ada,' said George. 'I love you, Ada. Will you marry me?'

A moment passed that seemed to George a lifetime.

'Of course I will marry you,' Ada Lovelace said.

★

Three days later the Martian airship touched down upon the cobbled vastness of the Royal London Spaceport at Sydenham.

Bedraggled passengers, their finery gone, their high-blown spirits deflated, shook George and Ada by the hand and traipsed down the gangway to be greeted by bewildered onlookers.

'Darwin,' said George to the monkey close at hand. 'Would you care to be the best man at my wedding?'

'That will not please the professor,' said Ada, laughing as she said it.

'*That* to the professor,' said George, making a rather rude gesture.

'I suppose we must speak with someone in authority,' said Ada. 'Explain, well, *everything* really.'

'Let us do it then,' said George in reply. 'And then we will take a hansom and I will introduce you to my family. It is a long time since I have seen them. I hope they will be as happy to see me as I will be to see them.'

Together they strolled down the gangway, Darwin hard on their heels.

They had not strolled a further ten yards, however, when they heard certain sounds behind them that caused them to pause in their tracks and turn back.

Those certain sounds were of engines, roaring into life.

'Oh no!' cried George. 'He would not.'

But he had.

As George and Ada and Darwin looked on, the Martian airship, now piloted by Professor Coffin, who waved at them through the windscreen and displayed the casket of jewels that Ada had been given as a going-away present, lifted off, swung about and soared away into the sky.

35

ealous officialdom saw to it that things did not go exactly how George had hoped that they would. That he and Ada were immediately arrested and led away in handcuffs for interrogation lacked somewhat for the 'triumphal homecoming' that he had had in mind. He and Ada had, after all, brought back the survivors of the *Empress of Mars* safe and sound and once more to England. That at the very least had to be worth a medal or two and a tea of sweets with the Queen. The handcuffing and the frogmarching lacked for a certain dignity and suitable gravitas. And George became a most grumpy George when he found himself tossed into a pokey cell.

He called out for justice and demanded that he might speak with someone of high office in the Government of the realm. A spaceport guard in an ill-fitting uniform entered George's cell and struck him down with a steam-driven truncheon, which he assured George was 'quite the latest thing'.

At length George was conveyed to the low office of a minor body in charge of passport control. His handcuffs were removed and he was flung into a chair before a crowded office desk. George's guard left the room, informing George that he would be waiting outside and no funny business would be tolerated. The minor body viewed George Fox across the crowded desk.

George was asked to produce his papers.

George explained that he had none.

George was then told that in order to enter England he would need to display papers of indenture and permission to travel. An entry visa, accompanied by letters of recommendation, sealed with the authorisation of at least three diplomatic envoys and a license for the unclassified hairy-boy that—

'It is a monkey!' protested George. 'Darwin, my monkey butler.'

The minor body ran his fingers down the passenger list of the *Empress of Mars*. 'Lord Brentford had a monkey butler called Darwin,' he observed. 'And Lord Brentford is numbered amongst the deceased.' He gave George a very hard look and then made notes with a hand-driven pen that was *not* the latest thing.

'And you claim that you were a passenger yourself on the *Empress of Mars*?' said the minor body.

'I was,' said George. 'And where is Ada Lovelace?'

'Ah yes,' said the minor body. 'Your accomplice.'

'My *what*?' asked George.

'Your partner in subversion and crime. I understand that she too claims to have been a passenger on the *Empress of Mars*, but her name does not appear on the passenger list.'

'Ah,' said George. 'Oh dear,' said George. 'I can explain,' said George also. But he was not altogether certain that he could. Not to the satisfaction of this minor body, who clearly took his job most seriously.

'Look at you,' said this body. 'Your accomplice is

dressed in her undergarments like some music hall floozy and not only do you sport a suit that is clearly two sizes too small, but you do not wear a hat!'

The minor body made big notes of this scandalous sartorial faux pas.

'I suspect, sir,' said he, 'that you are a Prussian spy, or indeed one of the American anarchists whom I am informed by the survivors attacked the *Empress of Mars* in New York.'

'This is absurd,' said George. 'I rescued these people. Ada and I rescued them. Ask any of them, they will tell you.'

'Ask *them*?' asked the minor body. 'Are you quite bereft of your wits? Those survivors are members of the aristocracy. One does not trouble the likes of them with such trivialities.'

George made a most exasperated face. He was most exasperated.

'No, hold on, hold on, hold on,' cried George. Suddenly seeing a light at the end of what looked to be a *very* long dark tunnel. 'My name is on the passenger list. Oh yes, indeed it is.'

'Is it now?' asked the minor body. 'So what is your name, pray?'

'My name is George Fox,' said George Fox. '*Lord* George Fox, so you can just release me now, give me a nice cup of tea and then allow me to return to my aristocratic country seat. Go to it, my good man.'

The minor body stiffened slightly in his chair. 'A lord?' said he. 'You?' said he. 'In a suit like that and no hat?' said he also.

'I am a survivor of an airship wreck,' complained

George. 'But I *am* on the passenger list. Go on, look me up.'

The minor body turned pages. Most slowly indeed he turned them. But presently he paused in his turning and uttered a single, 'Oh.'

'Yes,' said George. 'Oh indeed. Now release me and bring me some tea.'

'Lord George Fox,' said the minor body, and he began to smile.

'Splendid,' said George. 'And I am pleased that you are able to affect a detached attitude and see the humour of your own folly in doubting me.'

The minor body looked up at George. 'Not as such,' said he. 'You see, I have here,' and he held up just what he had there, 'a warrant for the arrest of Lord George Fox, issued by the Penge Constabulary at the request of a number of tailors and outfitters with whom this very Lord George failed to settle before he boarded the *Empress of Mars*.'

The minor body intoned the list. 'Jonathan Crawford, suiting to the gentry. Elias Mainwaring, purveyor of quality canes and umbrellas. Louis Vuitton – manufacturers of superior luggage.' And several others that George had quite forgotten but had no particular wish to be reacquainted with.

George Fox groaned and his striking chin sank towards his chest.

'We have you, sir,' said the minor body, 'in the parlance of the *Police Gazette*, "bang to rights" and no mistake.'

George did further groanings.

'Do you have anything to say for yourself before I call back the guard to return you to your cell?'

George felt hard put now to think of *anything*.

'I will have to ask you to turn out your pockets,' said the minor body. 'It appears that the guards have neglected to search you. Can't have you producing a set of skeleton keys and making your escape, can we?'

George shook his head. 'I suppose you cannot,' he said.

George rooted through his pockets and produced his few meagre possessions, his gold watch, a handkerchief, this trifle and the next. He placed them before him on a slightly less crowded area of the minor body's desk.

'Is that everything?' asked the minor body.

'Everything!' said George, with a dismal nod.

The minor body poked about amongst George's personal belongings, took up something and asked George, 'What is *this*?'

George viewed the item the minor body held in his hand. A slim glass phial of colourless liquid topped by a screw-on cap.

'Ah,' said George, and a faint smile flickered at his lips.

'I really do have to ask you,' said Ada Lovelace as she and George were driven away from the Royal London Spaceport, not in a police wagon but in a rather nice landau carriage drawn by matched black geldings, 'exactly how you achieved this.'

'Wave back at the nice minor body,' said George. 'He is bidding us good fortune.'

Ada waved. 'Just how?' she asked of George.

'Charm?' suggested George. 'Force of personality? Justice, perhaps?'

Ada kissed George on the cheek. 'So *not* the Scent of

Unknowing,' said she. 'Which is what *I* would have employed.'

They shared a moment of carefree joy and George Fox treasured this moment.

'So,' said Ada, 'my bold adventurer and husband-to-be. Whither are we bound?'

'Well,' said George, and he made a certain face, 'we are both in rags and penniless too, so there is only one thing for it.'

'Beg on London Bridge?' said Ada. 'Surely not.'

'No,' said George. 'Do what those in their teens have done throughout this century and will probably continue to do throughout centuries to come, when they are in financial trouble. Go home to Mum and Daddy.'

Ada Lovelace made a face, the perfect match of George's.

'Yours or mine?' she asked him, thoughtfully.

'In our present state of dress, I am thinking *yours*,' said George.

There can sometimes be a terrible problem with dates. Getting dates right, remembering dates. George had no trouble remembering that Ada Lovelace was the daughter of Lord Byron. She had told him that she was and he had seen the newspaper cutting. George had not, however, mentioned at the time that he had 'done' Lord Byron at school. And that Lord George Gordon Byron, the sixth Baron Byron, had been born in seventeen eighty-eight and died in eighteen twenty-four. And that this was now eighteen ninety-five and Ada could scarcely be more than eighteen.

'Regarding your father,' George asked, as the landau moved through the pretty village of Penge, passing, so it chanced, the new police station. 'According to history books and indeed his memorial in the Poets' Corner of Westminster Abbey, Lord Byron died in eighteen twenty-four.'

'And precisely what point are you making?' asked Ada.

'That was seventy-one years ago,' said George. 'Yet you claim to be his daughter and have a newspaper cutting that apparently confirms this.'

'And?' said Ada.

'You do look younger than seventy-one,' said George.

'Flatterer,' said Ada.

In a perfect world, thought George Fox, *all* matters would be resolved. And resolved satisfactorily. The good would be rewarded for their goodness and the bad punished accordingly. Questions that demanded answers would receive them. Puppies would never grow up and Planet Earth would sail through space upon the wings of joy.

'You have no intention of explaining it to me, have you?' George asked Ada.

'None at all, dear George,' the girl replied.

Ada named a fashionable street in Mayfair and requested that the driver of the landau take them there. The matched black geldings trotted, the weather was pleasant, countryside passed to the outskirts of town and London loomed ahead.

'It has all been such an adventure,' said Ada. 'Have you enjoyed it, George?'

'In truth,' said George, 'now that we are back in London and safe, I suppose that I have.'

'*Suppose* that you have?'

'I definitely did.' George gave Ada's hand a squeeze. 'It was fearful at times. But I met you. And I found my fate, as it were. Saw the statue of Sayito that is older than time and the most sacred object in the universe. Although I never actually saw the book, and it was prophesied that I would. But all is well that ends well. And it was quite an adventure.'

'You will not be seeking employment from Professor Coffin again?' Ada asked.

'That scoundrel!' George made a very sour face. 'I feel certain that he will now have retired from the show-man's profession and will live most comfortably for the rest of his life when he sells those jewels that were yours.'

'If there was justice in this world,' said Ada, 'then he would find no happiness from his evil. But I care not for him, nor the jewels. I care only for you.'

George Fox got a lump in his throat. He had never been so happy.

The landau moved on towards fashionable Mayfair and George held great hopes for the future.

36

ery impressed was George with the Byrons, a fine Bohemian crowd, who inhabited roomy apartments and seemed artful, arty and gay.

The house had somewhat gone to seed, but the rooms were brightly muralled in a style that was just then coming into vogue: Brit Art, otherwise known as Primitive. No great skills were employed, or required, just the necessary enthusiasm.

George viewed a mural in the hallway that most enthusiastically extolled the joys of onanism. George was a little taken aback, but after all, these *were* the nineties. The *fin de siècle*.

There were a great many Byrons, so it seemed to George. Some coming, a few going, but most just lolling about upon chaises longues, puffing at long-stemmed opium pipes and making the occasional languid gesture to imply that their absinthe glasses needed refilling.

As, to use one of Mr Oscar Wilde's expressions, a 'lifestyle', George could find much to recommend it. Especially for himself, after all his recent vicissitudes.

As to exactly how each and every one of these Byrons was related to Ada, George could only guess. Most referred to her as 'dear child' and kissed her tenderly.

George found, much to his surprise and satisfaction, that his grimly shrunken suit received neither mockery nor contempt. He was in fact complimented upon the novel nature of his look – 'such a biting social statement, my dear, a triumph of irony' – or asked whether it was 'the very latest thing' and where such a suit could be purchased.

George felt rather at home with the Byrons, and they with him.

Ada wasted no time in outlining her present position. She gathered together those Byrons who were capable of perambulation and told them how things would be. She meant to get married to George, she said, as soon as this could be arranged. George was a writer himself (this intelligence came as something of a surprise to George), but until he had received his first advance from his publisher, he would have to live here. As this received no objection, Ada went on to say that George and herself were presently penniless having lost all that they possessed when the *Empress of Mars* went down.

This did have to be explained to the Byrons, who rarely paid any attention to the actual 'news' pages of newspapers.

So, continued Ada, she would require an advance on her bridal dowry to purchase necessary necessities. George needed more sober apparel to visit his publisher. And she, much as it would not have bothered her to do so, could *not* walk the streets of London clad only in vest and corset and bloomers.

A sharp intake of breath had been occasioned upon the part of the Byrons with the coming of the words 'bridal dowry'. Ada added that naturally such a bridal dowry amounted to little more than a *very* short-term loan, as much of George's *large* publishing advance would be lavished upon his new family.

A Byron named Lord Billy finally wrote out a cheque.

A Byron named Lady Elsie gave Ada the loan of a frock.

A day or so later, George and Ada took tea at the famous Ritz. An announcement of their forthcoming marriage had been posted within the society pages of *The Times* newspaper and George had borrowed money from Ada's dowry to buy her an engagement ring. Nothing of outrageous price, but a pretty thing in itself.

George and Ada sat in the elegant tea pavilion of the Ritz, which was furnished in the Oriental style: black lacquer, white enamel, chinoiserie and dainty chintz.

George wore a dark and elegant morning suit that had been paid for in cash from a tailor that George had *not* previously visited. Ada wore the most delightful confection of rich dark-red velvet. Full skirt with bustle, dainty cape and quilted bodice, miniature top hat with tiny afternoon goggles.

Ada glanced at her engagement ring and smiled a smile upon George. 'What time is your appointment, dear?' she asked him.

George took out his gold watch and perused its face. 'An hour from now,' he said. 'At half past four.'

'And you do know what to say?'

'Of course I do.' George patted at a little sheaf of papers. 'I have written out a brief synopsis of our adventures together. Leaving out, of course, anything that either of us might find embarrassing. Putting emphasis upon the *exciting* side of it all.'

'And have you made any mention of the subterranean Martians?'

George made so-so gestures with his hands. 'I am in two minds,' he told Ada, 'whether to sell, if sell indeed I can, this book as a fictional adventure, rather than a true-life tale. I do not know whether it would be appropriate to use the word "Martian" at all.'

'Perhaps just Lemurian, then,' said Ada Lovelace. 'The wreck of the *Empress of Mars*, escape from cannibals and flying monkeys, the discovery of the most sacred object in the universe and a lost civilisation – this book has much to recommend it, I am thinking, without making mention of Martians. You must judge the publisher's reaction when you outline it to him. Use your intuition.'

'My *intuition*?' said George. 'Perhaps *you* should be visiting this publisher.'

'George,' said Ada, '*I* would certainly *not* be believed. I would appear a mere slip of a silly girl. Publishers are men and they like to publish other men. You will be fine. Everything will be fine.'

'Not one of my favourite phrases,' said George, 'but everything *will* be fine.'

They enjoyed a delightful tea of cakes and crumpets washed down with Twinings Afternoon Blend and a glass of chocolate-flavoured port to give George a little perk in the right direction.

At precisely four-thirty, George Fox entered the offices of Leonard Smithers. A gentleman with a reputation for publishing a more racy brand of literature, Mr Smithers had published the work of Aubrey Beardsley, Oscar Wilde, Max Beerbohm and the sinister Aleister Crowley.

George considered that this was the man to publish his fabulous tale.

The interview did not last long. Leonard Smithers was a man with a certain reputation. A man who took his luncheons in a mostly liquid form. A man who enforced a spoken opinion with a thrown object. A volatile fellow.

When George left the office of Leonard Smithers, a short half-hour after he had entered it, he did so with a certain faltering step. Things had not worked out *exactly* as he had hoped.

Certainly George *had* received an advance. And a very *large* advance too. The cheque that now fluttered in his fingers sported several zeroes. But George felt saddened too regarding this advance.

Mr Smithers had *not* been impressed by George's tale, whether pitched as fact or very-far-fetched fiction. He knew a thing or two about the occult, he told George, and was well aware of the legends surrounding the Japanese Devil Fish Girl. One of his authors, a Mr Crowley, had written a piece regarding this singular deity. The mother Goddess to all mother Goddesses. The mother too of God himself, as some religions claimed. It was whispered by those in the know of the occult world and inner Government circles that the ecclesiastics of Venus had recently launched an expedition to seek the statue of this Goddess. That they actually knew the location of the island on which it was to be found. But that also too the Jupiterians sought Her. That it was becoming a political issue which might lead to an interplanetary incident, and that something called a 'D notice' had been posted, forbidding any mention in newspapers, magazines or books regarding this matter.

George had been most surprised to hear all this.

Mr Smithers then suggested that perhaps George had in fact been sent by a rival publisher, seeking to sell him something that when published would cause Mr Smithers to be put out of business by the arrival of certain Gentlemen in Black, who would close down his office and carry him off to Heaven only knew where.

Mr Smithers had asked George whether he knew of the term 'conspiracy theory'. George had told Mr Smithers that he did.

And then George went on to say that if it was the case that nothing regarding the Japanese Devil Fish Girl could be published, that actually suited him very well and he would be happy to amend his manuscript to rename her the Cantonese Goldfish Girl, if needs be.

But it was at about this time that Mr Smithers, well in his cups and foaming somewhat at the mouth, openly accused George of being an agent for the Gentlemen in Black and hurled a clockwork ashtray at his head.

'Get out of my office and stay out!' he shouted at George.

So, as George strolled along Threadneedle Street, towards the Bank of England, where he intended to open an account with Mr Smithers' cheque, he did so with a certain faltering step. And a certain degree of sadness.

It is not a pleasant thing to have a publisher hurl an ashtray at your head and rant and rave about getting and staying out. Why, if it had not been for the employment by George of a slim glass phial of colourless liquid topped by a screw-on cap, George might not have got nearly so large an advance.

So George did not exactly laugh all the way to the

bank, but thinking of Ada and their wedding day, he did smile just a little.

'The Cantonese Goldfish Girl?' said Ada Lovelace. Over an intimate supper for two in the kitchen of the Byron household.

'I had no choice,' said George. 'I do not wish Mr Smithers to get into any trouble. There seem to be some political issues involved.'

'Well, naturally there would be, George. Do you not think that every race in the universe would seek to possess the most sacred object in the universe? Seek to take it to their own world?'

'I had never really thought of it that way,' said George. 'Do you think then that if the Venusians knew where the statue was, they would try to steal it?'

'I have absolutely no doubt of that at all,' said Ada. 'I read *The Book of Sayito*, remember. The Venusian version claims that the statue was originally on Venus and was stolen by iconoclasts.'

'I do wish I had read this book,' said George.

'Well,' said Ada, 'I suggest that you and I keep very quiet about the temple on the island. Let us think of more cheerful matters. When are you having Darwin measured for his best man's suit?'

'Tomorrow,' said George. 'If I can ease him away from his opium pipe. He seems to have settled into this house more as a guest than a butler. He will not do anything for me any more.'

'Ah,' said Ada, 'then you did not hear. It was announced in the *Tatler* – Lord Brentford left the bulk of his fortune to Darwin. When the redecoratings are completed at Syon House, Darwin will be moving there.'

'Well, that is a happy ever after for Darwin,' said George, raising a glass of red wine in his hand and toasting the monkey's good fortune. 'What do these redecoratings consist of?'

'The rose arboretum in the great conservatory is being uprooted and replaced with banana trees.'

Darwin the monkey ex-butler seemed to enjoy being measured for his best man's suit. He flicked through the tailor's catalogue and indicated that he would also like a tweed shooting jacket with matching plus fours, a linen suit, a panama hat and two pairs of red silk pyjamas.

The tailor, who was a regular reader of the *Tatler*, opened an account for Darwin and then drew his attention to a new range of headwear, aimed at gentlemen of modest hat size.

Days passed one upon another, and the wedding day drew near.

And George Fox woke up upon a particular morning to find that it had arrived.

George had taken temporary lodgings with Darwin at the estate of the late Lord Brentford, as it was not really the done thing to live in the same house as your intended. Even if her family *were* of Bohemian bent. The banana trees were planted now and George even helped to install a few climbing ropes in the ballroom and place a number of small empty cardboard boxes in the late lord's study for Darwin to put on his head when he felt in the mood.

George breakfasted, bathed and dressed in his finery.

Tactfully parted Darwin from a cardboard box to which he had become romantically attached and then helped the ape into his spiffing attire.

Examining themselves in one of the great hall mirrors that Darwin had not bespattered with dung, they nodded in agreement. A regular pair of toffs.

The service itself was to be held in St Paul's. Not actually *in* the cathedral, but at a coffee house around the corner. It was a Bohemian thing. A Byron family thing.

George did not mind really. Although he had not lost anything of his piety. George *had* become a believer. But he felt that God would understand. God had, after all, spared both him and Ada. God had been good to George.

The carriage of the deceased Lord Brentford was an old-fashioned, high-wheeled affair. But it held to considerable dignity and the horses were thoroughbreds.

Darwin dismissed the coachman and insisted upon doing the driving. George was not altogether enthusiastic about this, but, he reasoned, reasonably enough, that he and Ada had got this far together and that nothing was that likely to stop them getting married.

'But you will drive *very* slowly, just in case,' George said to Darwin as they climbed into the carriage.

Darwin raised his tiny top hat, then thoroughly whipped up the horses.

Through Brentford, Kew, Chiswick and Hammersmith they travelled. And many stopped to marvel at the sight.

George raised his hat to the gawpers and settled back on the plush leather seating. There had been no accidents thus far.

The problem began just near Hammersmith Bridge.

There were a great many carriages and omnibuses and hansom cabs and fellows on penny-farthing bicycles and steam-powered automobiles. And all were jammed up together and very stopped indeed.

'Do we have a horn to honk?' George asked.

Darwin glanced towards a pile of horse dung in the road.

'No!' said George. 'No throwing. Just honking, that is all.'

But they had no horn, and although many others had, and honked these with a vengeance, the traffic moved not a single inch, which caused George great concern.

'We must not be late,' he said to Darwin. 'I wonder if we might perhaps detach one of the horses and gallop it along the pavement?'

Darwin looked most enthusiastic. George set to the task.

He almost had the horse detached when a London bobby happened by.

'Having trouble, sir?' this bobby asked.

'My wedding day,' said George, 'and all the traffic has come to a standstill. I am proposing to ride this horse along the gutter. This would create no problem, would it at all?'

'That would hardly be sporting, sir, now would it?' asked the bobby. 'You might just be trying to get to the front of the queue. Some of these people have been queuing all night. They will not take kindly to you pushing through.'

'I am trying to get to my wedding,' said George. 'And what are they all queuing for anyway?'

'Come now, sir,' said the bobby. 'You are not

pretending that you don't know, surely? Where have you been, outer space?' And he laughed. Heartily.

'I am so glad I amuse you,' said George, 'but I have been rather involved in organising my wedding of late. Is it some sporting event or royal occasion?'

'Well, certainly Her Majesty will be attending. It is after all the kind of thing that only occurs once in any lifetime.'

George had the horse detached now and was climbing onto it. 'Well,' he said to the bobby, 'I am sure it must be something terribly exciting, but it holds no interest for me whatsoever. I have my wedding to attend.'

'You will kick yourself if you miss it,' said the bobby. 'It will only be in London for a week, before it is toured to every capital city in the world. Tickets are a guinea a piece but worth every penny, I've heard.'

'I am sure it must be,' said George, 'but I must be off.'

The bobby, however, held hard on the horse's reins. 'They say that She is the most beautiful thing in all of creation,' he said. 'Brought to London by the world's greatest explorer and archaeologist. Who, having endured terrible hardships, conquered all and won Her for the Empire.'

'Most beautiful thing?' said George slowly. 'Won Her for the Empire?'

'Professor Cagliostro Coffin,' said the bobby. 'Hero of the Empire. Lord Coffin as he will be when he has received his knighthood from the Queen for bringing the statue of the Japanese Devil Fish Girl to London.'

37

'h for the love of God, no!' cried George. 'He has stolen the statue of Her.'

'Calm down please, sir, if you will,' said the bobby, still retaining a firm hold upon the horse's reins. ' "Stolen" is such an ugly word. It is not technically stealing if you are a British archaeologist and you acquire items of historical significance in the savage realms and liberate them to civilisation.'

George gawped somewhat at the bobby. 'You have no idea just how awful this is,' he told him.

'No, sir, but I soon will – I have ordered a copy of Lord Coffin's book. He has apparently written a thrilling account of his deeds of bravery. How he constructed an airship and set out in search of adventure. And of the heat ray he installed upon his airship, with which he exterminated all the cannibals and flying monkeys on the island, before he liberated the statue. How—'

But George had heard quite enough.

'Darwin,' he called, and the monkey leapt up behind him. And, 'Away,' shouted George and dug his heels into the thoroughbred's glossy flanks.

'Hold on there, sir,' bawled the bobby, finding himself dragged and tumbled. 'You can't just go—'

But his helmeted head struck the rear of a carriage and he sank into unconsciousness.

George shouted, 'Tally-ho,' and, 'Fly like the wind,' and, 'Get me to the church on time,' and other implorements of haste upon the part of the horse. Now freed from the shackles of plodding carriage service, this equine beasty put its best hoof forward without further encouragement and plunged along the pavement.

Ladies and gentlemen, pram-pushing nannies, children with dollies and hoops, a Pomeranian doggy or two and Biff the performing bear – all took to leaping, dodging, scurrying, fleetly sidestepping and otherwise and everywise moving at speed from the path of the onrushing charger.

Darwin the monkey clung to George and chattered away in joy. George clung grimly to the horse's reins, and the knowledge that he had never actually learned to ride a horse, nor even sat upon one before, was never far from his mind.

It is a fair old gallop from Hammersmith to St Paul's.

The crowds grew thicker the closer George drew towards Wren's mighty cathedral. And the coffee shop just around the corner.

The horse leapt with ease a hot-chestnut stand that barred its way and also a Hokey-Pokey Ice Cream seller. A child distributing pamphlets jumped nimbly aside, his pamphlets spiralling into the air, a blurry cloud that met George full in the face. He snatched one away from his eyes and glanced at what was printed upon it.

The Japanese Devil Fish Girl

THE GREATEST ATTRACTION OF THIS OR ANY AGE

Eminent Professor's Archaeological Find

EMPIRE'S GREATEST HERO DISPLAYS THE MOST ANCIENT AND SACRED STATUE IN THE UNIVERSE

• For one week only • 1 gns All classes • Open 24 hours •

WEST NAVE • ST PAUL'S CATHEDRAL

George did terrible sighings and dug his heels in harder.

George was late for his wedding. But still he was there before Ada. But soon the lovely girl arrived looking radiant in a wedding gown of the Pre-Raphaelite persuasion. Hair garlanded with wild flowers and silken trappings that might have graced Lady Guinevere when she married the great King Arthur.

'You came upon horseback,' said Ada. 'How romantic.'

'Have you heard what he has done?' cried George. 'He has stolen the statue. Stolen the most sacred object in the universe.'

'Yes,' said Ada, gravely. 'And, as I am sure you realise, in so doing he has committed the Great Blasphemy. And I do not have to tell you what that is going to cause.'

'So what do we do?' asked George.

'Well,' said Ada, 'I do not know about you, but I intend to get married.'

'What?' went George. 'What?'

'If the Martians attack,' said Ada, lowering her veil, 'it is to be hoped that they will do so *after* the service. Do you know how many fittings I had for this dress?'

George Fox nodded his head slowly. And then he shrugged his shoulders.

'So,' said Ada Lovelace, poking George in the ribs, 'are you going to marry me or not?'

George Fox said, 'I certainly *am*,' and extended his arm to her.

The service proceeded very much in the manner of the horse that George had so recently ridden. Which is to say, speedily. The cleric employed, a Reverend Schnorer, seemed to be somewhat the worse for drink and in something of a hurry.

'Apparently,' said Lord Billy Byron to George, as he swayed gently in his direction, 'he has a ticket to see this Great Attraction around the corner at St Paul's. The Japanese Codfish Woman, or some such nonsense. Have you booked anywhere nice for your honeymoon?'

George Fox ground his teeth meaningfully. The Reverend Schnorer rushed on through the service.

It was a nice enough coffee house, furnished in that style known as eclectic. Which is to say, 'a bit of everything, really'. Fine old wood panelling, colonial cane chairs, Turkish coffee tables, some wicker platters of fruit. George could not help thinking how fiercely all of this would burn when it was inevitably struck by a Martian heat ray. He jigged slightly from one foot to the other. He was anxious to do something. *Anything*. Anything to stop the potential Apocalypse that might well be shortly to occur.

George's thoughts all now became confused. A great separation occurred within them. A delineation of priorities. He was getting married here. In fact, in a few short moments from now he would actually *be* married. And then he could concentrate on what must be done. And here came the great divide.

Confront Professor Coffin? Demand and force him to return the holy statue?

Or engage in those sensuous marital joys so beloved of honeymoon couples?

George was not actually a virgin. After all, he had worked in a number of fairgrounds, where one is inclined to meet the sort of girl you do *not* take home to mother. And Ada, he suspected, might just have 'a history' of her own. Especially if she really was at least seventy-one years old—

George halted all his thinkings in mid-flow. They were getting out of control. Nuptials first, then consummation of the marriage. *Then* save the world from a very bitter end.

Pleased that he had at least got his priorities right in the face of considerable distractions, George, at the Reverend Schnorer's request, placed the wedding ring upon Ada's finger and rattled through his vows.

★

The ceremony completed, Byronic children threw rose petals. Aunties, uncles and whomsoevers popped the corks from champagne bottles and the gentleman who owned the coffee shop showed up and asked just what everyone thought they were up to on his premises.

'They did not actually book these premises then?' George asked of his wife. *His wife!* George grinned very proudly.

'I think that,' said his wife, 'to use one of Mr Wilde's expressions, it was a "cost-cutting exercise". I see the reverend leaving – I just have to go and have a word with him outside.'

George Fox shrugged and kissed his wife and smiled and smiled some more.

'How does it feel, young fellow,' asked Lord Billy Byron, 'to be married to so lovely a girl as she?'

'It feels wonderful,' said George. 'I only hope that—' Then he paused. What could he say to this fellow? That London would shortly be under threat once more of destruction by Martians? That it was partially *his* fault? George gave a little shiver. Perhaps the consummation of the marriage *would* have to be postponed after all.

A glass of champagne was thrust into George's hand and George took it gratefully.

Lady Elsie fluttered her fan at George. 'Please do not think me prudish,' said she.

'By no means,' said George, bewildered by this remark.

'It is only that your best man is apparently copulating with that potted plant.'

George awaited Ada's return. The owner of the coffee shop now engaged him in chit-chat.

'Actually, I am sorry that I missed your wedding,' he said to George. 'I hear from my manager that it was a positive hoot. What with the drunken vicar and everything.'

'You really had to be there to truly appreciate it,' said George.

'I know the Byrons well enough,' the coffee-shop owner continued. 'Typical toffs. Never put their hands in their pockets if they can possibly avoid it.'

'They have been very generous to me,' said George.

'I wonder whether any of them are likely to shell out for tickets for the Great Attraction. I'll wager not. I had to queue all night to get mine. Which is why I arrived here so late.'

'How interesting,' said George.

'I expect you won't want to hang about here for too long,' said the coffee-shop owner, elbowing George in the ribs and winking lewdly at him. 'You've a frisky young filly there that needs breaking in, I'm thinking.'

'Actually,' said George, 'there is something I would like to speak to you about in private.'

Presently Ada Lovelace returned and smiled warm smiles upon George. 'Any of that champagne left for me?' she asked a nearby Byron.

The nearby Byron shook his head. 'We drank the lot,' he said.

'I have not touched my glass,' said George. 'Here, share it with me.'

'My noble knight upon horseback,' said Ada. And taking the glass she raised it to George. 'To my brave and noble husband.'

George shared the champagne and soon it was gone

and then George looked at Ada. 'What do you think we should do now?' he asked her.

'What do *you* think?' Ada replied. 'You are the man of the house now, after all.'

'You really *mean* that?' asked George in astonishment. 'Am *I* now in charge of *you*?'

Ada Lovelace shook her head. 'Did the thought excite you?' she said.

The blush that rose to George's cheeks implied that yes, it had.

'You are thinking that perhaps we should repair to the marital bed?' said Ada, squeezing George's arm.

'The thought had crossed my mind.'

'Along with certain others?'

'Regarding the professor, yes.'

'I think, my dear,' said Ada, 'that pleasure must wait upon duty. We must confront the professor. We must demand he return the statue.'

'My thoughts exactly,' said George.

'Which is why we will require this,' said Ada Lovelace. Flourishing something for George to look at.

'It is a ticket to see the statue,' said George as he looked at it. 'But how—'

'I had words outside with the Reverend Schnorer. He did not part with the ticket willingly. I had to punch him very hard and knock him out.'

'You wonderful girl,' said George. 'See this.' And he now flourished something.

'You have a ticket too,' Ada said.

'Indeed,' said George, 'and now I suggest that we say our goodbyes to all before either the reverend or the coffee-shop owner regain consciousness.'

38

indly, some members of the excited and ever-growing crowd actually did move aside as George and Ada sought to push to the very front. Some even cheered the happy couple and a cockney chimney sweep sang them a verse of 'The Old Bamboo' as they squeezed by.

Politeness, however, was being put to the test as purveyors of souvenirs and pamphleteers waving placards extolling the wonders of what was to be seen competed for attention with the vendors of sweetmeats, rough lemonade, gutta-percha dolls, candy canes, straw dogs, photographic portraits of Her Majesty the Queen and sundry saucy postcards. Bunting arced between lamp posts, and what George and Ada instantly recognised to be the commandeered Lemurian airship circled overhead, broadcasting stirring anthems, recorded upon wax cylinders, through its brass-horned public address system.

'Bad,' said George to Ada. 'All of this, so very bad.'

Ada's wedding wreath of flowers had fallen from her head. Her hair was tousled and her silk dress crumpled. To George she had never looked so utterly ravishing before and he prayed, with no small desperation, although with little hope of success, that all matters pertaining to the Japanese Devil Fish Girl's statue might be reconciled before bedtime this evening.

'Move out of the way, please,' George shouted. And in a moment of inspiration that should really have reached him sooner, added, 'We are to be married in the south aisle of the cathedral and we are late. Please move.'

Nannas in the crowd cooed kindness at them. Young bucks winked their eyes at George. But they were making progress now, so George shouted more such lies and pressed on regardless.

The cathedral rose before them, Wren's masterpiece filling up the sky. The great portico with its Corinthian columns, beyond which loomed the striking dome, second only in size to that of Michelangelo's dome of St Peter's Basilica in Rome.

The twin towers that reared up to either side of the portico were inspired by Borromini's Roman church of Sant'Agnese. The glorious stonework was all over ravaged though by the guano of London's feral pigeons.

A massive canvas show banner had been stretched between the twin towers. It covered much of the portico and rippled very softly in the breeze.

The Greatest Wonder of the World
The Japanese Devil Fish Girl

George gazed bitterly up at it.

'How did he get permission to display the statue in

St Paul's?' he asked Ada. 'Would not the word "Devil" tend to put off the church hierarchy?'

'I expect he went straight to the top,' said Ada, elbowing her way forwards as she did so. 'An audience with Her Majesty. I don't know how he did it, but he did.'

'We are quite near to the front now,' said George. 'Should we just sort of blend into the queue, do you think?'

Ada had already blended, so George slipped in beside her.

'Oi there, deary,' said a lady in a straw hat. 'Are you pushing in front of me?'

'We have special tickets,' said George. 'And as you can see from our fine apparel, we are members of the upper class.'

'Well la-di-da,' said the lady. 'And there was me thinking that you were nothing but a jumped-up barrow boy with ideas above his station.'

'Nothing could be further from the truth,' said George, craning his neck to see how far he now was from the door. 'I am a lord and this is my lady wife.'

'Well, may all the saints preserve us from scrofula, buboes and palsy, syphilis, gangrene and gout. And there was me thinking that you were none other than young George Fox who ran away from home rather than put in a decent day's work on the fruit and veg barrow as his dad and his granddad had done for years before him.'

'Mum,' said George.

'You're a very bad boy,' said the mother of George. 'But you seem to have done all right for yourself. Could you lend me half a crown?'

But then the crowd took a certain surge forwards and George lost sight of his mother.

'Who was that?' Ada asked.

'I think it was my mother,' said George. 'Though it might have been my dad.'

Ada's request for an explanation was lost in the push of the crowd. 'Hold on to me tightly, George,' she shouted. 'We cannot be parted now.'

Inside the cathedral it was cool and calm and almost silent. A reverent hush descended on all as they passed through the great arched portal. The smell of incense hung faintly in the air, mingling with the scents of elderly woodwork, brass polish, tapestried kneelers, candle wax and that certain fragrance only found in churches.

To George's amazement he saw that pews had been cleared and stacked to the sides, and that a great 'inner temple' had been erected to house the marvellous statue. This, however, was no pious work of holy art. More a crude showman's booth, constructed of canvas and scaffolding and painted with symbols of numerous religions.

George saw something else up ahead and touched at Ada's elbow. A party of Venusians, perhaps numbering a dozen, tall and erect with their ostrich plumes of albino hair rising above their grave-faced heads and their perfumers gently swinging from their long, slender fingers. They had nearly reached the canvas booth and stood like marble statues.

'This is all going to end very poorly,' said George, 'if they seek to reclaim the statue for their own people.'

Ada Lovelace nodded her head. 'And see up there,' she said.

George looked up and noted a group of beings huddled as best they could huddle in the gallery above the choir stalls.

'Burghers of Jupiter,' said George. 'And yes – I surely recognise them to be the survivors of the party that accompanied us to the volcano.'

'Move along, please,' said a verger with a yellowed face and deep cadaverous eyes. 'There's thousands queuing to see what must be seen. Hasten along now and do not hold them up.'

George and Ada took several paces forwards. George called back to the verger. 'Sir,' he said, 'might I take a moment of your time?'

The verger shuffled up and nodded his jaundiced head.

'The man who brought this great wonder to England—'

'Professor Coffin, the mighty explorer and hero of the Empire.'

'Yes,' said George. 'That very fellow. Is he in attendance with the statue?'

'Indeed yes.' The verger's head bobbed like a mad canary's.

'So he sits within that booth?'

'The sacred shrine, yes.'

'Might I ask one more thing?' said George, and proceeded to ask without waiting for permission. 'What is *your* personal opinion of the statue? You are a man of faith. What do you believe it to be?'

'It is Sayito,' said the verger. 'All truly devout Christians who have studied the Apocrypha know of Sayito.

Moses received the knowledge of Sayito when he received the Ten Commandments from God upon Mount Sinai. The story goes that when he descended from the mount and found the Israelites worshipping a brazen calf, he flung down the tablets of stone, including a great grimoire dictated to him by God. *The Book of Sayito*, that grimoire was called. And it was pieced together and is said to still exist, written in a universal language that all can understand.'

'So who do you believe Sayito to be?' George asked.

'The Mother of God. The Grandmother of Christ. We kneel in this great cathedral and we worship God Almighty. But God Almighty, He worships Sayito.'

A chill ran through George Fox and his teeth gave little chatters. 'Thank you for your time, sir,' said George to the verger and he and Ada moved forwards.

'I do not suppose,' George whispered to Ada, 'that some kind of plan is now forming within that extraordinarily beautiful head of yours?'

'I was thinking,' Ada whispered in return, 'that *that* is a very large stained-glass window.'

'Very large,' said George. 'And noted for it.'

'Large enough to perhaps accommodate the nose of an airship. Say if someone was to crash one, perhaps the one that circles above, through it, connect lines to the statue, tow the statue out into the sky and away at speed to its temple.'

'That is an outstanding plan,' said George. 'I foresee a number of difficulties. But then no doubt so do you. And no doubt also you have plans for how they might be surmounted.'

'Not really,' said Ada. 'I just made up the first thing

that came into my head in the hope that it might inspire *you*. Oh look, it would appear to be our turn.'

The Venusian party had entered the 'inner temple', seen what there was to be seen, made hasty abeyances before the holy statue and then been hustled out by two burly 'protectors'. They left the 'inner temple' as George and Ada entered it. The looks upon their faces lacked for their usual composure.

Burning censers flanked the beautiful statue. The flames reflected in rainbow hues about the golden Goddess. If anything, She looked even more beautiful than the first time George had seen Her. But there was something about that uplifted face, a sadness, a vulnerability that George had not seen before.

Ada Lovelace caught her breath and curtseyed unconsciously before the holy sculpture. 'Oh George,' she whispered. 'She really does look very like me.'

'Well, my, my, my,' came a most familiar voice. 'If it is not my dear friend and fellow traveller, George. And if my senses do not deceive me, he has married the lovely Ada.'

George looked up towards the canvas awning that served as a sloping ceiling. There, amidst lofty scaffolding, was a sort of throne chair, bolted to safety and containing the unsavoury personage that was Professor Cagliostro Coffin.

'You swine,' said George simply. But simple can often say so very much.

'That is no way to speak to your *ex*-business partner. Have you seen the crowds, George? Thousands of Rubes. I shall be a millionaire by the end of the week. And six months from now—'

'There may not be a six months from now,' called

George. 'Do you not realise what you have done? You have committed the Great Blasphemy. The Martians may even now be rising from the volcano crater in their war craft to murder us all.'

'Oh please, George, *do* give me *some* credit.' Professor Coffin laughed. 'I am not a fool, far from it. There will be no Martian attack. The volcano is, how shall I put this, *somewhat full*. I purchased many, many, many boxes of explosives before I returned to the island. If any of the Martians survived the enormous rockfall, it will take them many years to dig themselves out.'

'You fiend!' cried Ada Lovelace.

'Oh come now, my dear,' returned the professor. 'I have brought the greatest treasure in the universe to London. Her Majesty is awarding me a knighthood. My autobiography will, I believe, top the list of best-selling tomes for years to come. A fiend, you think? Me? Surely not. I am Professor Coffin. Hero of the Empire.'

George Fox felt himself at a loss for words.

Ada snarled at the man who sat above.

'I do wish we could chat some more,' called down Professor Coffin, 'but so many people are queuing and anxious to see my treasure that I regret you must take your leave.'

'I will be back,' called George and he shook his fist. 'You have not heard the last of me.'

'Oh, on the contrary.' Professor Coffin leaned most forward in his throne-like chair. 'You fail to understand. You will be taking your leave now, but you will *not* be returning. You cannot be allowed to wander abroad telling who knows what kind of tales about me. I regret to tell you, George and dear Ada, that this is a final farewell.'

Professor Coffin clapped his hands. 'Gentlemen,' called he.

Two unsavoury types, none other than the burly protectors, appeared, one from either side of the statue's base.

'Allow me to introduce you to my business associates,' called Professor Coffin. 'This gentleman is Bermondsey Bob, the bad bruising bare-fist brawler.'

Bermondsey Bob grinned evilly and gave a little bow. He was big, brawny and sported hands the size of Christmas turkeys.

'And this is his companion Limehouse Lenny, the Laughing Lepidopterist.'

George said, 'Lepidopterist?'

'A geezer 'as to 'ave an 'obby,' growled Limehouse Lenny. 'For when 'e ain't owt mutilatin' corpses and a-droppin' of small children down wells.'

'Quite so,' said George.

'Show him your cut-throat razor, Lenny,' cried Professor Coffin.

Limehouse Lenny showed his razor. It was a very large razor.

'Mr Bob and Mr Lenny will now escort you from the premises.' Professor Coffin rose from his chair and gave a little bow. 'Please do not make a fuss about this. It would be almost blasphemous to shed blood upon holy ground. Farewell to you, George, farewell to you, Ada. We will not be meeting again.'

39

da and George were led from the inner temple. They were nudged along a stone corridor and out through a small door into the cathedral yard. A yard that was surprisingly quiet, given all the thousands who mobbed about the cathedral's front. Here was a little island of peace in the midst of a human sea.

A four-wheeled funeral cortège carriage with blinds at its windows and high black plumes to each corner stood at the centre of the yard, with two rather wretched-looking black ponies attached to the shafts.

'On board,' demanded Bermondsey Bob, giving George just a hint of the biffings to come with a monstrous fist. 'We're goin' on a little journey, we are.'

'A one-way journey,' said Limehouse Lenny, laughing as he said it.

Ada turned upon the deadly duo. 'Gentlemen,' she said, 'I do not believe for one moment that such fine specimens of manhood as yourselves would harm a helpless female.'

'You'd be surprised at the depths we'd stoop to.' Bermondsey Bob did sinister grinnings.

'Especially me,' said Limehouse Lenny. 'I'm a ravin' nutter, me.'

Ada winked at Limehouse Lenny. 'You're very hand-some,' she said.

The Laughing Lepidopterist, a leprous brute with a broken nose, few teeth that were not blackened stumps and a single eye to call his own, viewed the lovely tousled woman with interest.

George looked aghast at Ada, but she merely squeezed at his hand.

'There's little I would not do for a beau like you,' she said to Lenny.

'And what about *me*?' asked Bermondsey Bob.

'Oh, you too,' said Ada, fluttering those gorgeous lashes of hers.

The East End thugs made atavistic gruntings.

'Perhaps within the carriage,' said Ada. 'One at a time? Or together?'

George's jaw was on his chest.

'Could I have my perfume, dear?' asked Ada.

George Fox managed a, 'What?'

'My perfume, dear. You have it in your waistcoat pocket. A slim glass phial of colourless liquid with a screw-on cap.'

'Ah,' said George. 'Yes,' said George. 'And here,' said George, 'please take it.'

And he withdrew from his pocket the slim glass phial that contained the Scent of Unknowing.

'And I'll take *that*,' bawled Bermondsey Bob, snatching it from George's hand. 'The professor warned us that you might just have this in your possession and that it would be best to relieve you of it should it so appear.'

George Fox made a desperate face. He was a desperate man.

'You did not drop your h's when you made that little speech,' Ada observed.

'Nah,' said Bermondsey Bob. 'We do all that simply for effect. East Enders don't speak in that fashion to each other, only to strangers. But then neither myself, nor my, to use one of Mr Oscar Wilde's terms, "life partner" Lenny here, would wish to engage in any unsavoury sexual hanky-panky with you in the carriage.'

'Gag me with a spoon,' said Limehouse Lenny.

'So,' Bob continued, 'no more old nonsense. Into the carriage and away to the river, where you will be weighted down with stones and sent off to feed the fishes.'

'Gor blimey, guv'nor,' said Limehouse Lenny.

'Gor blimey, guv'nor indeed, my friend.' Bermondsey Bob did urgings forward. Ada and George did climbings into the carriage. Limehouse Lenny shinned up to the rear and took up the driver's whip.

Exactly how the carriage managed to evade the crowds and find its way almost at once onto open roads was beyond George's comprehension. And as the blinds were down over the carriage windows, he would never know whether even his wildest speculations, should he actually have them, were founded in fact.

George and Ada sat in the carriage's rear seats, Ada clinging to her love and looking every bit the damsel in distress, George trying hard to affect the stiff upper lip of a Hero of the Empire, but failing for the most part dismally.

Opposite them sat Bermondsey Bob, manicuring his nails.

'I do not suppose,' George whispered to Ada, 'that you have any more plans at all?'

Ada Fox shook her head in sadness. 'None whatsoever,' she said. 'But in all fairness, I do feel that we had, to use another of Mr Wilde's expressions "milked that particular gag for all that it was worth".'

'I do not really wish to end my days feeding fishes,' whispered George. 'And I certainly will not stand idly by and let any harm come to you. I will think of something.'

'Do you think blue or purple?' asked Bermondsey Bob of a sudden.

'Excuse me?' said George. 'What?'

'I was talking to your wife,' said Bermondsey Bob. 'Purple, or blue, for my tailcoat and matching accessories? When the professor goes to the palace to receive his knighthood, Lenny and I are to accompany him as his personal escort. I was just wondering which would be an appropriate colour for my turnout.'

'Surely black,' said Ada, through her teeth.

'Oh no, love, black is so "last season". Purple is said to be the new black, but I don't know. Purple tends to bring out the broken veins in my nose.'

'Are you sure that you two are in the right profession?' George asked. 'You would not be happier working in, say, the theatre?'

'No thanks, love. Too many old queens trolling about.'

The carriage bumped over a manhole cover and conversation ceased.

The carriage then did a bit more bumping and took a sudden veering to the right. Ada found herself upon George's lap, and Bermondsey Bob lost his nail file.

'What's goin' on 'ere?' he demanded to be told, back in character once more.

The voice of his life partner called down from above. 'Some raving loony in one of them new steam cars keeps bumping up against us.'

'Put a whip to the 'orses, Lenny,' called Bermondsey Bob. 'We'll outpace any clankin' steam car.'

Limehouse Lenny whipped up the horses and George fell back in his seat.

Bermondsey Bob lifted a corner of a window blind and peered out. 'Nothin' like a good old race between 'orse-drawn and 'orseless to prove the superiority of the 'orse,' said he.

'The man is a mass of contradictions,' Ada observed. 'I expect he had a very troubled childhood.'

And, 'Oooh!' now went Ada Fox, thrown up into the air. As speed was being gathered, with further bumpings taking place aplenty.

'Run 'im off the road!' cried Bob to Lenny.

'I'm tryin' to,' cried Lenny, trying to.

The race was well and truly on and Devil take the hindmost now. George glimpsed the steam car through the gap in the lifted blind. A rather sleek affair of polished metal with a glass dome mounted upon the top. George had never seen anything quite like it before and marvelled at its advanced design and clear ability to keep pace with galloping horses.

Lenny was whipping and yelling and bawling.

Bob dipped into his jacket pocket and brought out a small revolver.

George was going to remark that shooting at the steam car was somewhat unsporting, but he thought better of it and concentrated on clinging on to Ada as the carriage bounced every which way upon the cobbled road.

They had somehow reached Tower Bridge now, which looked for the most part deserted. All of London, it appeared, was crammed about St Paul's, eager to see the Wonder of the Ages.

On the bridge now was the carriage, the steam car still alongside. The steam car swerved and caught the carriage, which struck the side of the bridge. Clouds of sparks flew as the wheels scraped metal. Lenny jerked at the horses' reins, and the carriage slammed the steam car to the side.

Bermondsey Bob had the window down and was leaning out with his pistol in his hand. He let off a shot that missed the steam car, then one that struck and whined as it ricocheted.

George and Ada exchanged but a single glance. Before each grasped a leg of Bob and pitched him out of the window.

It might have been a satisfactory result if Bob had simply bounced into the road. However, he did not. He managed to hang on to the carriage door with a single hand, his feet kicking out at the steam car, still puffing with apparent ease alongside.

The ejection of Bob solicited much profanity from Lenny, who now tried to draw out a pistol of his own. His efforts were, however, hampered by the sheer chaos of what was occurring. The carriage was lurching and bouncing as the steam car plunged into it again and again, forcing it up against the bridge, raising more showers of sparks. And Bob was now somehow caught on the front of the steam car and—

There was a moment, it seemed, when all became

silent. And actions slowed from blurry madness down to the slowest of motions. A rear carriage wheel caught on *something* that ripped it from its axle. The carriage lifted and crashed down again, shattering the horse shaft and freeing the horses, which leapt on rather beautifully in this balletic slowness.

Bermondsey Bob lost his grip upon the carriage door and indeed upon being as he was swept most elegantly under the wheels of the steam car. Whose panting exaltations of steam appeared as Heavenly wraiths in this transcendent infinite moment.

Then speed renewed as with a crash and a bang as the carriage overturned.

George and Ada spun head over heels, then heels over head over heels. Limehouse Lenny was catapulted from his driver's perch, over the balustrade of the bridge and down to the Thames below. He howled terribly as he fell, but with the splash fell silent.

The carriage slid to a grinding halt. The steam car slewed to a stop before it.

The glass dome atop the steam car raised and slid back. Two men issued forth. Stern-looking, cadaverous men, all in black with pince-nez spectacles, lensed in a similar hue. They stalked to the side-fallen carriage, one front wheel still spinning lopsidedly around, climbed upon it and peered in through the open door.

'Everyone all right?' asked a Gentleman in Black.

The untidy huddle that Ada and George had become moved painfully. George said, 'Somebody help us,' and somebody did.

They were lifted carefully from the carriage and set down upon the road.

'Might I ask,' said George, most shaken up, as a

Gentleman in Black did dustings down at him, 'exactly why you did *that*?' And George raised his fists and prepared to make quite a fight.

'In order to save your lives,' said another Gentleman in Black. 'Would I be correct in assuming that I am addressing Mr George Fox?'

'Yes,' said George. 'But how—'

'And Mrs Ada Fox?' said the Gentleman.

Ada curtsied and nearly fell over.

'You nearly killed us,' cried George.

'Nearly but not quite,' said the Gentleman in Black. 'Which is how it should be, don't you think?'

George did not know quite what to think. George was most confused. And this confusion did not resolve itself even to the slightest degree when added to the further confusion that the Gentleman in Black's next statement accorded.

'Mr and Mrs Fox,' said he, 'the Prime Minister wishes to see you.'

40

r Gladstone sat once more in the secret room at Westminster.

Flanked once more by anonymous men of dark, funereal aspect.

To the right of them dwelt the great Charles Babbage. Red-faced, in his abundance of tweed, but no longer looking so jolly. Opposite Charles sat Nikola Tesla, with one arm in a sling. Next to Mr Tesla sat a man with a baby's face, the up-and-coming chap named Winston Churchill. And opposite *him*, Mr Silas Faircloud, the Astronomer Royal.

A Gentleman in Black knocked lightly upon the door to this secret room, awaited permission to enter, received same and ushered George and Ada Fox inside.

George Fox looked along the table. And there was Mr Gladstone.

'George Fox, I presume,' said he. And he made introductions all round.

George Fox nodded his head and said, 'Sir.'

'And this is your lovely wife?'

Ada Fox curtsied prettily. 'What are we doing here, George?' she whispered to her husband.

'If you will both be so kind as to seat yourselves, I will

explain,' said the Prime Minister. Whose hearing was most acute.

There were two seats at the door-end of the table. George drew back a chair for Ada and then seated himself.

'So good of you to join us, Mr Fox,' said Mr Gladstone. 'We find ourselves in a difficult situation and would be grateful for any assistance that you might offer.'

'Assistance?' said George. 'Why, certainly,' said George. 'But of what possible assistance could I be to you on any matter?' said George also.

'It is a complicated business,' said Mr Gladstone, 'but I will do my best to explain it in as simple terms as possible. I must first ask you to take an oath that nothing that is spoken of within these four walls will go beyond them, so to speak.'

'Certainly,' said George. 'Do you have a Bible?'

'We have something more than *that*.' Mr Gladstone touched a bell button upon the table before him. Shortly thereafter a panel in the oaken wall behind him slid open and a Gentleman in Black appeared carrying something swaddled in a red velvet cloth. He plodded about the secret room, then placed this something onto the table before George and withdrew the cloth in the manner of a conjurer. 'Wallah.'

George gaped down at what lay before him. It glittered as a rare gem. As a piece of a pharaoh's hoard caught in the beam of a treasure hunter's lamp. It was a little larger than an average pocket Bible, but exuded a quality of absolute pricelessness.

'*The Book of Sayito,*' he said. 'I thought somehow it might be bigger.'

Ada gazed at the wonderful book. The cover of gold

embossed with unearthly gems. 'It is identical to the one I read in Lemuria,' she said. 'It is *The Book of Sayito*.'

'A *Book of Sayito*,' said Mr Gladstone. 'We are aware of at least five others. But for all we know there may be thousands, millions even, scattered throughout inhabited worlds across the universe.'

'Goodness me,' was all that George could say. But he gently placed his hand upon the cover of the holy book and swore a vow of secrecy.

Ada did likewise.

Mr Gladstone continued, 'As you must know, Mr Fox, the sun never sets upon the British Empire. Two-thirds of this world are under our benign control, as is the planet Mars.'

George nodded thoughtfully and wondered what was coming.

'As you will also know,' continued Mr Gladstone once more, 'after the failed Martian invasion, the British Empire carried the fight to the Red Planet and defeated the Martians there. Ambassadors from Venus and Jupiter made their appearance before Her Majesty Queen Victoria and an era of interplanetary trade and peaceful commerce commenced. Now, Mr Fox, what you will *not* know is that the British Government, or at least certain members of it, had been aware of the existence upon *this* planet of men from Venus and Jupiter long before the Martians invaded. A secret department called the Ministry of Serendipity had been set up to monitor their movements, investigate the supernatural, para-normal, outré and untoward. With a view to, how shall I put this, increasing the viability and protection of the Empire. If magic or suchlike actually existed, or functioned, then the Empire should have it as a resource. Surely you would agree?'

'Certainly,' said George.

'The Ministry employed spirit mediums, astrologers, diviners of future events. Some proved to be charlatans and were summarily dismissed. Others, such as Mr Macmoyster Farl and his father, were genuine and a great deal of valuable information was gleaned from them. These mediums had thought that they were communicating with the dead. They were, however, actually receiving telepathic messages from the ecclesiastics of Venus.

'I will not bore you with all the details. The crux of the matter is that the ecclesiastics have been seeking something for millennia, something they claim was stolen from them.'

'The Japanese Devil Fish Girl,' said George. 'The statue of Sayito.'

'Precisely so, Mr Fox. The book before you is one of the grimoires written in the universal language. It is the Bible to countless races, within this solar system and beyond. The Venusian search led them eventually to Earth. They telepathically communicated the plans for a machine. Would you care to continue, Mr Babbage?'

'I would,' said Mr Babbage. 'And hello to you again, Ada dear.'

'Ada dear?' queried George.

'I met Mr Babbage during our flight back from the island, George. We talked about mathematics. I believe he intends to employ me to help him work on his new Difference Engine.'

'I would be honoured,' said Mr Babbage. 'But to continue with the story. A Mr Phineas Barnum put up the money to construct this machine, the Hieronymous Machine it was named. A device, I was led to believe, that would act as a communicator with the dead. In fact, it was a locator. It sent a beam of energy all around the world in order to locate the statue of Sayito. Do not ask me how it functioned. I have to confess it was beyond my abilities to comprehend its workings. However, the energy that it transmitted apparently reached Mars. And as you might expect, the folk of Mars also had *The Book of Sayito* as *their* holy book. And *they* believed that the statue was stolen from *their* planet. And so they launched their attack upon Earth to reclaim it.'

'I did know some of that,' said George. 'But certainly not all.'

'This treasure,' said Mr Gladstone, 'now resides within St Paul's Cathedral. Where it will continue to reside, I will have you know—'

'Professor Coffin intends to tour it around the world,' said George.

'Professor Coffin,' said Mr Gladstone, 'is presently being hailed as a hero of the Empire. But both you and I know him for the scoundrel that he really is. Mr Fox, Mr Macmoyster Farl made a prediction that *you* would find Sayito, did he not?'

'He did, sir,' said George Fox.

'And you told the professor of this prophecy and he financed the expedition to find the statue?'

'He thought She was a living being. He sought to exhibit Her. He is, of course, now doubly happy as She is not living and so does not need feeding or paying.'

'But I understand there have been complications.'

'Are you speaking of the Martians that inhabit Lemuria?' George asked.

'I am,' said Mr Gladstone. 'Professor Coffin was not at all forthcoming regarding the inhabitants of the island. He skirted right around the issue, a most slippery individual.'

'But what do you want of me?' asked George. 'I can tell you all I know about those Martians down there. And I can tell you this – if they are able to leave that island they will, and they will seek to destroy us all.'

'Because they claim the statue to be theirs?'

'Indeed.' George nodded. 'And what they read in *The Book of Sayito* is that they are the forces of Good and we are the forces of Evil, and they will destroy us in a mighty Apocalypse.'

'Such as I feared,' said Mr Gladstone, and he took from his pocket an oversized red gingham handkerchief and mopped at his brow with it. 'I have to confess,' said he, 'that we are in a pretty pickle and no mistake. A party of Venusians visited the statue today—'

'We saw them,' said George.

'And a party of Jupiterians also.'

'We saw them too,' George said.

'Both parties reported back to their respective embassies in Grosvenor Square. And both of their ambassadors have sent me letters.' Mr Gladstone lifted these letters, then let them drop from his fingers. 'Both these letters demand the return of the statue,' said he.

'Difficult,' said George. 'I suppose you should probably have it returned to the Venusians. The Jupiterians appear as a race less religiously fanatic in their nature.'

Mr Gladstone nodded. 'No,' he said.

'No?' asked George.

'Precisely, no. Do you not think that explorers of the British Empire have sought Sayito? All manner of men have sought Her. Sir Richard Burton, Professor Challenger, Doctor Livingstone, Allan Quatermain. All sought, all failed in their searches. You, however, were successful. How would *you* account for that?'

'I would say sheer luck,' said George. 'But all luck long ago fled this dismal episode. Except for meeting Ada, of course.'

'There must be some reason,' said the Prime Minister, 'why *you* should be the one to find Her. I believe that Mr Macmoyster Farl's prediction went—' Mr Gladstone sought notes before him, '—"Upon your shoulders will rest the future of the planets".'

'Yes,' said George. 'I recall *that* line only too well.'

'The question is,' said Mr Gladstone, 'how will your shoulders be employed in this matter?'

'I will certainly do anything I can to help,' said George. 'If you would care for my advice, I would say, give the statue to either the Venusians or the Jupiterians. Let them sort out the matter between themselves. Elsewhere and not upon this planet.'

'There may be wisdom in your words and I will bear them in mind,' said Mr Gladstone. 'But for now and for the foreseeable future, the most sacred object in the entire universe will stay *exactly* where it belongs. In St Paul's, in London, at the heart of the British Empire.'

George Fox bit at his upper lip. Ada leaned across and squeezed his hand. 'Prime Minister,' she said. And Mr Gladstone nodded. 'I really do feel that you should heed my husband's words. Perhaps it might be decided by a show of hands around the table.'

'Are there any more matters that must be discussed?' Mr Gladstone asked of Mr Babbage.

Ada Fox did foldings of her arms. 'Well, *really!*' she said.

'We need whatever information Mr Fox can give us regarding the martial strength of the Martian inhabitants of Lemuria,' said Mr Babbage. 'Anything at all will be helpful. I understand Mr Faircloud here has alerted the observatories around the world to "keep watching the sky".'

'I have,' said Mr Faircloud. 'If anything untoward appears in orbit around the planet we will be notified.'

George stood up and protested. 'And do *what?*' he asked. 'The Martian weapons were far superior to our own. Who knows what awful death rays and killing beams the Venusians might possess?'

'Negotiations are ongoing,' said Mr Gladstone.

'Negotiations over *what?*' George asked.

'Young man,' said Mr Gladstone, '*I* am the Prime Minister of England. I will not have *you* demand answers of *me.*'

'This is all madness,' said George. 'We will all be killed.'

'Things must move slowly and precisely through diplomatic channels,' said the Prime Minister. 'The ambassadors of Venus and Jupiter have made certain requests. These must be looked at, discussed, amended, reviewed. Committees must be formed to discuss procedures. Areas of discussion and negotiation must be broadened. These things are not to be rushed. No decisions must ever be made hastily. Such is the nature of democratic government.'

George Fox rolled his eyes and sat back down.

'We need to be in command of *all* relevant information,' said Mr Gladstone. 'Which is why you are here: to help by telling all that you know. But big decisions must be left to big men. Negotiations over the statue may take weeks, months, years, decades even. So much red tape. So many departments that must be consulted. Leave it to us to make decisions, Mr Fox, and all will be for the best. You mark my words.'

George Fox rolled his eyes once more.

A knock came at the door.

'Come,' called the Prime Minister. And a Gentleman in Black entered, bearing letters on a tray.

The Prime Minister received the letters, dismissed the Gentleman in Black, opened the envelopes that held the letters, read the letters to himself, then leaned back in his chair.

'It would seem,' said he, to one and all, 'that our discussions must now take a different tack, for as of—' he brought out his pocket watch and studied its face '—five minutes ago, both Jupiter *and* Venus have declared war on us.'

41

r Winston Churchill now rose to his feet and bowed.

His baby face smiled sweetly as he declared that the time for empty words had passed and that he personally would take charge of dealing with the alien threat. Immediately. And have it all done before bedtime.

George, at least, applauded *this* timescale.

'Mr Gladstone,' said Mr Churchill, 'might I be so bold as to propose that you elevate me to the rank of Supreme Commander of all land, sea and air forces, that I might expedite matters swiftly and conclusively?'

Mr Gladstone scarcely paused. 'Why, certainly, sir,' he said.

'The responsibility will be mine,' said Mr Churchill, bringing out his cigar case, selecting a fine Havana and slotting it into the corner of his mouth. 'I have planned for such an eventuality as this. The Martian invasion caught us with our trousers around our ankles, so to speak. My apologies for the metaphor, dear lady.'

Ada smiled at Mr Churchill. *What a lovely fellow,* she thought. *How nice it would be to give him a little cuddle.*

'This time,' said Mr Churchill, 'we are ready.'

'Are we?' asked Mr Gladstone. 'This is the first that I have heard of it.'

'It is ten years since the Martian invasion,' continued Mr Churchill, lighting up his cigar and puffing great plumes of smoke in Ada's direction.

What an absolute rotter, thought Ada. Correcting her earlier unspoken opinion.

'During these ten years,' said Mr Churchill, 'I have initiated a defence strategy. With the aid of Mr Tesla and Mr Babbage here.'

'Gentlemen?' asked the Prime Minister.

Mr Tesla said, 'The Martian weaponry was superior to our own because they employed ionisation principles utilising a cross-polarisation of beta particles through the transperambulation of pseudo-cosmic anti-matter.'

Mr Babbage nodded in agreement. 'And very big Zo Zo guns,' he said. 'It is all very technical.'

Mr Gladstone mopped at his brow once more.

'The upshot,' said Mr Churchill, puffing further smoke around and about, 'is that heat weaponry of a most destructive nature is available to us for use against any invading armies.'

'And the British taxpayer paid for this?' asked Mr Gladstone.

'Sir,' said Mr Churchill, 'the British taxpayer pays for *everything*.'

Mr Gladstone nodded and asked Mr Churchill whether he might have a cigar to smoke also. As did Mr Babbage *and* Mr Tesla.

Ada, who was now growing somewhat green in the face, asked whether a window might be opened. But Mr Babbage drew her attention to the singular lack of windows in the secret room. Which, at least, meant that *he* acknowledged her question.

'Please continue, Mr Churchill,' Mr Gladstone said.

'A ring of steel,' said Mr Churchill, 'about the city of London. There are gun emplacements installed at secret locations all about the city. They can be manned and made active within a very short period of time.'

'Do so,' said Mr Gladstone. 'Excellent cigar,' he added.

'Thank you, sir. We also have new mobile ground weapons. The Mark Five steam-driven Juggernaut tank, for instance. A fleet of armed airships standing by at Croydon Aerodrome. Our off-world attackers will get more than they bargained for. *Some* chicken, some neck, I am thinking.'

'Regarding the chicken?' Mr Gladstone asked. 'I fail to understand.'

'A catchphrase,' explained Mr Churchill. 'Everyone has one nowadays. Mr Wilde has, "Nothing to declare but my genius". Little Tich says, "Ay-up, Mrs Merton, it's only a saveloy." I am working on one that goes, "Never in the field of human conflict has so much been owed by so many to so few. Some chicken, some neck." '

'I prefer the one about the saveloy,' said Mr Gladstone. 'But feel free to employ as many catchphrases as you wish, as long as the job gets done.'

'Well, thank you, Prime Minister.' Mr Churchill bowed once more, but as he was now all but invisible behind the pall of cigar smoke, no one saw him. 'I might ask,' he called out through the fug, 'that anyone with a security rank beneath A-One be asked to leave the room, as matters appertaining to top-secret business must be discussed.'

'I assume that means us,' said Ada, coughing fitfully.

'We will wait outside,' agreed George, coughing also.

Blue smoke followed them into the corridor. A Gentleman in Black swung shut the door and stood before it, a large gun in his hand.

Ada ceased coughing and fanned at her face. 'What should we do now?' she asked of George.

'Get away from *here*,' said her husband. 'I do not know how much credence can be given to Mr Churchill's claims, but I do know one thing.'

'And that is?' Ada asked, as George took her arm and steered her down the corridor.

'That this building must be very high on the list of targets, for both the Venusian and Jupiterian forces.'

'Time to leave,' said Ada Fox. 'Hurry, George dear, please.'

From the cold and cloistered world that was Westminster, George and Ada emerged into a London bathed in sunlight. A London joyous of the Empire that surrounded it. Proud of its achievements. Certain in the knowledge that it would ever prevail.

Here was London in the full throes of celebration. Whipped up to a frenzy of excitement by the arrival of the most sacred object in all of the universe. This London feared nothing. This London was of England. And England was for ever.

George put his arm about his wife's shoulder. 'All will be well,' he told her. 'Somehow, all will be well.'

A ragged paperboy approached them with his papers.

'Special edition, guv'nor,' he cried out.

'All about the statue, is it?' George asked as the lad approached.

'Nah,' said the paperboy. 'It's about the outbreak of war.'

George purchased a paper and held it before him.

WAR

it read, in letters big and bold. And then went on in a polite and solicitous fashion to inform the population of London that regrettably a state of war now existed between Great Britain and the forces of Venus and Jupiter, which together formed an 'unholy alliance' and an 'Evil Empire'. London, however, was well defended. But in order to guarantee the safety of its citizens, it would be appreciated if they would repair to places of safety – to wit, the platforms of the newly constructed London Underground Railway System – at the sound of an air-raid siren.

'Air-raid siren?' Ada queried. 'What is an air-raid siren? Some kind of singing lady in a pilot's uniform and high heels?'

'Mm,' went George, thoughtfully. 'I am sure we will find out. But let us hope it does not come to that.'

'I think Mr Churchill is a man of deeds rather than words,' said Ada. 'I do not think diplomacy will win the day.'

They stood and looked up at Big Ben. The clock was striking four. 'Time for tea, I think,' said Ada Fox.

'Tea?' asked George. 'At a time like this?'

'What better time could there be?'

★

They strolled together arm in arm along the streets of London, both aware now just how precious their surroundings were. Each storefront, café, restaurant or pub seemed suddenly something that must be clung to, treasured. Each somehow fragile, its very existence as frail as a bubble of soap.

'The thought of all this being destroyed,' said George, 'is making me feel quite sick.'

'Tea will help for certain, then,' said Ada.

As they strolled further they saw folk clutching the special-edition newspapers, pointing, raising fists towards the sky. And snatches of conversation came to them as folk walked briskly by.

'Never trusted those Venusians.'

'A rum lot. Should never have been allowed here in the first place.'

'Down here, taking our jobs and our women.'

'Send them all back to their own worlds.'

'Wipe out the lot. Extend the British Empire.'

George held Ada firmly by the arm. They stopped before a Lyons Corner House.

'Come,' said Ada. 'We'll sit and talk. Perhaps we'll think of something.'

It was somehow even worse within the Corner House for Ada and for George. Polite folk taking tea and making gentle conversation. Waiters, well dressed and attending with pride to their work. A string quartet playing a medley of popular songs. Palms in pots and crisp white linen on the tabletops. The mundane made achingly precious, through the fear that it all might be taken away.

They were shown to a table, sat down before it, accepted the afternoon menus.

Ordered tea.

'I am thinking,' said George, 'about the plan you mentioned in passing, whilst we were in the cathedral, regarding the acquisition of the airship and the abduction of the statue. That plan is seeming more and more to me like a winner. What do you think?'

'I think,' said Ada. And then she paused. 'What is that rumbling sound?'

Knives and forks upon the tables rattled. A framed portrait of Queen Victoria fell from a wall. The string quartet became silent. The rumbling grew and teeth were set on edge.

George Fox leapt from the table. 'Earthquake!' he shouted.

Which perhaps was not for the best.

Genteel folk now rose to their feet and made for the door in haste. A terrible squeezing and squashing of bodies occurred.

'Back door, do you think?' asked Ada, as the rumbling grew.

'No,' said George. 'Now would you look at *that*.'

The source of the growing rumblings now was apparent. Visible beyond the high front window of the Corner House, a gigantic vehicle hove into view, bulbous, built of steel with many rivets. A Union flag fluttered above a great raised turret that bristled with several odd-looking guns. High chimneys belched out smoke and steam. Iron wheels grumbled at the cobblestones. Upon this mighty war craft rode the soldiers of the Queen, coats of red and buttons brightly polished. The folk who were jammed in the doorway cheered. What hats could be reached for were flung into the air.

'That, I assume,' said George, 'would be a Mark Five steam-driven Juggernaut tank.'

'And more behind,' said Ada. And there were more behind. Many more. The great war wagons trundled by on their huge iron wheels.

George and Ada returned to their table. The waiter brought them their tea.

'You will have to excuse me, madam,' said he, as he poured with a trembling hand into a rattling cup. 'I will have to serve you quickly, before I away and join up. Would you care to accompany me, sir?' he asked of George. 'Together we can sign on with the Queen's Own Electric Fusiliers and fight for Queen and country and the Empire.'

'I will give the matter some thought,' said George. 'But, as you can see by our manner of dress, we were only married today and we do have plans for later.'

'Quite so, sir.' The waiter poured tea for George, then bowed and turned away.

'Matters are accelerating at preposterous speed,' said George.

'Perhaps it *will* all be over by bedtime.' Ada winked at him.

George said that he hoped it would and then drew Ada close. 'I have a confession to make,' he told her.

'You do not share the tastes of Mr Oscar Wilde?' said Ada.

'No!' said George. 'I do not. But I took something. Something that I should not have taken. But I felt that I should.'

'So that is where my spare pair of bloomers went.'

'No,' said George. 'Be serious, please. This is most

important.' And he drew from his pocket a certain something. 'I stole *this*,' he said.

Ada touched the certain something. *'The Book of Sayito,'* said she.

'I *had* to take it,' said George. 'The prophecy says that I will read from it. Perhaps there is something in this book that will save the day.'

Ada smiled at George and said, 'I put my trust in you.'

But then a terrible sound was to be heard. A sound that had never before been heard in London. A vile screech of a sound, prolonged, fearsome, strident. It jangled the nerves of all and set their teeth to grinding.

Folk, who had returned to their tables, were rising once again, flapping their hands and making the faces of dread.

'What is that appalling racket?' Ada asked of George.

'That, I fear,' said George, 'is the air-raid siren.'

42

'h no,' cried Ada. 'It cannot be. It is all too soon.'

And indeed it was true that things *were* occurring with a most disturbing rapidity. The declaration of war. The special-edition newspaper. The arrival of the Mark 5 Juggernauts. The banshee cry of the air-raid siren. All too fast indeed.

'What do we do?' asked Ada of George. 'Run to an Underground station?'

'No,' said George. 'I do believe not. Come with me, if you will.'

There was never going to be any doubt that Ada would accompany George. It was little more than a turn of phrase. George took Ada by the hand and when the patrons of the Lyons Corner House had squeezed themselves into the street and run screaming towards the nearest entrance of the London 'Tube', he and Ada took their leave with many a fearful skywards glance and much speed in their steps.

It would later be reported in the press that a veritable armada of Magonian cloud-ships had for several weeks been orbiting Planet Earth. That thoughts of a planned invasion had lurked within the snow-capped heads of the visiting Venusians. That the ecclesiastics who had been aboard the ill-fated *Empress of Mars* had been in search of Sayito all along. These things *would* be made known. But to Mr Churchill and those now in the cabinet war room, these things should have *previously* been known.

Within the war room, bunker as it was, deep beneath the streets of London, Mr Churchill lazed in a wicker chair. Cigar at full bore between his lips. A glass of port at his elbow. A monkey on his knee.

'Get down, Darwin, if you will,' said Mr Churchill. 'And please don't move the flags about on the war-board map table until I tell you to.'

The ex-monkey butler of the late Lord Brentford, close chum of Mr Churchill, had called by at Westminster in search of George. Using that special seventh sense for which simians are so noted, Darwin had found himself reunited instead with that old friend of his late lamented master, Mr Winston Churchill. And having nothing else planned for the afternoon, had accompanied Mr Churchill to the war room.

Darwin fished a monogrammed cigarette case from the waistcoat pocket of his best man's suit and helped himself to a Spanish Shawl, a perfumed cigarette.

A curious whistling sound was now to be heard. Mr Churchill reached for a speaking tube. The subterranean war room should have been fitted out with Mr Tesla's new telephonic communication system, but Mr Churchill had spent the allocated funds on weaponry. So speaking tubes remained, and there were many indeed to choose from, being connected as they were to all manner of important secret locations. The blower at the other end of this particular speaking tube, whose blowing was raising the whistling sound, was located at an observation post atop the Crystal Palace on Sydenham Hill. He was gifted with a particularly strong set of lungs and a very loud voice indeed.

'Mr Churchill,' came his voice to Mr Churchill's ear.

'Not so loud,' said Mr Churchill. 'There's no need to shout.'

'Sydenham Hill position here, sir,' came the voice once more in a more moderated manner. 'Magonian cloud-ships moving in from the south, sir. I can count nearly twenty, but there may be more.'

'Ah,' said Mr Churchill. 'They intend to raze the spaceport. Darwin, if you please, put one of those big yellow flags on the war-board map at the location of the Royal London Spaceport.'

Darwin deposited something at that location.

'Ah,' said Mr Churchill once again. 'Well, I suppose that will have to do for now.' He spoke once more into the speaking tube. 'Open fire from the Crystal Palace battery as soon as you have the cloud-ships within range.'

'Yes, sir,' said the voice. And that was that for now.

Ancient generals in exaggerated uniforms swirled brandy in large balloon glasses and looked towards Mr Churchill for orders. None were presently forthcoming, so they continued with their conversations.

Darwin sucked on his cigarette. The sky grew dark over Sydenham.

They appeared to be almost transparent. Fragile, delicate forms. Sails frail as the fins of tropical fish. Wispy superstructures. But the cloud-ships of Magonia moved across the still, blue sky of late afternoon in a close formation, their trajectories arrow-straight, their helmsmen in perfect control. Did they truly move by the power of will alone, the power of faith, these Holier-than-Air craft? Or through some subtle aetheric fluid? Some all-pervading universal force as yet beyond the human understanding of even such luminaries as Mr Tesla and Mr Charles Babbage? How?

At an order unspoken, two cloud-ships broke from the formation, swung down from on high, gained a vivid solidity and swept in low towards the Royal Spaceport.

Those aboard could not have been aware of the whirring of gears. Of steam-driven pistons engaging and iron doors drawing back. The twin fountains before the Crystal Palace ceased their aquatic displays. The water-bearing statues shuddered and moved aside. From out of the fountain's pools rose armoured gun ports. Brass-muzzled heat-ray cannons swung into view.

Gunners donned their range-goggles. Adjusted their focus settings. Were given the order to 'Fire'.

Simultaneous discharges of red-raw energy belched from the brazen muzzles, swept down the hillside, over the spaceport and onto the low-flying cloud-ships. Flame engulfed the fabulous craft. Shrivelling the gossamer sails. Wreaking horrid destruction. Billowing smoke, ravaged and broken, the cloud-ships fell from the sky. Down to the cobbles of the landing field to die in pools of fire.

First blood to the Empire of the Queen.

Ladies and gentlemen, taking afternoon strolls upon the lawns before the Crystal Palace, applauded enthusiastically. News of the start of Worlds War Two had yet to reach the suburbs.

'Splendid stuff,' called gentlemen in tweeds. Assuming this to be an unscheduled afternoon entertainment. 'Jolly good show,' and, 'Most convincing,' and, 'I say, there is more.'

A vast and ghostly vessel, the flagship of the fleet perhaps, dipped its prow and then released a shower of crystal spheres. Like swollen hailstones, down from the sky they fell. And into the great hall of glass. Explosions ripped along the length of the Crystal Palace, erupting into the blueness above in a firestorm of destruction. Girders melted, sank, dissolved, wonders of the Empire turned to dust. Within brief seconds little remained.

The Crystal Palace was gone.

The Jovian warships lay somewhat further away from the Earth. They were harboured on the dark side of the moon, in garrison towns that had existed there for many hundreds of years. Jupiterians were noted for their jolly dispositions, which to a degree had been rightfully attributed to their gift for planning ahead. Jovian garrisons were stationed upon the dark sides of moons that swung in orbit around all the habitable planets of the solar system. Including Mars.

Word of the declared war reached the garrison stationed upon the Martian moon of Phobos through the medium of Jovian pigeon post. The space pigeon, a species not native to Earth, inhabited the depths of space and had been domesticated by the burghers of Jupiter as an ideal form of speedy message transportation. Space pigeons, their flight-bladders filled with solar wind, travelled at close to the speed of light.

Portly admirals of the Jupiterian battalion on Phobos perused the message lately arrived by speedy space bird, mounted up their chunky-looking ships of war and dropped down to the undefended planet to purge it with ease of Earth folk.

The air-raid sirens ceased their awful cry. London was a city now of empty streets. A ghost town drained of life. Now and then the sound of breaking glass was to be heard as some looter took the opportunity of a lifetime.

Shots soon followed on as armed police patrols sought out their prey. Dark wraiths moving but fleetingly in the dreadful stillness. The horses of abandoned hansoms munched away in their nosebags. Earthly pigeons circled overhead. A flyer advertising the Japanese Devil Fish Girl drifted on the breeze along the Mall.

George and Ada skulked within the shadow of a butcher's awning. Peering at the all but silent streets.

'We must be very careful,' said George. 'I have no wish that we be shot as looters by mistake.'

'So where are we going?' Ada asked. 'You have not told me yet.'

'To St Paul's Cathedral. To the statue.'

'And then what?'

'I intend to give it up,' said George. 'It may not truly belong to the Venusians. I do not believe that it truly belongs to anyone. It belongs to itself. But if it remains in London, I fear that things will become far worse than when the Martians invaded.'

'Do you remember that?' asked Ada. 'Where were you when it happened?'

'In the East End of London,' said George. 'I never saw

any of the Martian tripods. Only the refugees. Thousands of them streaming into the capital seeking safety. I remember the sadness.'

'It must never happen again,' said Ada.

'No,' agreed George. 'And we are in the midst of all of this. I am very much to blame. That statue could have remained undiscovered by the "civilised world" for another thousand years.'

'It was fate,' said Ada. 'All of this is fate. Do not feel too badly, George. If there is anything that is within your power to do in order that the day be saved, you, I trust, will do it.'

'By bedtime?' George asked. Hopefully.

'That might be asking quite a lot.'

'There,' said George, pointing. 'Two policemen with rifles. Let us slip into the back alleyways and make haste to St Paul's.'

'And then?'

'Somehow end this war,' said George. 'Upon my shoulders, so I have been told, rests the future of the planets. I must do what I can to end this war.'

Ada nodded. 'Yes indeed.'

'And,' George added thoughtfully, 'war. What is it good for?'

'Absolutely nothing,' said Ada Fox.

Evening was coming, borne, it so appeared, on summer winds. The great dome of St Paul's darkened with the setting of the sun. George and Ada edged their ways down alleys whose grim impoverishments had guided the pen of Gustave Doré. Here was a London never viewed by tourists. A dark forbidding place of crime, poverty and hopelessness.

A more cynical George might have reasoned that areas such as this would do well to be destroyed by fire-breathing spaceships. That they might be destroyed and forgotten. New housing built to home the poor in a manner more humane.

But such thoughts never entered this George's head. All was precious to him now. London, rich or poor, life and, above all, Ada.

'Look,' whispered Ada. 'Above St Paul's – the stolen Lemurian airship still remains.'

'Then perhaps we will succeed.'

But sounds of distant cannons reached their ears. Cannon fire and then explosions slowly drawing nearer.

'Whatever we can do,' said George, 'it would be best that we do it now.'

Magonian cloud-ships hung in the sky above Penge. Sunset tinting diaphanous sails. Glinting in the golden eyes of sky-sailors. Languid fingers, frail as twigs, toyed at weird controls. Sparkling spheres descended to the village far below.

A gout of flame, an awesome force and Penge in but a moment was gone from England's soil.

The red soil of Mars was blistered and black. Settlers from Earth dead or dying. Space pigeon post carried orders and Jovian battle craft arose from moons and turned their prows towards the planet of blue.

And in the midst of the bluest of seas a mighty volcano erupted. Not from lava came this fearful shock, but through weapons of monstrous design. The work of alien tentacles. And Martian ships of aerial war rose up into the heavens. Engines of ghastly destruction, these, they swung in the sky and set a course for London.

43

peaking tubes whistled in the war room bunker and Mr Churchill held one to each ear. He passed on messages to General Darwin, the ape he'd commissioned to aid him throughout the campaign, by sticking coloured flags into the big war-board map on the big war-room table.

The elderly generals in their exaggerated uniforms grumbled and mumbled to each other. They were 'Old Contemptibles' all, veterans of many a map-sticking campaign. So this was the much vaunted 'progress' that they had been hearing about, was it? Usurped from their map-sticking pinnacles of power by a damned monkey!

The damned monkey in question, now being a monkey of not only high social standing but military rank, took immediate offence to the mumblings and grumblings against him. But not being gifted with the powers of verbalisation, he vocalised his contempt through the medium of dung.

A response perhaps somewhat overused of late, but one which nevertheless always got its point across.

'General Darwin,' called Mr Winston Churchill. 'When you are done with that, would you please wash your hands and stick a very large blue flag to the south of the Croydon Aerodrome?'

General Darwin saluted and went to the washroom.

To the south of Croydon Aerodrome a bloated copper-coloured craft wallowed in the sky. It had dropped down towards Croydon at a most alarming speed, red and glowing as it parted from space to enter the atmosphere. Like a flaming meteor it fell to the Earth. Then it put on its air brakes, swerved and drew up short.

The craft was, by nothing more than coincidence, the precise length that the Crystal Palace had so recently been. And there were similarities in shape also, as this craft was not only fast, but it was bulbous too. Waves of energy flowed from its propulsion system, superheating the air about the ship of space to create the effect of a shimmering mirage.

The orders Mr Churchill had delivered via the speaking tube system, to the gunners in their turrets all about the aerodrome, differed in no way from the orders he had delivered to every gunner at every other location.

'When the enemy comes within range, fire at will.'

The Croydon battery opened up into the evening sky. Rapier blades of searing force slashed at the Jovian warship.

But the hull was tempered to resist the heat of atmospheric entry and these beams did little to trouble the swollen craft.

But now a klaxon call rang out across the aerodrome. The amplified voice of an adjutant called, 'Scramble, chaps, and chocks away.' Captain Bigglesworth, who had *not* gone down with his ship, the *Empress of Mars*, was squadron leader of the armoured airship company stationed at Croydon. He marched across the cobbled airstrip, meerschaum pipe firmly clenched between fine white teeth. Silk scarf of similar whiteness all a-flap about his neck. One of those new leather flying jackets with the high sheepskin collar, adding that little extra sleek sartorial something that might not have already been amply catered for by his abundant handlebar moustache, black leather flying helmet and exclusively customised brass flying goggles, courtesy of Dogfish, Marmaduke and Gilstrap, goggle-makers to the gentry.

'Pip pip, chaps,' called Captain Bigglesworth, adopting the new and singular patois of the Flying Service. 'Bandits at five o'clock and it's half past seven now, some giraffe, some neck, doncha know.'

The gunners in their turrets lashed the alien craft with fire. The Jovians retaliated, slender missiles seeking out their targets. Captain Bigglesworth and his company of airmen took to the sky and engaged the enemy in combat.

That enemy of honesty, that fiend in human form, Professor Coffin paced before the statue. The golden Goddess so beautiful and perfect to behold seemed now to be so very sad of face. Professor Coffin glanced up at the wonderful visage. Was that actually a tear that had formed at the corner of an emerald eye? Surely not. A mere trick of the light, nothing more.

Professor Coffin paced further and muttered to himself. It really had *not* occurred to him that either the ecclesiastics of Venus or the burghers of Jupiter would actually go so far as to declare war against the Earth. He had seen himself touring planets with the statue. Achieving vast celebrity upon each world he visited. Receiving medals of distinction. Being feted by off-world royalty. Being entertained by glamorous concubines. An interplanetary war was, to say the least, a tiresome inconvenience.

But then Professor Coffin gave himself up to optimistic thinking. If the British Empire triumphed in this war, as they had indeed triumphed in the last one, the Empire would extend itself to the populated worlds. Their peoples, now conquered and wholly compliant, would shell out their entrance fees. There would still be fortunes to be made.

'Things will be for the best,' said Professor Coffin. 'Things will be for the best.'

'Best foot forward, chaps. Do the hokey-cokey and poke my ailing aunty with a mushroom on a stick,' cried Captain Bigglesworth, as there were still many wrinkles to be ironed out in the new patois of the Flying Service.

'Strafe those Jovian bounders,' he continued. Which was near enough.

The Croydon squadron were not, however, making any particular impact upon the Jovian man-o'-war. Sleek missiles streaked from its rotund underbelly, striking home at an English airship and dropping it to the ground. The Jovian craft seemed all but invulnerable and Captain Bigglesworth was about to order a strategic withdrawal when help arrived from a most unexpected quarter.

A Magonian cloud-ship of the Venusian strike force skimmed overhead, its masts draping vapour trails across the evening sky.

Crystal spheres discharged on the Jovian man-o'-war.

A mighty explosion, blinding white, dazzled the heavens above.

'Bravo, old chap,' cried Captain Bigglesworth. 'A friend in need is a friend in need and all that kind of turkey muffin guff.'

Crystal spheres now swept in his direction.

Captain Bigglesworth swung the ship's wheel and took to evasive action.

Evasive action was a tactic quite unknown to Martians. These lately risen Lemurian fighters knew neither fear nor concept of surrender. Their aircraft, heavily armed and crowded to the bulwarks with warriors anxious only for battle, the utter destruction of their enemies and the return of their sacred statue, streaked over San Francisco and continued at improbable speed towards London.

And in London, George and Ada reached St Paul's. The sky above was night dark now, the dome a silhouette of deeper black upon it. Above the dome and tethered by a cable hung the Lemurian airship, twin to those that swept across America.

Before the great cathedral doors, George halted. Once more he took Ada in his arms.

'Know only this,' he said to her. 'Whatever happens next to me, never forget how much I love you.'

'That sounds like a fond farewell,' said Ada.

'Well,' said George, 'we must part company here. I must face Professor Coffin alone.'

'Oh yes?' said Ada. 'And why might that be?'

'Because of the danger,' said George.

'Oh,' said Ada. 'And I am a stranger to danger, I

suppose? A helpless little woman who must fret while her big brave man deals with the wicked villain?'

George looked down at Ada Fox. 'Well, it *was* worth a try,' said he, 'but I did not for one moment expect it to work. Come quietly with me now then and we will see what we can do.'

General Darwin, doing things that he should not be doing with red flags, was called to some attention by young Winston.

'Darwin, my dear fellow,' he said to the monkey. 'There is a war on, you know, and your assistance would be valued at this time.'

Darwin bared his teeth and bounced and gestured at the map.

'Ah, I see,' said Mr Churchill. 'You are trying to tell me something. What is it, boy, a small child trapped down a well? A party of Abyssinians locked in a water closet?'

General Darwin rolled his eyes and then renewed his gestures.

The elderly generals who had been deprived of their map-pinning duties were clustered all about the big map spread across the big map table. Winston rose from his comfortable chair and elbowed several aside.

General Darwin spread his arms above the flag-stuck map.

'Ah,' said Mr Winston Churchill, drawing deeply upon his cigar and releasing a great gale of smoke to envelop all and sundry. 'I see your cause for concern, my dear Darwin. London, it would appear, is completely surrounded.'

And it was as true as a terrible truth could be.

Yellow flags signifying Venusian forces arced to the south and the east. Blue-flagged areas to the west and north displayed the air forces of Jupiter.

'A pretty pickle,' said Mr Winston Churchill, 'but not, I feel, a desperate circumstance. As our American cousins would have it, it will shortly be like "shooting fish in a barrel".'

And these were no idle words upon the part of the great militarist. For dug-in close to the capital's heart were many fortifications. And these armed with modified weaponry of a most fantastic nature. The work of Mr Charles Babbage and Mr Nikola Tesla.

Electrical weaponry, this, involving many valves and capacitors. And many great 'power-up' levers that had to be swung into place using both hands, which gave life to much electrical crackling between steel balls high upon towers of pale ceramic insulators. Operators in special goggles of greenly darkened glass threw the 'power-up' levers, marvelling at the cracklings of electrical force. Others peered through telescopic sights, which offered night-time vision via the medium of pseudo-cosmic anti-matter transperambulation.

A Jovian warship moved silently above the Thames, coming from the direction of Kew. A fine hunter's moon shone down on its globulous upper parts. The Thames reflected moonbeams to its armoured underbelly.

Its captain might have taken in the sudden flashings ahead. Taken them to be some vehicle moving over the Hammersmith Bridge. But before the misinterpretation of those flashings could be reinterpreted into the positive threat that they truly represented, it was all too late.

The new electric street lighting of Hammersmith

dimmed as colossal fistfuls of power were sucked from the grid and hurled with devastating force from Mr Tesla's futuristic weapons.

The Jovian spaceship, girdled in blue flame, reared like some startled, swollen creature stung by a deadly insect. It circled, rolled, turned its bloated belly to the heavens and plunged into the Thames.

The water foamed, bubbled and boiled. The Jovian ship exploded.

A mighty cheer rose up from those upon the Hammersmith Bridge.

A mighty cheer and a great, 'God save the Queen.'

And the Queen was being blessed now in many parts of London. The electric guns spat bolts of man-made lightning to the sky. Striking home on many an alien spacecraft.

Magonian cloud-ships withered and crumpled. Folded in upon themselves and died. Venusian commanders, appalled by this turn of events, cast aside their tranquil mien, bawled furious orders to retreat and drew their ships on high and out of range.

From there to drop their crystal spheres with terrible effect.

On Hammersmith and Shepherd's Bush the crystal spheres rained down. An eight o' clock performance by Little Tich at the Shepherd's Bush Empire was rudely interrupted by the building's utter destruction. And the award-winning architectural triumph that was the gentlemen's lavatory on the green – a favourite haunt of Mr Oscar Wilde when *The Importance of Being Earnest* was playing at the Empire – became nothing but the fondest of memories.

Gentlemen of the West London Fire Brigade stoked up the fireboxes of their steam-driven tenders. It was likely to be a very long night.

Firemen offered up their prayers and donned their great big helmets.

The dome of St Paul's, a helmet of faith perhaps, was now being lit sporadically by flashes of flame. Explosions on high and roaring fires below. The chaos of war was drawing nearer to the great cathedral. Beyond the stained-glass windows, sheets of artificial lightning, hurled from Mr Tesla's guns, fragmented the sky and challenged the light of the moon.

Within the inner temple, Professor Coffin, all alone, was very hard at work. He had removed the canvas awning that covered this blasphemous showman's booth and he was high on a gantry dismantling the scaffolding, cursing as he did so to himself.

'Damned fools!' he cried, and loudly too. 'All of them, stupid damn fools. Fear not, my lovely,' he called to the statue. 'I will save you from harm. We'll make away from here in haste and head to safer parts.'

'No,' came the voice of George Fox, firmly. 'That you will never do.'

Professor Coffin turned to view the young man on the gantry.

'George,' he said. 'Well, this is some surprise.'

'Yes.' George nodded. 'It must be, as you sent my wife and I to our deaths.'

'There must be some misunderstanding, my boy.' Professor Coffin danced a little. 'I merely wished for those fellows to lock you away for a couple of days. Where are they, by the by?'

'Both dead,' said George. A-smiling as he said it.

'Ah.' Professor Coffin nodded. 'That is most unfortunate.'

'For *you* certainly,' said George. 'London is under attack. People are dying and it is *your* fault. I will offer you a choice that you do not deserve. Leave the cathedral now, alone, walk away and I will make no attempt to stop you.'

'Or?' asked the professor. 'I am intrigued.'

'You have committed a crime so heinous,' said George, 'that there can only be one just punishment for you. Resist me and attempt to steal the statue once more and I swear that I will kill you where you stand.'

'Kill *me!*' Professor Coffin made flamboyant gestures. 'Such bluff and bluster, young man. You have not the stomach for such gruesome stuff. You are but a boastful boy.'

George Fox glared at the professor. 'The enormity of what you have done still seems to evade you,' he said. 'And I can understand that you might harbour doubts as to my sincerity. So we will put it to the test. Descend the ladder now and depart the cathedral by the time that I have counted to ten, or I will fling you from the gantry to the tiled floor beneath.'

Professor Coffin shook his head. 'George, George, George,' he said to George, 'what has become of us both? Such travelling companions were we. Such adventures we had.'

'One . . . two . . . three . . .' went George, and, 'Four-five-six . . .'

'Is there nothing for it, my boy? Must it come to this?'

'Seven,' went George. 'Eight,' went George. 'Nine,' went George.

And—

Professor Coffin yanked a pistol from his pocket.

'Ten, I suppose it is,' he said. And fired it point-blank into George.

44

ackwards staggered George, a look of horror on his face, a smoking hole in the breast of his wedding suit jacket. He tried to utter words, but none would come. His knees gave beneath him and he sank to the boards of the gantry.

'*No!*' Ada screamed.

The professor turned quickly, for she'd been sneaking up behind him.

'You too?' said he, but then he said no more. Ada high-kicked the gun from the showman's hand, swung about once more with her foot and swept the legs from under him. Professor Coffin lost his balance, clawed at the air, then with a scream that sounded scarcely human, fell to the cold tiled floor beneath. He struck with a sickening, bone-breaking thud and lay very still indeed.

'George,' cried Ada, springing forwards to her love and flinging herself to her knees. She lifted George's limp-necked head and cradled it in her lap. 'My darling George,' she wept. 'My darling, do not die.'

George could manage whispered words. 'Give them the statue,' said he.

'The Venusians?' asked Ada, tears streaming down her face.

'Bring down the airship,' George managed. 'Crash it through the windows, haul the statue out and let whoever cares to take it do so.'

'George, don't die. You can't die.'

'Please,' said George. 'Just do it. If you can.'

Beyond the stained-glass window, Magonian cloudships drifted upon high. Twinkling spheres of light sparkled down from them. Parts of inner London now took fire.

'I will not fail, George,' said Ada. 'But please do not die.'

'I will try my best,' said George in reply and with that fainted away.

Ada Fox gently eased George's head back to the gantry planking. Rose, made a face of terrible determination and gave forth an atavistic scream. Then she tore away the encumbrances of her petticoats and bustled skirts, shed her jacket, ripped free her bodice and stood for a moment, a Valkyrie in corset and bloomers. A girl adventurer. Gorgeously tousled.

Ada climbed onto the scaffolding, shinned higher. Balanced on its highest cross-beam and then, upon no more than a wing and a prayer, flung herself towards the rail of the Whispering Gallery. Onto this fearlessly she climbed, then from there to a tiny door that led to the outside of the dome.

Alone stood Ada under troubled skies. Above swam Jovian spacecraft like horrid copper carp. Crackles of electricity leapt towards them from the Tesla guns. The stolen Lemurian airship hung close at hand, mere feet above the great dome's peak. Moored by a heavy cable, but not an impossible climb for such a lady as she.

A wind was whipping up now and nesting pigeons all about Ada took to sudden flight.

The adventuress in the corset and bloomers wiped away tears from her eyes. A fierce determination electrified her body. Ada took to climbing up the dome.

It was vast and there was little purchase. A safe enough place to moor a stolen airship. Ada scrabbled higher. Great booms beneath announced that the Mark 5 Juggernauts were aiming their cannons aloft. Shells exploded over her head as some lethal firework display.

Ada noted with some satisfaction that the attacking sky-craft were giving St Paul's Cathedral a very wide berth. Neither the ecclesiastics of Venus nor the burghers of Jupiter wished to harm the holy statue. In this at least she was offered some safety to go about her task.

With fingernails broken and fingers bloodied and torn, Ada gained the very summit of the dome. Wind lashed about her now, threatening to fling this frail form of a girl away into the sky. But Ada took a mighty breath and climbed up to the airship.

'Airships?' queried Winston Churchill. 'Fleets of Martian airships?'

'Seen over New York five minutes ago,' said Mr Nikola Tesla, 'the message transmitted to my personal receiver—' he held up same, a slim, flat box of brass with many buttons, '—via trans-Atlantic wireless telecommunication. I have installed communicating devices in Ten Downing Street, Windsor Castle, Buckingham Palace and the apartment of a lady named Lou, whom I met at the music hall.'

'Impressive,' said Mr Winston Churchill.

General Darwin cast covetous eyes towards the brass contraption.

'How many Martian airships?' asked Mr Churchill.

'My contact counted fifty, maybe more.' Nikola Tesla shook his head. 'We may not win this war.'

'We will win it,' quoth Mr Churchill. 'We will fight them on the beaches, in the parlours and up the back passages. We will never surrender. Some chicken, some neck. Some giblets.'

'Still needs a bit of work,' said Mr Tesla. 'I am thinking to make my departure now, if you have no objection. I have been working for some months past upon a time machine. I think now might be the moment to test its capabilities.'

'You do that,' said Mr Churchill. 'And if you get it working, come back yesterday and tell me about it.'

Mr Tesla carelessly thrust his personal telephonic communicator into what he thought was *his* trouser pocket, saluted Mr Churchill and left.

Mr Churchill chuckled to General Darwin. 'An impressive feat of sleight of trouser,' he complimented the ape. 'Kindly lend the thing to me – I have to speak with the Queen.'

General Darwin offered Mr Churchill one of those old-fashioned looks.

'Yes, all right,' said Winston. 'Perhaps after I have spoken with the lady known as Lou.'

The whistles on the speaking tubes now shrieked in ill harmony.

Winston Churchill shook his head and lit another cigar.

In the eye of a smoking hurricane, on the flight deck of the airship, Ada Fox acquainted herself once more with the on-board controls. Flying the craft would be easy, for the Martian pilot had unknowingly shown her how. First, release the cable that moored the airship. Ada flung the lever, shot the bolt.

The craft lifted rapidly. Ada Fox applied herself to steering the ship down. She felt that perhaps she might have but a single attempt at this. Crashing the airship through the stained-glass window might well rupture the gas bag. Hooking up the statue and hauling it out into the night was something that would have to be done speedily. There were perhaps terrible flaws to this plan. Insurmountable flaws.

The actual act of desecration, of destroying the beautiful window, meant very little to Ada. Windows, any windows, could be replaced. Balanced against all of the rest of London, the window seemed a tiny sacrifice.

But hauling out the statue was another matter entirely.

What if it was to be damaged?

What if she accidentally destroyed it?

And then a sudden thought came unto Ada. On the face of it, a terrible thought. A mad and desperate thought. An iconoclastic thought. What if she was to purposely destroy the statue?

Blow it up?

Smash it utterly to pieces?

Destroy it beyond all repair?

Surely then there would be nothing left to fight over.

Surely then the alien craft would simply fly away.

As Ada brought the airship low and backed it away from St Paul's, preparatory to taking a great rush forward at the window, she mused upon just what might happen if the statue simply ceased to be.

It was, if one thought about it dispassionately, *only* a statue. As the stained-glass window was really *only* a window.

A religious faith that was sincere and devout did not depend upon the existence of some manufactured object. True, the claim was that the statue had never been created. That it had always existed. But it *was* only a statue. Wasn't it? Ada Fox took very deep breaths and clung to the controls. Haul it out, or smash it up?

A terrible dilemma.

But then, of course, Ada had seen the statue. Had witnessed its mind-rending beauty. Its absolute perfection. Its aura of the divine. Could she, Ada, really destroy such a thing? Did she have the right?

'One way or the other,' said Ada, 'something is going to happen.'

She disengaged the air brakes, jammed her foot down onto the accelerator pedal and clung for the dearness of life as the airship thundered forwards.

Again there came a moment. Of silence and of peace. When everything happened in the slowness of slow motion. Serenely, with queer dignity.

The nose cone of the airship ploughed into the cathedral window.

Images of saints and stern apostles. The Christ child in his virgin mother's arms. God Almighty clothed in golden raiment in the heavens. Noah in his wondrous ark and Samson as the pillars part. Angels at the dawn of man, the Architect's celestial plan. Eve and Adam in the garden, tempted by the evil serpent's charms . . .

. . . all rendered in a thousand glorious hues of tinted glass, struck and shattered by the airship's entrance. Spiralling shards and fragments of the holy tableaus, rent and violated, torn and tumbling. Light of sky-borne fires flaring in about the vast intruder. The nose cone of the airship jamming fast. Engines dying at the touch of Ada's hand.

What was to be done had to be done and as the Martian war craft gained the English coastline Ada scrambled down a landing line from the airship and ran at speed to re-enter the cathedral.

The devastation she had wrought was sickening. But Ada could think only of George. That she might do what she must do most quickly, then return to him and pray he was not dead.

Ada tore away the remaining canvases from the horrid inner temple.

Gauged the statue's height and whether it might feasibly be hauled away without bringing down all the scaffolding upon it. And without bringing down all the scaffolding upon George.

There would be room.

A cable connected between the statue and the prow of the airship could, if pulled with sufficient care, ease the statue out, then carry it aloft.

Ada Fox did shakings of the head. It was all clearly ludicrous, the chances of actually getting the statue out without destroying it hopeless at best.

Ada slumped down and began to cry. It simply could not be done.

'A little too much for you, my dear?' The voice of Professor Coffin echoed hollowly in the vast cathedral hall. 'But thank you for your work so far. I will take charge of matters from here.'

Professor Coffin had regained his pistol. He limped

towards Ada, bloody of face, his left arm broken and twisted.

'Allow me to direct,' said he. 'The cable you require is coiled within the statue's hollow base. Kindly remove it and I will instruct you how to link it up. I am somewhat wounded, thanks to you.'

Ada hesitated. She glared at the professor.

'Perhaps your husband still lives,' crowed the evil showman. 'Be advised that I will not hesitate to shoot you dead, should you play me false.'

By the light of the high church candles and the flaming braziers that flanked the passive statue of the beautiful Sayito, Ada swung open the stone doors at the statue's base, dragged out the heavy cable, did as the professor ordered. Followed his instructions.

Instructed simply to 'fire when ready' all about London, gunners trained their weapons on the sky. Chaos reigned above and great confusion. There was no doubt in the minds of the Earthbound gunners that the alien forces were now not only bombarding the army of the British Empire, but indeed each other. Terror weapons buzzed and flashed, cloud-ships fell and bulbous craft exploded. The devastation was spreading now across the face of London, for every wounded craft, no matter its planet of birth, fell upon the city spread beneath it.

Beneath the airship's nose cone, Ada stood. Perspiring, bedraggled, utterly ravishing. The cable had been connected, the statue now could be dragged out into the night.

'Well enough, young woman,' said Professor Coffin. 'You are truly of heroic stock and quite a beauty too.

Why not throw in your lot with me? I was born to adventure and so were you. Together who knows what we might accomplish. What marvels we might achieve.'

'I would rather die,' said Ada Fox.

'That is exactly what I expected you to say,' said Professor Coffin. 'Your husband is dead and you must join him in this death.'

And so saying he aimed his pistol at Ada and pulled on the trigger.

45

da closed her eyes.

A shot rang out and echoed.

Ada did not fall.

She heard a thump, a clatter of steel.

She opened her eyes and beheld.

Professor Coffin was slumped on the floor. George stood over him, glowering down at the body.

'I hit him with a scaffold pole,' said George. 'I think I might have killed him, but it is probably all for the best.'

And then George cried, 'Ada!' For Ada had fainted away.

He awoke her with a kiss, as any gallant knight would do. Her eyelids fluttered and her green eyes opened.

'George,' she whispered. 'You are alive. You are alive. But how?'

'Saved by this,' said George Fox, and he pulled from the inner pocket of his punctured wedding jacket *The Book of Sayito*. 'Its metal cover deflected the bullet. The force, though, knocked me out.'

'The book,' Ada whispered. 'A miracle,' she said.

'That I would agree with,' George said, 'for I know full well that I did *not* put the book in *that* pocket.'

'Oh, George.' The two embraced.

Ada, tears in her beautiful eyes, said, 'You must help me, George. Together we can move the statue, drag it into the open.'

'No.' And George raised a high hand. 'Disconnect the cable,' he said. 'The statue must *not* be moved.'

Ada said, 'Are you all right? The statue must *not* be moved?'

'I had a revelation,' said George Fox. 'I have seen the light.'

Light as air, fast and deadly, Martian forces closed upon London. Mr Churchill had now pulled the whistles from the speaking tubes. He and General Darwin were into their second bottle of port, the map table upon which they lolled a matted tangle of colourful flags, with several stuck in the end of Darwin's cigar.

The militarist and the monkey were all that remained in the war room. The elderly generals in their exaggerated uniforms had fled; Mr Tesla had gone to whenever he might have gone.

'We are doomed,' slurred Mr Churchill. 'Damned unfortunate, as it happens. It will look bad on my record.'

General Darwin toasted Mr Churchill.

'But you,' Mr Churchill continued, 'are my bestest friend.'

General Darwin broke wind tunefully.

Both were reduced to giggles.

But Martians knew not laughter, only vengeance wanted they. Vengeance and Sayito's safe return. The Lemurian airships swept in low from the west, laying waste to everything before them. Guns and tanks and troops and British airships. Cloud-ships of Magonia and Jupiterians too. The devastation was epic. It was biblical.

'A revelation,' George Fox continued. 'The book saved my life, do you not see? The book did it. It saved my life because it is my destiny to read it. That is what the prophecy said, that I would read the book and that the future of the planets would depend upon me.'

'But I do not understand.' Ada clung to George now. The walls of the great cathedral shook with the shockwaves of explosions. Shrapnel whined. Mark 5 Juggernauts thumped at the sky. The heavens were in flames.

'It is what I have to do,' said George. 'Now is the time – the time that the book should be opened and I should read from it.'

The whirling hulk of a Jupiterian man-o'-war collided with the dome of St Paul's, tearing away a mighty section and opening the cathedral to the Hell that reigned above. Lath and plaster, stone and gilt-girt timber tumbled into the nave. None fell on the holy statue. None on Ada and George. Above the ragged hole, elemental forces roiled and twisted in a firmament of fire. Within the cathedral, before the statue of Sayito, there was a sacred calm.

George Fox opened the book.

The letters on the pages, lit by the flaming censers, danced as curious hieroglyphics, mystical and quaint. But as George stared they straightened, changed their form that he could read the verses of the Revelation of St John the Divine:

*And there was war in Heaven. Michael
and his angels fought against the dragon;
and the dragon fought against his angels.*

Magonian cloud-ships engaged the Jupiterian war craft. And the sails of the Magonian ships fluttered as dragons' tails. Though those who stood upon the decks looked very much as angels.

*And I stood upon the sand of
the sea and saw a beast rise
up out of the sea, having seven
heads and ten horns and upon
his horns ten crowns, and upon
the heads the name of
Blasphemy.*

And the Lemurian craft that had risen up from the island in the sea bore down upon the inner city of London. Tongues of flame licked out upon all. The End of Days had come.

Ada looked desperately to George as a great crack shot up above the fractured window and spread across what remained of the dome. The roaring of the battle was deafening. The End of Days *had* come.

George held the book in trembling hands and read once more aloud.

*And there appeared a great wonder
in heaven; a woman clothed with
the sun, and the moon under her
feet, and upon her head a crown
of twelve stars.*

And George and Ada looked up towards the statue of Sayito. And the helmet of the Japanese Devil Fish Girl was no longer to be seen. Instead there was a great wonder. Upon her golden head she wore a crown of twelve stars. Beneath her feet the crescent of the moon.

The pages of *The Book of Sayito* moved of their own accord. Turned to display the words of other gospels. Gospels not of this Earth.

> *And she shall rise at the saying*
> *of the sacred word. At that*
> *word through which all might*
> *be achieved.*

'She will rise?' said George. 'What does that mean? What is the sacred word?'

The great cathedral shook, rumbled to its very foundations, preparing itself, as it were, to crumble into dust.

'The sacred word,' cried Ada Fox. 'I know the sacred word. The sacred word is LOVE.'

And in the midst of Hell's own mouth, the fury in the sky and all about, that silent moment came once more. That sacred silence born of the sacred word.

No more were to be heard the sounds of battle.

No more the crash of buildings, nor the fire of falling craft.

As George and Ada looked on, rapt in wonder, awe-struck into silence of their own, the statue of Sayito moved.

The huge angelic wings spread wide, the feathers glistening rainbow colours, twinkling as with stardust.

The delicate hands of the Goddess closed one against the other, fingertips touching, palms together, held in an attitude of prayer. The lovely face smiled down on George and Ada. The emerald eyes fixed them with a look of utter love.

The statue – now a living Goddess – rose into the sky.

And there, amidst the heavens, Sayito spoke. Spoke in every language there had ever been, would ever be. The universal tongue, most understandable to all.

'Shame,' cried She, in every given language. 'Shame unto all who violate peace. Who seek to possess what can never be possessed. I would slay you for your blasphemies, for your hatreds of one another, for all your petty grievances. I should wipe this very ring of planets clean as I have done before and I will do again. And truly so I would, if not for *them*.'

And Sayito gestured towards the war-torn cathedral below and all knew through Her sacred power that She spoke of George and Ada.

> 'Two children of Love,' said Sayito, 'have spared
> you all from my wrath. Treat them
> kindly, if you would ever seek salvation. I
> go now to other worlds, but know that I
> have spoken and know that you have seen
> me, and mend your evil ways for evermore.'

The book shook in the hand of George, urging him to read once more from its pages.

> And I saw a new heaven and a new earth:
> for the first heaven and the first earth
> had passed away.

The night sky parted, golden light poured down in sweeping shafts. As George and Ada looked on, the entire cathedral shone with a heavenly radiance. And on high, Sayito, wings spread, golden fish-scaled tail so gently waving, ascended into the vastness of space and the glorious golden light. And there was a sound, as of angels singing, and then the light faded and Sayito was gone.

Sight and sound returned to normalcy. Flames and firestorms guttered, died away. Alien craft hung motionless above.

And then, with no words spoken — for what indeed could be said? — the commanders and captains of the skyborne warships turned their faces to the heavens, raised their craft above the clouds and set courses for their home worlds.

George and Ada stood for a moment, then they knelt to pray. *The Book of Sayito* in George's hand melted into nothing and was gone.

The Second War of Worlds was at an end.

There would not be another.

There would only now be peace.

46

ord and Lady Fox took the carriage out for a Sunday spin.

Lord George would dearly have liked to do the actual driving, but their weekend house guest General Darwin OBE (in reward for services rendered to the Crown for valiant deeds involving flag-sticking in the face of overwhelming odds) had taken the reins, and made known by the baring of teeth that *he* would do the driving.

It was a pleasant Sunday in May, though, ten months since the terrible war between worlds. Lady Fox cradled upon her knee their one-month-old son, named Connor.

It was as if the war had never occurred. That war which had been prompted by the stealing of a Goddess and concluded by a suitably *deus ex machina* ending. A great project of restoration had been put into force. All had worked together.

Those terrible slums about St Paul's were gone. New and decent housing for the poor were built. And all over London the damage was repaired, gardens were tended, windows shone, there was a brightness to all. There was a love for this London, this new London. All played a part in her revival. All would feel the benefit.

The horses trotted gently and Lord George settled back beside his wife and child. These days treated him well. He was a man of social status now. Knighted by Her Majesty the Queen for his role in saving the Empire. Author of a best-selling autobiography. Husband to a beautiful wife. Father to a wonderful son.

George looked proudly to his beautiful wife. It was she who had spoken the sacred word. She, who looked so like Sayito, had spoken the word that was love.

Other adventures might well lie ahead for George and Ada.

Ada now worked for Mr Babbage, designing logic patterns for his new Difference Engine. But her adventurous nature still bubbled up and having a child would scarcely still this bubbling.

George was toying with the idea of perhaps purchasing a spaceship, that they might adventure abroad across the galaxy. He had put this possibility to General Darwin and General Darwin seemed keen to sign aboard.

The carriage moved to the high street of Hounslow. The yearly fair was on. George Fox thought back to his not too distant past. To the stinking pickled Martian in its tank. That all felt now so very long ago. He had come so very far since then.

Darwin drew the carriage to a halt and gestured with a hairy hand towards the milling crowd. George looked on and there he spied a ragged shuffling figure. This figure had the aspect of a beggar, though the clothes that he wore, though ragged now, were of expensive stuffs. He limped along, his head bowed low, but there could be no doubt.

'Professor Coffin,' George Fox whispered. Ada raised her head.

The professor limped to a grubby showman's booth, entered same and vanished from their sight.

Lord George read the sign that hung above the tent-flap entrance.

PROFESSOR COFFIN'S
CELEBRATED
FLEA CIRCUS

'And so are the mighty fallen,' said George. 'Drive on, Darwin, if you please.'

The monkey took the reins in hairy hands. But then, it seemed, he sought to fight against some inner demon. Strained against some primal urge that would not be resisted. Darwin gave up the unequal struggle, produced dung, and prepared to throw it.

George Fox raised a hand and said, 'No, do not.' He dug into the pocket of his waistcoat and produced a golden guinea. 'Throw this instead.'

Darwin grunted, but George remained firm.

Darwin flung the golden coin.

'Now please give your hands a wipe and drive us back,' said George.

And Darwin did so. At speed.

THE END.